HE WOULDN'
THEIR INTIM

Drew followed the enticing line of her back, tracing Lezlie's gentle curves. His hands lingered on her neck, looking for the wedding band he'd found hanging from a small gold chain the last time he'd touched her.

It wasn't there. Had she finally broken free of her dead husband's memory?

Lezlie's eyes darkened as she looked into his face. "Make love to me, Drew," she murmured.

"I want to. God knows I've never wanted anything more in my life. But I don't want there to be any regrets, any second thoughts...."

"There won't be," whispered Lezlie, silencing him with a kiss. Drew's response was no longer tempered, but filled with all the raw passion he'd denied. Sweeping her off her feet and into his powerful arms, he carried Lezlie toward her darkened bedroom.

MORE THAN YESTERDAY

Angela Alexie

A *SuperRomance* from
HARLEQUIN
London · Toronto · New York · Sydney

All the characters in this book have no existence outside the imagination of the Author, and have no relation whatsoever to anyone bearing the same name or names. They are not even distantly inspired by any individual known or unknown to the Author, and all the incidents are pure invention.

The text of this publication or any part thereof may not be reproduced or transmitted in any form or by any means, electronic or mechanical, including photocopying, recording, storage in an information retrieval system, or otherwise, without the written permission of the publisher.

This book is sold subject to the condition that it shall not, by way of trade or otherwise, be lent, resold, hired out or otherwise circulated without the prior consent of the publisher in any form of binding or cover other than that in which it is published and without a similar condition including this condition being imposed on the subsequent purchaser.

First published in Great Britain in 1985 by Harlequin, 15–16 Brook's Mews, London W1A 1DR

© Angela Alexie 1984

ISBN 0 373 70140 3

Printed and bound in Great Britain by Cox & Wyman Ltd, Reading

**To my daughters, Lisa and Christy,
who make each day
more than yesterday.**

CHAPTER ONE

"Dr. Garrett... Dr. Lezlie Garrett, please."

The summons startled the young woman standing at the nurses' station. She snapped the chart shut and picked up the phone. Her expression was thoughtful, her deep gray eyes still riveted to the chart. She reopened the chart, and made a quick entry while balancing the phone on her shoulder.

"This is Dr. Garrett." She pulled a notebook from the pocket of her white coat and hastily made a note of what the operator said. "Yes, I have it. Thank you."

Her voice was clear and efficient. "Mrs. Lawrence, tell Billy Jansen I'll be in to see him in a little while. I'll be on the surgical floor if you need me."

"Yes, ma'am." Thelma Lawrence, the head nurse in Pediatrics, watched Dr. Garrett walk briskly down the corridor. She, like half the staff of the small hospital, was plagued by curiosity about the attractive psychologist. Dr. Garrett kept to herself, doing her job with an efficiency many of the nurses appreciated. She had been on staff at the private Riverview Hospital for over a year, yet no one knew any more about her now than when she had first arrived. But one thing had to be said. Lezlie Garrett was one good doctor. Thelma couldn't understand why someone with Lezlie's qualifications would choose to work in a private institution rather than gaining a position at one of the larger metropolitan hospitals in Atlanta. Riverview had an excellent reputation for handling minor surgeries, outpatient care, emergencies and obstetrics, but it could not offer the opportunity for recognition as a fully equipped medical center could. Still, it didn't seem quite right for Dr. Garrett to bury herself in work. Some people needed work, the nurse thought, returning her attention to the medicine tray she was preparing.

Lezlie entered the elevator, pressed the button for the seventh floor and leaned against the cool metal wall. Automatically she smoothed wayward auburn tendrils that had escaped the fashionable French braid she wore twisted into a complex knot at the back of her neck. The hairstyle accentuated her smooth forehead and small ears. She was always very conscious of her appearance, and so was every other doctor, she admitted ruefully.

Ever since she had accepted the position of psychological evaluations director at the hospital on the outskirts of Atlanta, she had felt she was being evaluated...scrutinized for some shortcoming or failing. So she not only paid particular care to her patients, but to her appearance. She wore her professionalism as determinedly as she wore a white smock. She had had her share of lines and come-ons from colleagues the first few months after coming on staff, but her aloofness eventually diverted even the most amorous admirer. The truth was, she didn't want involvement of any sort. She didn't need it. She had worked hard to earn her degree in psychology, then her master's and a Ph.D. She had put up with smug young interns year in and year out, and fended off their ribald flirting and pursuit with cool disdain. Her work was all that mattered to her...now. She was twenty-nine, unattached and unencumbered, and that suited her just fine.

The elevator slowed and then stopped. She walked down the hall, her heels clicking quietly. Several physicians glanced around, smiling wistfully at her rigid posture, which was belied by the gentle sway of her slim hips. The strappy heels accented long slender legs and trim ankles. If it wasn't her figure or intelligence that attracted them, it was her eyes. The dark gray pools held a hint of sadness above finely shaped cheekbones, and her small mouth with its pout of concentration revealed a sensuality even her aloof attitude could not diminish. But the word was out. Dr. Lezlie Garrett was not interested in anything but professional relationships.

Dr. Charles Sanders stood outside a small cubicle at the end of the hall. He smiled with obvious relief when he saw Lezlie.

"Boy, am I glad to see you." He ran a hand through his salt-and-pepper hair. "I've got a patient, a twelve-year-old girl named Merri Bradinton...an appendectomy. But I don't want to put her under until she's calmed down."

"What about her parents..." Lezlie started to inquire.

"It's a rather complicated story, Lezlie. I've put a

call in to Drew Bradinton and he's on his way. But I'm really getting behind schedule. I'm due to leave for a medical convention, so I'm going to get scrubbed up while you talk to her. For God's sake, see if you can calm her down. I would put it off altogether until Drew gets here, but I don't want to risk the appendix rupturing. Then we'd be in a real fix."

"I'll see what I can do." The soft smile completely changed Lezlie's features. Charles Sanders was one of a few close friends she had made in the past two years. He had gained her friendship through respect for her work. Never once had his behavior been demeaning or insulting. He considered her a colleague who shared his devotion to a demanding profession—all the more remarkable since Lezlie's speciality was combined with an ability to logically approach young patients and their families and diminish their fears of treatment, even when, at times, their fears were warranted.

The door whooshed as Lezlie entered the small room. Quiet sobs came from the young girl on the surgical bed. Merri, Charles had said her name was. She was small for a twelve-year-old, her soft blond hair framing a pale face where large teary blue eyes looked fearfully at Lezlie.

"Hello, Merri," Lezlie stood beside the bed, smiling down at the terrified girl. "Has Dr. Sanders explained what he has to do?"

Merri brushed away her tears as she hiccuped. "He said he has to op...operate and take out something that's making me sick. I don't feel sick now."

"That is because of the shot you had a little while

ago." Lezlie leaned against the bed. "Would it help if I told you exactly what is going to happen?"

"I don't kn-know." The small timid voice revealed every ounce of fear welled within the young girl.

Slowly and in terms Merri could understand, Lezlie explained what the appendix was and why it had to be removed. Then she outlined without embellishment the steps that would bring about its removal. "So you see, Merri, if it isn't taken out now, you could get a lot sicker. And by the time it's over, your father will be here."

The rapt attention Merri had given Lezlie for the past five minutes evaporated. The pain that riddled the child's face was palpable. "He can't be here," she said, her words slightly slurred from a preoperative injection. "He never can. He says it's not my fault, but it is. I heard what they said."

Lezlie was momentarily confused. Whom was Merri referring to and what did she think was her fault? Lezlie could only assume it was something to do with her father. But what about her mother? Why hadn't Mrs. Bradinton come to be with her daughter? None of the questions had answers. Afraid of upsetting her further, Lezlie decided not to mention why no one was standing by to offer the girl support and ease her fear.

"I'm sure he will be," Lezlie said with conviction. "But until then, will I do?"

"You?"

"I can be your substitute family. I'll be here when you go into surgery and I'll wait until it's all over and you wake up."

"You will?" The hope in the simple question touched Lezlie.

"I'll be right here," she smiled.

"Promise?"

"I promise," Lezlie said, aware of a flicker of doubt in the girl's eyes. "But you have to promise me something."

"What?" Merri asked warily.

"No more tears, okay? And I want you to try your very best to be brave. I know it's a lot to ask, but will you try?"

Merri was thoughtful and then nodded. Explaining the surgery and giving her a goal had worked. The child was no longer focusing on being afraid, but on trying not to be afraid.

A nurse poked her head around the door and then motioned two orderlies to wheel the bed into surgery.

"You'll be here?" Merri asked suddenly, her fear resurfacing for a moment.

"I'll be here," Lezlie reassured her, noticing Merri's shyness as the girl looked away. Lezlie leaned over and kissed her smooth forehead, soft butterfly lashes touching Lezlie's chin. As Merri was wheeled out of the room to the surgical suite, Lezlie was rewarded with a brilliant smile and a quick wave. Lezlie thrust her hands into the pockets of her smock. No child should have to face such an ordeal with only strangers to allay her fears. With purposeful strides she approached the nurses' station and asked for Merri Bradinton's chart. She glanced over the admission information, noting that Andrew Bradinton was listed as father, but under the mother's name was the notation "deceased." A sigh of relief whistled through her clenched teeth that she had not mentioned the girl's mother.

"Who filled out this admission form?"

The nurse glanced up from her desk. "Dr. Sanders. He's known the family for years."

"When was Merri brought in?"

"About noon, I think."

It was almost four o'clock. Surely her father could have made it to the hospital by now, Lezlie thought. "Has Mr. Bradinton called?"

"Not that I know of. I know Dr. Sanders was in a panic trying to reach him. I think he did and got verbal permission to operate."

"Then why isn't he here?" Lezlie murmured. Her anger was mingled with disbelief that not only had Andrew Bradinton not arrived, he hadn't even bothered to call to find out how his daughter was. All she could remember was Merri's comment: "He can't be here...he never can."

Granted, an appendectomy wasn't exactly a life-threatening procedure, but any surgery held unforeseen risks. And since he was Merri's only parent.... A heavy sigh lifted Lezlie's shoulders as she replaced the chart.

"When and if Mr. Bradinton arrives, would you tell him I would like to speak with him. I'll be in the lounge on the third floor."

The nurse nodded, her mouth slack at the controlled anger in the clipped request. From the telephone on the third floor, Lezlie left the message with the operator that she could be reached in the lounge. Then she called her secretary to bring her some files to go over during the wait. But after Jean had brought the requested files, Lezlie could not concentrate.

The clock ticked away the minutes, which seemed to drag endlessly. Lezlie repeatedly checked her own watch. Nearly an hour passed. She paced from the window to the door, hesitating at each for a moment before going to the other. Then Charles Sanders called down from surgery.

"The floor nurse told me you were waiting," he said, and Lezlie could imagine his smile. "She's fine and should be down in a little while. Tell me, has Drew arrived?"

"Not yet," Lezlie said. "Listen, Charles, about her parents—"

"I'll explain it all when I come down," Dr. Sanders interrupted. "It'll be another half hour. Hopefully by then Drew will have arrived."

"Hopefully," Lezlie echoed, remembering her words to Merri. She checked in with her office, but there were no messages. She flipped through one magazine after another, her frustration increasing. How could any parent be so insensitive? If Merri were her child she would have been at the hospital for her regardless of business or anything else. The fact that Merri only had one parent made it all the more important that her father understand her needs. But Merri's situation was not all that unusual, Lezlie knew. She had come across the same pattern many times during her practice.

Lezlie was standing at the window when she heard

the ping of the elevator. She turned, watching as a man reached the desk. His thick sandy hair was windblown, and there was a haggard look in the way his tie hung loosely and the top button of his shirt was open. Lezlie saw him in profile as he addressed the nurse. He glanced toward the lounge and looked at Lezlie. He said something to the nurse and crossed the corridor, his eyes never leaving Lezlie.

In one swift motion, he had discarded his coat and tossed it across the back of the chair. "I'm Drew Bradinton. The nurse said you might have some more-detailed information about Merri." His voice was deep, timbered with a throaty rumble.

Lezlie's stomach tightened as she watched him. He was obviously tired and somewhat impatient. "Dr. Sanders just called down from surgery—"

"Is Merri all right?"

"Physically, yes," Lezlie answered. "Dr. Sanders consulted me about Merri."

Suspicion lined his wide forehead. "Consulted you for what?"

"Merri was extremely upset, Mr. Bradinton. Dr. Sanders asked me to try to calm her down before he began surgery."

The directness of her tone caused his eyebrows to lift, then lower over his incredibly blue eyes...eyes very much like his daughter's, Lezlie thought.

"Perhaps this isn't the time or place, Mr. Bradinton, but you should be aware that Merri may require more attention than the average child. It is difficult enough to lose one parent, but when the other is too busy or preoccupied to be available, it can lead to serious problems. I tried to reassure her...."

"What are you talking about?" Drew demanded. "In what way did you reassure her?"

"Mainly by assuring her that you would be here when she woke up. I'm glad I wasn't proven wrong. It seems a stranger has more faith in her father than she does."

"What?" The question seemed to explode from him. "Who the hell told you I was her father?"

Lezlie's composure slipped, but she answered calmly, "It's on her chart, Mr. Bradinton. I didn't have a chance to read her file because of the urgency Dr. Sanders felt."

"And just what is your job? Are you Dr. Sanders's assistant, an intern...what?"

Lezlie bristled and was instantly on the defensive. "I am Dr. Garrett, Mr. Bradinton. I am on staff here as a psychologist. My speciality is adolescent disorders."

"Well, perhaps you should have taken the time to do your job properly, or had Dr. Sanders fill you in. He might have enlightened you about some rather pertinent facts about Merri." A volatile anger threatened, emanating from him as though the leash he held on his temper was a fine thread that could snap at any moment. "You might have learned that both of Merri's parents were killed less than a year ago. I am Merri's uncle and guardian. And if I could have reached here a moment sooner, I would have. Any more advice?"

Lezlie was absolutely speechless. The enormity of

her mistake was obvious. She could have complicated an already-bad situation. A blush of humiliation crept up to spot her cheeks. "I do apologize, Mr. Bradinton," she started.

"It's a little late for that," he charged. "Had you done your job properly, there wouldn't be any need for an apology or for me to wonder just what damage you've caused. Your blundering can only be called irresponsible for any doctor, but for a psychologist, it borders on negligence. I'm glad Dr. Sanders is more attentive—at least I didn't have to worry about her physical welfare."

Lezlie was stung by his sarcasm and her conciliatory manner dissolved. "Perhaps I should have demanded Merri's file before complying with Dr. Sanders's request, but as I said, he wanted to proceed with the operation as quickly as possible. I don't think your niece was too aware of my mistake since she was already sedated. She may not even remember it."

"Don't count on it," Drew said succinctly. "Now if you don't mind, I would prefer to see Merri alone when she comes back."

"But I promised her I would be here—"

"I'll be here, Dr. Garrett."

Lezlie did not move, but his request was academic as the gurney bearing Merri was wheeled into the hall. Lezlie smiled warmly when the orderly stopped next to them.

"You did stay," Merri breathed, still groggy from the anesthesia.

"I promised, didn't I?" Lezlie touched her arm,

checking the steady pulse before the cool fingers closed over hers. Drew stepped up beside Lezlie.

"Hi, sweetheart. How are you feeling?"

The soft smile on Merri's face held a hint of shyness. "Hi, Uncle Drew. I feel sort of funny and my stomach feels tight."

"That's the bandage," Lezlie explained. "Remember we talked about it?" Merri nodded. "It's going to feel like that for a while, until the stitches come out."

"Can I see them?" Merri asked, her child's curiosity bubbling forth.

"There will be plenty of time for that later... maybe tomorrow. I have to leave now, Merri, I have some work to do."

"Will you come back?"

Lezlie smiled and smoothed a stray curl from the small forehead. "Of course."

"Tomorrow? I want to see my stitches."

"Tomorrow it is. You be a good girl and do what the nurses tell you. Deal?"

Merri nodded sleepily.

Lezlie turned around, coming face-to-face with Drew Bradinton. His narrowed eyes raked her from head to foot before settling on her face. Lezlie wouldn't give him the satisfaction of a further apology. She nodded curtly, then walked briskly down the hall. Lord, had she ever made a mess of things. She hated inefficiency, and she certainly hadn't given proper consideration to routine. The next time, she fumed—the next time the attending physician had better come file in hand. She stood at the elevator, still berating herself when Dr. Sanders emerged. His smile dissolved.

"Is anything wrong with Merri?"

"No, but her uncle is fit to be tied," Lezlie replied. "I wish you had mentioned that her parents were dead. Understandably, Mr. Bradinton is furious because I reassured Merri her father would come. Hopefully, she was too sedated to remember."

Charles didn't seem particularly surprised but he shook his head. "I'm sorry, Lezlie. I know how short Drew can be at the best of times. I'm on my way to see him now and I'll explain the situation. There's something else I want to discuss with him concerning Merri. Would you be willing to counsel Merri if I can get Drew to agree?"

"We didn't really hit it off—" Lezlie smiled ruefully "—but I will say that she has a problem concerning her parents."

"You might have realized that a lot sooner had I given you her file," Charles said. "She has been complaining of stomachaches for almost a year. They started just after her parents' deaths. Drew thinks that the appendix is the explanation. I'm not so sure. I'll get back to you in a little while."

Lezlie started to get into the elevator and then swung around. "I thought you were leaving...."

Charles smiled. "I got a later flight. You'll be in your office?"

Lezlie nodded and watched as he walked away. Lezlie's office was in the medical building adjoining the hospital. Her secretary had already gone for the day, so Lezlie went over some of the files on her desk, making notes or dictating a brief paragraph to be typed into the file. But her thoughts kept wandering to Merri. Losing a family could be devastating. And while she had only seen Drew Bradinton briefly, he didn't seem quite the type to give Merri the emotional bolstering she needed.

Lezlie was leaning back in her chair, still lost in thought when the phone rang. Charles had spoken to Drew and asked Lezlie to join them in the hospital cafeteria.

Lezlie placed the notes to be typed on Jean's desk. There was an air of quiet solitude in the wing of offices and in the corridors. But crossing into the hospital, the mood changed as visitors talked quietly in the halls or sat in the lounge areas, waiting.

The cafeteria was on the first floor. Only a few visitors were scattered among the tables. Charles sat in the far corner with Drew Bradinton. The intensity of the conversation was visible in Charles's deep frown and expressive hands. As she drew closer, she overheard part of their conversation.

"Listen, Charles, I know you're working out of concern for Merri, but I don't have any faith that counseling will change anything. This is just something she has to work through, and besides, the surgery did prove that there was something wrong with her physically."

"It doesn't prove that the appendix has been acting up for almost a year, Drew. And it's obvious you can't handle it alone."

"What I don't want to have to handle is some pipe-smoking, Freudian shrink confusing Merri more than she already is."

Lezlie was standing just behind him. Her calm voice caused him to turn suddenly. "That's a bit stereotypical, if you ask me," she said with a smile.

Charles chuckled, then winked at Lezlie. "We all have our secret neuroses, right, Lezlie?"

Lezlie slipped into a chair, her expression serious. "Mr. Bradinton, are you aware that Merri feels she's to blame for her parents' deaths?"

Drew's level stare met and held Lezlie's. "What did she tell you?"

"Nothing specific, but when I erroneously reassured her that her father would be at the hospital, she said no and that it was her fault. At the time, I didn't make any connection to her parents because I had assumed her father was alive."

"Did she say anything about me?" Drew asked quietly.

"No...why?"

"Just after my brother's and his wife's deaths, Merri blamed me. I think she still does in a way." The admission seemed to drain Drew as he ran a hand through his thick unruly hair. "I suppose you will want to know all about her."

"That may be the usual way," Lezlie said gently, "but I would prefer to approach Merri differently. I want Merri to tell me how she has felt during the past year without adult rationalizations for her behavior. I will need some information about her life before her parents died and how they died."

Drew stood up, his chair scraping the waxed

linoleum floor. "Well, we'll have to discuss it over dinner. I haven't had a thing to eat since early this morning. And while the food here would suffice, it's hardly appetizing." His unwavering blue eyes captured and held Lezlie's. "Any suggestions?"

Lezlie wanted to discuss Merri but not in the relaxed atmosphere of a restaurant. "We don't really have to do this tonight," she said quickly. "You could come by my office sometime tomorrow. I am sure I will have some time open."

"That may work for you, but not for me. I have to spend most of the day trying to straighten out the mess I left in Denver. Since I'm going to be here for a while, I have to find someone who can fill in for me."

Drew left her little choice as he picked up his coat and looked at her expectantly.

"You might try the Galleria just up the street," Charles offered, smiling slyly at Lezlie. "But then you would know more about it than me, Drew." Lezlie glanced over her shoulder as Drew guided her out of the cafeteria.

The warm spring evening was refreshing as they emerged from the hospital. Lezlie's hours were usually long, and during the winter months, it was usually dark by the time she left her office. But with the approach of summer, it was still daylight outside. The silver-blue haze of twilight made everything seem more poignant: the scent of the flowers, the gentleness of the breeze whispering through the beautiful dogwood trees. Lezlie often spent a warm evening in her garden, which was little more than a small plot behind the house she owned a few miles from the hospital. The way her responsibilities were burgeoning at the hospital, she had little time to enjoy anything other than her work. But she was not complaining. Her work was her solace, her salvation and her pride. It was enough.

Drew interrupted her distracted thoughts. "My car is over here."

"Mine's over there." Lezlie motioned in the opposite direction.

"Are we going to argue over whose car to take?"

Lezlie couldn't help smiling. "No, I'll meet you at the restaurant. It's only two blocks down on the right."

"I know where it is," Drew commented, a hint of impatience in his deep voice.

The restaurant was an open-garden style with large windows overlooking the expressway. The dark green walls with arches of glossy white enamel and the tiled floor gave the room a coolness not achieved through air conditioning. The tables were set with white linen, and a vase of greenery held a lovely fragile orchid. Lezlie felt oddly uncomfortable as Drew held her chair, his hands touching her back as he pushed her closer to the table. He sat across from her, the flame from the candle globe shadowing his strong rugged features. The waiter appeared immediately, placing their menus on the table next to Drew.

"Would you like a drink?" Drew asked. Lezlie declined and he ordered a Scotch.

Drew leaned forward, his arms resting on the table. "I feel I owe you an apology. Charles explained about the urgency with which he called you in without informing you about Merri. I'm not usually so short-tempered, but you caught me flat-footed when I got to the hospital."

"Apology accepted, if you will accept mine in return."

"Done." That simple word did a great deal to dispel the tension between them, and Lezlie tried to relax.

"What did Charles mean when he said you would know more about the Galleria than he did?" she asked in an attempt to keep the conversation going.

"My brother helped design this complex," Drew explained. "He was an architect. He had some unique ideas that he worked on for several years—his dream project, he used to say. I heard about the proposed complex and suggested it might be perfect for Greg's plans. It took Meredith and me six months to convince him to submit his designs." A slight smile played across Drew's smooth mouth. "You should have seen him when he got the letter from the investors. They loved it, especially his idea of using only Georgia marble for the walls and floors of the hotel lobby. The budget, if you could call it that, was staggering. So, Greg worked with their architects and this is the outcome. Unfortunately, he never saw it completed."

Lezlie had seen write-ups about the Galleria, and had watched it develop from a wooded hillside into a mélange of buildings filled with exclusive shops and restaurants, and what some were calling the most luxurious hotel to be built in Atlanta. "Your brother designed this?" she asked incredulously.

"Parts of it. Of course, after he died, I stepped in to explain some of the details that had been left to the last minute. And there was another project in Denver. I have tried to keep his contracts intact, as well as my own."

"You were partners?"

"No, though that was always what we planned when we were growing up. I have my own construction company. I had hoped that Greg would come up with the designs and I would build them. But childhood dreams are often just that...dreams. And there were other things that would have made working that closely difficult."

"What things?" Lezlie prompted.

"Is that the lady or the doctor asking?"

"Well, it might aid me in helping Merri if I knew the relationship between you and her father."

A wry smile curved his mouth. "Why don't you want to know about the relationship between Merri and me?"

"I do, but I am more concerned about how she took her parents' deaths."

"How would you expect her to take them?" he countered. "It was damned hard. She isn't the same little girl anymore. It's almost as though part of her died with Greg and Meredith. She's closed a door on herself and on me."

"Do you know why?"

Drew looked up, his piercing eyes boring into hers. Lezlie had an unexpected glimpse of pain, of heartbreak and anguish, but in the briefest moment it was gone, concealed in the mind of the man whose large hand surrounded the glass, a hand so powerful that his fingers could easily shatter it. "Yes, I know why," he said quietly. "Do you want any details?"

Lezlie shook her head and asked instead how Meredith and Greg Bradinton had died. It had been a car accident, one of those freak things that happens so unexpectedly and so needlessly. Greg and Meredith had been out to dinner with Drew. They had parted, and Greg and Meredith had picked up Merri at the sitter's. Merri had been asleep on the back seat when Greg had lost control of the car during an argument with Meredith. The car had gone down an embankment, flipped several times, but Merri had been thrown clear before it burst into flames. Merri had been unconscious when help arrived, but had come to just long enough to see the inferno in which her parents had been trapped. Miraculously she had suffered only a concussion and a broken leg.

Oh God, Lezlie cried inwardly, remembering the day two years ago that had forever changed her life. What Merri had been through sounded so familiar, so painfully familiar. Lezlie's mind groped for a direction to the conversation—anything to stop her own thoughts. "Do you know what your brother and his wife were arguing about?"

Torment and grief mingled on the strong features. "I have an idea. We had been discussing something over dinner earlier that evening."

"Do you think Merri heard any of the argument before the accident?"

"I don't know for certai.., but I think so."

The waiter was hovering discreetly. "I think we should order," Lezlie suggested.

"I have suddenly lost my appetite," Drew said quietly. "The steak here is excellent, but I think I'll settle for a lobster salad."

The food was delicious, the atmosphere relaxed and Drew's company pleasantly exciting. It had been a long time since Lezlie had been out with a man, any man. It didn't matter that this man was a patient's guardian. She learned a little more about Drew through dinner. His parents had died only a few months apart. His father had apparently lost interest in living without his wife. Drew had been twenty-three, Greg twenty-one and still in college. No sooner had Drew graduated from the Georgia Institute of Technology than he received his draft notice. Rather than be drafted, he had enlisted. While Greg was going through his graduation ceremonies, Drew was tramping through the jungles of Vietnam, trying to survive. He had spent three years in Vietnam: the first two learning to live day-to-day before he was captured and imprisoned by the Vietcong. All that kept him going during the endless months was the thought that when he returned home, he and Greg would start that business they had always planned. In fact, before he had even arrived in Atlanta, he had decided on the name for the business, Bradinton Design and Construction. But, of course, that had all changed. A lot had happened in those three years. Greg had married, moved to Denver and established his business, Bradinton Architecture. And there were circumstances, extenuating circumstances each brother accepted, making it impossible for them to work closely. It was best that they kept their lives separate. So, Drew had remained in Atlanta and started his own company, Bradinton Construction. Each was successful in his field, yet Drew felt the void of a dream unrealized.

"But to answer your question, though Greg and I weren't as close as we once were, we were brothers. There is nothing I wouldn't have done for him, nor he for me. Without going into detail, I can say a family matter came up just after I left for Vietnam." Drew toyed with his coffee cup. "Greg was forced to make a decision. Right or wrong, it caused some bad feelings on both sides over the years. But I have never discussed it with anyone but Greg and Meredith." Drew placed his napkin on the table. "Any more questions?"

Lezlie shook her head, glad to end the conversation that had both mystified and fascinated her. Whatever had happened between the brothers had changed their relationship, and she couldn't help but wonder what was the cause, and had it perhaps affected Merri's opinion of her uncle.

"So, tell me about Dr. Garrett," Drew prompted. "Charles had a lot of good things to say about you and your work. He mentioned you could have a job at any hospital in the city. Why Riverview?"

Lezlie shrugged self-consciously. "I interviewed with some of the larger hospitals and observed their departments. Riverview offered what I really wanted—the opportunity for progressive extended treatment, which is nearly impossible in the larger institutions.

I think that was what made me decide to accept the position at Riverview. I have time to work with each of my patients as closely as needed without being overloaded.''

"And that's important to you?"

"It's what I studied to do," Lezlie said simply.

When Drew suggested a tour of the complex, Lezlie readily accepted. They ambled through the mall of shops and boutiques, game room and restaurants and down a hallway into the lobby of the exclusive hotel connected to the complex.

"This is where my brother's designs were incorporated the most," Drew said quietly. Soft beige marble dominated the modernistic spaciousness of soft hues and abstract art. A sunken oyster bar with deep wine-colored carpeting was enclosed by a low, plant-lined wall, and dominated the center of the lobby. Glass elevators glided quietly up the interior while an open-air café offered a restful moment or impromptu meeting place for guests or visitors.

"It's all a little overpowering," Lezlie commented, her gaze lifting from floor to floor to the domed blue-glass ceiling.

"I guess it is. I just wish Greg could have seen it completed."

Silence fell over them as they ascended to a second level where a small open piano bar was flanked by the many conference suites. They studied the art between the suites, slowly making their way back toward the mall. When some rowdy conventioneers pressed into the narrow hall, Drew shielded her from being jostled by the crowd. His arm had slipped protectively around her waist. Warm sensations flooded Lezlie's skin when she glanced up at his strong face and his ice-blue eyes locked momentarily with hers. He returned her smile, guiding her beyond the crowd. Her face was flushed, her skin warm and tingling where his fingers touched lightly but firmly. She could almost imagine how possessive those hands could be, how gentle yet demanding.

Lezlie's thoughts slammed to a halt. What in heaven's name was she doing speculating about Drew Bradinton in such a manner! She was a grown woman with experience at passion, not some love-seeking adolescent with a first crush. She didn't have the slightest interest in a relationship of any kind. She never wanted to depend on anyone ever again, to become comfortable and at ease with one person only to lose them without warning or preparation. It hurt too much.

The vision of a face shot through her mind, dulled by time but still clear. Michael, who had been her best friend, her lover... her husband. The memories washed over her, the years, the happiness and the tragedy. She had shut herself off and denied her own sense of loss for so long. Their friends had slowly stopped calling, stopped trying to get her involved with other things and other people. The career she had worked so hard to achieve had become her focus. She had laid it aside just after her marriage to Michael while he completed his own education. Then it had been her turn. It was funny that after all this time she could still recall the strain, the hours of study as she achieved her master's in psychology and then her doctorate. And though Michael had tried his best to accept her impending career as she made out her resumé, there were times when he resented her driving ambition to do something more with her life than be his wife. All of it faded as she remembered the day he died, the incredible numbness that had kept her from shrieking, from going completely to pieces. That had come later, in the dark lonely solitude of night, and then in the office of a colleague where all the guilt and anguish had been painstakingly revealed, analyzed and discussed until Lezlie could deal with the pain and pick up the pieces of her life.

Drew was watching Lezlie curiously. She was miles away, absorbed in some thought he could not even guess. He felt the tremor of her arm and noted her pallor. He leaned down. She hadn't even realized they had stopped walking. "Lezlie?"

She glanced up slowly, his face only inches from hers. The warmth of his chest was pressed against her shoulder. He held her close, alarmed by the strange expression in her eyes. She glanced around, realizing people were staring. She moved away, her thoughts now under control. Whatever it was that had brought such a strange reaction, Drew knew she would not share it. He tried to smile and, shakily, she did also.

"How about an ice cream?" he asked, momentarily confusing her with the abrupt diversion. He took her hand and led her to the ice-cream parlor near the exit. A moment later she held a cold concoction of several flavors; a rich chocolate, a creamy cherry and vanilla. His cone was every bit as delicious.

He suddenly looked years younger as he licked the

cold ice cream and sighed with exaggerated pleasure. "A kid would kill for this," he mumbled between licks.

"I was just thinking the same thing." Lezlie smiled, her distraction completely forgotten. She was in control again, and she was glad that Drew had not questioned her. She had enough solicitous inquiries about her welfare to last a lifetime.

"You know, one of the clearest memories I have is my father taking Greg and me to the ice-cream parlor on Saturday afternoons during the summer. He could have been mowing the yard or doing chores, but he never forgot our trip to the store. And, we might have been playing at neighbors, but no matter what we never really let him forget as we dashed home."

"Children are creatures of habit," Lezlie commented. "You do something more than once, you may as well resign yourself to it becoming part of the routine, unless you are ready to fight to change it."

"Didn't you have any 'habits,' as you call them?" Drew asked mischievously.

"I only remember one: playing in the attic on rainy afternoons. My parents owned an old home with the greatest secret places—big closets, cupboards...."

"Are they still living?"

"My father died about five years ago. My mother still lives in Atlanta, but she travels a lot." Lezlie smiled ruefully. "She calls me between trips to be certain I am eating properly and taking care of myself."

"Don't knock it," Drew remarked.

"Oh, I'm not. My mother is one of the most together people I know. She always seems to see things in true perspective. She puts it down to a healthy dose of common sense, but she is very secure being alone. And she's always been there when I really needed her, especially when...."

"What?"

Lezlie shrugged and looked away. "Oh, she's just very sensitive," she said quickly.

Drew felt she had been about to say something that would give him some clue about what had upset her so strongly, but she didn't continue.

They walked leisurely toward the exit. It had grown dark and the parking-lot lighting cast everything in a surrealistic glow. Newly planted trees and shrubs looked out of place against the large buildings. Drew walked her to her car, laughing when she looked up to thank him for dinner and, actually, to her surprise, what had been a very pleasant evening. He extracted his handkerchief, dabbing at the smear of ice cream on her chin.

"I always was a messy ice-cream eater." Lezlie smiled, completely at ease with him. The smile left Drew's face slowly as she looked up at him, momentarily lost in the shadowed blue eyes. The buildings and parking lot receded. Lezlie felt as if they were the only two people in the world, wrapped in the starry moonlight. Her heart was suddenly in her throat. She was both afraid and excited by the intensity in the eyes that still held her captive. And she suddenly admitted she was dangerously attracted to Drew Bradinton.

What was it this man did to her, she thought, that she was unable to move away from him? He beckoned to her without words, but the silent entreaty was far more powerful. For a long moment he looked into her twinkling eyes, then studied her face. His gaze lowered to the soft lips. Lezlie knew he was going to kiss her, and though it was crazy, she would not stop him.

CHAPTER TWO

LEZLIE FELT NO THREAT or intimidation as his face lowered slowly toward hers. He kissed her tentatively at first. But the coolness of his mouth did not dispel the rush of heat through Lezlie's senses. The muscles along his spine tensed when her hands slipped around him. The gentle kiss deepened into a searing exploration. Longing swept through Lezlie and robbed her of every ounce of reserve. Her body reacted spontaneously: her heart began to pound and a strange rushing noise filled her head.

Drew gripped her narrow waist, and his fingers pressed into the small of her back, exploring her with a deftness that included a gentle pressure from her shoulders to her hips. He trailed butterfly kisses along her flushed cheek. Drew sighed heavily before he kissed her again, this time with a tempered fierceness that left Lezlie leaning limply against him. It was as though she were dying and being reborn in the arms of a man she hardly knew. Her arms hugged his broad back as she pressed closer. A faraway sound drifted toward them and it was a moment before Lezlie realized they were no longer alone.

"Easy, Lezlie," Drew said, drawing away from her slightly.

His words were like a splash of cold water. But a short distance away, a group of people stood on the curb, watching them with silly indulgent smiles. *They must think we are lovers,* Lezlie thought with a shiver of alarm.

Lezlie stepped back to break the embrace. Embarrassment flooded through her. She could not believe what she had just allowed to happen. But she hadn't merely allowed it, she corrected honestly. She hadn't discouraged him, she might even have encouraged him, and she had enjoyed the embrace...much more than she should have.

Drew was staring down at her, a quizzical frown on his face as he studied the conflicting emotions on hers. "Has anyone told you how incredibly beautiful you are?" he asked softly, his gaze sweeping her hair, her face and then settling on her eyes. His hand gently kneaded the nape of her neck. It was a gesture as sensual as a kiss.

Lezlie had regained her control entirely. "Don't," she said quietly. "Listen, Mr. Bradinton...."

"Don't you think we have passed the stage of such formality?" Drew asked, an amused quirk tilting his smooth lips.

"What just happened was a mistake, Drew. I don't usually behave this way and certainly not with the relatives of patients."

"Then they don't know what they're missing," Drew teased. "And it's nice to know I have the same effect on you as you have on me."

"I think we should have an understanding," Lezlie said quickly.

"We do," Drew said. He was leaning toward her, his intention plainly visible in his smiling eyes as his finger lifted her chin.

It would be so easy, Lezlie thought, *so easy to allow him to sweep me away.* The parking lot was once again deserted, but Lezlie had no intention of being party to such a display again. She could barely think as it was. If he kissed her once more, she wasn't certain what might happen.

"No," Lezlie blurted. She struggled to control her riotous emotions. "What just happened wasn't very professional of me, and...."

"And you pride yourself on handling everything, even your personal life, in a responsible manner?"

Lezlie tried to find any hint of censure in his words, but there wasn't any. "Yes, I do."

Drew smiled warmly. "There are some things that defy logic, Lezlie. What just happened is one. And I get the feeling your professionalism is a shield. Against what...me? Or you?"

"I don't think there is any need to discuss it," Lezlie said coolly.

"Then what do you suggest?"

"Nothing. Let's just forget it happened."

"That may prove a little difficult," Drew said. With teasing lightness his finger traced the line of her chin, lifting her face until she was staring directly into his eyes. "In fact, I don't think I can forget it." She didn't answer, and for a moment he seemed puzzled. "Why are you afraid, Lezlie?"

"I'm not afraid of anything," Lezlie answered defensively. She wasn't afraid of Drew, but she was terrified of the emotions he had stirred. "It's getting late," she said lamely.

Drew opened her car door, but before she started the engine, he leaned into the opened window. "It won't help to deny it, Lezlie. That never solves anything. And what happened between us won't simply go away." Without warning, he leaned forward and kissed her lightly on the mouth. Her sharp intake of breath drew a smile from him. "See?" Drew chucked her lightly on the chin. "Sleep well, Doc."

Lezlie drove away, glancing once in her rearview to see Drew standing in the same spot, his hands thrust into his pockets. *Oh God,* she thought frantically, *how in the world could I have allowed this to happen?* She hadn't exactly given him the impression that she was immune to him as a man. In fact, he probably thought she was his for the taking, once he worked his way around her resistance. Which as it was didn't amount to much, Lezlie thought derisively. But she would be better prepared to deal with her reactions the next time she saw him. She had no intention of becoming an easy mark for any man, she told herself, much less the relative of a patient.

Lezlie felt more secure, yet that security held a niggling doubt that she would be able to remain completely unaffected in Drew Bradinton's presence. She would concentrate on her work, on her sessions with Merri and her other patients. She would allow no time for the thoughts that troubled her now.

Her house, a spacious stone-and-wood ranch style, was dark and depressingly empty as Lezlie pulled into the driveway. She unlocked the front door, threw on a light, kicked off her shoes and dropped her purse on the sofa. Cane-backed, dark blue velvet chairs accented the pattern in the pillowed couch. Brass tables and glass lamps gave the room sparkle while large ferns and a fig tree near the sliding patio doors provided a rich burst of color.

The soft beige carpet felt good under Lezlie's stockinged feet as she continued on down the hall and into the bathroom. She slipped out of her clothes, then fumbled with the pins in her coiled braid while water filled the tub. Her hair rippled down her back, a wavy mass of chestnut curls. Michael had often said her hair was one of her sexiest features. How he had grumbled when she had begun to experiment with styles that would tame her thick, waist-length hair and make her look more professional.

Professional. Lezlie frowned into the mirror. That word was cropping up more and more. And she couldn't push aside what Drew had said—that she wore her professionalism like a shield. Against what?

Against involvement, against caring, against pain, Lezlie admitted frankly. And she was a good enough judge of people to know that a relationship with Drew Bradinton would bring all those things, because he would expect nothing less than everything. And Lezlie wasn't capable of giving it all, not again. If he wanted to think she was afraid of her own sexuality, that was fine with her. She had never worried about what people had thought or said of her, except where her work was concerned. Besides, Drew would never believe that while she was attracted to him, she already knew such a relationship couldn't go any further. She couldn't become involved again...she just couldn't!

The steamy bathroom was playing havoc with her hair. Lezlie leaned over, brushing it briskly. A thin gold band swung from a chain around her neck. She touched it gently, not needing to look at the inscription in the wedding ring to remember the words Michael had had inscribed. She twisted her hair into a loose knot, added a few drops of bath oil to the water and slid into the slippery wetness, letting the heat work on her tense muscles. She closed her eyes, her mind drifting in a dreamy void until a face flashed in her mind's eye. The laughing blue eyes offered excitement, charm and promise. Without realizing it, her fingers traced the contour of her mouth as she remembered how Drew's kiss had made her bones feel as though they were melting.

How could she respond so strongly to someone she hardly knew? It didn't make any sense. She had loved Michael Garrett with all her heart. They had shared so much: dreams, ambitions and caring. She had enjoyed their lovemaking, but never had she felt so completely defenseless over a stupid impetuous kiss. She sat up in the tub and reached for a towel, running the cloth briskly over her flushed skin. That was what had made the kiss so exciting. It had been an impulse, an impetuous curiosity, which heightened the excitement. Lezlie shook her head. She had to stop thinking about it and trying to analyze it. She would just forget it. After all, it had only been one kiss, for heaven's sake.

Lezlie donned a floor-length robe and tied the belt as she padded through the house. She poured a glass of orange juice and sat down on the sofa to read over some of the files she had brought home. Within the routine was safety. A moment later, a quiet meow interrupted her concentration. A cat as black as night itself sat at the patio sliding doors. Beelzebub, one of the neighbors' pets, was a frequent visitor to Lezlie's house, as well as every other house on the street—a real mooch. But tonight she was glad for his company, such as it was.

"Well, cat, what have you got to say for yourself? Am I the only one home tonight?" Her question was met by an impatient meow as the animal rubbed his back against the screen. She slid the screen back, smiling. Beelzebub strolled in as though her home was his private domain. He leaped onto the sofa and when she sat down again, he curled up in her lap as he had done so many evenings before. Lezlie absently scratched his head as she continued her reading.

Lezlie had just decided to go to bed when the phone rang. Carol Stanton, the night-duty nurse in Pediatrics, identified herself.

"There's a problem here, Dr. Garrett. Mr. Bradinton was in to see Merri. I went by the room several times and thought she was asleep. But then I heard her crying. I gave her a little while, but she's still at it. I was going to call Dr. Sanders, but he has Dr. Carver standing in and your name was also listed on her chart."

"Has she had any medication?"

"No, she was still under the effects of the anesthetic until a little while ago," Carol said before reading off the medication listed on Merri's chart. "She says she's not in any pain. But I could call Dr. Carver and order her a sedative. It might calm her."

"Maybe I should talk to her first," Lezlie said. "I'll be there as soon as I get dressed."

"Thanks, Dr. Garrett. And I'm sorry to have bothered you."

"It's no bother," Lezlie said. She slipped out of her robe on the way to the bedroom, then donned a pair of slacks and cap-sleeved knit shirt. She slipped on casual sandals and a moment later had wound her hair into a soft twist. She wore very little makeup, and only brushed a light coat of lipstick across her lips before scooping up her purse and heading through the house to put out her visitor and lock up.

The drive back to the hospital took less than ten minutes. As she walked into Pediatrics, Carol glanced up, smiling gratefully. Merri's room was at the end of the corridor. A light shone from the partly opened door and Lezlie could hear the muffled sobs. She could remember times when, as a girl, she had buried her face in her pillow to smother her own tears. The memory became more poignant as she walked into the room to find Merri smothering her sobs in the same way.

Lezlie touched the girl's shoulder, but Merri didn't look at her. Instead, she turned her face deeper into the pillow. "What's all this, Merri?"

When Merri didn't answer, Lezlie became concerned. "Do your stitches hurt? If so, I can ask the nurse to loosen the bandage."

Merri shook her head. "He promised he would come back and he didn't."

"Who?" Lezlie asked.

"Uncle Drew. He said he would come back later. I waited and waited."

"But he did come back," Lezlie said quietly. "He was here just a little while ago. The nurse saw him in your room." Lezlie sat down on the edge of the bed. "You must have fallen asleep waiting for him."

"Then why did he take so long?"

Lezlie looked into the beautiful face marred by a petulant pout. "That's not really fair, Merri." The simple comment brought a suspicious glance from Merri. "Tell me, Merri, do you like your Uncle Drew?"

"He's all right, I guess."

"How long have you been living with him?"

"Since my parents went away last summer," Merri answered dully.

Lezlie recognized the common euphemism for death: the sense of desertion, of being left behind, which many people felt. For the next half hour, Lezlie asked Merri simple unthreatening questions. She learned that Merri was in the care of a housekeeper most of the time. Drew was often out of town or arrived home late. There weren't many children in the neighborhood where they lived, which was an exclusive suburb north of the city. Lezlie could only conclude that Merri had not adjusted very well to being moved from Denver. The school year was nearly over, but she had not mentioned any particular friends the way children often do. Lezlie's last question was more delicate.

"Merri, do you want to tell me about your parents?"

"No."

Lezlie noted the sudden shift in Merri's mood. The child suddenly became tense and withdrawn. There was undeniable anger in the direct answer. "Why?" Lezlie prodded.

Merri turned on her side. "I'm getting sleepy now."

The abrupt change in Merri's attitude made it apparent that she was not happy with her life, and that she was angry at her parents for leaving her. Hers was not an abnormal reaction. Lezlie tucked the sheet and blanket around the little girl. She whispered good-night, but before she reached the door, Merri stopped her.

"Are you still coming tomorrow, Dr. Garrett? I haven't seen my stitches yet."

"Yes, Merri. Now go to sleep."

The hall was dimmed and quiet, the night-shift nurses going about their duties with unhurried efficiency. Carol Stanton was at the nurses' station.

"What time does Dr. Carver usually do rounds?" Lezlie asked.

"It varies, but he's usually here between eight and nine."

"Did you make a notation on her chart about calling me and the reason?"

"Yes." Carol's features softened. "She seems like such a sweet child."

"She is, but she has quite a chip on her little shoulder. I was planning a session with her tomorrow, so I'll be here about eight. But if something should come up beforehand, just give me a call."

"I wonder if Mr. Bradinton will be back in the morning," Carol mused wistfully. "He is one attractive man, and I have a friend on the day shift who will absolutely melt...."

"I suppose he could have that appeal," Lezlie commented.

"What's not to appeal?" Carol chuckled, but she straightened when she realized she was overstepping bounds, especially where Dr. Garrett was concerned.

Lezlie was reminded of how that appeal had affected her. She was also aware of Carol's lengthy scrutiny. But Lezlie didn't want to stand around gossiping, and certainly not when the subject was Drew Bradinton. It was late and all Lezlie wanted to do was fall into bed.

Once again, she set out for home, fighting and almost conquering a familiar loneliness. Silently, she wished her mother were in town. She really needed to be with someone close to her even if it was just for a casual lunch or dinner. She had had so many friends at one time, but one by one they had faded away... or had she gradually pushed them away? She had tried to stay in touch; she had attended the usual dinners and parties, but everyone seemed so careful around her that it made her uncomfortable. And the fact was she had become a single in a world of doubles.

THE TELEPHONE RANG at exactly seven o'clock. Lezlie was sitting in her bright yellow-and-green kitchen sipping a cup of coffee. A warm smile settled on her face when she recognized the caller's voice.

"Hi, mom." As if on cue, her mother had called to check on her.

"Lezlie, dear, is everything all right there?"

"Of course, mom. But I'm glad you called. I've missed you."

"I've missed you, too," Margaret Hall said, and Lezlie could envision her mother's smile and then concerned little frown. "I had the strangest feeling something was wrong."

"You know, it's funny, mom. But I was just thinking last night I'd like to talk to you and voilà, you call. I see your radar is still sharp." They both laughed at the familiar joke. Ever since Lezlie could remember, her mother had known if she was worried or if she had a problem almost before Lezlie knew it herself. For a few minutes her mother talked about her trip and one of Lezlie's relatives whom she had been visiting for the past two days. The conversation was easy and pleasant.

"Did you have something in particular you wanted to talk about, Lezlie?"

"Not really, mom. It can wait until you get back."

"Are you sure, dear? You don't sound quite like yourself."

"Yes, everything's all right. I'm just a little tired. I had a late call last night. I was just about to get dressed to go to the hospital. But it will be good to see you."

"Well, I should be back the middle of next week and we can meet for lunch."

"That sounds fine," Lezlie said, but she couldn't deny her spirits had lifted.

Lezlie's mood was brighter when she hung up the phone. *Don't knock it.* The words Drew had said flew into her mind. She hadn't meant her comment as a complaint. While she and her mother didn't see each other that often, they shared a very special relationship, each woman independent and going her own way, but always there for the other when needed. Lezlie understood her mother's love for traveling. For years, Margaret Hall had kept house, giving everything of herself to her husband and her child. And now that she was alone, it was her turn to do exactly what she wanted. Truth be known, Lezlie was glad that her mother had found the diversion traveling offered. And it gave them so much more to talk about than they'd had in the past.

Lezlie rinsed her breakfast dishes, straightened her kitchen, then watered the plants sitting on the sill of her kitchen window. She stared out the window, watching the wind whip the last remnants of winter across the grass. She really had to get her yard cleaned up this weekend. It was beginning to look a little like a small jungle. But it was her jungle, she thought, contented.

The morning shift at the hospital was as busy as the night had been quiet. Twice as many nurses manned the station to help with patients' baths, updating the charts, preparing medication, orders for x-ray or testing, while orderlies quickly changed bed linens or removed breakfast trays to the huge carts in the hall.

Lezlie had just arrived when she found Dr. Carver already on the floor. He stood outside Merri's room, his brow furrowed in concentration as he read over her chart. He glanced up when Lezlie stopped next to him.

"Have you seen Merri yet?" Lezlie asked.

"I was just going in. Trouble last night?"

"Nothing I couldn't handle," Lezlie said. "I was planning a session with her this morning, so I thought I would catch you beforehand. She is really excited about seeing her stitches."

"Aren't they all?" Dr. Carver stated blandly.

Lezlie didn't care for Dr. Carver's jaded attitude, but she followed him into the room. There was no sign of the previous night's upset on Merri's face. Excitement sparkled in the child's eyes and Lezlie was amazed by the change in Dr. Carver when he entered the room. He was a different man when he put his bedside manner into practice. No sooner had he removed the bandage than Merri shyly said she had to go to the bathroom.

Lezlie exchanged a glance with Dr. Carver. They both knew there was a full-length mirror on the back of the bathroom door. Lezlie held Merri's arm while she slipped her feet slowly to the floor. A perplexed frown settled over Merri's eyes and she looked up at Lezlie, her hand holding her abdomen.

"It feels like everything's going to fall out," Merri said.

Dr. Carver hid his smile behind the chart.

"Well, it won't," Lezlie reassured the girl, but she couldn't suppress a chuckle. Merri's smile brightened her whole face. She slipped her hand into Lezlie's and walked with her slowly across the room. Inside the bathroom, Lezlie closed the door. Merri stood before the mirror, lifted her gown on one side and stared, wide-eyed at the black thread crisscrossed across the neat incision.

"Will the stitches be there forever?" she asked in alarm, unable to break her transfixed stare.

"No, Dr. Sanders will take them out in about a week. Then, when the incision is all healed, there will only be a thin line where the stitches are now."

"Boy, that's neat," Merri remarked. "I can't wait to show Uncle Drew. He's coming to have lunch with me. He says it will be like a picnic."

"That sounds fun," Lezlie said.

"Can you come, too? I'm sure Uncle Drew will have enough. He always gets more than we can eat."

"I'm afraid not," Lezlie said. The last thing she wanted today was to see Drew Bradinton. She would have to see him eventually to give him a report on Merri and a session schedule, but not this morning...not after what had happened between them the previous evening. She wasn't ready to handle his confidence in her attraction to him...or to deal with his pursuit. "I have patients I have to see today," she explained when Merri continued to stare at her. "But I can drop by to see you while you're here in the hospital, and once you go home, you can come to see me and we'll talk."

"What about?" Merri asked, her expression guarded.

"Oh, whatever you want to talk about. You can tell me about the things that make you happy, what you like, about school, anything you want to."

"Like a best friend?" Merri asked.

"Sort of," Lezlie answered, aware that she must make Merri understand that while they could be friends, theirs would also be a doctor-patient relationship. "Can you make it by yourself or do you need some help?" Lezlie asked, reminding Merri of the excuse she had given Dr. Carver.

Merri dropped her eyes, smiling slightly. "I didn't really have to go. I was afraid he would put the new bandage on without letting me see."

"Well, now that you've taken a peek, I suggest we get you back to bed so Dr. Carver can get on with his rounds. And if he says it's okay, we can take a walk down the hall."

A short time later, Dr. Carver left Lezlie alone with Merri. "Can we go for a walk now?" Merri asked, ready to leave the bed.

"In a minute," Lezlie answered. "I want to talk to you first. Merri, do you know what a psychologist is?"

"No."

"A psychologist is someone who talks to people or who listens to people who have problems or things that hurt them. That is what I do. I am a psychologist. And while I want us to be friends, I also want you to talk to me. When you're ready I want you to tell me about your parents. I can understand—"

"No, you can't," Merri blurted. "Nobody can. They left me...."

"No, Merri, they didn't leave you, they died," Lezlie said firmly. "You can't blame them. It was an accident...."

Merri turned away, tears threatening. "I don't want to talk about it."

"All right," Lezlie said gently. She lifted Merri's chin and looked directly into the child's blue eyes. She didn't usually use her own experience to gain the confidence of a patient, but it could save a great deal of time with Merri if the little girl realized that what had happened to her was not an isolated incident... that other people had faced the same kind of loss. "I want to tell you a secret, Merri. I do know how you feel...maybe better than anybody else. Because what happened to you also happened to me."

"It did?"

"Yes, and it took me a long time to believe it had really happened. So you see, I know how much it hurts. And sometimes it helps to talk to someone about what hurts. And that's what I want you to do. You don't have to until you want to, but it has been put off a long time. Unless you've talked to your uncle."

Merri shook her head. "He asked me, but I wouldn't tell him."

"Wouldn't tell him what?"

Merri hedged, her eyes darting away from Lezlie.

"There's only one other thing I want you to know, Merri. I'm going to be your doctor, but I also want to be your friend. We'll work toward that, okay?"

Merri nodded, not quite ready to accept Lezlie. But trust would come in time, Lezlie mused. She stood up. "How about that walk?"

Lezlie moved the chair aside and was going to help Merri out of bed. But she caught a slight movement out of the corner of her eye. Turning around, she faced Drew Bradinton. He was leaning in the doorway, his eyes locked on her with such intensity that she felt a shiver settle in the pit of her stomach. How long had he been there? How much had he heard of what she had said to Merri? She was the one who wanted to hedge now.

"Good morning, Dr. Garrett." Drew walked into the room, no sign of intimacy in his incredibly blue eyes or his tone. Lezlie could have sighed with relief.

"You're early," Merri chirped, giggling when Drew lifted her gently off the bed and held her for a moment. "We were just going for a walk. Dr. Carver says I should. Will you come, too?"

"Why don't you and your uncle go, Merri? We can go another time."

"I want us all to go," Merri protested.

"Then we will," Drew announced, his inquiring glance swinging to Lezlie. He set Merri on her feet, her small hand completely lost in his. Merri extended her other hand to Lezlie.

"I got to see my stitches this morning," she babbled excitedly. "Boy, are they neat! Lezlie says it will be a week before they are taken out. And then there will be a scar, a little one."

Merri chatted happily as they walked the length of the hall and then back. Drew had glanced up in surprise when Merri had called Lezlie by her first name. A simple shrug and a smile had answered his silent question. But Lezlie avoided meeting his eyes as they walked. She listened to Merri, all the while aware of Drew's unwavering perusal. The longer he stared at her, that unreadable question sparking in his eyes, the more uncomfortable Lezlie became. She found herself wishing she had a patient to see or some task that would give her an excuse to escape. Rescue came quite unexpectedly. They were nearing the nurses' station when the nurse leaned over the desk.

"You have a telephone call, Dr. Garrett."

Drew and Merri continued along the hall. Jean, Lezlie's secretary, relayed a message that Mrs. Hawkins had called about rescheduling her daughter's afternoon session for this morning. Lezlie checked her watch, reset the appointment for Lori Hawkins, and then popped into Merri's room to say goodbye.

"I'll be back tomorrow," she said when Merri frowned.

"Can't you come back for our picnic? Uncle Drew is going to bring all kinds of things."

"I wish I could, but I can't today. Maybe another time."

"We'll hold you to it," Drew said. For the first time since his arrival, Lezlie was aware of the challenge in his eyes. She waved to Merri and walked quickly toward the elevator. She had just pushed the button when a hand caught her arm and brought her around.

"I need to talk to you," Drew said, his voice a low rumble.

"I was wondering how long the act would last," Lezlie said.

"What act?"

"The one where you act like I'm the doctor and you're the patient's relative."

"Do you want me to act otherwise?"

"No," she said quickly. "But neither do I want to talk to you."

An amused smirk curved his mouth. "Well, that may be a little difficult considering that you are treating my niece, and of course, I have questions."

"Oh," Lezlie said quietly, embarrassed that she had misinterpreted. "I have patients until late this afternoon. You could come by my office then."

"Fine," Drew agreed, glancing beyond her to the open doors of the elevator. It was empty and when Lezlie walked through the doors, Drew quickly followed.

His hands were on her shoulders the moment the doors slid shut. "What do you think you are doing?" Lezlie demanded.

"I just wanted to say we can talk about Merri in your office, but since you are such a stickler for protecting your reputation, where do you suggest we talk about us?"

"There's is no 'us.'" Lezlie said flatly.

"Not yet," Drew drawled, "but there will be."

The confident promise took Lezlie off guard. "Why, of all the conceited, egotistical...."

"It is not conceited or egotistical to recognize what happens between us. The trick is to accept it for what it can be."

"No, thanks," Lezlie said quickly. He was leaning over her, trapping her against the walls of the confining elevator.

"Why not? Give me one good reason why we shouldn't see each other. Well?"

Lezlie folded her arms over her chest. "Well, what?"

"One good reason," he reminded her playfully.

"I am treating your niece."

"Besides that," Drew corrected. "That's not a reason, it's an excuse."

"Look, this is getting us nowhere," Lezlie stated.

"I agree." Drew smiled.

Lezlie had had enough of the silly game. "Mr. Bradinton, to put it simply, I am not interested...."

Drew towered over her, his face only inches above hers. "Aren't you?" He said it so quietly she had to strain to hear. "I keep remembering a woman I held in my arms for a brief moment, a woman who, for some reason, wants to deny her own sexuality. I haven't forgotten."

Neither have I, Lezlie thought. She had dreamed of Drew last night, dreamed of a kiss that went on and on without end, but without fulfillment. Even now her lips began to tingle. He was so close that she could see the fine lines around his eyes, the dark hairs within the sun-bleached arch of his eyebrows. And then she made the mistake of looking directly into his eyes. She was trapped, caught as securely as a snared rabbit. She became lost in the sky-blue irises, befuddled by the promise of passion that glittered and glowed more brightly than any candle. She could feel his warm breath, smell his alluring cologne and see the naked longing beckoning in his eyes.

Drew sensed Lezlie's disquiet from the rapid rise and fall of her breasts and the way her eyes skittered away and then returned. And her vulnerability was almost tangible. She seemed to be holding her breath, waiting for him to act. To kiss her, he wondered, or to move away? He didn't know which. As certain as he was of what he wanted, she seemed just as uncertain. He touched her chin, then traced the line of her trembling mouth. The air vibrated between them, charged with the electricity of desire and doubt on her part; passion and determination on his.

"You don't ever have to be afraid of me, Lezlie," he said quietly.

Lezlie finally found her voice. "I'm not," she said honestly. It wasn't Drew she was afraid of, but the commitment a relationship would demand.

"Good," he murmured.

Lezlie had a twinge of disappointment when he straightened, for his lips never once touched hers. A dull ache replaced the rippling sensations. She smoothed her hair and cleared her throat, feeling as though she had walked in and out of a dream those few minutes in the elevator. The doors opened and no one in the lobby could have the slightest suspicion of what had transpired. Drew walked at her side, touching her briefly to catch her attention.

"I'll see you at three."

Lezlie nodded dully, watching as he walked away. Lord, what was she going to do? Being around Drew was like playing with dynamite. The fuse was lit and racing, threatening an explosion that would rock anyone near. Perhaps she should suggest another psychologist for Merri. Then she wouldn't be thrown together with Drew.

"You can handle it," she mumbled, yet something warned her to steer clear of situations that could unleash the vortex of emotions swirling within her.

CHAPTER THREE

BY TWO-THIRTY THAT AFTERNOON, Lezlie was as close to a nervous wreck as any self-respecting psychologist would ever admit to being. Although she had taken a copy of all the pertinent information in Charles Sanders's file on Merri and had read it thoroughly, she went over it once again. There were some notes about the treatment given to Merri in Denver after the accident; the leg had healed nicely, the concussion had been minor. But as Charles had said, there were remarks concerning an inordinate number of ailments: a slight case of anemia, some headaches. But what stood out was the unrelenting complaint of stomachache. It was a common adolescent manifestation of emotional stress. The file revealed only what had happened to Merri in a physical sense, not the pain she had buried.

When the intercom buzzed, Lezlie jumped. Well, he was punctual, Lezlie thought. Unwittingly, she braced herself for his entry into her office. His eyes swept the plush carpet, the glass-and-wood desk, dark blue sofa and chairs and the bookcases that sided her desk. He took a chair in front of her desk, his attitude totally focused on a discussion of Merri.

"I have gone over Dr. Sanders's files and the reports he received from Denver," Lezlie started. "I have to agree with Dr. Sanders that Merri's chronic complaints of stomachaches have very little to do with the appendix. It isn't unusual for someone who is suffering emotional stress to project that stress into a physical ailment. After having talked with Merri this week, my opinion is based on some obvious facts."

"Such as?" Drew asked quietly.

"First, that Merri feels a great deal of grief and guilt over her parents' deaths, to the point that she can't even discuss it. You can't deal with a problem unless you can face it. And the fact is, Merri hasn't faced it yet. Has she talked to you about it all?"

"Merri has been pretty withdrawn ever since the accident," Drew answered. "I've tried to talk to her, but she has made it clear she doesn't want to talk, at least not to me."

"One thing has also become very clear," Lezlie went on, consulting her notes. "Merri is not a typical twelve-year-old. When I first met her, my first impression was that she was younger than a girl of pre-teen age. And through our discussions, I have found that she doesn't share the interests of most girls her age: the current fads in clothes, music or an awareness of boys. She hasn't mentioned any special friends or activities, but you may know of something."

"Merri seems to prefer being alone," Drew said. "I've tried to get her involved in school activities, but she doesn't show much enthusiasm for anything."

"That isn't as unusual as you may feel," Lezlie

said quietly. "Since Merri is carrying around a lot of guilt and probably anger, she is denying present happiness in an attempt to hold on to the past. Therefore, the process of maturing has been interrupted. I would be able to learn more about this during therapy, and if I could gain her trust and encourage her to tell me about her parents, it could reverse her immaturity. Unfortunately, for the present, she adamantly refuses to discuss her parents."

Drew stood up and walked to the window. He gazed outside into the warm sunshine.

"Mr. Bradinton, should I treat Merri, there would be times when I might ask you to verify things she tells me. Or you would need to support aspects of the therapy, even if you disagree with the method. The main thing at this point is that she receive help." Lezlie stared at his broad back. "I know Charles recommended that I counsel Merri, but I thought I should allow you the opportunity to choose another psychologist. I can assure you I won't take your decision personally."

Drew swung around. "Why?"

"Well, considering the way things began...."

Drew scowled, and Lezlie sensed the anger she had seen once before. "That's ridiculous and you know it," he said shortly. "Merri has already become very fond of you. You have seen her through a very trying time. And for that, I am indebted. But let's get one thing clear, Lezlie. Taking yourself off the case has nothing to do with the way things started with you and Merri. It's what happened between you and me that has you worried."

Lezlie looked at her hands as Drew turned his back on her and stared out the window. She wasn't aware that he was trying very hard to control his temper. He had accepted all Lezlie said concerning Merri with stoic silence. But when he turned around, there was a haunted look in his eyes and a tightness around his firm mouth. He wanted to tell her what might be the cause of Merri's reluctance to discuss what had occurred the night of the accident. Drew wasn't certain himself that Merri had overheard her parents, but if she had, it would explain her behavior. Yet he had to consider Lezlie's preference to learn what troubled Merri from Merri. What if Merri had overheard Greg and Meredith and suppose she blurted it to Lezlie? Could he make Lezlie understand? Suddenly, it was very important that she did. But he would not tell her. Perhaps once she came to know him better, it would be easier.

"How often are you going to want to see her?" Drew asked, deliberately avoiding her comment about another psychologist.

"We're getting a good start, and I'll continue to visit her room each day. Once she is released from the hospital, it is more or less up to you. I would suggest twice a week—more the first week or so, when she's back home, if she wants it. I want to have enough contact without pushing."

"Merri said you were going to be her friend—"

Lezlie intercepted his question. "She's had quite a few doctors, and they haven't really helped her. I've explained that I will be her doctor, but what she also needs is someone who can just be a real friend.

Does she ever talk about any particular child at school?"

Drew shook his head. "I've suggested that she invite someone home, but she never has. Her teacher has tried to get Merri involved with the other kids, but Merri hangs back."

Lezlie was somewhat surprised. For some reason it hadn't occurred to her that Drew might be so deeply concerned as to talk to Merri's teacher and encourage new friendships. Obviously he was more complex and more sensitive than Lezlie had originally presumed.

"Do you know when Merri will be discharged from the hospital?" Lezlie asked.

"Charles said it would be a few days."

"Then we can set up a schedule of appointments for after she's had her stitches out."

Drew smiled suddenly. "I think she'll be sorry to see them go."

"Yes." Lezlie chuckled. "I've seen the healing process better than I ever have before."

"Was there anything else about Merri?" Drew asked.

Lezlie hesitated, certain that the moment they completed the discussion of his niece, his usual bantering challenges would return. She shook her head and nothing happened. He started to leave her office, but caught her stunned expression when he reached the door.

"I'm beginning to think this may be a good thing for Merri, and that she has the right person helping her. And I wouldn't want you to be misled, Lezlie.

Just because I decided to conduct myself in the manner you requested doesn't mean anything has changed." He grinned and winked at her before disappearing.

THE RESTAURANT was crowded with the noontime rush. A hum of conversation and laughter hung over the tables as waitresses moved briskly with subdued haste. Margaret Hall checked her watch. As usual, Lezlie was late. She shook her head, knowing that her daughter was driving herself. But her realization didn't alter the fact that she still worried about her child. The hardest thing Margaret had done in her entire life was to let go of her daughter, entirely and without reservation. She had seen some of her friends cling to their children, clutch them so tightly that the young people had been barely able to breathe. She hadn't wanted that for Lezlie, nor really for herself. And she was proud of all that Lezlie had been able to accomplish. They were separate yet forever connected through their relationship, one that burdened neither of them.

Lezlie rushed toward the table, breathless and flushed. "Hi, mom, sorry I'm late." She leaned over to kiss her mother and then slipped into the booth. "How was New York?"

"The same as usual—frantic. Your Aunt Jane sends her love. I think we saw most of the shows on Broadway, and we went shopping...you know, the usual." Margaret eyed her daughter critically. "So, how are you?"

"Fine, busy though."

"Are you taking care of yourself? You look thinner."

Lezlie smiled with true affection. Impulsively she reached across the table and squeezed her mother's hand. "Yes, I am thinner. I've been working some overtime lately."

"And your social life?"

"Is the same," Lezlie reported.

"Honey, it's so easy to let one thing get control of your life. I know it's none of my business, but I think it would do you good to get out more."

"I love my work, mom. For the present, it's all I need."

Margaret put up a slender hand. "All right, dear. I guess what I was trying to say is that work can't compensate for companionship."

The waitress interrupted their conversation to take their orders. But the moment she walked away, Margaret leaned forward.

"Lezlie, you wanted to talk to me about something when I called. I could feel it. Is there anything wrong?"

"Not really, mom," Lezlie evaded. "I have taken on a new patient...."

Now it was Margaret's turn to smile. "Since when does a new patient make you sound as though you need to talk to someone?"

"I suppose I was feeling lonely, but your call was enough to get me past it." Lezlie leaned forward, her arms folded on the table. "Oh, mom, you should see her. She lost both her parents last year. She's just so...so...."

"So much like you two years ago."

The remark was direct, and true. "I guess so," Lezlie murmured, but excitement shone in her eyes. "I know I can help her deal with it, or at least accept it. I had you to help me. But she doesn't have anyone except an uncle she doesn't know very well. She blames herself and her parents for leaving her. She needs someone who can understand, and while I don't doubt that her uncle loves her, she doesn't really trust him yet."

Lezlie rarely discussed her cases with anyone. But when she did, she was careful not to mention names. Lezlie quickly explained how she had come to be involved with Merri and how Dr. Sanders had talked with Drew Bradinton.

Margaret's bright eyes narrowed perceptively. "What's this uncle like?"

Lezlie sipped her tea and hedged artfully. "I don't know really. He is extremely busy handling the affairs of the girl's parents and his own business. Perhaps that explains why he hasn't been with her a great deal. And he feels his niece blames him to a certain extent."

"Isn't that all fairly normal, to try to find some justification, some reason for death?"

"I suppose. Over dinner last week, her uncle told me that there was some kind of argument between her parents. That might have caused his niece's attitude." Lezlie did not notice her mother's slight smile. "He was convinced that the appendix was the cause of her complaints of stomachaches that started just after her parents' deaths."

"And it wasn't?"

"Charles Sanders doesn't think so and neither do I. I think it was her way of getting attention. The appendix was just an unlucky coincidence. She was released from the hospital a few days ago, but we'll continue the sessions." A determined gleam filled Lezlie's eyes. "With a little time and patience I can get through to her and make her see she's not to blame."

Margaret smiled. "I know you will. You can not only sympathize, but empathize. It would be easy to become emotionally involved. You can offer advice and support, but it is still a singular adjustment."

"I know, mom. But if I can just make that adjustment a little easier for her, then I will have accomplished a lot." The waitress had placed their orders on the table. Lezlie bit into the thick juicy hamburger. "So, tell me about the plays you saw."

Their conversation through lunch was one of critiques, opinions and anecdotes about the entertainment industry in general. Lezlie laughed easily at her mother's amusing comments about her spinster aunt. Their meeting was a pleasant interlude to Lezlie's hectic schedule. And as always happened when she was with her mother, the sense of loneliness she occasionally felt dissolved. She drew comfort from her mother's company. Perhaps it was because her mother didn't expect anything of her. Margaret Hall only wanted what was natural, for her only child to find happiness. And Lezlie had already decided that she would treat Merri Bradinton as she had been treated by her mother after Michael's death—with gentle comforting, compassion and care. Before parting, they made a tentative dinner date for a week from Sunday.

Lezlie returned to her office, her mood lighter, her smile easy and relaxed. The afternoon passed quickly as she dealt with a variety of problems, seeing one young patient after another. One cried woefully while another glared at her with rebellious defiance. But she gave each the same patience. She had just seen her last patient for the day when her intercom buzzed. Jean told her that Mr. Bradinton and his niece wanted to see her if she had a moment. Lezlie's hands trembled as she smoothed her hair. She was halfway across the room when the door opened.

Drew's presence seemed to fill her office. He was dressed casually in crisp gray slacks, a cream-colored Oxford shirt and a soft, cranberry-colored pullover sweater. His thick sandy hair was tousled by the wind. Lezlie avoided his appraising scrutiny by leaning down to speak to Merri.

"Hi, Merri. How are you feeling?"

"Okay. I just got my stitches out. It hurt."

Before Lezlie could offer a comment, Drew put his arm around his niece's small shoulders. "But she was very good about it. So when she asked to come and see you and where you work, I thought it might be all right."

"It is." Lezlie smiled.

"Is this where I will come to see you?" Merri asked. Lezlie nodded and then remained silent as Merri walked around the room, surveying the pottery on one shelf of the bookcase and the parchments hanging on the wall. She sat in a chair and bounced up and down before smiling at Lezlie. "It's nice. Blue is my favorite color."

"Mine, too," Lezlie admitted honestly, but even if it wasn't, according to studies done, blue was a relaxing color, and that had contributed to her decision to use it in her office. The walls were a pale tint of blue that matched the carpet.

Lezlie was very aware of Drew, even though he remained apart from them, his arms folded across his chest. "Tell me, Merri, what are you doing now that you are home?"

Merri grimaced. "Schoolwork. Uncle Drew went over and got my books and assignments from the teacher. I'll never get it all done. Dr. Sanders said I can go back to school for the last couple of weeks. I got a card from the kids in my class, and Mrs. Cates baked me a cake."

"Mrs. Cates is our housekeeper," Drew explained. "Which reminds me, we should be getting home, Merri. She will have dinner ready in a little while."

"She gets all bent out of shape if you're late," Merri confided and Lezlie laughed.

"Merri, why don't you wait outside for just a minute? I want to ask Dr. Garrett something." When they were alone, Drew's eyes swept over Lezlie. The light from the window highlighted her dark hair as wisps fell across her cheek and shoulder. It was all he could do to keep from kissing her soft mouth. He shoved his hands in his pockets and sighed. "I have a favor to ask," he said. "I have to go out of town next week so I won't be here for Merri's first sessions with you. My housekeeper will be staying over, but she doesn't drive. Is there any way you could schedule Merri as your last appointment of the day, and see her at the house? I know it's an imposition...."

It was unusual, Lezlie thought, but not impossible. "I think I can arrange it. How long will you be gone?"

"A little over a week. If I knew Merri was up to it, I would take her with me, but it's a little soon after her surgery."

"Have you explained that to her?"

"Yes, but I'm not certain she understands. I've spent every minute with her since the operation, but I can't let the business slide completely." Drew smiled. "She's really a great kid, although she's still a little standoffish."

"Did you see her very much before her parents died?" Lezlie asked.

"Not as much as I wanted to," Drew said. Lezlie thought she detected an edge of bitterness in his voice. But why? Perhaps it was because if he had seen more of Merri through the years, coming to live with him might not have been so traumatic for the child.

Lezlie hadn't realized that Drew had closed the distance between them and now stood only a few feet away, his eyes boring into hers. "Sometimes I feel I have spent my entire life doing the right and equitable thing in a given situation when I might have been better off to follow my instincts. What do you think?"

"I think it would depend on the situation," Lezlie said, suddenly unnerved by his nearness. "And who else happens to be involved," she added quickly. He hadn't even touched her, yet she felt as though she was being caressed as his voice washed over her.

"And what if the situation involved a very beautiful psychologist whom I find utterly irresistible?"

"Then my suggestion would be to resist at all costs."

"Oh, lovely lady, you don't know what you're asking," Drew said, but his light tone was belied by the intensity in his eyes.

"Mr. Bradinton...."

"Drew."

"All right...Drew. You have to stop this—"

"What?" he asked innocently.

Lezlie couldn't bring herself to put into words the subtle or not-so-subtle pursuit she felt. "My first concern is your niece, as it should be. She is my patient. And this verbal game you're playing is very unnerving."

"There, was that so hard to admit?"

"What?"

"That I unnerve you. That is only half of what you do to me."

"So you've intimated before," Lezlie said, unable to stop her response to his amused grin. "You have a very bad habit. You don't listen very well. Regardless of what you feel or I think, Merri comes first. Are you listening?"

Drew nodded.

"I don't want to become involved with you—"

"Because you are Merri's doctor and it wouldn't be professional," he supplied.

"That's part of it."

"And what's the other part?"

"That," Lezlie said calmly, "is personal and something I don't wish to discuss."

"Maybe you should."

Lezlie felt trapped just as she had in the elevator. "It wouldn't change anything, Drew."

"Are you always so certain?" he said gently, lifting her chin so that she was forced to look at him. "I get the distinct impression that you may look at me, but you don't really see me. You try very hard to keep me in the safe little category of Merri's guardian. Perhaps if you would give yourself a chance to get to know me, you wouldn't think I am an insensitive clod who's only after your body...."

"I don't," Lezlie murmured.

"Don't what? You don't want to know me better or you don't think I am insensitive clod."

"Both," she returned calmly. "I don't have time for personal involvements."

"Nor the inclination?" he teased.

"Nor the inclination," Lezlie confirmed pointedly. It was impossible to feel as steady as she sounded when he looked at her with such a warm smile and those twinkling eyes.

"I think you should reevaluate your position. You know what they say: 'All work and no play....' But we'll do it your way for the time being." Before she could utter a response, he had touched her lightly on the cheek, then turned and walked across the office. "I'll call you when I get back. If you should need me, Mrs. Cates knows how to get in touch with me." He hesitated at the door and looked at her. "Take care of my girl."

His smile was enough to melt the coldest heart, and Lezlie was fairly seared. She was glad to be through for the day for she couldn't have concentrated on another appointment if her life depended on it. Was each meeting between them to end on a personal level? His playfulness and unrelenting persuasiveness was hard to resist. And the truth be known, Lezlie couldn't help responding to his warm personality.

Lezlie left her office, stopped at a nearby grocery store and then headed for her workout at the spa.

"Hi ya, Doc," said Patti Cach, one of the exercise instructors, as she hurried toward Lezlie. Patti was slender and her lithesome figure was shown to advantage in the scanty leotard. Lezlie had met her on her first session at the spa. It hadn't taken long for them to become friends. Lezlie could still remember how she had tried unsuccessfully not to laugh when Patti had introduced herself, for her last name was pronounced "cake."

"I know, I know," Patti had said wryly. "My folks had a weird sense of humor. I got ribbed all through school about my name."

Lezlie's attention snapped to the present when Patti took her arm. "You look a little strung out, Lezlie."

"My schedule has been really tight," Lezlie said. "And what I need is a good workout."

"Say no more," Patti said with a grin, leading her through the maze of exercise equipment. "You've got just enough time to change before the class. Your friend got here just a while ago." Patti chuckled. "She may be ready to quit by the time you get started."

A popular song with a heavy beat pounded through the speakers in the exercise gym as Lezlie headed for the locker room.

Donna Blair called out from a position on the floor. "Leave it to you to be late," she puffed. "Come on before they kill me." Donna continued with the leg raises. "Oh, God, every muscle is screaming and I just started. I'm going to need a physical therapist."

"I can recommend one," Lezlie joked.

"Very funny," Donna drawled. "You of thin bodies have no pity for us that don't."

Lezlie laughed and shook her head. She had met Donna Blair two days after beginning work at the hospital. Donna headed a private school for mentally retarded and autistic children. It was an endless, often thankless, undertaking, but Lezlie had to come to know that it was the slightest accomplishment or progress of her students that repaid Donna for the many hours of hard work. Donna was totally absorbed in her "kids," as she called her students. She and Lezlie often met for lunch and sometimes for dinner when Jim, Donna's husband, was out of town. Lezlie was in awe of the unwavering patience Donna's job required, but Donna waved away her praise with a laugh and a joke about having taken a course, Patience 101, during college.

When Lezlie returned to the exercise room, Donna

was on her way out. "I'll see you in the Jacuzzi," Donna said with a grin, and Lezlie nodded. Music pounded through the ceiling, the beat offering a steady rhythm. Lezlie did a couple of warm-up stretches before joining the more vigorous exercise routine. For the next thirty minutes, Lezlie stretched, twisted and kicked until she felt her tension easing away. Patti's constant banter kept everyone going even though they might be winded or perspiration was running down their straining bodies. When the class ended, Lezlie leaned over, puffing heavily. A few minutes later she went to join Donna, who was relaxing comfortably in the swirling bubbling water of the Jacuzzi.

"If you ask me, this is a far better way of reducing stress than by wearing yourself out doing things a body wasn't meant to do." She looked at Lezlie's thin figure, then at her own. "Well, at least not this body."

"You're being too hard on yourself," Lezlie said. "You can't expect results immediately. It takes time and a good routine...."

"Thanks, but no thanks." Donna grimaced and then grinned mischievously. "Besides, Jim's not complaining."

"He wouldn't dare," Lezlie commented, slipping into the square ceramic tub. The warm water swirled around her, tickling her skin. "Ooh, this is wonderful."

"See? Why wear yourself out, right?" Donna scooted down until the water lapped at her chin. Her short blond hair curled riotously and drops of water shimmered on her face.

For a while they talked about nothing in particular, the conversation progressing idly from Jim's latest fiasco while trying to fix a leaky faucet, to Donna's plans for a summer vacation. And then Lezlie found herself talking about Drew and his attitude toward her. Donna listened without comment.

"I just don't know how to get through to him that I'm not interested in getting involved. He is constantly challenging me in a playful way, and promising what will happen between us. And no matter what I say to put him off, he turns it around to mean something entirely different. It's unsettling to say the least, and I won't lie and say he isn't attractive. But I feel so trapped when he makes it clear what he feels will inevitably happen between us. He senses I'm afraid, and the truth is, I am."

"Then tell him why," Donna said easily.

"It's none of his business," Lezlie snapped. "I just want him to leave me alone. I think we have reached a tentative understanding because of Merri. I can't treat her and be involved with her uncle. But somehow, I don't feel he is convinced."

"You can handle it," Donna said confidently.

"That's what I keep telling myself."

"Well, if you're that attracted to him, which you obviously are, perhaps you should reconsider."

"You're beginning to sound like my mother," Lezlie teased. "I'm not going to wither away just because I prefer to remain alone."

"No one is saying that," Donna said. Donna was the only friend aside from Charles Sanders who knew the truth about Lezlie's past and her struggle to put her life in order. "But she may have a point, Lezlie. Everybody needs someone." Donna raised her hand before Lezlie could utter a word. "I know, I know. You have me and you have your mother and you have your work, but it isn't the same, Lezlie. Have you thought about talking to Dr. Harvey?"

Dr. Harvey was the psychologist who had counseled Lezlie after the accident. As a student of psychology, Lezlie had appreciated an objective point of view. Dr. Harvey had provided that and more. But Lezlie had not seen him in well over a year.

"I think I have been more concerned with getting through the present," Lezlie said. "And I haven't really needed to see him. He said it would take time...."

"It has been two years," Donna said gently. But when Lezlie frowned, she quickly changed the subject. "How about having dinner with Jim and me tomorrow night?"

Lezlie smiled. "I would love to, but things around the house are literally falling apart. Can I have a rain check?"

"Sure," Donna said easily. "If I don't get out of this oversized bathtub soon, I'm going to be as shriveled as a prune." She raised a foot to expose her wrinkled toes, then made a face of disgust. "I knew it. Jim has just about figured out that I'm not working out anything in this place but the Jacuzzi. This will cinch it."

"Well, you just tell Jim not to judge it until he's tried it." They headed in to the showers.

Donna draped a towel across the shower door.

"Actually, I have been wanting to talk to you, Lezlie. Jim says I shouldn't get involved but it's damn hard when one of my kids is at stake. Do you remember me telling you about Elizabeth, one of the autistic children? She started at the school about a year ago?"

"The last time you talked about her, you said she was making progress, though it was slow."

"Yeah, it still is. The problem is her parents are considering having her institutionalized. When they brought Elizabeth to me I cautioned them not to expect miracles. They had the medical definition of autism, but it's still an emotional adjustment for people to accept and deal with a child who lives in her own world, who won't speak or respond to affection. It's almost as though they've given up."

"Was there some specific thing that happened recently to discourage them?"

Donna nodded. "Everything was going pretty well until a month ago when Elizabeth started showing some previous behavior patterns, like banging her head against a wall. It's the first time she's reverted to such behavior in six months or more, but it doesn't mean her treatment is all for nothing. I can't seem to make them understand."

"Maybe you should appeal directly to the mother," Lezlie suggested.

A heavy sigh escaped from Donna. "That's just it. It's the mother who wants to find an institution. I understand that it's frustrating and hard on her. She's given up a career to take care of Elizabeth and they have other kids whom she may feel she is neglecting.

The father's agreeing because he can't be there to help her out and she can't handle it alone. The mother has handled it for almost seven years now, and I suppose she's just really tired and burned out. I don't know how to make them see that Elizabeth is making progress."

"That may be true, Donna, but you have to see it from their viewpoint, too. Having a child is difficult in itself, but coupled with special needs, it becomes more difficult and other children are a factor."

"Then what can I do?"

Lezlie was thoughtful for a minute. "Have you suggested that the mother find a very special housekeeper and go back to work? It would be less expensive to hire a housekeeper than it would be to pay for care in an institution, and it would provide an outlet for the mother. But, either way, Donna, you can't really get emotionally involved."

"That's what Jim keeps saying, but it's so hard not to. I really feel that Elizabeth is making progress."

"I know, but it is a decision her parents will ultimately make, and the more emotionally involved you are, the more difficult it will be for you."

"I suppose you're right, but I think I may talk to them one more time and use your suggestion of a housekeeper. It is an alternative and one I hadn't thought about."

"When are they supposed to tell you their decision?"

"They're coming to the school Monday, but I may give them a call tonight. They can be thinking about the alternative over the weekend."

"If you want to talk later or on the weekend, I'll be home."

Donna's smile dimpled her chin. "Thanks, Les. I really appreciate you listening."

"What's a good psychologist all about?" Lezlie teased, but she grew more serious. "I hope it works out, Donna."

"So do I," Donna breathed.

It was nearly dark as they left the spa and headed toward their cars.

Lezlie returned Donna's wave as she threw her bag into the back seat of her white Mustang. She headed home to cook a light supper and settle down with some long-overdue reading of new theories in psychology.

CHAPTER FOUR

LEZLIE'S FIRST SESSION with Merri went far better than she had anticipated. She'd left her office after her last appointment, and was more than a little impressed when she had pulled into the driveway of Drew Bradinton's house. It was an extremely large house built of cedar and odd-sized glass windows. Mrs. Cates, a matronly woman in her fifties, opened the door. Her wiry gray hair stood out around her face, and she wiped her hands on a large apron.

"You must be Dr. Garrett," she said. "Merri's out back. You want me to call her?"

"No, if you will point the way, I'll join her there." Lezlie followed the housekeeper, but couldn't help a quick inspection of the rooms she passed. The large living-room area with a cathedral ceiling had the most unusual fireplace Lezlie had ever seen. The hearth was of natural stone and the mantel of antique pine. Above the mantel was an unusual geometric panel of wood and inlaid brass.

The soft tan-and-rust accents and the various woods interspersed with plants gave the room a warm comfortable atmosphere. Lezlie's glance wandered to the stairs and the balustered landing, which she assumed connected the bedrooms of the upper landing.

Merri was in the backyard, rocking slightly on a swing near a narrow creek. A cedar-and-glass playhouse stood to one side, and there was what looked to be a newly constructed wood-and-metal gym set. The grass was lush and soft beneath Lezlie's feet as she thanked Mrs. Cates and headed toward Merri. A sudden empathy for the child assailed Lezlie as she watched the slow lazy movement of the swing. Merri sat staring blankly into the grassy creek.

"Hello, Merri." Lezlie continued her approach when Merri turned around. Lezlie was coming to recognize the guarded expression Merri wore when she felt threatened in some way.

"Did your uncle tell you I would be coming here, Merri?"

The girl nodded.

Lezlie pretended an exaggerated interest in the yard. A split-rail fence separated Drew's property from that of his neighbor. Heavy flowering rosebushes crept along the fence posts. The yard had an air of seclusion provided by the dense red-tipped bushes. "It's nice here," Lezlie said.

"I like it," Merri commented.

"I'll bet it isn't very similar to Denver. Did you have a yard like this where you used to live?"

"No, we had a pool."

Lezlie sat down on the swing. "Merri, is anything the matter?" When Merri shook her head, Lezlie prodded gently. "C'mon, you can tell me. Remember, we were going to talk."

"But I don't feel like talking."

"Then we don't have to. Is there something else you want to do?"

Merri was thoughtful for a moment, and then smiled tentatively. "I could show you my room."

Lezlie smiled in return. "I would like that."

After the uncluttered decor in the lower rooms of the house, Lezlie was actually taken aback when she walked into Merri's room. It was all ruffles and lace. There was a canopied bed, and dolls and stuffed animals occupied every nook and cranny. A shadowbox shelf was crammed with dozens and dozens of miniature ceramics while a corkboard held a collage of pictures and photographs. The total effect was a bit overpowering and it took Lezlie a moment to find her voice.

"Isn't it great?"

"Great," Lezlie murmured.

"It's almost exactly like my room at home," Merri said, the first trace of a smile on her mouth. Merri took Lezlie's hand, guiding her around the room and pointing out each special item of the assorted collection.

Lezlie didn't have to ask Merri to talk about her parents. *She must have everything her parents ever gave her in this one room,* Lezlie thought, troubled. She had surrounded herself with mementos and reminders and that disturbed Lezlie. Why had Drew allowed her to put together such a morbid shrine? How could Merri accept a new life when she must be constantly reminded of the past? Lezlie studied the photographs tacked to the corkboard. Greg Bradinton resembled Drew, but Greg was thinner, his face more open. Meredith was as beautiful as Lezlie had assumed she would be; soft blond hair, expressive eyes and a pretty smile.

"Which one of these pictures is your favorite?" Lezlie asked.

"Oh, I like them all. I took some of them out of the scrapbook." Merri described where each photo was taken or some little anecdote about the occasion. For a short while, she was just like any other little girl.

"You don't have any of your uncle up here?" Lezlie pointed out.

"These are just pictures of *us*," Merri explained simply. "I have a picture of Uncle Drew over there."

On the third shelf of her bookcase was a snapshot of Drew with Greg when they were young boys. Disheveled clothes and toothless grins spoke of carefree days and mischievous thoughts. Books lined the other shelves: bedtime storybooks that were for a much-younger child than Merri. The room was a tangible verification of Lezlie's diagnosis of immaturity.

"My momma used to read me a story every night," Merri said quietly. "Sometimes I read them and can remember just how she would say the words."

Lezlie spent a long time with Merri, and then Merri led her on a tour of the house. Lezlie was uncomfortable walking through the rooms that had the stamp of Drew's personality firmly embedded on them, and her unease increased when she stood in Drew's bedroom. She could smell the lingering scent of his after-shave and almost feel his presence amid the soft rust-and-gray colors. The huge room had a fireplace sided by floor-to-ceiling windows that overlooked the yard. Lezlie would never have known the oak bed was a water bed if Merri had not run across the room and jumped onto it. The spread undulated crazily.

"Should you do that?"

Merri grinned. "Uncle Drew doesn't mind. My dad wanted to get one after he saw Uncle Drew's one time. But my mom said a water bed was deprived...."

Lezlie had to stifle a laugh. Obviously Merri's mother had meant depraved. Still, it was a strange thing to say. By the time Lezlie was ready to leave, she felt she had learned more about Merri than would have been possible in many sessions in her office. She was standing at the front door with Merri when Mrs. Cates came toward them from the back of the house.

"Mr. Bradinton is on the phone, Merri." Lezlie had heard the phone ring, and as Merri ran to answer the call, she opened the door to leave. "He said he would like to talk to you, too, Dr. Garrett. The phone is this way."

After shutting the door, Lezlie followed Mrs. Cates into the kitchen where Merri was propped on a stool. "I will, Uncle Drew. Yes, she's right here."

Merri handed the phone to Lezlie. "I thought I might find you still at the house," he said quietly. "How's Merri? Did the session go okay?"

"Fine on both counts," Lezlie said carefully. She

noticed that Merri hung rather close. "Merri has been showing me her room...."

There was a moment's pause. "Pretty awful, huh?"

"Oh, yes. And we've had a nice visit."

"And how are you doing?" Drew said, a personal warmth radiating through the line. "Are you thinking about me?"

"It would be a little hard not to at the moment. I am standing in your kitchen."

"Miss me?"

"No," Lezlie said coolly, but she was not as calm as she sounded.

"Didn't anyone ever tell you it's a sin to lie?"

"Who says I am?"

"I do, but we'll talk about it when I get back."

"Yes, I think that would be a good idea," Lezlie said, meaning more than a personal discussion, but unable to say so with Merri listening to every word.

And her meaning had not been lost on Drew. "I can guess that Merri is close by. Should I call you later? You could give me your home number."

"That isn't really necessary. Why don't you call me when you get back?"

"Oh, I'll be talking to you before then," Drew promised. "Will you put Merri back on so I can tell her good night? Good night to you, too, Lezlie."

"Good night." Lezlie passed the phone, trying not to listen to Merri promise to behave and to do as Mrs. Cates instructed.

Merri gave an exasperated sigh as she hung up the

phone. "Gosh, you'd think I was gonna run away or something."

"Does your uncle have reason to be afraid that you would?" Lezlie asked without quite knowing why.

Merri looked completely puzzled. "Where would I go?" she asked, her tone soft and dejected.

LEZLIE CONTINUED THE SESSIONS, carefully arranging her schedule so she would not be on call at the hospital during her visits with Merri. She found Merri was far more at ease when they talked in her room, surrounded by reminders of her parents. Perhaps Drew had made an unwitting but excellent suggestion by asking Lezlie to call at his house. Merri told Lezlie about her school friends in Denver, about the neighborhood where she had lived, the vacations she had taken with her parents, but never once did she mention the accident. At times Lezlie was unnerved by the way Merri often talked about her parents in the present tense. By the end of the week, Lezlie had decided on a definite course of treatment with Merri. The first thing seemed to be to convince her to alter her behavior... and to redecorate her bedroom.

As had become habit, Drew called before Lezlie left his house after their Friday session. He talked to Merri and then asked to speak with Lezlie. He was at the Denver airport, waiting to board his flight home.

"Lezlie, I want to talk to you... really talk about Merri without all the cautious hints. I may be in late. Can I call you then, or will you be in your office tomorrow?"

"Are you worried?" Lezlie asked quietly.

"I don't know exactly, but there's something in Merri's voice when I talk to her, an excitement I haven't heard for a long time. Is she making progress? Is that it?"

"Maybe you had better call me later," Lezlie suggested, waiting while Drew got a pencil to write down her home number.

Lezlie spent a few minutes with Merri and then headed home. She hardly tasted the chef salad she whipped together. And as much as she didn't want to admit it, she was looking forward to Drew's call. The contact between them during the week had been brief and had almost exclusively concerned Merri. But there was a steady undercurrent Lezlie could not deny when his deep voice became more personal. Why should Drew Bradinton affect her in such a way? Granted, he was good-looking, charming and quite appealing with his dry humor and smiling challenges. Was she really that afraid of becoming close to a man? The mere thought of a relationship made Lezlie's stomach lurch crazily. Yes, she was afraid of an entanglement that could lead to the kind of dependency she had decided she didn't want. She didn't need anyone to give her life value or purpose. She was self-confident and self-sufficient. Involvement brought emotional commitment. And that was what she had tried so hard to avoid and had done so successfully, until now. The feelings she was discovering she harbored about Drew were overwhelming in one sense yet enticing in another.

Angrily, Lezlie put her dishes in the sink, flipping off the lights as she headed through the house. She wasn't going to think about it any longer. She would take her bath and then curl up with a good book—anything but a steamy romance would suffice.

Lezlie had just stepped out of the shower when she heard her phone ringing. Hastily she wrapped a towel around her sopping hair and pulled on a terry robe. The low rumbling voice that greeted her wiped away whatever anger she had fabricated.

"I thought maybe you had decided not to talk to me," he said calmly. "Have I caught you at a bad time?"

"Actually, I am dripping all over the carpet at the moment. I was in the shower."

"I can call back...."

"No," Lezlie said quickly—too quickly, she realized as she closed her eyes and groaned inwardly. "I know you want to talk about Merri."

"Among other things. Perhaps we should do this in person."

Lezlie could imagine Drew sitting in his den with its bleached-pine paneling and leather furniture and the photographs of the various buildings she assumed he had built. There were other photographs on one wall, including the Galleria complex, indications of the pride Drew felt in his brother's work. Drew's hair would be tousled from the trip, the lines around his eyes more obvious.

Lezlie's thoughts were running in a dangerous vein and, mentally, she shook herself. "I really don't have a great deal to tell you other than some opinions." She brought Drew up-to-date on her sessions with Merri, mentioning how Merri had supplied a lot of information just by talking about the things in her room. "Have you ever noticed how she talks about her parents in the present tense?"

"I figured it's a game she's playing," Drew answered.

"It's more than that. Merri doesn't want to admit that her parents are dead and as long as she speaks of them in the present tense, they won't be. Her bedroom is another denial."

"Any ideas?"

"A few," Lezlie answered. "But it will take time. First, I have to get her to open up a little more and tell me about what happened. She hasn't even mentioned the accident, and I want her to be more confident in me before I bring it up."

"Is there anything I should do?"

"Not at the moment. Actually, I feel very encouraged. I may need some support from you once I get her to open up, which may leave her vulnerable to some overwhelming emotions...and she will need you, too."

"I'll be there for her," Drew promised.

Lezlie could almost feel the weariness in his voice. "Did your trip go well?"

"That depends on who's on the receiving end of the problems. This time it happens to be me. Besides some trouble with the subs, the owner isn't too happy that I'm not on the site twenty-four hours a day. I'm glad this one is almost finished."

For the next few minutes, Drew explained the design of the luxury-apartment building and some of the problems he had encountered. "Subs" was short for subcontractors who were hired for a specific job by Drew, the general contractor. Lezlie was amazed at how very little she knew about construction. But then she didn't imagine Drew knew very much more about her profession. Other than their mutual interest in Merri, they had very little in common.

Lezlie snapped back to the present when she heard Drew chuckle. "Now that you've listened to me ramble on about what a rotten week I had, Doc, the least I can do is return the favor."

Lezlie laughed. "Actually, I had a good week."

"I'm glad one of us did," Drew said wryly. "By the way, you have a nice laugh. In case I haven't said it, thanks for seeing Merri here."

"You're welcome," Lezlie replied, an inner alarm going off at the easy sharing.

"How about letting me show my appreciation... say over dinner. I want to spend tomorrow with Merri, so what about Sunday?"

"I already have plans," Lezlie said truthfully. But it was also just as true that her mother wouldn't mind if she were to cancel their tentative date.

"Still holding to the rules, I see." There was no anger in Drew's voice, only amused resignation.

"It's for the best," Lezlie said, but the comment sounded lame even to her ears.

"You're the doctor," Drew returned. Then more quietly, "I'll talk to you soon."

Slowly, Lezlie hung up. She had been sitting on the side of the bed, but now she was stretched on the spread. Even though it was late, she wasn't the least bit sleepy. She could remember the fatigue in Drew's warm voice. "Still holding to the rules," he had said. Was it for the best, she wondered. With a burst of nervous energy, she slid off the bed, finished toweling off, then went to sit in the backyard to let the warm night air dry her hair. She leaned back in the chair, draped her hair over the back and stared up at the stars. A gentle breeze caressed her face and she sighed deeply. Another long empty weekend stretched before her. She made a list of things to do on Saturday: a session at the spa, grocery shopping, cleaning her house. It all was so terribly exciting, she thought wryly. She found herself wishing that Drew would find some excuse to call her on the weekend. But he didn't.

MONDAY MORNING dawned overcast and muggy. By the time Lezlie had reached her office, a downpour had unleashed itself. She ran across the parking lot, trying in vain to avoid the puddles of water. Her feet were soaked to the ankles.

Jean was already at her desk. She looked up and smiled. "Wet out there, huh?"

"That's an understatement," Lezlie returned, wiping the moisture from her arms where she already felt the chill of the air conditioning. "Any calls?"

"A few." Jean followed her into the inner office. "Dr. Sanders called. He got back this weekend and wanted an update on Merri Bradinton. And Mr. Bradinton called about Merri's appointments for this week." Jean went through the other messages, then laid them on Lezlie's desk.

Lezlie checked her appointment book. She didn't

have a patient due for almost an hour. "I'll handle these messages and then call Dr. Sanders. Did you give Merri's schedule to Mr. Bradinton?"

"Yes, he will have her here today and Thursday at three."

Lezlie noticed that the times had been listed in her appointment book. She picked up the phone and called Charles's office, and they agreed to meet for coffee.

The cafeteria was crowded. Lezlie scanned the tables, locating Dr. Sanders when he waved at her. She threaded through the tables, smiling when she noticed that he had already retrieved her coffee.

"How's the harried doctor this morning?" he asked with a grin.

"A little less harried than usual," Lezlie returned.

"And how is Merri?"

"She's doing fine. I counseled her at her uncle's house last week because he was out of town. It was very enlightening." Lezlie described Merri's room and some of the child's personality traits that had come to her attention during the week. Charles simply shook his head.

"It's really sad, but I'm glad Drew agreed to treatment." Charles sipped his coffee. "Drew and I played a few holes of golf yesterday. I thought it was a little out of character for him when he called...until I found out why he had invited me. Seems he wanted to talk about you."

"Me?" Lezlie asked.

"Oh, he was pretty coy about it. He asked what I knew about you and I told him you were one of the finest, most-intuitive psychologists I've come across in a long time." Charles chuckled, his eyes twinkling merrily. "Somehow, I don't think that was what he was after." Then he saw the concern on Lezlie's face. "Oh, you needn't worry, Lezlie. I didn't tell him anything about your personal life. That's not my place. But if you will permit a friend an educated observation, I would say the man is interested in more than the psychologist where you are concerned. Has he let you in on it?"

"He has made certain overtures," Lezlie said cautiously and Charles nodded. "But it is nothing I can't handle."

"A little word of warning, Lezlie. I've known Drew since he was a boy. He was headstrong and determined even then. He's an unusual man, used to getting his way, eventually. I've never known of an instance where he failed...well, I should qualify that. There was one thing a long time ago that was beyond his control. And since then, he has become more determined, more pragmatic. I just thought you should know."

"Did you know Merri's parents?"

"Yes, you see, Drew's parents were close friends of ours. We attended Greg's wedding, and then he and Meredith moved to Denver." Charles seemed lost in thought. "I often worried if Drew would understand...."

When he stopped talking abruptly, Lezlie's cup stopped in midair. "If Drew would understand what?"

Charles looked profoundly uncomfortable. "I

shouldn't have said anything, Lezlie. Just as I didn't feel I could tell Drew about you, neither can I tell you about Drew's personal life. All I will say is that Drew had just spent three years trying to survive the day-to-day hell in Vietnam. And when he came home, his life became a purgatory. He's a hard man to know, especially where women are concerned. Only one person seems to be able to soften the impenetrable shield he's put up... and that's Merri."

"Should I take that as a warning?" Lezlie asked lightly.

"No, just a little concerned advice. Usually Drew is rather closemouthed about the women in his life—and there have been more than a few—and the fact that he approached me...." Charles spread his hands, cocking his head to one side.

Lezlie actually laughed. "Well, you needn't worry, Charles, though I appreciate the thought. I have made it quite clear to Mr. Bradinton that I am Merri's doctor, and I'm not interested in having a more-personal relationship." Lezlie glanced at her watch. "I really have to go, Charles. And I appreciate the warning."

As they walked out of the cafeteria, Charles extended a dinner invitation. "Myra thought it might be nice. We haven't seen you over at the house for a while."

"Can I take a rain check, Charles? I really have a lot to do this week. I'm repainting two rooms in the house."

"You're a better man than I am," Charles started and then smiled ruefully. "Better woman," he corrected.

"I should hope so." Lezlie laughed, hurrying off to her office. But her humor rapidly evaporated as she thought of Drew Bradinton. What gave him the right to inquire about her, she thought furiously. He had his nerve trying to use Charles to find out about her. For a while she mulled over how she should handle the situation with Drew, but when Donna Blair called just before lunch, obviously upset and needing to talk, Lezlie's thoughts were with her friend. The two women arranged to meet after work. Throughout the rest of the day, a steady stream of appointments wiped Drew out of her mind.

The session with Merri went smoothly, until Merri pulled out some snapshots of her parents. Lezlie studied the snapshots as Merri told her about their vacation the summer before.

"The photos are very nice, Merri." Lezlie leaned forward in her chair, folding her hands together. "Merri, I want you to think about something. I know how much you care about all the things in your room, but don't you think it would be better if you packed some of them away? Sometimes too many reminders of happy times... happy times that are in the past, can be upsetting for a person without the person really knowing it. Do you know what I mean?" Merri shook her head. "Well, I know how much you loved your parents and how much you miss them. Everything in your room only reminds you more of that. Don't you think it might be better to choose some of the most special things, and put the others away?"

"I d-don't know."

"Will you think about it?"

"Yes," Merri answered quietly, and her soft blue eyes met Lezlie's. "But do I have to put them away?"

"Only when you are ready to. Why don't we talk about it again on Thursday?"

A moment after Merri had left her office, Drew stuck his head into the opened door. "How did it go today?" he asked quietly.

"Fine. I should know pretty soon just how much Merri trusts my judgment," Lezlie answered.

"I'm sure she does," Drew said with a smile.

"Then she is easier to convince than her uncle," Lezlie quipped.

"What does that mean?"

"Just that I don't appreciate your going to Dr. Sanders about me. If you have questions about my qualifications, ask me. But you have no right to inquire into my personal life."

"I only wanted to know why you've constructed a wall around yourself. I thought there might be a reason."

"Perhaps to protect myself from men like you," Lezlie mumbled grudgingly. "And even if there is a reason, it is hardly any of your concern."

"Who says you need protection?" Drew had walked into the office and was now beside her desk. Lezlie stood up, but he took her wrist.

"Every time I get close to you, you turn tail and run," Drew said. "It's getting to be a habit."

"Well, considering that I cannot convince you to leave me alone, it is my only option."

"Not the only, just the easiest." Drew brought her forward slowly, his eyes locked with hers.

Lezlie stood her ground as his smooth mouth curved into a smile. She would not retreat, not this time.

Drew leaned toward Lezlie, fully expecting her to react. He could recall the breathless fear in her eyes that day in the elevator, but there was no fear now, only a challenge he would not turn down. When she dropped her arm and turned away, he brought her back around.

Lezlie had not sensed the seriousness of her error in judgment until Drew leaned over her and captured her lips beneath his. The kiss was a prelude to an onslaught on her senses. Drew slipped his arm around her waist, drawing her firmly against him. His other hand held her chin, his fingers caressing her cheeks and forcing her mouth to open to his. Trapped so securely within his arms and against his unyielding body, Lezlie could barely move, and she had no such inclination. She kept her hands at her sides, her nails digging into her palms to break through the sensual spell he was weaving.

Drew's arm rested intimately between her breasts, and Lezlie's breath caught as his tongue touched her softened lips, seeking the gentle curve of her bottom lip before exploring further. His fingers were as light as a feather on her throat, exerting a light caressing pressure.

But as his hand left her throat, brushed past her breast and slid along her side to her hip, Lezlie was quickly losing control. And she was soon aware that

Drew had little control himself when he pulled her against him, her thighs pressed hard to his. Drew held her securely as his strong fingers explored the curve of her back and her hip, before settling possessively around her waist.

She wasn't even aware of her blouse being pulled from the waist of her skirt until the warmth of his hand against the bare flesh of her back caused her to shiver. The callused skin of his palm was rough while his touch was agonizingly gentle.

"This is insane," Lezlie murmured, her breath mingling with his. "I don't think—"

"That's right," Drew interrupted. "Don't think. You're in no danger, Lezlie." His hand caressed her chin while his eyes roved her flushed face. "Tell me what you're feeling right now, and tell me that it's wrong."

How could anything so incredibly wondrous be wrong, Lezlie questioned. "I can't," she said honestly, her chin quivering in anticipation. His mouth hovered so near, and yet it seemed an eternity before his lips touched hers.

A quiet groan died in Lezlie's throat. She opened her mouth beneath Drew's, accepting a complete exploration as her tongue met and welcomed his. His breath was warm and ragged against her face and the spicy scent of after-shave heightened her awareness of him. It was the scent she had come to know as his, mingled with his own warm masculine smell. His hair was crisp and vibrant beneath her fingers, and the slight roughness of his face chafed hers.

Drew had no doubt of her desire. Her arms were

wound around his neck, every inch of her body crying out for release from the tension that coiled tighter and tighter within her. Her body fit beautifully with his, her softness driving him beyond all coherent thought. She was so incredibly responsive, her flesh quivering to his touch. Yet there was an air of vulnerability about her. Perhaps some would have taken advantage of it, but he didn't want to sweep her away in a moment of passion. He wanted her full and unequivocal understanding before beginning an affair that, if handled without consideration, could end as quickly as it had begun. Lezlie was an intelligent sensitive woman, usually in control of her own actions. But even Drew was having difficulty quelling an urge to carry her to the couch on the other side of the room.

He leaned back on the edge of her desk, drawing Lezlie with him. Her body was nestled between his legs as he pressed his face into the fragrant curve of her shoulder and then kissed the soft skin of her neck.

Lezlie arched against him, her fired sensations not yet cooled. Drew's arms were wrapped tightly around her hips.

"Do you have any idea what you're doing to me?" Drew murmured.

"Some," Lezlie said quietly. Her knees were shaking and she was glad he held her so securely or she might have slid to a heap at his feet.

"What do you suggest we do about it, Lezlie?"

It was all Lezlie could do to concentrate on what he was saying, much less give a coherent reply. "Drew," she attempted to answer, and then she simply shook her head.

Drew's intense concentration on her neck subsided. He leaned back slightly, moving her so that he could look at her. "You can't still be serious about no involvement. Surely it's obvious that I want you...perhaps more than any woman I've ever known."

Lezlie straightened. "The next thing you'll be saying is it's love...this thing between us."

Drew became rigid, the muscles in his shoulders tensing. "I don't need to lie, Lezlie. We both know it's chemistry." He stood up, negligently straightening his tie. "Besides, I don't use such ploys. I was in love once, or at least I thought I was. But the way things ended up, I wonder if I even know what love is all about." Drew watched as Lezlie straightened her own appearance. "And I'm beginning to wonder if we are two of a kind."

"What do you want from me?" she demanded. Then she qualified the question, "Besides what is obvious."

"Why don't you try being honest with yourself and with me? Forget the labels or excuses. Maybe if we were to get to know each other, the other issue would take care of itself." Drew shook his head. "But you won't even give it a chance, will you? I would certainly like to meet the guy who hurt you so badly that you can't even accept another man at face value. He did one terrific job of messing you up."

"That's not fair," Lezlie started.

"Very little is," Drew said cynically.

"Boy, if that isn't typical. A woman doesn't want anything to do with one man, and he immediately assumes it was another man who got her fouled up in the first place."

"And it wasn't?"

"No," Lezlie said. "At least not in the way you mean." Lezlie walked a few feet away and then swung around. "Let's just say for the sake of argument that I disregard everything and become involved with you. Where would that leave Merri? How could I possibly be objective should she tell me something about you that you wouldn't like, but we might need to discuss? Just how would that work if we're involved? And how would Merri feel about confiding in me if she knew I was sleeping with her uncle?"

"So what you're saying is that if you weren't treating Merri in a professional capacity, you wouldn't feel as you do?"

"Merri is part of it, Drew. The rest has to do with personal reasons."

"Merri is just an excuse, Lezlie, and one I can understand. What I don't understand are the personal reasons that preclude any chance of our getting to know each other. Because it isn't merely a biological reaction, Lezlie. I don't know exactly what it is I feel about you, but I want to find out. Are you content to leave things as they are with no resolution? Or would it really be different if you weren't Merri's therapist?"

Neither question really had an answer. "I don't know, Drew," Lezlie said honestly. The truth was she didn't know. For two years she had managed to avoid the exact situation she was now facing with Drew. But she had not been as attracted to anyone as she was to Drew, nor had she met anyone as blatantly persistent. Those men who weren't threatened by her career were put off by her attitude...until Drew. He was ignoring her resistance, challenging her arguments and teasing passions that had lain dormant for a very long time. And the result was that Lezlie felt somewhat off-balance where he was concerned.

Drew considered the uncertainty in her answer. "Then what about a compromise?"

"What do you mean?"

"I accept that your position with Merri could be jeopardized to some extent. But once she is able to deal with what happened, the situation will change. So until then, is there any valid reason why we can't have dinner together on occasion—" Drew's quick smile crinkled the fine lines at the corners of his eyes "—if there's no threat of involvement? What do you say? Is it a deal?"

"Wouldn't it be simpler to just accept the situation as it is?"

"Not for me," Drew answered, and his quiet rueful tone shattered Lezlie's wariness, and she could not resist smiling.

"So what you're suggesting is that we be 'friends,' right?"

"I would prefer a lot more, but I'll settle for friends, for the time being."

"A friendship would certainly be unique."

"That's an understatement," Drew returned good-naturedly, and his brow furrowed in mock concentration. "And, if memory serves me, having a girl as a friend will be a first since I was seven years old."

"The thought of girls didn't disgust you?"

"Not that I can remember." Drew smiled.

"That figures," Lezlie teased.

"And what do you mean by that?"

Before Lezlie could answer the door opened. Merri poked her head through the crack, surveying them. "Are you ready yet, Uncle Drew?"

"Yes, Merri, Dr. Garrett and I are finished with our... discussion. Thursday at three, right?" Lezlie nodded, and Drew extended his hand. "Then we have a deal?"

Lezlie placed her hand into his and his fingers closed around the coolness of hers. "Aha, cold hands...."

"I don't put any stock in old wives' tales."

"There's one saying that I'm beginning to think may have some substance," Drew said mysteriously. "Someday I'll tell you about it."

Merri shifted impatiently and Lezlie refrained from voicing her curiosity. But as they left her office, Drew's smile lingered. Lezlie stood at the window, staring at the swelling traffic on the expressway in the distance. But her thoughts were still on the playful exchange with Drew Bradinton as she wondered what he had meant about old wives' tales. For the life of her, she couldn't figure out what he might have been thinking.

Lezlie suddenly remembered her date with Donna. Glancing at the clock on her bookcase, she expected Donna was already waiting for her. She grabbed her linen jacket and purse and rushed out of the office. Any further analysis of Drew Bradinton would just have to wait. Besides, she had her doubts that Drew would settle for an uncomplicated friendship. But time would tell and she had no doubt whatsoever that the game would get old. Somehow the thought bothered her.

DONNA WAS INDEED WAITING for Lezlie, but there was no impatience in her attitude when Lezlie joined her. Traffic around the Marietta Square had been heavy and it had taken Lezlie two trips around the tree-shaded playground park to find a parking place. Shillings on the Square was a unique publike restaurant, which was dim and cool after the uncomfortable heat and the brilliance of the sun outside.

"You look as frazzled as I feel," Donna drawled.

"It's been one of those days."

"You, too?"

Lezlie nodded. "I had another run-in with Drew Bradinton. He has to be the most persistent man I've ever met."

"Do you want a drink?"

"Just coffee," Lezlie answered.

"So, tell me about your persistent admirer," Donna said. "He hasn't given up yet?"

"Hardly. Would you believe he actually went to Charles Sanders to ask about me?" Lezlie asked. "And that's only the beginning. We had made this agreement about no personal involvement while I was treating Merri, or at least I thought we had until this afternoon when he kissed me in my office—"

"He did what?" Donna interrupted, leaning forward. "What did you do?"

Lezlie could feel the blush creeping up her neck as she glanced at Donna. "I responded, unfortunately."

"Why, unfortunately? That just shows you there's something there."

"I've never denied that there is a physical attraction, Donna. Drew admitted it was chemistry and accused me of pigeonholing him in a neat safe place as a patient's relative. But chemistry just isn't enough."

"It's a good start. Do you have any idea how many relationships come about just because of that chemistry? Without it, why bother?" Donna shrugged. "It could lead to something more, you never know."

"Who says I want to find out?"

"I do," Donna said, "and you should. You forget, Les, I've seen you in action and you can put a man off with the best of them. I think this guy's persistence is a point in his favor."

"You do?" Lezlie grinned.

"For crying out loud, Les! How are you ever going to know if you don't take a chance?"

"That's my feeling. I don't want to take a chance, not again. And while I wonder about his motives, Drew said today that we could be friends."

"Uh oh," Donna said.

Lezlie glanced up. "Why do you say that?"

"You may have lost him already...."

"I never had him to lose," Lezlie cried.

"My point exactly," Donna answered succinctly.

"You're as impossible as Drew," Lezlie groaned.

Donna grinned, amusement lighting her eyes. "But I'm not as smart," she commented, having realized what Drew Bradinton might be doing in suggesting friendship. Through friendship Lezlie would have a chance to get to know him, and he would have a reason to stay in touch... a reason other than his niece.

"Since you are extolling the virtues of relationships, what was wrong when you called earlier? You and Jim having a lovers' spat?"

"You might say that," Donna said, taking a long sip from the ice tea she had ordered while waiting for Lezlie. "Actually it's more like a running battle that keeps getting dredged up. We've been going around and around about Elizabeth Clarke. He says I'm heading toward a letdown if I don't back off. I've talked to her parents several times during the week, but I don't think I'm getting anywhere. They haven't made a final decision yet, but Jim says I get too wrapped up in my students."

"You do, but if you didn't you might not get the results you want. Still, Jim is right, too. He just doesn't want to see you get hurt should her parents disregard your opinion."

"I know that here—" Donna said, putting her finger to her temple and then to her chest "—but not here. And I wanted to ask you a tremendous favor. I think it may help Elizabeth's parents, especially her mother, to talk to someone about Elizabeth, someone with an objective opinion. Maybe you could recommend someone?"

"You're really pulling out all the stops," Lezlie commented.

"If I don't, wondering if there was something I could have done but didn't would drive me crazy."

"Well, if her parents will agree to it, there are several counselors I could call," Lezlie said cautiously. "But you should be prepared that they may not go along with the idea."

"I just want to investigate all the options," Donna said. "I'll let you know, all right?" Lezlie nodded and Donna motioned to the waiter that they were ready to order. "So, what are your plans for the weekend?"

"Nothing terrifically exciting."

"Not because you weren't asked," Donna reminded her.

"I know, but I've been putting off this chore for months. This is the first free weekend I've had in a while, so I'm going to take advantage of it and paint the bedroom and den."

"Tell you what, I'll trade with you. Jim's got the weekend filled with tennis." Donna grimaced. "You go play tennis with him, and I'll do the painting."

"Thanks, but no thanks," Lezlie laughed, well aware of Jim's absolute passion for the game. He played with such fierce competitiveness that the majority of his partners had quit accepting his invitations. "I think painting will be much less strenuous."

"I was afraid you would say that. Guess I'm stuck on the courts for the duration."

"You'll survive," Lezlie teased.

Donna glanced in a heavenward direction. "Sometimes I wonder. But I'll tell you one thing. If he slams that ball at me just once, I'm going to really let him have it."

"Poor Jim," Lezlie chuckled.

"Save your pity for me, please. By the end of the weekend I'll have muscle strains and bruises a marathon runner could understand. No matter what I say, Jim runs me from one side of the court to the other."

"Then tell him to find someone else to play with."

"There isn't anyone left, or believe me I would have been on the phone days ago to round them up."

"Well, why don't you call me Monday and we'll see who fared the best."

"Or the worst," Donna commented shortly. But as they looked at each other, they suddenly laughed, sharing the easy comfortable laughter of close friends.

CHAPTER FIVE

THE HARDWARE STORE was jammed, which was usual for a Saturday morning. Lezlie threaded through the do-it-yourselfers and weekend handymen toward the paint department. Her list was in the back pocket of her jeans. She dug it out while waiting for the salesclerk to finish with another customer. She would get the rollers, pans, brushes and drop cloths while the clerk blended the paint she wanted. The color cards were marked: a light salmon for her bedroom and an oyster beige to cover the depressing shade of gray in the den. She would trim the windows and baseboards in the bedroom with an eggshell enamel for contrast. As she looked down the list, she grimaced doubtfully.

The clerk was an elderly man, and his wizened eyes surveyed his next customer. A baggy shirt was tied at her waist, and from the expression on her face, he wasn't certain she had decided what she wanted. "What can I do for you today?"

Lezlie glanced up and handed the clerk the color cards. "I need a gallon of each of the latex colors and a quart of the semigloss enamel."

The clerk glanced over the cards. "Thought maybe you needed some advice, but that's what I like...a customer who knows exactly what she wants. You wouldn't believe how many people I get in here who change their minds five times or more on a shade of paint."

"Yes, I would." Lezlie smiled, remembering the afternoon she had spent at the paint color chart a few weeks ago. She had taken at least twenty of the little color strips home to consider.

"Then, you're sure?" the clerk asked. When Lezlie nodded, he grinned. "I'll have it ready in a minute."

Lezlie wandered down the aisle of painting accessories. She was juggling two rollers and a variety of paintbrushes when a low voice from behind startled her and the tray she had just picked up dropped with a clang. Drew Bradinton stood in the middle of the aisle, grinning sheepishly. He seemed to pop up at the most unexpected moments! She crouched down to retrieve the utensils and to avoid the curious looks of other customers.

Drew squatted down in front of her. "Sorry, I didn't mean to scare you."

"What are you doing here?" Lezlie asked.

"I could ask you the same thing," Drew said. His faded jeans were worn and comfortable looking and the sleeves of his flannel plaid shirt were rolled up to expose hair the color of gold sunshine on his muscular forearms. "You planning on doing some painting?"

"No, I use these to make biscuits," Lezlie quipped, holding up one of the rollers. She smiled. "Fuzzy ones. It's an old family recipe."

"Remind me not to come to your house for dinner."

"Who said you'd be invited?"

"Isn't it usual when somebody does you a good turn that some reward is offered? Or have you already got help lined up?"

"Lined up for what?"

"To help you paint," Drew said simply.

"No...."

"Well, now you do."

"Oh, I couldn't ask you to do that," Lezlie said.

"You're not asking, I'm offering. You might as well take advantage of my expertise. It'll go a lot faster if you edge and I roll." Drew plucked a flat little pad off the shelf. "This is an E-Z Edger. The wheels let you paint corners and along baseboards without needing a steady hand. And it's a lot cheaper than a brush. Highly recommended for the beginner."

"I don't know if I qualify as a beginner, but anything that makes it easier is welcome," Lezlie said.

"I'll do my best," Drew said good-naturedly. "I've got a couple of things I want to pick up. I'll meet you at the checkout."

Lezlie had checked off the items on her list by the time the clerk brought her the three cans of paint. "You got everything?" he asked, grinning and placing the cans in her cart.

"I should think so," Lezlie answered.

"Well, have a nice day."

The checkout lines were five deep at each register. As Lezlie waited, the thought occurred to her that the day would indeed be more pleasant with Drew helping. Regardless of everything else, she did enjoy his company.

Drew ambled up and broke into the line behind Lezlie. "We're together," he explained simply when the man behind Lezlie started to comment.

"What's all that for?" Lezlie asked, referring to the various thin sheets of wood and plywood.

Drew actually seemed self-conscious. "It's something I've been working on for Merri. Her birthday is next month."

"What will it be?"

"A dollhouse. She may seem a little old for a dollhouse, but this one is special. Greg designed it." Drew stared steadily at Lezlie. "Do you think it's bad timing?"

"No, I think it will be a lovely gift, and a very special one, if I know Merri. By the way, what's she up to today?"

"She's at a friend's house," Drew said. "I was a little surprised, but this girl, Jill, has been after Merri to come over on a Saturday. I made certain her mother understood Merri would have to take it easy. So, lovely lady, you have me at your disposal for at least three hours, longer if Merri's having a good time. She's supposed to call Mrs. Cates. When I get to your house, I'll call and leave the number where Mrs. Cates can reach me."

Lezlie's turn had come and she placed her purchases on the counter, standing aside as Drew reached into the cart and put the paint on the counter. A few minutes later they were on their way to Lezlie's house, Drew's sleek Porsche following her white Mustang.

As Drew helped her carry in the bags, Lezlie recognized a sense of domesticity, and the feeling bothered her. But she wasn't going to jump to a wrong conclusion again. Drew had generously offered to help, and she would give him the benefit of the doubt that he would keep things on a friendly basis.

Drew glanced casually at the quiet tree-shaded street and then at Lezlie's house. It suited her, he thought. It was solid and traditional with contrasting touches such as ivy climbing haphazardly along the tree trunks in the pine island; large picture windows and a stained-wood door with an exquisite beveled-glass panel.

"Nice house," Drew said simply as he walked into the foyer.

"I like it."

"So, where do we start?"

"The bedroom. It's the biggest job so I'd like to finish it first."

"Very practical." Drew smiled, following her and setting the packages on the floor by the bedroom door. The furniture had already been moved far enough from the walls not to hamper their task. "I hope you didn't move all this yourself...or did you have some elves?"

"I doubt elves could have budged it," Lezlie said, ripping open the packages of plastic drop cloths. "It was all Jim could do with both Donna and me helping. But I'm beginning to remember why I put this task off last spring." Lezlie looked around and sighed. "I had decided to take time off to get some projects done... I opted for a vacation instead."

"Wouldn't it just be easier to hire someone?"

"I guess, but I've always done it myself... painting, wallpapering; I even sanded hardwood floors once." Lezlie hadn't thought about the first house she and Michael had owned, his handyman's dream, Michael had joked, but it had wound up being Lezlie's headache before she had gone back to school. But she had been proud of that house and of her taste when she had completely redecorated it.

"Why don't you go ahead and start edging the corners?" Drew suggested. "I'll put on the coffee."

"I can do that."

"I can roll faster than you can edge." Drew grinned. "Just point me in the direction of the kitchen."

"Back down the hall to the left. The coffee's in the cupboard next to the stove."

"I'll find everything. What about a stepladder?"

"It's in the broom closet next to the fridge," Lezlie called after his retreating back.

"Gotcha." Drew hummed happily as he dialed his house and left Lezlie's number with Mrs. Cates before locating the coffeepot, cups and coffee. He opened the window over the sink and was met by the shrill but pleasant chirping of birds. The kitchen, like the rest of the house, held a warm comfortable glow. Small glass bottles of amethyst, amber and cobalt glittered on the windowsill and pretty plants dotted the counter. The more Drew was seeing about Lezlie Garrett, the more he saw to like. But he had promised her they would be friends, and he intended to be the very best friend she had ever had... before he became her lover. The thought made him grin with high spirits as he carried a tray into the bedroom. He didn't realize his smile accompanied him.

Lezlie looked at him strangely. "What's so funny?"

"Oh, nothing really," Drew evaded, and then he chuckled. "But this would have been a terrific opportunity to get your phone number."

"But you have my number."

"Yeh, I know," Drew said.

Lezlie had stopped painting. "Drew, when we met that first day, didn't it even occur to you that I might be married?"

"Yes, it occurred to me, but if you were married, I certainly couldn't have kissed you, could I now?"

"No," Lezlie said quietly.

"Well, I had already asked Charles in a roundabout way when he was talking to me about Merri's therapy. What I didn't know was that you would fight an involvement with so much determination, but at least I know there's no one else."

No, there is no one else, Lezlie thought. *Not in the present sense, at least.* She turned back to the wall, listening to Drew's quiet whistling as he dipped the roller into the pan and began to roll the paint onto the wall with sure steady progress. They worked in silence for more than an hour. The bedroom was more than half-finished. Lezlie's hand was cramped and her shoulders hurt. She was just about to suggest a break when a call from the front of the house caused them both to stop.

"Hey, Les, I brought in the troops!" It was Donna's voice, followed by Jim's.

"Hey, that's some car in your driveway."

Jim and Donna Blair appeared at the bedroom door. Lezlie introduced them to Drew, who wiped his hands on a rag. Lezlie was aware of the quizzical frown Donna sent her way. "We ran into each other in the hardware store," Lezlie said quietly. "We were about to have coffee. You two want some?"

"I'd rather have a beer," Jim said turning toward Drew. "Didn't you play football for Tech. some years back?"

"Yes," Drew said simply.

"I thought the name sounded familiar. I was a couple of years behind you, but I never got off the bench." Jim smiled at Donna. "He was the hottest tight end in the region."

"Reaaally," Donna drawled.

The expression of surprise on Drew's face was priceless and Lezlie smothered a laugh.

"Can I get you a beer?" Jim offered hastily. "Unless you're out, Lezlie."

"No, there's a six-pack in the fridge. Help yourself."

As Jim disappeared, Donna smiled. "I didn't mean to embarrass you, Drew. Football season's been over almost three months but you'd never know it to hear Jim. Any excuse and he's off on a tangent."

Jim came back and handed Drew a beer. "You know, I was really surprised that you didn't turn pro," he said. "What'd you do after you graduated?"

"I enlisted in the marines."

"You're kidding?" Jim cried.

"It was either that or have Uncle Sam come after me."

"Oh, I see what you mean," Jim laughed. "Still, it's a shame. You could've been making a fortune playing for one of the pro teams. So, what are you doing now?"

"I'm in construction."

"Which end, the work or the management?"

"A little of both," Drew said patiently.

Lezlie felt as though Drew was being interrogated. She knew Jim was just interested in people, but sometimes he just didn't think about how he sounded. Donna often said it was because of his job as a salesman for a national computer company.

"So, what do you think?" Lezlie asked Donna, motioning to the still-wet walls.

"Oh, I love the color," Donna exclaimed. "This makes me want to spruce up our house."

"Oh, no you don't," Jim said. "The last time you started a fix-it project, I had to take a week off to clean up the mess you'd made."

"Grumble, grumble," Donna said teasingly. "Jim fussed the whole way over here. Seems he was planning to play tennis this afternoon."

"Well—" Jim began with a smile, obviously relieved that he wouldn't be put to work "—seeing as how Lezlie has all the help she could possibly need, we could still make the courts."

"Sure, Drew and I can handle this," Lezlie agreed, "but I appreciate the thought."

"Well, I guess that lets you off the hook," Donna said pointedly to Jim. "Let's get out of here and let them get back to work. I'll talk to you in the week, Les. Call me if I can help."

When they were alone again, Lezlie smiled apologetically. "I hope you didn't feel like you were on a spot, Drew."

"No, I meet a lot of guys like Jim. What's he in, sales?"

"How did you know?" Lezlie asked.

"Just a lucky guess."

"Jim's in computer sales, to be exact. He's really very nice. Once you get to know him, you find out he's not quite as intense as he seems. Donna grumps occasionally, but never seriously."

Drew retrieved his roller and headed for a far wall. "Do they have any kids?"

"Not their own, but Donna has a dozen very special children." Lezlie explained Donna's school and the enormous output of energy her friend's work required.

"I was wondering what you had in common," Drew commented.

Lezlie had finished edging all the corners before Drew finished. She retrieved the can of enamel paint and began to do the trim on the windows. When Drew was through, he watched her for a minute. Paint streaked her jeans and shirt and a smudge dotted her cheek. She didn't look the least bit like the professional Dr. Garrett at the moment. He found himself wondering about her. What had made her so defensive about relationships? Why did she prefer to remain alone instead of sharing her life with someone? Was her career really enough or did she fill her time with tasks and projects? Whatever the answers were to his questions, none of them really mattered. It had been a long time since Drew had felt strongly about a woman, but Lezlie had really intrigued him. She was a beautiful, obviously compassionate woman, who had shut herself off from emotion. Why? The question was on the tip of Drew's tongue, so instead of asking, he dug into his pocket for his keys.

"I've got an errand to run, Lezlie. I'll be back in a few minutes."

Lezlie glanced up and nodded, then returned to her painting. She heard the powerful surge of the Porsche engine as Drew pulled out of her driveway. Her bedroom was in the front corner of the house, and she watched the car until it was out of sight. She laid aside her paintbrush and wandered into the kitchen to get a fresh cup of coffee. Drew had left her kitchen as tidy as it had been; no coffee grounds scattered on the counter, the sugar back in the cabinet and the spoon in the sink. It was funny how different he was from.... Lezlie frowned. She was about to think how different he was from Michael, but that wasn't fair. She didn't want to compare them, to see the faults in her dead husband and find those within Drew. Michael had been on her mind a great deal lately, but Lezlie knew why. Next month it would be exactly two years since the accident.

Lezlie puttered around the kitchen, straightening things that really didn't need straightening, and she found herself wishing Drew would hurry back. Then she heard his car pull into her driveway. She met him as he came into the foyer.

Drew was carrying several bags. "What's all that?" Lezlie asked.

"I saw Harry's Deli on our way here. I don't know about you, but I need sustenance when I work." Drew headed into the living room, then squatted down on the floor. He pulled a paper tablecloth from one of the bags.

"What are you doing?" Lezlie laughed.

"We're going to have that picnic you couldn't make at the hospital. You did say another time, and this is as good as any." Drew had thought of everything, paper plates, napkins, even wine. "I didn't know what you like, so I got a very light white wine—" he said pulling out one bottle "—and a rosé. Which do you prefer?"

"I don't really care for wine, but I guess it depends on what you have in the bag," Lezlie said airily. "I couldn't possibly drink a white wine with beef."

Drew picked up on the easy banter. "Oh, a wine snob who doesn't even like wine. Well, you can have your choice. I have roast beef, ham or turkey sandwiches."

"I'll have turkey with rosé," Lezlie said, and Drew laughed.

"I should have guessed."

Drew had spread the tablecloth and was setting out the sandwiches as Lezlie sat down, crossing her legs. He had bought enough for a small army: sandwiches, pints of potato salad, coleslaw and a bag of chips.

"We'll never be able to eat all this," Leslie cried.

"Speak for yourself," Drew teased. "I'm nearly starved." He glanced around the makeshift table. "A corkscrew. I knew I forgot something...."

"I'll get one." Lezlie started to get up, but Drew put his hand on her shoulder.

"I'll go." As he stood up, his gaze caught Lezlie's and she smiled. He squeezed her shoulder, hesitating as her smile slowly faded. He sensed her reaction to his touch. More than anything he wanted to lean down and kiss her and replace that vulnerable stare with passion. Instead, he headed into the kitchen to find a corkscrew. When he came back, Lezlie was nibbling on her sandwich.

"Hey, this is a picnic, no serious thoughts." He sat down, crossing his long legs Indian style. "And that is no way to eat a sandwich. The trick is to take a big bite and then cram as much other stuff in as you can chew. Like this." Drew bit into his sandwich taking at least a third of it. Lezlie's eyes widened as he began chewing, his cheeks rounded as he took a bite of pickle and then a sip of wine.

Lezlie's smile bubbled into a laugh as he made a noise of satisfaction.

"Now you, with one alteration," he said, wiping his mouth. "I don't recommend the wine with pickle." Drew sucked in his cheeks and grimaced. Lezlie was about to bite into her sandwich when his hand covered hers. "No slouching, now."

Lezlie took as big a bite as she could and found chewing almost impossible. When Drew offered her a bite of potato salad, she shook her head, amazed when he attacked his own sandwich. She felt as though she might choke, but finally managed to chew.

"Surely you don't eat every meal this way," she said. "Your digestive system must be a mess."

"Old habits are hard to break."

"Maybe you should try."

"I have," Drew said. "It started when I was in college. You know, too rushed to eat properly if at all, and then in Nam the food went down easier if it was eaten quickly, and there wasn't much choice with snipers and all." Drew took a sip of wine, miles away with his thoughts. "Coming home was worse," he commented absently.

The quiet statement seemed an odd thing to say. "Why?" Lezlie asked.

Drew suddenly realized he had spoken aloud, and it was not something he wanted to discuss with Lezlie, not yet. "There is no training in the world that can adequately prepare anyone for the truths of war. I think a lot of people really didn't understand guerrilla warfare as it was in Vietnam. It was even harder on the soldier who was there, but on people sitting on this side of the ocean...well, how can you expect them to know how it feels to watch a child walk into a group of soldiers and detonate a grenade? It eventually made you paranoid."

Lezlie shivered at the thought. "I can understand why."

"I'm breaking my own rule for this picnic," Drew apologized. "No more serious talk." He unwrapped another sandwich and in deference to their conversation, he ate less hurriedly.

As they lingered over pastries, Drew told her about a picnic he had taken as a boy with his parents. They had gone to the Chattahoochee River, laid down their blanket and food and then dawdled near the riverbank. When they decided to eat, everything was gone, papers strewn around the blanket. The culprit was lying a few yards away, his stomach bulging with his feast. That was the last time they had ever taken Ralph, their dog, on a family picnic.

"Ralph?" Lezlie asked.

"Ralph," Drew confirmed. "He was the funniest dog, but smart. You know, I can still remember the look on that dog's face when my mother scolded him. Oh, he was a pitiful thing, but he wasn't sorry, not for a minute. He followed her around the rest of the day trying to make up, but she wouldn't have a thing to do with him."

Lezlie laughed when Drew related one of Ralph's escapades on laundry day when he had decided to play with the wet sheets hanging on the line. It was like a scene out of the Keystone Cops, everybody chasing the errant Ralph and nobody catching him. But Ralph had had tremendous fun playing the game.

Lezlie hadn't laughed so much in ages. Her sides actually hurt, but it was the best picnic lunch she could remember. True to his word, Drew had made sure there were no leftovers.

"I told you I was hungry," he said easily.

Lezlie had eaten more than she'd intended and she leaned back on her elbows. "This was a terrific idea. I'm stuffed." The wine had warmed her going down, and now she was content and sleepy. When she started to yawn, Drew uncurled his long legs and stood up.

"Oh no you don't. You're not leaving me to finish that other room alone."

"Just a few minutes," Lezlie groaned.

Drew reached down to take her hand and then hoisted her to her feet. "You quit now, you might as well call it quits for the day."

Lezlie sighed tiredly. She didn't notice how close she was standing to Drew until her head lolled forward and came into contact with his chest. His hand held the back of her neck, his fingers kneading gently. Before either of them realized the contented warmth between them, the telephone rang.

Lezlie's head came up to meet Drew's smile. "I thought the old 'saved by the bell' routine only happened in the movies."

"Did I need to be saved?"

"Not from me," Drew said gently. "You want me to get it?"

"It might be the hospital." Lezlie started into the kitchen, and Drew followed. The call was for Drew from his housekeeper. When Drew hung up, Lezlie was pouring a cup of coffee.

"Well, it seems Merri is having a good time. She called home and wanted to stay for dinner with Jill."

"You seem really surprised."

Drew was thoughtful. "I am in a way. It's just so sudden. A few sessions with you and she's making an effort. One of the doctors in Denver suggested counseling for Merri, but I didn't think it could help," Drew said honestly. "I thought I could help her through it. I guess I was wrong."

"It's not really a question of being wrong," Lezlie said.

"What do you and Merri talk about?"

"A lot of things, actually," Lezlie answered. "I've learned a lot about her life in Denver, or the way she perceives it. I am trying to get her to stop delving into the past, and to find a way to cope with a present situation that cannot be changed. Once she accepts the finality of the accident and realizes it's not really her fault, she'll be able to adjust. It does help that she has an uncle who is as interested as you are, Drew."

"Yeah, I guess," Drew said simply. He started to walk into the den and Lezlie wondered if she had said something to upset him.

Painting the den went much faster than the bedroom because the walls were half-paneled and shelves filled the wall beside the fireplace. But Drew was strangely silent. He was a complex man, Lezlie was coming to realize. He was warm and companionable with a good sense of humor. But beneath the exterior, she felt that he was also sad. She could imagine how the loss of his brother, coupled with anxiety over the new responsibility of his niece, could account for that sadness.

When they had finished and Drew was gathering up the brushes to wash them, Lezlie approached him. "Drew, I hope I didn't say anything a while ago about Merri to upset you. I understand how sensitive you are to Merri...."

"It wasn't what you said," Drew reassured. "But

there are some things from the past that could affect Merri, and that do affect me. Someday, when Merri gets beyond all this, maybe then I can tell you about them."

Lezlie had the same foreboding she'd felt when they had talked about his brother that night over dinner at the Galleria. Was the past somehow all jumbled up with the present? And was it the same circumstance that had made it impossible for the brothers to share their lives?

Lezlie's curiosity was about to get the better of her, and she quickly found a task to occupy her. She cleaned up the remnants from their picnic while Drew was busy at the sink.

"I don't know about you, but the smell of this paint is getting to me," Drew said. "You want to go out for pizza?"

"We just finished a huge lunch a little while ago," Lezlie cried.

"Actually, going out for pizza is just somewhere to go to get out of here until the paint dries," Drew said. "We could go to my house. I'm sure Mrs. Cates will fix us something."

An alarm went off within Lezlie. It would be too easy to accept Drew's offer. In fact, it would be too easy to become too content with his company. "Thanks, Drew. But I want to have a shower and go to bed early."

"Not in there?" Drew said sharply.

"No, I'll close off these two rooms. My couch can be made into a pretty comfortable bed."

"I have plenty of room at my house."

Lezlie smiled. "Thanks for the offer, and I really appreciate all your help. It would have taken me all weekend."

"What are friends for, right?" Drew said, his humor surfacing.

"Right."

He started to leave, but turned back around. "I guess I'll see you sometime this week."

"Tell Merri I said hello."

"I will," he said, waving quickly before he left. The house was suddenly very quiet and very empty. Lezlie went into the den and began replacing the books, bric-a-brac and pictures on the bookcase shelves and the mantel. But she couldn't stop feeling how Drew's presence had seemed to fill her house and had chased away the shadows of loneliness.

CHAPTER SIX

"I LIKED IT BETTER when you came to my house," Merri said bluntly. She fidgeted in the chair beside Lezlie's desk.

"Oh, why?" Lezlie's hands were folded on the desk in front of her.

"I don't know. There just seemed to be more to talk about."

"Merri, have you given any thought to my suggestion about your room?"

Merri began to twirl a curl of her hair, a trait Lezlie had come to know signaled apprehension within her young patient. Many children had little habits that were telltale of their moods. Merri was obviously still struggling with her decision.

"I just can't make up my mind what to put away," Merri said unhappily.

"Have you asked your uncle to help you?"

Merri shook her head. "He's going out of town tomorrow."

"I'm sure he'd be willing to help you, if you only ask him, Merri." Lezlie stood up and walked around to the front of her desk. "Tell me, did you have a nice time with your friend Saturday? What was her name?"

"Jill. Yeah, we had a pretty neat time. Boy, she's really boy crazy." Merri rolled her eyes and Lezlie smiled. Merri's blue eyes settled unwaveringly on Lezlie. "I think my Uncle Drew likes you."

"Oh?" Lezlie said, wanting to avoid the subject, but not able to say so.

"He said y'all painted your house while I was at Jill's."

"Not the whole house," Lezlie corrected. "Only two rooms."

"I heard Uncle Drew tell Mrs. Cates that he asked you to come over for dinner. He's never asked anybody to his house," Merri said self-consciously, "not since I came to live with him."

"Your uncle may not invite people over, Merri, because you haven't had enough time to adjust. He's wants you to be happy again. And he may feel you should be more comfortable with him before he brings his friends around."

"But I don't like it here," Merri said, a tinge of belligerence in her voice, followed by tears. "I want to go home.... I want things to be like they were before...before...."

"Before the accident," Lezlie supplied. "Can you tell me about it, Merri?"

Merri shook her head, misery written all over her face.

"Do you know what happened, Merri? Or were you asleep?"

Merri jumped out of her chair. "I don't want to," she said frantically. She was crying as she spun away.

Lezlie came up behind her and put her hands on

the slender shoulders. "It won't go away just because you don't want to remember, Merri. The anger and hurt you feel inside is what makes you so sad. Someday soon, I want you to be able to tell me what happened."

With unexpected suddenness, Merri threw herself into Lezlie's arms. Lezlie leaned over and put her arms around Merri. "I don't want it to be different like it is here."

"I know, Merri, I know," Lezlie consoled. "But it just isn't possible."

Merri sniffed and raised watery eyes to Lezlie's face. "Did your momma and daddy go away, too?"

So, Merri did remember that she had mentioned her own experience. She hadn't made any reference to it at all until now. "No, I lost my husband and—"

"You're married?" Merri said incredulously.

"I was," Lezlie answered quietly. "And like your parents, there was an accident. It took me some time to get used to being alone, but I had my mother. You have your Uncle Drew."

"Gee," Merri said, as though she had been told some precious secret. She hugged Lezlie tight, consoled and consoling, and the action touched Lezlie more than any words.

"I'm glad you're my friend," Merri said. Her smile held all the innocent trust only a child possesses. "You know, I told you my Uncle Drew was going out of town tomorrow." Lezlie nodded and Merri plunged ahead. "Well, Friday is Field Day at my school...and I can't play the games or anything...and I'll have to sit out...and I was just thinking...well, maybe you could come. All the other parents will be there and you could sit with me...it would be fun. Of course, we could only watch...."

"Whoa!" Lezlie smiled. "Are you asking me to come to Field Day?"

Merri nodded enthusiastically. "Will you... please?"

"I can't promise right now, but let me check my appointments and I'll let you know at our session Thursday. Okay?"

"Okay. But you will try? Please?"

"I'll do my very best," Lezlie promised. She checked her watch. Since Drew was leaving town, she considered telling him that Merri was having a hard time making a decision and his encouragement could help. But she decided against it. A discussion could wait until he got back. "Your uncle should be here in a few minutes."

"Uncle Drew isn't coming today. Jill wanted me to come play when we were done, so her momma's picking me up."

"Well, it sounds like you and Jill are becoming good friends."

"Yeah, I guess, but I sure wish she didn't talk about boys so much."

Lezlie waved goodbye to the little girl when her secretary came in to say Mrs. Moore was in the reception area to pick up Merri. Lezlie sat down at her desk and began to make notes of their session. Merri was making progress, she thought, with a deep sense of satisfaction. And once she made that definite first step, her treatment would progress even more quickly. Lezlie glanced over her previous notes, her attention on the "extended family" chart she made up on each of her patients. Merri's was sparse indeed. There were no grandparents, no aunts or uncles except Drew, and no cousins because Drew had never married. Drew's parents were dead; Meredith's parents had divorced when she was in school; Meredith hadn't seen her father since the divorce, and her mother had died a few years later of cancer. There was no extended family from whom Merri could draw support. The chart painted a very lonely picture. At least the child had an uncle who cared very deeply about her well-being and happiness. And he could be enough if only Merri would allow him to get close to her and carry some of the burden she bore on her little shoulders.

THE WEEK PASSED QUICKLY for Lezlie. Like Drew, Jim Blair was also out of town on business. Lezlie met Donna for dinner one night and on another they met at the spa. And between the two of them, they managed to put Lezlie's bedroom back in order. Donna was still troubled about her student, Elizabeth, being institutionalized. Her discussion with the girl's parents had at least bought some time. But ultimately, the final decision rested with them, and Donna's opinion would carry little weight.

"You know I hadn't really given much thought to what Elizabeth's parents are going through until you said what you did. Even though I wouldn't agree with their decision to institutionalize, I understand their reasons."

"Well, you have done all you can, Donna."

"I wonder," Donna mused, but she forced a brighter mood. "It's just the waiting that's hard. You know, sometimes I wish I had gone into a field where the results and rewards didn't take years. But then I look at the few who are making strides and...I don't know. It sounds corny."

"Why should it be corny to admit that what you've chosen to do is worth all the effort? If it weren't for a sense of accomplishment and purpose, nobody would be doing anything in this world."

"They would if they wanted to eat. That reminds me." As Donna and Lezlie pushed and strained to move the dresser back against the bedroom wall, Donna puffed out an invitation to a dinner party she and Jim were having.

"I don't know," Lezlie said uncertainly. "Most of the people you know are married, and I always feel a little out of place."

"You don't have to come alone," Donna suggested. "You could bring Drew."

"Asking Drew is liable to cause more problems than not."

Donna stood up, rubbing her back. "How did you ever work around your attraction to him, and more, his to you? Oh, he played it very cool when we were over, but every time he looked at you he gave himself away." Donna whistled softly. "If Jim were to look at me that way, I would absolutely melt."

Lezlie didn't comment on how Drew affected her. Donna would only badger her more about allowing a relationship to develop. "Actually, it was Drew who made the suggestion that we be friends. He finally understands that while I am treating Merri, I can't be involved with him."

"I think I would have found another doctor for my niece," Donna said bluntly. The look Lezlie shot her made her hold her hand. "Okay, okay, it was only a thought. And I know you really want to help her. But contrary to the advice you gave me, I think you are getting personally involved, Lezlie. And I'm not saying it's bad. I just hope Drew is a patient man."

Lezlie hoped so, too, but she immediately pushed the idea aside. She thought about Drew Bradinton more than was wise under the circumstances. At odd times during the day, he would pop into her mind and break her concentration. Donna's comment caused Lezlie to wonder, was she becoming too close to Merri's case? No, she thought, attempting to be honest. It was the circumstances of Merri's loss that made her special in Lezlie's eyes; the similarity of Merri's feelings to her own in the past. So much of her practice was filled with overindulged, underattended children, rebellious teens fighting a desperate battle to gain their parents' attention, the emotional problems or trauma of a broken home, or of a remarriage. And she hadn't become overly sympathetic. But Merri's case was different.

"Hey," Donna interrupted. "Where did you go?"

"What?"

"Well, you certainly weren't here. You didn't hear a word—"

"I'm sorry," Lezlie said. "I was just thinking about a patient...."

"Bet I can guess which one." Donna grinned.

Lezlie picked up a pillow and tossed it at her friend. "You're incorrigible."

"No, just observant," Donna said simply. Secretly, she was delighted by what was happening. For the first time since she had met Lezlie, her friend was genuinely interested in someone other than her patients. The wall Lezlie had built around herself was beginning to crack. Lezlie might not admit to it, not yet anyway, but it was there. And if Donna was any judge of character, it wouldn't be long before Drew Bradinton was as special to Lezlie as his niece had become.

FRIDAY WAS A BRIGHT and beautiful day. Lezlie left her office just before lunch and headed for Merri's school. She had told Merri at their Thursday session that she would come. The playground was already filled with excited screaming children. The races were about to start. Lezlie parked her car and started across the grass. Merri suddenly bolted out of a group of girls and hurried toward her.

"Hi!" Merri said cheerfully.

"Am I late?"

"No, nothing's started yet." Merri slipped her hand into Lezlie's and pulled her toward her classmates. The children looked at Lezlie curiously, but their attention was quickly diverted as the teacher called for them to line up. Merri led Lezlie to a spot set off from the rest of the groups and they sat on the grass to watch the games. The noise was deafening and the excitement contagious.

"There's Jill," Merri said, pointing out her friend. "She's one of the fastest runners in school. We'll win the relay without sweat."

The spectators shouted and cheered at the end of each race, and yelled encouragement during the contests. The sun was warm with only a slight breeze to ease the heat and Lezlie removed her lightweight jacket. The teachers didn't look at all as Lezlie imagined they must for class. They sported Bermuda shorts, culottes, tennis shoes and caps. Merri explained there was a volleyball match set for after the races: the sixth-grade teachers against the seventh-grade teachers. The principal was on one team; the assistant principal on the other. It was a yearly challenge and one Lezlie knew would give the children a great deal of fun.

"Oh, this is the sack race!" Merri exclaimed. "It's the only one I wish I could do. It's so much fun."

The teams divided into groups of two, each child putting one leg in a burlap bag. There was a great deal of stumbling, fumbling and laughing. Lezlie was completely enjoying the day when a flash of red caught her eye. A child had moved away from his mother and was running onto the playground. His hair blew across his round flushed face and he squealed with delight as his mother ran after him. Pain clutched Lezlie's chest. The little boy reminded her of other Field Days, of warm sunshine and messy clothes. Lezlie looked away. She had been so sure she could handle being around the children, but just the sight of a little boy in a red shirt and blue jeans brought bittersweet memories.

"Lezlie, are you okay? You look sorta sick."

"I'm fine, Merri, just a little hot."

Merri had looked beyond Lezlie. "There's Uncle Drew," she said, obviously surprised as she pointed toward the parking lot.

Lezlie turned around. Drew was coming toward them, his jacket hanging across his shoulder from his finger. He was loosening his tie and undoing the top button of his shirt. The breeze tousled his hair and tie, but he looked completely at ease as he leaned down and touched Merri's cheek.

"You're not overdoing it, are you, pumpkin?"

"No, we've just been watching." There was a caution in Merri's voice that Lezlie hadn't heard before.

"I thought you would be out of town until tomorrow," Lezlie commented.

"I got through a little sooner, so I went ahead and caught a flight."

"How are things going in Denver?"

"Pretty good, actually. Another month or so, and the project will be finished." Drew squatted down beside Merri. "So who's ahead?"

"The seventh grade," Merri grumbled.

"Then you should be a shoo-in next year," Drew consoled. "How would you like a ride home after school?"

"Are you going to stay?" Merri asked him.

"I'm here."

After the sack race, the volleyball game was getting under way. Merri went over to talk to Jill and Lezlie took the opportunity to talk to Drew.

"Drew, have you noticed that Merri is worried?"

Drew was watching his niece. "She had seemed quiet lately. I've asked her if there's a problem at school or what, but she's still reticent about talking to me. Is it something important?"

"It is to Merri." Lezlie started to explain, but before she could mention their session, Merri came back and sat down.

The volleyball game caused a great deal of excitement among the children and by its end the teachers were overheated and winded. But it had been a terrific upset: the sixth-grade teachers beating the seventh by two points. The children shouted and clapped, and the principal, a short balding man in his fifties, bowed in response to the applause. Then the teachers began calling their students into line to return to the classroom to get their things before the buses arrived.

Lezlie gathered her jacket and purse as Merri hopped to her feet. "I'm really glad you came, Lezlie," Merri said happily. "I'll be out in a few minutes, Uncle Drew." Merri skipped off to join her classmates.

"Was anything wrong when I got here?" Drew asked.

Lezlie knew she must have seemed strained, but she shook her head. "No, but if I had known it would be this warm, I would have dressed for it."

"I know what you mean," Drew said. Perspiration dotted his forehead and his shirt clung to his back. "Listen, I'm glad you came, too. If Merri had told me she had invited you, I wouldn't have felt so bad about not being able to get here sooner."

"She didn't tell you?"

Drew smiled ruefully. "There's a lot Merri doesn't tell me, Lezlie. But I can wait."

Lezlie wouldn't tell him about Merri's indecision. Maybe if she left it alone, Merri would go to her uncle on her own. "She will turn to you eventually, Drew," Lezlie reassured. "It's just a matter of time."

"Patience was never really one of my virtues—" Drew said, then smiled "—but I'm learning." Drew's meaning applied to more than Merri's turmoil. He was also being patient where Lezlie was concerned, more so than he had ever been before. He didn't want just an affair, which was what he had thought initially. He wanted much more from Dr. Lezlie Garrett, and he was prepared to wait as long as it'd take to get through to her.

"She is making progress, Drew. She is opening up a little more with each session." Lezlie had wanted to reassure Drew, but once again she felt she had said the wrong thing. She had no way of knowing that Drew was dreading the day that Merri confided completely in Lezlie. Because Drew was almost certain that Merri knew a lot more about the past than she was saying. It was as though he was waiting for a time bomb to go off, and he had to stand by silently and wait.

"Well, I guess I better get back to work," Lezlie said brightly.

"Thanks again for being here. It means a lot."

"Anytime." Lezlie headed for her car, but she could feel Drew watching her. Like the night in the parking lot at the Galleria, he stood with his hands thrust into his pockets, and then he ambled toward the front of the school.

Lezlie was awakened the next morning by a pounding knock on her front door. "What in the world?" she mumbled. She threw back the covers, shivering in the morning chill. It was nine o'clock on Saturday, her only morning to sleep in and she was irritated at the disturbance. If it was some door-to-door salesman, she would give him a piece of her mind. She pulled on her robe and stumbled down the hall, cursing when she stubbed her toe on the table in the foyer. Swinging the door open, her anger dissolved.

Drew stood on the doorstep, momentarily speechless. Lezlie's hair was unrestrained, rippling in a tangled mass of curls. Her soft velvet robe clung to her slender figure. A fluff of lace was visible above where she clutched her robe at the waist with one hand while sweeping her hair back over her shoulder with the other. Her appearance was far different than he had expected. "I need to talk to you," he said brusquely, but he was having difficulty keeping his temper and his thoughts under control. He stepped into the house and closed the door.

"I would like to know what in the hell is going on, Lezlie. I think it's about time you explain some things."

"What are you taking about?" Lezlie started.

"Your bright idea that Merri strip her room. She's sitting in the middle of her room with a couple of boxes, packing up practically everything—the same things she couldn't bear for me to leave behind in Denver." Drew's anger rose when Lezlie smiled. "I don't know what you can find to smile about, lady. But that is one miserable little girl I left back at the house. All she would say is that it was your idea. And it's tearing her apart to do it."

"Drew, if you'll just calm down, I can explain." Lezlie headed back through the house. "But if you don't mind, I'll put on some coffee first."

Drew remained silent as Lezlie moved around the kitchen, but she could feel his angry glare following her. The coffee was perking and Lezlie set the cups on the table. *What a way to start the morning,* she was thinking to herself.

Drew sat down, his whole body rigid. "So, explain, would you?"

"This is a first step for Merri, Drew, and it's a big step. It's natural that she would be upset. But you have to look at it from her point of view. In essence, this is a first step in saying goodbye to her parents...."

"How can you know that?" Drew demanded. He stood and paced to the counter, still angry. He hadn't seen Merri so upset since she had come to live with him. "How can you possibly know how the child feels, Lezlie?" he said quietly, and he faced her squarely. "Sure, you deal with children's problems, but books and education can only give so much. You live here in this empty house, bare of any mementos or memories, and yet you tell me this is a first step for Merri. Toward what, Lezlie, complete misery? Because that's what it is for her." Drew raked a hand through his hair. "I think I may have been wrong to consent to this," he mumbled. "Merri may have been making progress, but this will undo any of the good. You may have experience as a therapist, Lezlie, but as a woman, I wonder. This seems very cruel...."

Lezlie's hands had begun to shake and the tremors quickly traveled through her. He had said her advice was cruel, she thought incredulously. He didn't know the meaning of the word. Cruel was doing something that hurt someone intentionally, but what Merri was doing was necessary to put her life back in order. And Lezlie knew better than anyone else just what a hard thing it was to do. Drew was watching Lezlie, a concerned frown lining his forehead.

"Lezlie, I didn't mean to offend you...."

"Offend me?" Lezlie questioned shortly. "You haven't offended me, Drew. You've made me angry because once again you're questioning my qualifications. Don't you know that I wouldn't do anything to harm any of my patients? Or do you feel it would be better for her to go on surrounded by a morbid shrine of reminders? Because that's what that room is. And I can tell you one thing. I am better qualified to treat Merri than anyone else. You want to know why, Drew? Do you want to know?" Lezlie asked, her voice a little shrill. "Well, I'm going to show you how I know what Merri's feeling...."

Lezlie swept out of the kitchen and Drew followed, surprised by her quick display of righteous anger. As he walked into the den, he noticed that the room had been put back in order, the empty shelves and mantel holding several photographs. There were pictures of a young boy and a man, happy and laughing. Drew studied each one for a moment; then a baby picture and one of Lezlie with the man.

"You see, I can sympathize with Merri because I've been through it, Drew. My husband and my son drowned two years ago. And I couldn't do a thing to help them." She hadn't verbalized the truth in a long time, and the words still brought the old anguish and fleeting sense of guilt. Tears filled her eyes, and she wished she could run away and find a place where the truth wouldn't hurt her, but she carried it within.

"Oh, God," Drew groaned, and he closed the distance between them. Lezlie was rigid when he grasped her shoulders, but he could feel the tremors. "Lezlie, I'm so sorry. I had no idea."

The pity Lezlie detested from anyone sounded even worse coming from Drew. "I don't want your pity, Drew. I've managed to deal with the accident. My own experience was the reason I agreed to see Merri," Lezlie said, choked by emotion. "No one who hasn't been through it can know what it's like to lose someone, to have your whole life changed in an instant."

Lezlie had begun to cry and Drew pulled her into his arms. As he rested his cheek on her head, he stared at the photographs. So many things about Lezlie were now explained, so many questions answered. Drew finally understood her fear of a relationship and commitment. Drew didn't pity her; he was sorry for her pain and the suffering she must have known to have become as closed to involvement as she was now. But he also understood the inner strength she possessed. She had taken on a case that must be a continual reminder of her own loss, a loss that would make anyone fearful and cautious of being hurt again. He understood so many things now. He held her tightly, willing to give whatever comfort he could as he stroked her hair and whispered soothing words.

Lezlie pressed into the solace Drew offered. It had been such a long time since she had been held as Drew was holding her now, with tenderness and compassion and caring. The loneliness she had tried so hard to deny rushed over her and she clung to him as she might to a life preserver. She felt secure wrapped in his arms, his lips touching her hair and his strong hands holding her tightly. Her sobs finally subsided and Lezlie took a shaky sigh. When she raised her tear-streaked face Drew smiled tenderly.

"Better?"

Lezlie nodded and before she could wipe the tears from her cheeks, Drew had swept them away with his thumb. Drew was suddenly lost within the tear-bright eyes. He wanted to draw her into him to make her forget his hurtful accusations and harsh words. Her mouth was slightly parted and her bottom lip still trembled, and he could not stop himself. He leaned over and claimed her soft lips in a sweet kiss.

Lezlie could not resist, nor did she even try. Her eyes fluttered closed and her breath expelled in a sigh of desire. Longing ached within her as his mouth settled firmly over hers, his tongue touching and exploring. She slid her arms around him, awed by the rush of molten fire that swept her away in a blaze of desire. What she experienced when Drew kissed her was like nothing she had known before. Sex for her had been pleasant and satisfying—a mutual sharing heightened by deep love. But her reaction now had little to do with sharing. She was in peril of losing herself to a passion as equally demanding as Drew's, and she did not care. A spiral of pleasure radiated from the deepest, most-secret place within her, twisting and turning through her senses. She wanted to be closer still—to feel his touch on every inch of her skin. She wanted to be made love to, oh, God, how she wanted....

Drew caressed the length of her body from her breasts to her hips, drawing her even more tightly to him. It was as though they were of one mind, one body, singing a melody of promised ecstasy.

Lezlie clutched his shoulders, stretching her body upward to meet the kiss she had dreamed of, which was now a reality. Drew pushed the robe from her shoulders and replaced the soft material with his lips.

"I want to touch you," he whispered breathlessly, and Lezlie could not make herself object as her robe slipped unheeded to the floor. She was beyond protest or denial even when he turned her away from him. But she soon learned why. He lifted her hair and ran his lips along the tendons of her neck while his hands had free access to her body. Lezlie leaned back against him and he turned her head as he brought her mouth to his. His hand lightly explored the soft curve of her waist, the flatness of her stomach before beginning an agonizingly slow descent. Only the silkiness of her nightgown denied him full possession of whatever he wanted.

"Drew," she breathed against his mouth.

"Don't say anything," he returned and he swept her into his arms for a kiss that left her shaking and pliant in his embrace.

Drew was about to carry her to her bedroom when a glint of gold caught his eye. He lifted the slender chain, planning to do away with any obstruction to the intimate exploration he intended. The sight of the wedding band was as staggering as a blow. He dropped his arms from around Lezlie, quickly setting her feet on the floor, and stepped back to put some distance between them.

"Drew, what is it?" Lezlie asked, confused by his strange behavior.

"I thought your telling me about your family meant that you trusted me and were over the past. But you're not, are you, Lezlie?"

"What do you mean?"

"That," Drew said, pointing to the ring she wore.

Lezlie took the ring in her hand, then looked up at Drew. "I had forgotten about it. After the accident, I couldn't take it off, but it brought so many questions. So I put it on the chain."

"And you still wear it. That in itself says a great deal, Lezlie. I had hoped it would be right for us, but it isn't. Not yet. Maybe it never will be." Drew shook his head. "You're obviously still in love with your husband, or you wouldn't still wear that ring. But you're in love with the memory of love, Lezlie."

"My husband and son were very special to me," Lezlie said.

"Yes, but they can't share the present or the future. They are part of the past, and if I've learned anything in this life, it's that there's nothing that can be done to change the past, and it can sure as hell wreck the future if you try. But what you've done is worse. You've condemned yourself to life in an emotional vacuum. There's an adage in your profession: 'Physician heal thyself.' I think it applies to you. Nobody can do it for you."

As Drew walked out of the den and out of the house, Lezlie sank weakly into a chair. "I thought I had," she said quietly, shaking not only from reaction to his comments, but from the unquenched desire still teasing her. But Drew's opinion brought doubts she couldn't dispel as she stared at the photographs of Michael and their son, Mike. Was Drew right? Did her mother see the same thing as Drew? Was she nurturing a memory of love? Had all her efforts to pick up the pieces of her life been for nothing? Or had she merely channeled her energies away from an emotional commitment, while telling herself it didn't matter? Had she deluded herself with the belief that she had had one great love—two actually—in her life and that they had been enough?

Lezlie's head had begun to pound and she rubbed her temples. But couldn't he understand, couldn't Drew see that she was afraid to love and lose again? If she did and anything were to happen to end it for any reason, she wasn't certain she could survive it...not a second time.

Lezlie was stepping out of the shower when she heard the phone ringing. She didn't want to talk to anyone, but she had no choice. She was on call at the hospital. Drew's contrite voice answered her quiet hello.

"Lezlie, I said some things I shouldn't have," he apologized. "And I shouldn't have left the way I did." There was a pause before he continued even more quietly. "Tell me about Michael."

"I don't think it will make any difference."

"It might, Lezlie. I didn't have any right to judge you, and I did. But it's only because I thought you couldn't trust me, or your own feelings. But we're friends, more than friends I hope, and now I'm in more of a frame of mind to listen. Can you tell me about Michael, and your son?"

Lezlie was thoughtful for a moment. "Are you coming over?"

"No, I thought it would be easier this way."

Lezlie was relived that he was no longer angry. "What do you want to know?"

"Anything you want to tell me," he answered.

Lezlie didn't know exactly where to start, but suddenly she began to talk. She and Michael had met in college. She had been a sophomore, he had been in his third year of law school. They had married six months later. Michael had a part-time job in a law firm as a gofer, but that couldn't support them, so Lezlie had worked, too, and gone to school at night to finish her degree. Michael, Jr. had been born a year later. The day he was born was the most fantastic day she could remember.

It had been a struggle at first, but her family had helped out and they had been happy. Her mother had taken care of Mike while Lezlie continued to work. Once Michael had passed his bar, she quit her job and resumed her own schooling on a full-time basis, having decided to continue with graduate work. There was no way to describe those hectic, sometimes frustrating, often pleasant days of the next few years. They had bought a house in an older suburb with a wonderful fenced yard and given Mike his first pet. "The whole catastrophe," Michael had called it, their situation, quoting a line from the movie *Zorba the Greek*. Lezlie had completely renovated the house, which seemed to be in a perpetual state of disrepair. A private joke had developed between her and Michael that if she had wanted a handyman for a husband she should have married one.

Michael, Jr. had been five when she completed the requirements for her doctorate, and she had spent a whole summer doing so many of the things she just hadn't had time to do before. When he started kindergarten, she had begun to look for a job. Michael had advised her to go into a family counseling clinic, but after a few months she found she was more interested in the children's problems than those of the parents. So, she had struck out on her own. She had applied at several hospitals and waited for replies to her applications. And before she started a new job, she had wanted to go away for a few days.

Lezlie could still remember vividly her cajoling pleas as she had pestered Michael until he relented and agreed to a few days at the lake. She wished now she had never suggested the outing and that Michael hadn't agreed.

She and Michael, with little Mike, had gone away with two other couples, men who worked in the same law firm and their wives. She was so excited: three whole days on the lake with a boat for skiing and a cozy cottage. It had been a perfect weekend until the last day. She still couldn't explain why she hadn't wanted to go out on the boat that morning. Maybe it was because it was cooler than usual or the water was choppy, but Michael had ignored her protests.

It had all happened so fast. They were racing across the water, the wind whipping from the storm that threatened, when they smacked a wave from the wake of another boat. Mike was beside Lezlie one moment, the next he was in the water. She had screamed to Michael and he had turned the boat. For a moment, she hadn't been worried. Mike had on a life jacket, but her heart had nearly stopped when she saw that somehow Mike had slipped out of it. She could still remember the numbing fear that closed around her as she looked at Michael. He had shrugged out of his own life vest and gone after his son, so sure as he dived into the water. It was the last time she had seen either of them alive. She would have gone in herself, but the others had stopped her. The men went into the water after her husband and son, but there had been no trace of them. It was crazy, unreal, and the unbelievability of it had stilled her cries of anguish. At any moment, she kept expecting Mike and Michael to splash through the surface of the dark waters. The hours that followed were a nightmare. Rescuers were called, but they had no success.

Lezlie coughed through a lump in her throat. Every moment of the torment of those next hours was forever etched in her mind. She would never forget, never. Their bodies had been found the next day. The investigators said the fall from the boat had knocked Mike unconscious and he had drowned; her husband had struck his head on some object upon entering the water. It was so incredible, but it hadn't taken long for reaction to set in. The nightmare had only begun.

The details of the funerals were handled by her mother, and Lezlie had floated through it all in a haze of tranquilizers and sleeping pills. She had walked through their house, surrounded by all the possessions of a family that no longer existed, and she thought she would go insane. She ranted at the unfairness, cried over the senseless loss and blamed herself for suggesting the trip. She even blamed Michael for insisting they go out that morning. She went into fits of crying and despair and it was her mother who finally helped pull her out of it. Lezlie had tried to deal with the tragedy alone, but finally accepted that she couldn't. She had sought counseling to voice all the anger and bitterness and guilt. For three months, those sessions were all that sustained her until she could face, deal with and dispel her own sense of guilt. And therapy had eased the grief.

Slowly, she had begun to accept the finality of her child's and husband's deaths. Soon after that, she had come to work at Riverview. Her work kept her from thinking, from remembering and from hurting so badly.

Drew had listened without speaking. "It really wasn't your fault, Lezlie. It's just one of the freak things that happen, like Meredith and Greg. There is no rhyme nor reason."

"Unfortunately, I couldn't see that at the time. I kept looking for some explanation when there wasn't one." Lezlie was lost in an old thought. "And no one could truly understand what I was feeling...until one day, I met a woman sitting in the counselor's waiting room. She was in her forties, I guess, and she was trying to deal with a divorce where the husband had taken the children one night and left town with them. I think that was the turning point for me. Because I finally realized I wasn't the only one who was suffering through some tragedy. It would make more sense to you if you had been married and had been that close to someone for a long time...."

"I was almost married once," Drew said. "But it didn't work out."

"Why?"

"I don't know. Bad timing, I guess. Sometimes I wonder what would have happened if I had gone ahead. We'd been going together for a couple of years, and I was seriously thinking about popping the question. Then I got my draft notice. I couldn't see it. Getting married for a few weeks and then leaving for however long, or maybe never coming back. I just didn't think it was fair."

Lezlie wished she could see his face. "Then you think it was a mistake that you held off?"

"In one respect, I suppose. She married someone else."

"Oh," Lezlie said quietly.

"I think I missed having a family, a kid when it might have been important."

"But you could have married since then."

"Sure, I could've had my pick," Drew bragged, and then he laughed. "But I didn't meet anyone who has a back like yours."

"What?" Lezlie said, taken off guard.

"Didn't you know? I have this thing for backs, especially when they curve in so enticingly just above the waist, like yours."

"And how would you know that?" Lezlie asked, trying to sound serious. "I was wearing my coat the first time I saw you."

"I could still tell."

"How?"

"By the way you walk, of course."

"Of course," Lezlie agreed.

"And I also happen to like slim legs, trim ankles, upturned noses and big gray eyes."

"My, you were observant. All of that on the first meeting."

"You bet. And it almost undid me. My dream woman, a walking, talking, angry reality, if you remember."

"I remember," Lezlie said.

"So what did you like about me right away?"

Lezlie was becoming uncomfortable with the teasing exchange. "Who says I liked anything?"

"I do," Drew said matter-of-factly. "There was something, right?"

"We-ll," Lezlie drawled, pretending to pause. She knew exactly what had attracted her to Drew. It was not one or two parts of his anatomy, but more a sense of strength, of command and presence that had caught her interest. "It wasn't any one thing," she stressed. "I think it was your confidence, an almost egotistical overconfidence. Yes, I'm sure it was that."

"Egotistical? Egotistical?" Drew cried. "You can't be serious."

"What would you call it, then? Obnoxious might be a better word, or how about overbearing?"

"Okay, okay, I'll settle for overconfident. Have I dispelled my bad impression since then, I hope?"

"Oh, I think so."

"That's something then."

"That's quite a lot, actually," Lezlie rejoined. "I don't usually change my mind about a first impression."

"You mean you put aside your prudishness for little old me?"

"Prudishness?" Lezlie exclaimed, and the roar of laughter that followed made her smile. "Touché, as Charles would say."

The verbal sparring had completely erased Lezlie's gloomy mood. "Better watch it or I'll add incorrigible to the description...."

"That may apply, too," Drew admitted. "I'm glad we've talked, Lezlie. I didn't want to leave things the way they were."

"Neither did I, Drew."

"And in case I didn't say so, I'm sorry I rousted

you out of bed, although you did look delightful. I almost forgot my reason for coming over in the first place. I promise I'll call next time."

"I hope there isn't a next time," Lezlie said ruefully. "I don't think I could start many mornings like I did today."

"A cold shower helps," Drew offered with amused suggestiveness.

Lezlie wasn't about to admit that that was exactly what she had done. "I'll keep that in mind," she commented.

They talked for a moment more before Lezlie hung up. She bounded off the bed, slid into her jeans and shirt, passing the washer on her way to the kitchen.

"Ugh," she mumbled. It was too pretty a day to stay in and do laundry. She grabbed her purse and headed out for an afternoon of shopping. And she knew just where she would go. She picked up the phone and punched out the numbers quickly.

"Hi, mom, I thought you might want to go shopping."

"I thought you had all kinds of chores."

"I do, but I'm not going to do them. I want to go to the Flea Market."

"Oh, I thought you meant shopping shopping, not poking around those dusty places," Margaret groaned.

"Where's your sense of adventure?"

"The same place as my good sense. I'll be ready in thirty minutes. I have to change."

"I'll pick you up then." Lezlie hurried around, doing some of the smaller chores until it was time to leave.

CHAPTER SEVEN

THE FLEA MARKETS and antique shops around Atlanta were a true smorgasbord for antique buffs. Around the perimeter expressway were three huge markets that had been converted from large retail stores and offered the largest selection of antiques in the South. Lezlie could spend hours rummaging through the booths. She ambled unhurriedly, all the while keeping an eye out for the unusual little bottles she had begun collecting years earlier.

Musty odors and dust clung to the old furniture and other items that had been hidden away in some attic until coming forth in a second bloom of appreciation, and mingled with the odor of fine oil polish. There were shops of glass and crystal, of old brass lamps and beveled mirrors, dark somber paintings and huge pieces of furniture from another era. And it all held a fascination for Lezlie.

Even Margaret had to admit that she enjoyed browsing. She followed Lezlie up and down the aisles that were named after streets in Atlanta: Peachtree, Piedmont, Paces Ferry, West Wesley, Roswell. Sometimes she just looked at the fragile lace linens from another era, their delicate patterns discolored by age, and other times she remarked, "Oh, Lezlie, look, my mother had a tureen just like this one," or "This table is just like the one that used to sit in the hall at your Great-Aunt Emma's."

Margaret watched her daughter as they strolled along the aisles, glancing into one shop and then another. There was a nuance, some slight but perceptible shift in Lezlie's mood that had caught Margaret's sharp eye. Unless she was mistaken, Lezlie's usual seriousness was modified by a quick easy smile. And there was a becoming flush on her cheeks and a bright sparkle in her eyes. Margaret wondered if something had happened to make Lezlie happy again...or was it someone?

"How's your new patient doing?" Margaret asked as they browsed. "I know you were worried...."

"She's doing very well," Lezlie said brightly. "In fact, she came to a major turning point today."

"Oh?" Margaret prompted.

"Yes, her uncle was over this morning." The comment caused Margaret to glance up from a table of old costume jewelry. "He was pretty upset about a suggestion I had made because it was difficult for his niece to see it through, but she did. I think Drew understands now."

Margaret didn't miss the name, nor the slight smile that accompanied her daughter's explanation. She rarely resorted to subtle prying, but Lezlie had become so defensive in some respects, especially when questioned about her social life. And if there was something about this man Drew that had brought color and sparkle to her daughter's face, Margaret didn't intend to jeopardize it by asking. So she chose another tack to appease the curiosity that was about to get the better of her. "I imagine that should make things a great deal easier for the uncle and his wife."

"Adjusting to a new mother is one problem the girl doesn't have. The uncle's not married," Lezlie said, distracted by an unusually fine armoire of dark mahogany and beveled mirrors. She missed the smile that curved her mother's lips.

"You know, if I had my way, I'd probably furnish my whole house in antiques," Lezlie commented wistfully. She ran her hand along the smooth rich wood of the huge wardrobe. The craftsmanship was incredible; the piece built to last generations.

"Then why don't you?" Margaret asked. "You have some lovely pieces now."

"Oh, yes," Lezlie drawled, "like the claw-footed chair you had in your attic?"

Margaret grimaced. "I had completely forgotten about that."

"I think Michael wished you had forgotten you had it at all. God, how he hated that chair," Lezlie said with a grin. "He said it reminded him of sitting on the back of a gargoyle."

"They were lion claws," Margaret corrected.

"I know that and you know that, but nothing could convince Michael that it wasn't a replica of some ancient beast of prey that should never have been reproduced in the first place, and certainly not as furniture." Lezlie had started to laugh. "And the vase Aunt Louise sent us for our wedding...the one with black dragons on it?"

Margaret was laughing now. "Whatever happened to it?"

"It's in the attic, still in its original box. Michael said it was ugly enough to give a ghoul nightmares." Lezlie slipped her arm around her mother's shoulders, and they giggled like schoolgirls. "Oh, and that wild-colored wall hanging from Peru...."

Margaret collapsed with laughter as Lezlie went down a well-known list of things opened, gaped at and then promptly put away, out of sight. It was so good to see her like this, Margaret was thinking. Lezlie might not have had siblings but she had an abundance of aunts with Margaret's four sisters; two of whom traveled extensively and sent the most outrageous and useless presents for any occasion.

"Oh, Lord," Margaret sighed, breathless. "I haven't thought about that wall hanging in years."

"Neither had I," Lezlie agreed. "But if I ever redo the house, I might find something to give a room a unique flair...."

"I don't know if 'flair' is the right word," Margaret said. "Eccentricity might be better. No dear, stick with your own taste and you'll be safe."

Lezlie wandered to the next shop. She had wanted to furnish the home she shared with Michael with antiques, but even if the cost hadn't deterred her, Michael's preferences had. And now it seemed so impractical to get rid of the perfectly good furniture she already had. But maybe, someday.

Her mother was looking through a shop of memorabilia when Lezlie spied a shelf on the back wall of the booth. Several small bottles were clustered to one side. Carefully, she picked up each in turn. Two had small cracks in the bubbled hand-blown glass and another was chipped. The last was an amethyst much like the one she had over her kitchen sink.

"Pretty, aren't they?" The proprietor smiled politely. "The small ones are getting harder to find, and when you do, they're usually damaged."

"I noticed," Lezlie said, but she was suddenly drawn toward an unusual lamp on one of the tables in the booth. "Oh, how lovely," she said.

The proprietor followed her. "It is an unusual piece. You can tell it was originally an oil lamp, but it's been skillfully converted for electricity."

The brass of the lamp was dark with age, but the beautiful amethyst glass base sparkled beneath the delicate silk shade where tiny embroidered flowers seemed to dance along its edge. Lezlie couldn't resist it. The lamp would be a beautiful addition to her bedroom—and perhaps a beginning to realizing her wish. As she was writing out a check, the proprietor chatted easily.

"You know, if you really like the old glass, there's a shop up in Roswell, off Highway 19, that has a terrific collection. Actually, it's where I bought the lamp, and the owner has excellent prices. You might want to drive out there."

"Drive where?" Margaret asked, walking up at the tail end of the conversation.

"This gentleman was just telling me about a shop in Roswell that specializes in glassware."

"Well, we've seen all that's here. Why don't we ride out that way and take a look. Then we could stop for lunch somewhere."

The suggestion made Lezlie smile. "I thought you would have had enough of musty antiques."

Margaret shrugged nonchalantly. "Once you've been rummaging around for a while, you don't mind the dust so much. Besides, I may luck up on something I've been thinking about for a while."

"What?"

Margaret looked uncharacteristically ill at ease. "You'll laugh."

"No, I won't. I didn't know there was something you had been wanting. What is it?"

"A rocking chair," Margaret answered cautiously.

"You want a what?" Lezlie cried, and she unsuccessfully smothered a laugh.

"See, I told you you would laugh."

"No, no," Lezlie said, and then she shrugged. "It's just hard to imagine you sitting in a rocking chair, knitting or sewing," she explained. She smiled impishly. "Where would you put it, on the porch or in front of the TV?"

"Very funny," Margaret said.

"You have to admit, mom, it doesn't exactly fit your image."

"Yes, well I spent a lot of pleasant hours in the old one I used to have. I believe you have it now."

Lezlie was properly chastised. The rocker her mother referred to had been her mother's until she had given it to Lezlie when Mike was born. "Mom, there's no reason you can't have it back. If I had known you wanted one...."

"I don't want it back, dear. But that corner of my room has looked a little empty. Besides, you may have need of it again someday." Margaret could have bitten off her tongue the moment the words were out, but the closed expression she'd anticipated did not descend over Lezlie's features.

"Why don't we head up to Roswell? Maybe the shop there will have something." Lezlie smiled apologetically. "And I didn't mean to laugh."

"I know, dear," Margaret said, and then she chuckled. "I guess it would be a bit of a surprise to find me sitting in front of the TV, knit one, purl two."

The afternoon was comfortably warm as Lezlie maneuvered through the traffic on Roswell Road. Just north of Sandy Springs, the traffic lessened and she drove the left lane, amazed at the amount of development taking place. Condominiums, office parks and stores were opening up faster than she could have thought possible. She was looking at an office-condominium project when the sign at the road made her turn. Bradinton Construction was emblazoned in bold black letters. Lezlie caught a glimpse of Drew's car parked near a long trailer.

"What is it?" Margaret asked, leaning forward.

"Oh, nothing," Lezlie answered. "I just can't believe the construction going on along here." But her stomach did a dizzy little dance. It was strange to drive by Drew's workplace and know he was there. She wondered if he was immersed in paperwork, or if he was in one of the buildings. Lezlie stopped for the traffic light and continued to study the cluster of buildings in different phases of construction.

The sun was in her eyes, and even shading them

with her hand didn't help. But she could tell from one of the buildings that it would eventually be an impressive office park in a Williamsburg style with a dark brick. Funny, she had thought Drew would build the modern glass-and-concrete monstrosities that were so popular. It seemed that making erroneous assumptions about Drew Bradinton was becoming a habit.

Drew was standing on the third floor of the building shell. The foreman had gone to get a specific set of plans from the trailer. Leaning against the metal beam, Drew cupped his hand to light a cigarette and then stared idly out at the traffic on Roswell Road. His thoughts were rambling and disoriented as he tried unsuccessfully to push the mental image of a bewitching auburn-haired woman from his mind.

Drew was actually relieved that he had called Lezlie after he had stormed out of her house. Walking out had been a juvenile thing to do, he chastised himself, but he had been confronted with a fact he had in no way anticipated. It should have occurred to him that anyone as lovely as Lezlie would have been in love; might have been involved; could have been married. But he was so obsessed by her complete disinterest and rejection that he hadn't even considered what might have caused her withdrawal from emotional commitment. He knew about withdrawal. He had done virtually the same thing ten years ago when he had returned from Vietnam. The shock of war and months of imprisonment had taken their toll, but what waited to be revealed at home had been more devastating than the ravages of any war. He had been cheated, he thought, and the feeling of emptiness had taken a long time to be rid of. It had taken time and a great deal of self-evaluation for him to come to terms with the unchangeable fact that his brother had married his girl in his absence. And once he had pushed his pride out of the way, he had understood why they hadn't told him, not at first nor later when he had been listed as missing in action.

Drew had always held a belief that unless a person pursued a certain thing in life, only occasionally was there a definitive reason for the events within his life. Often there was no reason at all. Some people called it fate, others saw it as chance, Drew saw it simply as the nature of life itself. The philosophy had seen him over every hurdle placed before him—even when a series of events resulted in tragedy and the accompanying guilt that served no purpose other than to inflict misery upon those who took its weight. He had meant what he'd told Lezlie about the past ruining the future. He'd had firsthand experience. But he would leave no part of his intentions for a relationship with Lezlie to chance.

Drew dragged deeply on his cigarette, the smoke swirling around his face as he gazed at the traffic. A small white sports car caught his eye, but it was the driver who held his full attention. The sun had turned her hair to molten copper and he saw her raise her hand to shield her eyes. He smiled slowly as he tossed his cigarette through the nonexistent wall.

No, he wouldn't leave a future with Lezlie to chance. There was too much at stake. She had touched a tiny place within him that no one had ever reached before. She was so different from the women who had filtered through his life over the past few years. She was a survivor. Not without scars, perhaps, but a survivor nonetheless. And Drew had just the balm for her troubled heart... and his.

When the light changed, the Mustang pulled away and was soon out of sight. Still, Drew stood musing over his thoughts. He wasn't even aware that Mac had returned, the rolled plans clutched proudly in his hand.

James MacClaine, called Mac by everyone who knew him, was a reed-thin man with a quiet nature. In his midforties, his face was deeply tanned and etched with lines deepened by exposure to the weather. He'd worked for Drew from the inception of Bradinton Construction, having worked his way up through the crew to foreman. There wasn't one aspect of construction about which he didn't have an expert knowledge, from laying a foundation to studding a building to painting and Sheetrocking an interior. Whenever there was something that needed to be done, Mac was the one to see it through. But his boss's recent absentmindedness was about to test Mac's patience.

"I don't know what's gotten into you lately, boss," Mac grumbled, extending the plans toward Drew. "They were right there on the desk."

"Thanks, Mac," Drew said, unrolling the plans and placing them on an improvised table of sawhorses and plywood. He secured the edges with scraps of lumber, then leaned over to check the architect's configurations for the interior walls of the second floor.

"I already checked 'em," Mac said.

"I'm sure you did," Drew answered absently.

"I made sure the dimensions were marked off properly."

"I wasn't questioning that, Mac," Drew said.

"Then what?"

"I guess I'm double-checking myself."

Mac's grin split his face into a sea of grooves, and his black eyes twinkled. "I been wonderin' what's going on with you," he gibed. "Must be a touch of spring fever."

"Spring's almost gone."

"Yeah, but not the fever, huh, boss? You know, maybe you need to take some time off. Head to the beach for a few days and maybe a few bikinis, if you get my drift."

"You're as subtle as a lead balloon." Drew grimaced. "But I can't take the time now. Maybe when this project is closer to completion."

"That's what you said on the last two," Mac censured. "You can't keep working at this pace. Five jobs in the last year, not counting that one in Denver.... Hell, I need a vacation." Mac shoved his hands into the tight back pockets of his faded jeans, his scrawny shoulders hunched. "We could head out for a beer, or two if you've a mind...like old times."

The suggestion had been hard for Mac to make. Over the years, members of Drew's construction crew had come and gone, but Mac had held fast. Many a night Drew remembered relaxing with Mac and some of the other men over a few beers. But he had been too busy the past year, and Mac's invitation was a gentle reminder. Drew rolled up the plans. "Well, what are we waiting for? You can tell me how Bonnie Jean keeps you straight these days."

Mac hung his head, but his smile did not escape Drew's notice. "Oh, you know Bonnie Jean. Can't predict what that woman's gonna do from one day to the next. One thing, though, her temper's still the same. She can still tongue-lash me better than any man can whip me, I can tell you that."

"How long have you been married now?" Drew asked as they walked through the partially constructed building.

"All my natural life," Mac said with exaggerated chagrin.

Drew laughed in total amusement. Everyone who had ever met Bonnie Jean took an immediate liking to her. Any occasion of bad temper was easily overlooked because of her bigheartedness, but her sharp tongue was legendary and a constant source of ribbing for Mac. Even Drew hadn't escaped its scathing edge when, on one occasion, he'd brought Mac home in less than sober condition.

"Maybe over that beer you can tell me what's bothering you," Mac suggested. "I'll bet it's women trouble."

"Not women," Drew corrected ruefully. "Just one woman."

"She must be something to get you so distracted."

"Yeah." Drew smiled. "She's something all right." As Mac climbed into his truck, they agreed to meet at Jake's, a small neighborhood bar a few blocks away. Pulling away from the construction site, Drew wondered where Lezlie had been going.

LORILEI'S EMPORIUM was a beautiful old house north of the small square of Roswell, but not quite at the area known as Crabapple Corners. Lezlie pulled onto the gravel driveway, impressed by the renovated Victorian home with its angular lines, freshly painted veranda and carved latticework. The small sign in the window was the only identification verifying that this was the house they sought. A tiny bell jangled gently when the door was opened. Walking inside was like walking back in time. There were rich dark colors everywhere and the few pieces of heavy brocade furniture were obviously lovingly tended. There was none of the usual clutter so common in an establishment dealing in antiques. Every antique was displayed as it might be in any home; each vase or bowl was positioned upon a table with no other pieces to challenge or diminish its beauty.

"Hello!" Margaret called, and a voice immediately answered from the upstairs.

"Hello. Feel free to browse. I'll be down in a minute."

Lezlie soon found that the front room was the only one furnished in the heavy Victorian mode; each room had a distinctive period. She didn't know enough about antiques to determine the exact era or definition of Chippendale or Sheraton or Hepplewhite, but she could appreciate fine pieces of any style. The kitchen held an assortment of pine cupboards, washstands and pieces of primitive art, while the dining room was decorated as any English estate might be in elegant dark mahogany and burled walnut, complete with a beautiful carpet displaying a design of birds. Two other rooms held antique bedroom groupings. One set was a light oak, but it was the second bedroom that caught Lezlie's breath. The delicately carved four-poster with its canopy of lace was of dark mahogany. The pattern on the posts was repeated along the edge of a chest and a dresser and a small dressing table.

"That man at the flea market wasn't exaggerating. This place is incredible," Margaret said quietly as she walked into the room behind Lezlie. "Oh, my," she breathed. "This room is lovely."

Lezlie looked inside a cabinet that held a collection of glass. She spotted a group of exquisite small bottles, including one of a rare ruby red, which she didn't have. There was also a pair of vases only three inches tall. The hand-painted bouquet on each was very detailed and she imagined how the light would dance through the soft colors. She had decided to buy all three when an ornament in the window caught her eyes. It was a brilliant piece of stained glass with a white milk-glass unicorn in its center. Without knowing quite why, she picked it up to add to her purchases.

"Whoever owns this shop definitely has excellent taste," Lezlie commented. A voice from behind startled her.

"Thank you." The proprietor was much younger than Lezlie had expected. Her raven-black hair was tied back by a bright blue scarf. She wore a long peasant-style skirt, which almost reached her sandaled feet. She smiled graciously as she glanced from Margaret to Lezlie. "I'm Lorilei Sandler. Is there anything in particular I can show you?"

Lezlie was incredulous. She looked at the woman again, not sure she recognized her without the fashionable makeup and stylish clothes that had been her trademark. "Lori?" she cried.

Lori squinted toward Lezlie. "Oh, pooh," she said in exasperation. "I can't see a thing without my glasses."

"Well, I see that hasn't changed," Lezlie teased.

Owlish, blue-tinted glasses dangled from a chain around Lori's neck. She perched them on her nose and peered toward her visitors. Her face broke into a wide smile. "Lezlie! I can't believe it!"

"I hardly recognized you," Lezlie said.

"I have changed quite a bit," Lori agreed, "but I'm still as blind as a bat or I would have known you right away... except for the hairstyle, which is fantastic. I wish I could learn to do a French braid, but I'm still not much on patience."

Lezlie had known Lori years ago when they were in school. After Lezlie's marriage they had seen each other occasionally, but as so often happens between people, they had lost touch. "Is this your shop?"

"It was the last time I paid the mortgage." Lori grinned.

Lezlie suddenly recalled her manners. "I don't know if you remember my mother, Lori."

"Of course. How are you, Mrs. Hall?"

"Fine, Lori. You have a lovely shop here."

"I'm trying."

"How did all this happen?" Lezlie asked. "The last time I heard, you were studying anthropology."

"A very impractical major unless you want to go into teaching or research, neither of which appealed." Lori smiled, and her smooth cheek dimpled. "I went to work for one of the galleries on Peachtree, but when my grandmother died and left me this house, I decided to see what I could do."

"You own the house?" Lezlie asked.

"Me and the bank," Lori answered wryly. "It took quite a bit of renovation to modernize it. I live on the second floor, which cuts expenses. And other than some trouble with a developer trying to convince me to sell my acreage for a shopping mall, I can't complain."

"The man at the flea market was very complimentary," Margaret said.

"I have a wonderful idea," Lezlie said quickly. "We were going to lunch from here. Could you join us?"

"I wish I could, but there's no one to see to the shop. Actually, the shop takes up most of my time, but I love it. Maybe we could get together another time. Say, I saw Michael with your little boy one day at the grocery store...oh, gosh, it must have been a couple of years ago...."

Lezlie's smile was weak, but the words came out more easily than she had ever thought they could. "That must have been just before the accident," she said. "I lost both of them."

Lori muttered a quiet oh.

"But what about you? Are you married?"

"*Almost* doesn't count, does it?" Lori grinned but there was a bitter edge in her voice. "I thought it was the real thing until I found out that while I was studying the evolution of man, he was studying anatomy, of the female variety, and his research was hardly academic, if you know what I mean. I'm only glad I didn't find out after we were married. I was never one to be a statistic. Maybe I'll try again someday, who knows? For the present, I'm content. But I want to know what you've been doing all these years."

Lezlie told Lori about her job, the children she felt she was helping and the fulfillment it gave her.

Lori nodded, understanding completely. "I've found the same kind of challenge in starting this business, even if it does seem to be one problem after another: a broken furnace, a power failure that shorts out my ancient television, or that builder's campaign to convince me to sell my property."

"You seem very happy," Lezlie commented.

"I am," Lori agreed, and she shook her head. "Remember all the times we worried over our futures and who we would marry? What a waste of time and energy. It all just sort of falls into place, doesn't it?"

"It seems to," Lezlie replied.

Lezlie and her mother were about ready to leave when Lori squeezed Lezlie's hand. "Let's don't let it be another eight years before we see each other." When Lezlie nodded, Lori smiled. "If you're not familiar with the area, or not up for fast food, there's a deli a couple of miles down on the right. The Garden Tree. It has an outdoor café. You can't miss it."

THE OUTDOOR RESTAURANT was crowded with groups of young people enjoying the warmth of the day in the sunshine. An iron railing enclosed a flagstone patio dotted with tables shaded by green-and-white-striped umbrellas. A welcome breeze dispelled the afternoon's heat as Lezlie and her mother glanced over the menus and decided on cold salads and ice tea.

"Lori seems very happy," Lezlie commented thoughtfully.

"She's very nice, and quite knowledgeable about antiques if her shop is any indication," Margaret added.

"Lori never did anything halfway," Lezlie said. "I don't have a doubt in my mind that her shop will do just fine. But it's funny. I always thought Lori would be the one to have a brood of children and a wonderful husband. I wonder if she's really so content?"

"She seems to be. Are you, Lezlie? Do you know, you've talked more about Michael and the past today than you have in the two years since the accident."

"The past has been on my mind a lot lately."

"Any particular reason?"

"I've been wondering about some things." Lezlie hesitated, searching for the words to voice her doubts. "Mom, did you ever think about remarrying after dad died?"

"What brought that up?" Margaret asked, more than a little surprised, but Lezlie only shrugged. "I don't know," Margaret mused thoughtfully. "There have been times when I thought about having someone to take care of. But whenever I imagine it, all I can see is your father. Maybe if I was younger it would be more important. I had almost thirty-five years with your father, and while it wasn't perfect, basically we had a good marriage."

Margaret smiled, the impishness of her eyes shedding years from her face. "But as Lori says, things seem to fall into place. I meet a lot of interesting people. Should there be someone else for me, I certainly wouldn't disregard it."

"What would you do?"

Margaret's eyebrows lifted. "I would probably try to find out if there was enough substance to it, or stamina within me, to sustain a relationship. At my age, I don't know if marriage would be a prerequisite. But it would take a very special man."

"How did you feel after dad died?" Lezlie asked suddenly. Lezlie had spent a lot of time with her mother after her father's death, but it had just occurred to her that she had never really asked about her mother's emotions. Lezlie had had her own family and now she wondered if she had been any real comfort to her mother. "Are you ever lonely?"

"Sometimes there's loneliness even within a marriage, Lezlie," Margaret said quietly. "One partner is busy or preoccupied and the other feels left out. But it isn't the same loneliness as having no one. At least if you are sharing your life, you can reach out to that other person and know they are there. But to answer your question, I suppose I felt much like you did after Michael died. And your loss was even worse with Mike...." Margaret smiled compassionately.

"I had had so much more time with your father, so I didn't feel as cheated as you did."

Lezlie glanced up and met her mother's warm gaze. "How did you know that was what I felt?" she asked quietly.

"Because that was what I felt for you. You had had only a few years with your family when it should have been decades. It's one thing to face death and understand it on an intellectual level, but emotions don't always fall in line. I was surprised to hear you speak so calmly about Michael and Mike to Lori."

"It is easier now," Lezlie confided. "Can I ask you one more thing?" When her mother nodded, Lezlie took a deep breath. "Did you ever feel you would be betraying dad's memory if you became involved with someone else?"

"It probably crossed my mind, but to be honest, it never worried me. Is that how you feel, Lezlie—that you would be betraying what you had with Michael if you became involved with someone else?"

"I'm not sure," Lezlie answered.

Margaret reached across the table and laid her hand over Lezlie's clenched fingers. "What is troubling you, Lezlie? Is there a reason for all these questions?"

"I guess I'm trying to put things in perspective, mom. I have met someone, someone I'm very attracted to. He's a very unique man, and I haven't felt this off-balance about anyone since Michael. But I can't get beyond a sense of suffocation at the thought of leaving myself open to hurt."

"Honey, you can't shut yourself off from people just because you might get hurt."

"That what he says. I think he understands how I feel now that I've told him about Michael."

"It's good you're able to open up about the past," Margaret said. "And there's no reason to rush into anything. You could take your time, get to know him better until you're more comfortable with him."

"There are some complications at the moment," Lezlie said, and she shrugged helplessly. "He's the relative of a patient."

"Oh," Margaret mused.

"At the moment, we're at an impasse. He does understand that my patient must be my first concern, and an involvement between us could become very ticklish."

"That depends on how you handle it, dear. Of course it could become more complicated if you lose sight of your priority, which for the present, is as you say, your patient."

"I don't want to lose my objectivity...."

"That will take care of itself if you place the welfare of your patient above the relationship with this man. Right?"

Lezlie's smile was slow but sure. "Right. You always seem to have such a calm outlook about things, mom."

"It's years of practice, dear."

"Maybe you should have my job."

"Not in a million years," Margaret said. "You say this man is unique. Well, I think you're pretty unique yourself. And in case I haven't said it in a while, Lezlie, I'm very proud of you and all you've accomplished."

Lezlie felt a swell of emotion and she swallowed hard. "Thanks, mom."

Margaret smiled warmly. "I wish that waiter would hurry up. I'm starving."

Their lunch passed pleasantly with Margaret going through a list of places she would like to visit before the summer was over. She couldn't decide which one she preferred. Lezlie opted for any of the spots near the beach.

"You always did like the beach," Margaret commented.

The rest of their lunch was taken up with reminiscences of summer vacations and family escapades. Lezlie and her mother fell into an easy silence during the drive back to her mother's house. Lezlie dropped her mother off, declining an invitation to come in. There was still time to get the laundry done, she decided grudgingly.

WHEN LEZLIE REACHED her own home, she placed her packages in a chair and, as usual, called her service for any messages. The receptionist gave her several, including two from Merri.

"She sounded really anxious to talk to you, Dr. Garrett," the receptionist said.

Lezlie immediately dialed Drew's home, wondering if he would answer, but it was Merri who did.

"Merri, this is Lezlie Garrett."

"Hi, Lezlie." There was a moment's pause before Merri said quietly. "I did my room today."

"So I heard," Lezlie said. "Your uncle came by earlier. How did it go?"

"Okay, I guess, but it sure looks different, sort of empty. I thought maybe you would come over and see."

"Today?"

"Is it too late?" Merri asked.

Lezlie was surprised by the request, but she concealed her hesitation. "Not really, but what about your uncle?"

"He's not here," Merri answered. "He had to work today. Can you come over...just for a little while?"

There was more in the request than a simple wish for Lezlie to see her room. Merri needed reassurance, and perhaps some word of approval for her accomplishment. Lezlie couldn't help feeling that it would be better if it was Drew offering the child reassurance, but it was more important that Merri receive it than who gave it.

"I'll be there in about fifteen minutes," Lezlie said.

"Okay," Merri answered, her voice noticeably more cheerful.

As Lezlie started out the door, she thought about what Merri had said about her room seeming empty. Smiling, Lezlie opened one of the packages and retrieved the stained-glass unicorn.

Merri was sitting on the front steps when Lezlie drove up. Merri bounded across the yard, meeting her on the driveway. Lezlie was glad to see that Merri wasn't as upset as she had sounded over the telephone.

"You made it in ten," Merri said with a smile.

"Ten what?"

"Ten minutes. I was timing you, and you got here in ten minutes. That's better than punctual, my teacher would say."

"How is school?" Lezlie asked.

"Fine," Merri sighed. "Only one more week and it's summer."

The delight in Merri's voice reminded Lezlie how time was often measured in a child's mind by breaks from routine such as vacation from school. As the last day of classes drew closer, the excitement would grow and then linger for the first few weeks of summer. Then the uncontainable delight would fade into the lethargic contentment of lazy days and sticky hot weather.

"Uncle Drew says I can maybe go to camp," Merri was telling Lezlie as they headed through the house. "Jill will be going, too. There's swimming and horseback riding and hiking."

"That sounds like fun."

"Yeah, everything but the hiking." Merri opened the door to her room and Lezlie stepped through. The change was not only remarkable, but startling. All the clutter was gone, the bookcase was no longer crammed, the shadow box now housed half of what had been in it before, and the stuffed animals that remained fitted into the seat of one chair in the corner of the room. Only three pictures remained, including the one of Drew and his brother as children.

"It is quite a difference, Merri," Lezlie said. "And it looks so neat."

"That's what Mrs. Cates said. She took the boxes

up to the attic." Merri looked around the room, and a sigh lifted her slight shoulders. "I guess it was kind of messy, and it does look better."

Lezlie reached into her purse. "While I was out today, I bought something that should look very nice in your window." She handed Merri the gift she had brought.

"Oh, it's terrific," Merri exclaimed. She held the present gently and then went to the window. The late-afternoon light filtered through the bright glass and shimmered around the unicorn, casting a rose pattern on the floor. Lezlie handed her the suction hook and they attached the pane to the center of the window. Merri spun around and threw her arms around Lezlie's waist. "Thanks, Lezlie."

"You're welcome," Lezlie said gently. "I thought you deserved a reward."

"A reward for what?" Drew walked into the room but stopped dead in his tracks. "Well, pumpkin, you have had a busy day."

"Look what Lezlie bought me." Merri pointed to the unicorn.

"Very nice," Drew complimented, and his warm gaze settled on Lezlie. "Was this a spur-of-the-moment visit?"

Merri shifted and her voice dropped to a shy whisper. "I called and asked her to come over."

Drew shoved his hands into his pockets. "Seems you had a busy day, too, Lezlie. I hope none of it was inconvenient."

Lezlie smiled to relieve the anxiety Merri was feeling. "Not at all."

"We seemed destined to be thrown together," Drew said, "even innocently. I saw you this afternoon. If I'd known you were going to be in the area, I would have asked you to stop by the site." Drew's gaze had become intense, almost probing. "That was you at the light?"

Now it was Lezlie who shifted uncomfortably. He had seen her. She wondered if he had been standing in some shadow watching her. Did he have any idea that she had been secretly hoping for a glimpse of him? "It's a very impressive complex," Lezlie complimented, hoping to disguise her self-consciousness. "How many buildings will there be in all?"

"Five," Drew answered automatically. "You should have stopped and I would have given you the guided tour."

Lezlie wished she had, too, but she didn't say so. "I wasn't certain you were there. I saw your car... but, I mean, well...." Lezlie had talked herself right into a corner with no graceful way out, and she groaned inwardly.

"I know what you mean," Drew said, his expression softening. "Since you're here, why not stay for dinner?" Lezlie started to refuse, but Drew's upraised hand stopped her. "As compensation for our taking up so much of your day off."

"Oh, yes," Merri squealed. "Please, Lezlie."

"I don't want to put you out, really...."

"It's no imposition at all, unless you have other plans," Drew said. "Mrs. Cates only has to set another place. Say you'll stay."

There was no excuse Lezlie's fuddled mind could

grasp in light of his warm invitation. And the truth was she didn't really want to go home and eat alone. The realization disturbed her. In the past two years, being alone hadn't bothered her in the least; in fact, she had thought she'd preferred the solitude to the intrusion of people. A great many things seemed to be changing, she thought, a little frightened by the prospect. Her solitary world was safe, without complications and emotion...or commitments. An 'emotional vacuum,' Drew had called it. Had she really spun a silken cocoon around herself and deluded herself into believing her life was happy? How could she have been completely content when just being with Drew filled her with a sense of expectation and bubbling pleasure? She felt very much like a butterfly emerging from her silken cocoon to discover that her world was not at all as she had so carefully constructed. The complicated discrepancies were impossible to unravel with Drew waiting for her answer.

"I'd like to stay," she said simply.

"I'll go tell Mrs. Cates," Merri said.

The moment Merri left, the room seemed to shrink around Lezlie.

Drew walked toward her, his eyes caressing her face as gently as his hand touched her hair. "I'm glad you decided to accept. I haven't seen Merri this happy in a long time."

Doubt crept into Lezlie's eyes. Was Merri the reason Drew had asked her to stay for dinner? But the question was shattered the moment she tilted her head back to look up at him. His expression was one of such intensity, such tempered tender fierceness, that it took her breath away.

Drew touched her cheek, a rueful smile tipping the corners of his mouth. "What are we going to do, Lezlie?" The question hung between them. "What happens when Merri gets past all this? She's come a long way...."

"But she still has a way to go," Lezlie said.

"I know, but the day will come when the only reason for us to see each other will be each other. I know what I want. What about you?"

The situation evidently bothered Drew as much as it disturbed Lezlie. "I don't know," she said honestly. "At this point, I'm just trying to get a grip on all the things that hadn't confused me before, Drew."

"Join the club." His smile widened and bubbled into a chuckle. He shook his head, laughter filling the bedroom and dispelling the tension. Lezlie responded to his humor and Drew slung his arm around her shoulders.

"I'm not being a very good host, am I? Plying you with questions and deep revelations when I should be plying you with wine." He twitched his eyebrows and gave her his most lecherous leer.

"I would prefer a beer if you have it," she said calmly.

Drew couldn't believe he had heard her correctly. "You're joking?" he scoffed, and Lezlie shrugged. "Beer?"

"It's an acquired taste," Lezlie offered.

"The more I learn about you, the more intrigued I become," Drew mumbled. "Beer! Who would have thought that a pretty, career-oriented modern woman would dare put such a concoction to her lips." He was herding her along the upstairs hall. "And such pretty lips, too."

"If it will make you feel better, I'll have wine," Lezlie offered playfully. "I wouldn't want to offend your masculine sensibilities."

"There is nothing in the world you could possibly do to cause that," Drew said confidently. "I just never imagined that when you offered Jim a beer that you kept it on hand for yourself. Will wonders never cease."

Lezlie simply returned his smile and silently answered, *I certainly hope not.*

CHAPTER EIGHT

IN ADDITION TO ALL HER other fine qualities, Mrs. Cates was an exceptional cook. The fried chicken, potato salad, fresh garden greens, corn bread and ice tea was a mouth-watering feast. As soon as dinner was on the table, the housekeeper left for home. Drew waved a drumstick at her as she said goodnight.

"You've outdone yourself, Mrs. C.," he complimented, and the usually dour Mrs. Cates actually smiled.

"You're very lucky to have someone like Mrs. Cates," Lezlie said when the front door had closed. She thought of all the people she knew who would give half their salary to have a housekeeper who was just as reliable and efficient.

"She spoils us rotten, doesn't she, Merri?"

"I wonder what's for dessert?" Merri asked.

"You have to eat all your dinner first," Drew said. "That's the rule." He glanced at Lezlie and explained. "On weekends Mrs. Cates always makes a special dessert. She never mentions it, but there's always some outlandishly fattening treat in the refrigerator on Saturdays."

Dinner was relaxed, and the togetherness might

have been unsettling if Drew and Lezlie hadn't bantered back and forth as he ate the succulent chicken with his fingers and encouraged Merri to join the conversation. Merri finally talked about school, then requested more details from Drew about the camp she and Jill would visit for three weeks in the summer.

"Jill's mother suggested it," Drew explained to Lezlie. "Jill really wants to go, but Barbara didn't want to send her alone. I don't feel too easy about Merri being away from home for so long."

"Oh, but Uncle Drew, I've already told Jill I'd go...and I really want to."

"What do you think, Lezlie?" Drew asked.

The question took Lezlie by surprise. Her biscuit was suspended between her plate and her mouth. Merri watched her expectantly. "I think it's a decision the two of you will have to reach."

"That's a very subtle way of not stating an opinion," Drew said.

"It isn't my place. I'm not a member of the family," Lezlie explained.

"No, but you're a friend and we would value your thoughts. Right, Merri?"

When Merri nodded, Lezlie felt cornered. "Well," she said, stalling for time to assemble her thoughts. "Firstly, I don't see why Merri shouldn't go to camp if she would like to. But on the other hand, Merri, I think you should take your uncle's feelings into account and try to understand."

Merri and Drew exchanged curious glances. "I believe that was the most unopinionated opinion I've ever heard," Drew said.

Merri chimed in, "Me, too."

"I can't say one of you is right and one is wrong," Lezlie explained. "And I don't want to be in the middle of what should be a family matter. Maybe I should put it another way. I think Merri should go to camp as long as it is acceptable to both of you. Is that better?"

Again, Drew and Merri looked at each other and said simultaneously with matching grins, "No."

"Then why did you ask?" Lezlie said good-naturedly and Drew started to laugh.

"I don't know," he said with a chuckle.

The honk of a car horn interrupted them. Merri hopped up from the table, then remembered her manners. "May I be excused, Uncle Drew? That's Jill."

"All right, go ahead and get your things. I'll take your turn at the dishes tonight, but you have tomorrow."

"Thanks." Merri headed out of the dining room. "Bye, Lezlie."

Suddenly Lezlie was completely alone with Drew. "She's off to spend the night with Jill," Drew explained.

As Merri passed the dining room, she called out to her uncle. "It's your favorite for dessert, Uncle Drew, apple cobbler and ice cream."

"Oh, I couldn't eat another bite," Lezlie groaned, and she started to push back her chair. "I guess I really should go, too."

"Oh no, you don't," Drew challenged, getting to his feet. "I don't mind doing dishes as long as there is someone to talk to. And you have to taste the dessert. Mrs. Cates will ask me about it Monday. She may not say much, but she expects her efforts to be appreciated."

"Well, we certainly wouldn't wish to offend your invaluable housekeeper." Lezlie laughed.

"She is definitely that," Drew said. "It took me three months just to find her. I had a part-time housekeeper at first, but it wasn't working out."

Lezlie picked up her plate and utensils. "What are you doing?" Drew asked.

"I'm taking my dishes to the kitchen."

Drew shook his head. "Company doesn't help with dishes," he said haughtily.

"I'm not offering to help with the dishes," Lezlie said. "I'm simply getting them there for you to do."

Drew rolled his eyes toward the ceiling, but amusement sparkled in his eyes. "I should have guessed," he commented, placing Merri's plate on his and heading into the spotless kitchen. Mrs. Cates had washed the pots and pans, so cleaning up was only a matter of rinsing the dishes and putting them in the dishwasher. Drew poured Lezlie a cup of coffee and she sat down on the stool at the breakfast bar. He dispatched the task with a brisk efficiency. They talked easily and Lezlie told him about her afternoon of antiquing and seeing an old friend.

"Would you like some cobbler?" Drew asked.

A pained expression accompanied Lezlie's refusal. "Maybe later, but I'm not making any promises."

"That doesn't surprise me," Drew said, but his

tone and manner held no malice. "Come on and I'll show you why I bought this house."

Drew poured himself a cup of coffee and headed through the living room and sliding glass doors to the deck. Half the deck was enclosed by screen, the other half was open. A table and a few chairs occupied the screened portion; lounge chairs were on the other. Drew motioned her toward a chair and he collapsed into another with a contented groan. It wasn't dark yet, and the hazy twilight was filled with the sounds of children playing up the street, a dog barking and the steady chirping of birds. As the sky darkened and stars began to twinkle, the sounds faded, leaving only the quiet breeze to rustle the trees and the sound of a babbling stream in the distance.

"This is nice," Lezlie said lazily.

A spotlight on the corner of the house illuminated one edge of the backyard. Drew's face was shadowed as he turned his head to look at Lezlie. Her eyes were closed and her arms rested easily on the chair. The moonlight made her face a shimmering oval, her heavy lashes shadowing her eyes. Her cheekbones seemed more pronounced and the curve of her mouth was an enticing sight. Drew's body stirred at the thought of his mouth upon hers, drawing all the sweetness and passion from her as he had both times they had kissed. She seemed so remote and unapproachable, lying so still, her body seemingly relaxed. Without thinking, he reached across the distance and his long fingers closed around her wrist.

Lezlie's eyes fluttered open, and she turned toward

him, her eyes heavy. A soft smile played across her mouth.

"I thought maybe you had fallen asleep."

"Not quite," Lezlie answered, trying to discern his features. "I can certainly see why you like this spot. It's very peaceful."

"The last thing I wanted was to put you to sleep," Drew drawled. His fingers were stroking her arm, producing sensual shivers. "Are you cold?" he asked.

Lezlie's negative answer made Drew smile. "Maybe we should come up with some activity to wake you up," he suggested.

"I prefer laid-back activities, none of this frantic race to keep up with all the latest physical-fitness stuff. A couple of times a week at the spa takes care of the stress." Lezlie yawned. "I am perfectly content."

"That makes one of us," Drew said ruefully. He added mischievously, "But I can think of a better way to relieve stress than exercise."

"Like what?" Lezlie challenged, unaware of the enticement she offered.

Drew leaned across the side of his chair, his hand sliding along her arm. "Do you really want to know?"

"No," Lezlie said firmly, but her heart had begun to hammer erratically.

Drew heaved himself off the chaise, gripping her hand. "Since you've had so much experience at redecorating, I guess I'll have to settle for some much-needed advice about the dollhouse."

"The what? Oh, that's right. How's it coming?"

"Pretty good, but I could use a woman's touch on the interior. I picked up some wallpaper and carpet scraps last week."

Drew's workshop was in the basement. Every conceivable tool filled the plywood wall and toolboxes. The dollhouse was nearly finished. The intricacy of its design made it seem like a work of art. It had two levels and the walls between the rooms were divided by a doorway finished with the tiniest strips of molding. An incredible banister led to the second level, its posts not much bigger than toothpicks. The roof had been shingled with individual pieces of cedar cut into the shape of an ice-cream spoon, and there was real glass in the many windows. Miniature columns supported the rounded portico entrance. There was even a small gold filial ornament over the door. The dollhouse was definitely not a toy, but a miniature home any eager collector of miniatures would admire.

"It is absolutely incredible," Lezlie exclaimed. "I can't see where you need any help at all." She leaned over for a closer look at the tiny rooms. Even the bathroom had a tile floor and was ready for the placement of the porcelain fixtures, which would be exact replicas of the full-size fixtures. "Do you already have the furniture?"

Drew stood just behind her, his shoulder brushing hers as he also leaned down. "I've bought a couple of things, but I thought Merri would get a kick out of choosing the furnishings. I have some material for curtains Mrs. Cates will make... once I make the final decision on the color schemes. So, lovely lady, I would appreciate your good taste."

The pieces of carpet and wallpaper were on one end of the workbench. Lezlie went through the papers first. The miniature patterns were varied: florals, stripes and light airy colors. "I can see why you need some help," Lezlie said. "You have too many to choose from."

Quickly she discarded the papers that were too bold for the tiny rooms or too difficult to work with colorwise. She had chosen her favorites for the kitchen, two of the bedrooms and the entry into the miniature house. She held a small pattern of tiny rosebuds and stems separately.

"Why don't you like this one?" Drew asked, indicating the rose paper.

"Oh, I do," Lezlie said. "I had already chosen it for the master bedroom."

The carpets were next: a soft blue for the living and dining rooms, green for one of the bedrooms, yellow for the other, and a dusty rose to compliment the rosebud paper in the master bedroom. The scraps of material were then a cinch to match to each room.

"You have saved me days of indecision." Drew smiled gratefully.

"Will you have it ready for her birthday? It's June 28, isn't it?"

"I certainly hope so. I have a month yet. I still have some work on the outside, and all the papering and painting inside...." Drew shook his hand. "I can hope."

"We could work on it now," Lezlie suggested. "At least we could get some of the rooms done."

"You wouldn't mind?"

"I wouldn't offer if I minded. I feel like we're decorating a real house." Lezlie's eyes sparkled. "Besides, it might keep your mind off other things."

"Only temporarily," Drew promised. "But you've got a deal, on one condition."

"What condition?" Lezlie asked warily.

"That you let me do something for you."

"But you have," Lezlie interrupted. "You've helped me with my painting."

"No, I mean something you would enjoy and that we could do together. And you'll let me plan it. A whole day of fun. Would you do that, Lezlie? Give me one whole day without any pressure for anything but relaxation and maybe getting to know each other a little better?" Drew's gaze swept her face, lingered on her mouth, then his smile dissolved. They were momentarily caught up in a silent exchange that required no explanation.

Lezlie had completely forgotten everything except Drew and his invitation. The thought of spending an entire day with him was both exhilarating and frightening, considering the attraction between them. She felt as though she was racing toward an uncertain end. But was the outcome of an affair with Drew really that uncertain?

"Will you at least think about it?" he asked.

Without hesitation, Lezlie nodded. She would be breaking her own rule, throwing all caution to the wind if she eventually accepted, but she was powerless before Drew's quiet but persuasive plea. She had only promised to think about it, and she could always say no when the time arrived if she decided not to risk a more entangling relationship than they had now. One thing she already knew was that she would indeed be thinking about it.

"So, where do we start?" she asked brightly.

Drew gathered up several cans of various materials: glue for the wallpaper, two cans of paint and one of a special adhesive for securing the carpet, and the utensils they would need. "We can work simultaneously. You start on the bedrooms on the right while I get some of the painting done over here. Then we can switch sides."

If Lezlie had thought putting up wallpaper on a standard wall was difficult, working within the confines of the small square rooms was a real job. "Thank heavens I can do a solid piece and cut around the openings." The thought of the traditional way of hanging wallpaper made Lezlie chuckle. "Could you imagine rolls of wallpaper scaled to size? What a headache that would be!"

"They've managed everything else," Drew answered, his nose and hand hidden within the room he was working on. "I think we painted your room faster than I'll be able to paint this," Drew agreed, holding up a narrow brush that looked strangely out of place in his large hand.

"Just be glad you didn't have to paint my room with a brush that size."

"I'd have been there a month," Drew countered and turned his head toward her. "Although that idea does have a certain appeal."

"Not to me. It was bad enough that it was messed up for a few days."

"What's a little mess between friends?" Drew teased.

"You wouldn't be so blasé, if you knew how uncomfortable my couch is to sleep on. I thought I'd never get everything back in place."

"Ah, a place for everything and everything in its place. That says a great deal in itself...."

"Oh, really?"

"Of course." Drew's tone was so confident that Lezlie stopped what she was doing.

"Such as?"

"Such as a leaning toward perfection, an inclination toward extreme neatness. Keep everything ordered and in place, and the world will run smoothly."

"Thank you, doctor," Lezlie said, inexplicably miffed by his casual air. "Any other findings during your amateur analysis?"

"It's not analysis nor is it amateur," Drew said. "It's one thing about yourself you can't hide."

"Who says I do?"

"I do."

"You do?"

"Yes, and you act as though I just accused you of something. There's nothing wrong with wanting order."

"Thank you," Lezlie said stiffly.

"As long as you don't take it too far," Drew continued. The stormy look in Lezlie's eyes made him smile. "This is all just a little friendly observation."

"Well, observe somebody else," Lezlie snapped.

She was angry at the casualness he maintained. She didn't feel accused, she felt criticized, and she didn't like it one bit.

"I would if I could, but I can't. You've mesmerized me, Lezlie, and it's a new experience, believe me. One I hope you'll learn about real soon." Drew turned her back toward her work. "Will you hand me that little screwdriver in the toolbox?"

Lezlie started to tell him to get it himself, but she was afraid she'd reveal just how angry he had made her. She fumbled through the various tools and when she located the screwdriver, she put it in his hand none too gently.

"Ah, the lady does have a temper," Drew said, amused. "I was beginning to wonder."

"I do not," Lezlie said defensively.

"Then what is this?"

"What?"

Drew stuck out his hand, feigning a pained frown. "The hole you just put in my hand with that screwdriver."

"I did not," Lezlie said, but she wasn't certain. "Did I?"

Drew's frown dissolved into a smile, and he chucked her cheek. "It wouldn't matter if you had. I wanted to see if you're always so damned controlled. I'm glad to see you have some simple failings like the rest of us."

Drew was obviously pleased with himself, but Lezlie didn't want to explore the possibilities of what he'd said. Still, she couldn't help admitting that what he had observed was the truth. She was neat, almost to a fault, and she did prefer order in her life, but he had baited her.

"Well, aren't you going to get back to work?" Drew asked innocently.

"I ought to tell you to take that screwdriver and—"

"Now, now, that wouldn't be very professional of you...."

"Will you quit?" Lezlie said sharply, and she felt the sting of tears. Usually she was in control, but Drew affected her strangely. One minute she was content and at ease, another she was walking on tenterhooks not knowing which way she was going to fall. "I don't need your observations or criticisms."

Drew was instantly contrite. "I didn't mean to sound critical. I was only teasing you."

"Well, you could've fooled me."

"Obviously, I did, but I didn't mean to hurt your feelings." Drew rubbed his chin thoughtfully, putting on his best Transylvanian accent. "Tell me, doctor, how can I make it up to you?"

"You can shut up," Lezlie replied, but her mouth twitched with suppressed laughter.

"Ah, a very good suggestion." Drew started back to work, but stopped. "I wonder what Count Dracula would have done if one of his victims had told him to shut up."

"I doubt any of them had a chance," Lezlie said.

"That was his secret," Drew said. He laid his screwdriver aside and caught Lezlie around the waist. "He would take them totally by surprise...."

Lezlie's hands were splayed across his chest where she could feel taut muscles rippling. Drew's exaggerated lascivious leer made her giggle. "You're crazy," she said.

"And before they could protest, he would seize the soft white flesh of their necks...." Drew's mouth swooped down, and he nuzzled the crook of her shoulder.

Lezlie squealed in surprise and laughter. But her amusement soon died as Drew's mouth clung to her neck, then brushed lightly along the tendon and tickled the hollow of her throat. Suddenly her hands were clinging to his shirt as his moist mouth teased and caressed.

"And he would drain away all their resistance," Drew ended thickly.

Lezlie moved her head, allowing him better access to the sensitive skin. The lower part of her body was pressed intimately against his. Sensations danced along her skin. The effect was devastating.

Drew inhaled the alluring fragrance that was hers alone, a mingling of soap and fresh flowers, of honey and sunshine. If he held her much longer with her warm pliant body responding so intensely, he couldn't be responsible for the natural course of events. His mouth teased the sensitive skin of her neck, and her bubbling sighs brought a smile to his lips.

"Next Saturday," he murmured.

Lezlie tried to rouse herself from her passion-drugged lethargy. "What?"

"We'll have our day next Saturday." Drew raised his head to look down into the heavy-lidded gray eyes that were focused on him. "Yes?"

Lezlie nodded heavily, trying desperately to control the racing of her pulse. Drew leaned down to plant a gentle kiss on the corner of her mouth. "We're not getting much done," he said with a wry grin.

"It's all these distractions," Lezlie said, taking a deep shuddering breath when Drew released her.

"There's only one that I know of," Drew teased.

"Maybe if we don't talk, we can work faster," Lezlie suggested.

"A practical suggestion," Drew agreed.

While Lezlie went through the motions of concentrating on her task, her mind raced in total turmoil. She didn't know how much longer she could tolerate these playful interludes with Drew. As it was her stomach was tied in knots and a slow ache still throbbed within her. But one thing had become very clear. If he had swept her into his arms and carried her to his bed, she wasn't at all certain she would have been able to stop him, even if she had been inclined to do so. She had no doubt that, physically, he wanted her very much—as much as she was coming to desire him. She watched him surreptitiously, his sharp features a mask of total preoccupation. The light played across his hair, highlighting strands of sun-bleached gold. His strong chin was thrust out as he surveyed his work with a critical eye. Lezlie had never really noticed how incredibly long his eyelashes were, but the light cast fluttery shadows on his cheeks. He was an intensely handsome man, his muscled body defying thinness, but beautiful in the angles of bone and sinew.

Lezlie mentally shook herself to break the train of her thoughts, which were running in a very dangerous vein. She wasn't aware that Drew had seen the puzzled contemplative expression on her face, nor did she see his slight smile. But it was a moment later that he began to whistle while he painted.

Lezlie didn't know how long they had worked. Her back had begun to ache and her eyes burned. But she had finished each of the rooms, and Drew was gluing in the last of the carpet.

"I don't believe it," Drew said, wearily rubbing his neck. "You must be wiped out." He glanced at his watch and whistled in surprise. "Good Lord, it's almost three o'clock."

"I'm glad tomorrow is my day off," Lezlie sighed, hiding a yawn. Was it only this morning that Drew had rousted her out of bed?

"Well, I can promise I won't wake you up," Drew said. "I don't know about you, but I'm hungry. Do you want something?"

"Cobbler would be good," Lezlie answered, trying to massage her back.

"I'll take care of that while you eat your pie," Drew promised, heading upstairs. He put two heaping helpings of cobbler into the microwave, then sat Lezlie in a chair. His strong fingers massaged and kneaded her tired muscles, bringing a groan of blissful relief from Lezlie.

"That's marvelous," she said sleepily.

"I'll take that as a compliment."

"It was meant as one."

When the bell of the microwave went off, Drew retrieved the two plates and they dug into the spicy apple cobbler. They talked easily about all they had accomplished and how surprised Merri was going to be. Even though she was tired, Lezlie felt good. As she rose to leave, Drew took his jacket from the coat tree.

"What are you doing?"

"Following you home," he answered simply.

"You don't need to do that."

"I know, but I will rest easier knowing you got home safe and sound."

Drew followed her out of the house, his headlights a reassuring gleam in her rearview as Lezlie drove down the dark streets. When she pulled into her driveway and pressed the garage-door opener, he flashed his lights and waited until he saw a light from inside the house. Lezlie was in her bedroom when she heard the quiet rumble of his engine as he drove away. She was too tired to do anything more than crawl into bed and pull the covers over herself. Whatever worries or thoughts she might have had were wiped out by total exhaustion, and she was asleep the moment her head touched the pillow.

CHAPTER NINE

THE FOLLOWING WEEK was one of unusual upheaval. Summer vacation brought a rash of canceled appointments, rescheduling requests and patients who simply did not show up. Out-of-town vacations had been planned by some families while short getaways brought harried messages from mothers trying to plan everything. And some parents simply needed a break themselves from the winter-long schedule as children ran helter-skelter with the freedom of summer. For two days Lezlie had patients back to back from early morning until late evening; for two others, she sat in her office trying to catch up on her notes.

Friday turned out to be an almost useless day. By midmorning, Lezlie had brought her notes up-to-date, checked the appointments for the following week, made a grocery list, balanced her checkbook and done any other task that would help pass the dragging hours. Merri was to be her only appointment for the day.

The idle hours during the week had given Lezlie a lot of time for thought—mostly about Drew Bradinton. It wasn't really difficult for her to admit that she truly liked Drew. He amused her, teased her and made her laugh, and he had also made her angry. And when she became angry, it often brought tears. She hated to lose control of her emotions, especially in front of people, and even more in front of Drew. She was extremely concerned about what he thought of her, not in a professional sense as had been the case with almost everyone for the past two years, but personally. Her staunch position of no involvement was slowly crumbling under the onslaught of Drew's intense personality. There was no way to deny that Drew elicited an emotional response from her; one she thought she had silenced. But with the acknowledgment of her fondness for Drew came a sense of fear, which Lezlie could not overcome so easily.

It wasn't very often that Lezlie was called into the hospital on Saturday, but on the off chance she might be, she had arranged for another doctor to take her cases. And all week she had been looking forward to the outing Drew had cajoled her into. She wondered where they would go, what Drew had planned—all the thoughts of an excited young woman on a first date.

Lezlie had been daydreaming. She placed her hands firmly on the desk. "Enough," she whispered decidedly, trying to think of some task to take her mind off Drew and his proposed outing. She had just sat down in frustration when the door to the outer office opened.

Margaret Hall peeked into the office. "Well, I see Jean wasn't exaggerating. She said the week has been a little slow."

"Slow? It's been crazy. I'm glad summer vacation

only comes once a year or I would be out of a job." Lezlie stood up to receive her mother's affectionate kiss.

Margaret draped her lightweight jacket over a chair. "I was shopping at Cumberland and thought I'd drop in on you. But I called first. Jean said you only had one appointment, so I'm asking you to join me for an afternoon of shopping. We could really do it up right and waste the whole day at the Galleria."

"A lifesaver, that's what you are," Lezlie said. "A little while longer and I would have been dusting the shelves or something."

Margaret laughed. "Can I take that as a yes?"

"You may," Lezlie said. "The shops I've seen in the Galleria are marvelous little boutiques."

"Then you've been there?"

"Only once. The relative of a patient and I went to dinner to talk about his niece, and then we went on a short tour."

Before Margaret could comment, the buzzer on Lezlie's desk went off, and she went to answer. Lezlie turned back to her mother. "My last patient is here," she explained. "If you wouldn't mind waiting, mom...."

"Not a bit. It'll give me a chance to catch up on my reading." Margaret gathered her things and had just reached the door when it opened and Merri bounded into the room, followed by Drew.

"We didn't mean to interrupt," Drew started, obviously embarrassed.

Drew and her mother were face-to-face and Lezlie tentatively introduced Drew and Merri.

"It's very nice to meet you, Mrs. Hall," Drew said. "Lezlie has told me a great deal about you. It isn't often you meet someone and they match the mental picture you've put together."

"And I do?" Margaret asked. She was stalling for time, wanting a better look at Drew Bradinton. She had made a lot of connections since Lezlie had said his name. This was Drew, the man who had been at her daughter's house, had taken her to dinner and, to Margaret's thinking, had made an impression on her daughter when others had failed.

"Yes ma'am, you do," Drew confirmed. Margaret Hall carried all the quiet dignity and confidence he had discerned from Lezlie's comments about her. And looking into the older woman's face, he saw the same gentleness in her gray eyes as in Lezlie's. "The two of you have a very unique relationship, Mrs. Hall."

"I think so," Margaret said, her expression one of deep affection when she looked at Lezlie. "It was very good to meet you, Mr. Bradinton, and you, too, Merri. I'll wait for you in your reception area, Lezlie. I hope to see you again." She directed the last comment to Drew and it held a sincerity he understood.

As she left the office, she overheard Drew speaking quietly. "You haven't forgotten about tomorrow? You'll need a swimsuit and a hat, for sure. I'll pick you up at ten."

"It's supposed to rain."

"Hasn't anyone ever told you forecasting the weather is an inaccurate science, especially here in Atlanta...."

The amusement in Drew's voice caused Margaret to smile as she quietly closed the door. Any intention she had of passing the hour reading had flown from Margaret's mind and she sat down to wait. As her daughter had done earlier, she started to daydream too, her gaze focused somewhere in midair. So he was the one who was bringing the sparkle to Lezlie's eyes, she thought happily. Yes, it would have to be a man like Drew, she decided. He had the confidence necessary to overcome Lezlie's strict posture, yet she had discerned tenderness even in his teasing. Margaret found herself silently wishing him luck, though she didn't think for a moment that he needed it. Maybe Lezlie was really ready to put the past aside. Margaret silently prayed that was the case.

Alone with Merri, Lezlie listened to all that had happened since their last session. Merri was bubbling over with the excitement of the coming summer: visits to friends' houses, which now included two other little girls besides Jill, and, of course, the trip to camp.

"Have you and your uncle come to an agreement?"

"Yeah, instead of three weeks, we're going for two. That should be plenty."

"I think so, but it's even better that you reached an understanding."

"Well, if we went for the whole three weeks, I would miss my birthday. Uncle Drew says he has a surprise for me."

"I know," Lezlie said.

"You do? What is it?" Merri asked excitedly.

"Well, it would hardly be a surprise if I told you. And I don't think your uncle would appreciate it, either. After all, it is his present." Lezlie took the opportunity to ask Merri about her uncle.

"He took me over to some buildings he's working on, and we went to a place he said my daddy did the arch...arch...."

"Architecture," Lezlie supplied, and Merri nodded. "What did you think?"

"It was really big," Merri said, awed.

"It's quite an accomplishment," Lezlie agreed. "And what did you think of your uncle's project?"

"My dad says Uncle Drew is the best builder around," Merri said, "but I couldn't tell too much. Uncle Drew says the work will be finished by the time I start school." Merri pursed her mouth. "I just got out and he's already talking about when I start back."

"That's only to set the time frame for his construction," Lezlie said, and she broached another subject. "Merri, do you think your uncle wants you to live with him?"

Merri looked straight at Lezlie. "I guess so."

"Do you think he cares about you?"

Merri dropped her eyes and stared at her hand. "I guess so," she said with a shrug.

"Tell me what you like best about your uncle, and then what you don't like."

Merri was thoughtful for a long time. "I like him okay most of the time," she said sincerely. "We talk about school a lot. He's good at helping me with my homework, but I can't tell him things...."

"What sort of things?"

The interruption caused Merri to hesitate. "Well, about my friends and the way they act. They're awfully mean sometimes and I don't understand. It just isn't the same."

"The same as when you talked to your mother?"

"I guess," Merri answered quietly. "Uncle Drew wouldn't understand."

"I think he would if you gave him a chance," Lezlie said reassuringly.

"He doesn't know anything about kids," Merri said, and there was an underlying current of anger. "My dad says so. I heard him."

Lezlie leaned back in her chair, wondering when the conversation might have taken place. "When did your father say that?" Lezlie asked directly.

"One night he and momma were fighting. He was awful mad."

Lezlie felt that Merri was very close to admitting something important. "Was this the night of the accident, Merri?"

Merri nodded, hanging her head so that her blond curls concealed her face from Lezlie's scrutiny. Merri had overheard the argument as Drew had assumed, Lezlie thought, or she had at least heard part of it, and it had concerned her uncle. But why would Greg have said what he did about Drew's knowledge of children? An inadvertent comment made in anger could have caused Merri's reticence to trust her uncle, unless there was more to the argument. And Lezlie had a feeling of certainty that there was.

"My mom and dad fought a lot when Uncle Drew came to visit. I heard them in their bedroom, but I couldn't hear what they said. When he would go away, they wouldn't fight anymore." The admission had been a slow painful revelation for Merri, and she looked at Lezlie with uncertainty clouding her tear-filled blue eyes.

Lezlie quickly reassured her. "Grown-ups often disagree, Merri. It's part of two people being married. They are different people...."

"You don't understand," Merri said. "They were fighting about Uncle Drew...and me. Uncle Drew wanted my mom to take his side, but my dad said it was wrong...and it was about me."

"Do you know what it was about?" Lezlie asked.

"No," Merri answered, but from the tone in her voice and the way her eyes slid away from Lezlie's stare, Lezlie perceived that Merri did have some idea of the basis for the argument between her parents. For some reason, Merri preferred not to reveal it. *Whatever it is, it may be too much for her to deal with,* Lezlie assumed.

"Merri, if you could tell me one thing about your parents, and only one thing, what would it be?"

"That I love them," Merri answered, her voice almost a whisper.

"And if I asked you the same question about your uncle?"

The transformation that came over Merri's face was instantaneous. "I wish he had never come to visit. Then I would be at home now like it was...."

"So you blame your uncle for what happened to

your parents because they were arguing about him when the car went out of control?"

"He just shouldn't have come and upset my mom."

"Wasn't your father upset?"

"My dad would get mad, but he didn't cry like momma did."

All that Merri had told Lezlie only strengthened Lezlie's opinion that children were far more perceptive than most adults believed. Merri had seen a sequence of events, and though she might not have understood them all, she had been left with a definite impression of a family relationship.

"Merri, did you ever talk to your mother about your uncle?"

Merri shook her head. "She always went to bed after he left. She would get one of her sick headaches... that's what she called them."

"Migraines?"

"I suppose."

Lezlie thought over what Merri had told her, compiling the string of events that had brought Merri to the present. Only one thing did not make sense. What could Greg and Meredith have been arguing about that concerned Drew and Merri? What situation could involve the two of them? Was Drew too attentive to Merri during his visits? Were her parents concerned that he might spoil her? But Drew had said he hadn't seen Merri as often as he wanted, only a few times a year when his business took him to Denver, and even then only for a few days. Whatever was causing Merri's guilt was somehow rooted in the arguments she had partially overheard. There could have been a simple misunderstanding on her part. But how to get that through to her presented a challenge Lezlie would need to evaluate.

"Can I ask you something, Lezlie?" Merri's question brought Lezlie back to the present, and she could feel the pain in the next question. "How did you forget? About your family, I mean?"

"I didn't forget, Merri," Lezlie answered with gentle honesty. "I'll never forget them, but I had to leave them in the past, to understand that I couldn't be with them anymore, and my life had to go on without them."

"Do you still miss them?"

"Yes, but I'm not unhappy anymore. I was for a while."

The telephone rang suddenly. A moment later, Jean buzzed, something she wouldn't have done unless it was important. Lezlie listened in stunned silence as Donna's frantic voice came on the line, asking her to come to the hospital emergency room as soon as possible. Something dreadful had happened, and Donna needed her help. "I'll be there as soon as I can," Lezlie promised, somewhat distracted when she hung up. "I'm sorry, Merri...."

"But what did you do? How did you stop thinking about it?"

"There's no simple formula, Merri. For me, I think it helped that I went back to the place where the accident happened, and I said goodbye. I hadn't been able to do that before. What helps one person may not be the answer for someone else, and it really isn't possible for you to do the same thing."

"I guess not," Merri said quietly.

Lezlie came around the desk and smiled reassuringly. "It will get better, Merri, I promise. I know that's hard to believe, but time has a way of healing. You can't dwell on the things you can't change, and you can't change what happened. Wishing the hurt you feel would go away won't help, either. It will get easier, but you have to help it along, not by trying to forget what happened, but by remembering and putting whatever was said in its proper place. That's what I want to help you do. So, at our next session I want you to tell me what happened or what you remember the night of the accident."

She waited for some verification or acceptance from Merri, but none came. Merri had withdrawn into herself, into the safety of ignoring what she didn't want to hear, but Lezlie's suggestion was enough for now.

"Are we done for today?"

"I think so," Lezlie answered, "unless there's something in particular...."

"No, but you looked funny when you were talking on the telephone."

"That was a friend who needs my help. I have to go over to the hospital's emergency room. But I will see you Tuesday, maybe sooner."

"I'm leaving for camp next Thursday. Uncle Drew said to tell you I won't be here for two weeks." Merri stood up and headed toward the door. "I hope your friend's okay," she said sweetly before turning the handle.

"I'm sure she will be." It was a couple of minutes

before Lezlie was ready to leave, but when she walked into her reception area, her mother, Drew and Merri were still there.

"Is anything wrong, Lezlie?" Margaret had stood up, her face showing her concern. "Jean said that was Donna and she sounded very distraught...."

"There's some problem, but I don't know what it is yet."

"Can I help?"

"I don't think so, mom, but I appreciate the offer. I'm afraid our shopping is off. I have no idea how long I might be."

"Will you call me later? Just to let me know Donna's not hurt or anything?"

"Of course."

"Maybe I should go over with you?" Drew suggested.

"I don't think it's necessary." Lezlie hadn't wanted to sound aloof, but the truth was she was worried. What if something had happened to Jim, something serious... she didn't want to think about it.

"I'll come," Drew said, not leaving room for any argument.

"And Merri can come with me to the coffee shop," Margaret offered. "You meet us there as soon as you can?"

"Thanks, Margaret. Merri, you go ahead and have a snack. I'll be there in a little while."

Lezlie had a companion whether she wanted one or not, and she didn't have the inclination to think about the informality that already existed between her mother and Drew. She hurried out of her office and across the walkway into the hospital.

THE MOMENT she entered the emergency room, relief swept over her. Jim was standing with Donna near the waiting area. Another couple was nearby and the tension between them was obvious in the agitated motions of the two people. The woman was crying and the man looked as though he might explode. The woman suddenly covered her face and sank into a chair. Three children sat motionless, their wide uncertain eyes round disks in pale faces.

"If you hadn't fought us, none of this would have happened," the man said angrily, his frustration directed at Donna before he turned to comfort the woman in the chair.

Donna stood, held by Jim's embracing arm, and she looked at the floor and shook her head as he spoke quietly. When she saw Lezlie, she smiled weakly.

"I'm glad you're here, Lezlie." She looked beyond Lezlie and said hello to Drew.

Lezlie's eyes swept the huddled group in the waiting area. "What's going on?"

"It's Elizabeth, the little girl I told you about. Those are her parents, Ann and Bill Clarke. It seems Ann left Elizabeth alone for just a moment, and she got her hands on one of the kitchen knives."

"Oh, no," Lezlie said. "Is she badly hurt?"

Tears swam in Donna's eyes. "She nearly cut two of her fingers off. They're taking her into surgery. As you can imagine, if you didn't hear, her parents are really upset."

"What do you want me to do?"

"I know you don't counsel adults, Lezlie, but could you talk to Ann? She's nearly hysterical, and she won't listen to anyone. She just keeps saying how stupid it was, she knows she can't leave Elizabeth alone for even a moment, and she doesn't know how much more she can take. It might help if you talk to her."

"I can try, Donna. I don't know how much good it will do."

"Anything at this point couldn't hurt," Donna said.

As Lezlie went over to Elizabeth's distraught parents and introduced herself, Drew watched their reactions. At first they were anxious, then cautious, but a moment later the father moved away, allowing his wife the privacy she needed. When Lezlie sat down, Drew turned to Jim.

"I think I'll go for coffee. The two of you want anything?"

Donna shook her head, and Jim rubbed her shoulder consolingly. "Will you be okay, honey? I think I'll go with Drew and give him a hand."

As they waited for the elevator, a heavy sigh lifted Jim's shoulders when he saw Donna lean against the wall, her arms folded tightly across her chest. "God, I hate it when something like this happens. It tears the hell out of Donna."

"I take it this is one of the kids Lezlie told me about?"

"It's one of the kids Donna's grown very close to. She cares about all the children, but there are a few who touch her more deeply. Elizabeth Clarke is one of them."

On the way to the coffee shop, Jim explained the case to Drew, defining autism and its effects for better understanding. Autistic children were very hard to deal with because there was so little capability for communication, if any at all, and it took years to establish that communication. But some children did respond, and Donna had such hope for Elizabeth, eventually. But it was a slow, often frustrating process for everyone involved.

"Donna must have a very special personality to be able to draw them out," Drew commented.

"It goes deeper than that," Jim said. "Donna had a sister who was autistic, only there was less known about it then. She was in an institution and died of pneumonia when Donna was fourteen. I think Elizabeth reminds Donna of Tina."

Lezlie hadn't realized Drew had left until she glanced up and saw the drinks he had brought for the children, which they tentatively accepted after a nod from their father. She and Drew shared a fleeting glance. She appreciated his nearness and his thoughtfulness for the Clarke family. A lot of people wouldn't have bothered about people they didn't know, and that made Drew's kindness even more touching.

Drew handed Bill Clarke a cup of steaming coffee and put the cream and sugar on the fiberglass table. In the short time he had been gone, a noticeable difference had come over Elizabeth's mother. As she listened to Lezlie she became much more relaxed, nodding or making some comment, her hands resting unclenched in her lap. By the end of their conversation, she was even smiling, a weak smile, perhaps, but a smile.

Lezlie returned to where Donna was standing. "You okay?"

Donna nodded, and then hung her head, fighting tears. "Maybe I was wrong to take such a strong stand against institutionalizing Elizabeth," she choked out.

"It isn't an issue of right or wrong, Donna. I hope you don't mind, but I explained to Ann about your sister. She feels so badly about the institution, and now she understands why you've opposed it."

"I shouldn't let what happened to Tina overshadow my objectivity...."

"I don't think it's that extreme, Donna. You've just become emotionally involved, and that has left you open to disappointment. But not in this case." Lezlie smiled as Donna blinked up at her.

"What do you mean?"

"I mean that Ann is going to try a private companion to take the load off her, and I'll put her in touch with certain agencies who can find just the right person. And Elizabeth will continue at the school."

"Oh, Lezlie," Donna cried, and she threw her arms around her friend. "I'm so glad I called you. I knew your calmness would rub off on all of us."

"Well, will you quit crying now? There's no guarantee that it will work out."

"I know, but it gives Elizabeth another chance, and I'll work even harder."

"I know you will. I think Ann wants to talk to you."

Donna's quiet thanks was reward in itself, then she approached Ann Clarke and they clutched each other's hands. Lezlie's shoulders slumped. She was always so calm during a crisis, but when it passed, she often felt as if all her energy had ebbed away. And that was the case today. Warm hands caressed her shoulders and she glanced over her shoulder.

"Are you finished?" Drew's warm voice asked. His strong fingers offered silent understanding. Having seen the Clarkes comfort each other and Jim offer Donna his support, Lezlie wanted sorely to lean back against Drew and have him surround her with his strong arms, just for a moment. Instead, she smiled and answered that she was through.

"And I appreciate your tagging along, Drew. You diverted everyone's attention and it helped."

"Then I'm glad I tagged along, too. How about you? Tired?"

"Absolutely," Lezlie sighed. She waved to Donna and Ann Clarke before she and Drew headed downstairs to meet her mother and Merri. They were sitting in the coffee shop, a pad of paper in front of them. Ticktacktoe squares filled every inch of the paper.

"This child has a pattern," Margaret said, distracted. "I haven't won a game yet."

"It's been a long time since you played," Lezlie reminded her.

"Yes, but I am going to practice so that the next time I won't take such a beating." Margaret leaned over and patted Merri's hand, and Merri smiled brightly.

"Well, by the time you've mastered ticktacktoe, Merri will have another game," Drew interjected. "Merri, we had better be going, honey."

"Oh, do we have to? I'm having fun."

"We can do it again," Margaret said.

Lezlie remained silent even though she was thinking that one shouldn't make promises one couldn't keep, especially to a child. But in one brief meeting an easy rapport had developed; first between Drew and her mother, and now between her mother and Merri. The implications were obvious. Drew was slowly invading her life, unerringly insinuating his presence into her routine and winning over everyone close to her. She might have suspected his motives if he wasn't so genuinely concerned and prepossessing.

"Drew told me that it was one of Donna's students who was hurt," Margaret said. "Is she going to be all right?"

"I think everything will be fine," Lezlie said, and she attempted to mentally shake off the lethargy that had seeped through her. "If we're going shopping, we had better go, or we'll hit the rush traffic."

"Aren't you tired?" Margaret asked.

"Yes, but it seems I need a bathing suit," Lezlie said with a quick glance at Drew. He was the epitome of innocent silence as they left the hospital, only to be confronted with a torrential summer downpour. "Well, so much for our outing," Lezlie started.

"I have an alternate plan if it's raining," Drew said smugly. "But it won't ruin your day or mine."

"You sound awfully sure of yourself."

"I am, at least where the weather is concerned," Drew answered.

"No fear of the unpredictable?" Lezlie challenged.

"None."

"I wish I knew what the two of you were talking about," Margaret said, her eyes traveling skyward to the heavy dark clouds. "It's supposed to rain through the weekend."

"It won't," Drew said confidently, and both women laughed.

The rain added to the muggy heat, and the streets gave off wafts of steam as Lezlie drove home several hours later. On the seat beside her was a bag containing the bathing suit she had found, a black backless maillot. A fuchsia stripe ran from the right hip to the left shoulder and enclosed a splash of flowers in teal, gold and pink. Trying it on, Lezlie had been undecided because it clung so tightly, emphasizing her waist and the curve of her hips, but her mother had quickly dispelled her doubts... at least in the store. But the thought of wearing it in front of Drew rekindled her uncertainty.

"Everyone's wearing much less," Margaret had said. "And really, Lezlie, you should enjoy your youth while you have it. You'll be my age someday, and you'll wish you had."

"I hope you're not trying to say you're old," Lezlie teased.

"I don't have to say what is true, dear, by today's standards. I see it every morning in the mirror.

Everything today is aimed at the young. The only problem is that the inside woman doesn't match the outside."

"What do you mean?"

"Just that I don't feel any differently now than I did when I was, say, your age. And I couldn't have worn that bathing suit even then. So, take advantage while you can."

The conversation had prompted Lezlie not to listen to the little voice warning her against tempting Drew. Besides, the suit was beautiful, and was one of the few she had found that was both colorful and unadorned by a series of strings, which offered a greater chance of embarrassment should they untie unexpectedly.

The rain came and went through the evening, dripping from the eaves and trees and splashing on the patio where Lezlie stood looking out into the inky blackness. She stared idly into the puddles, watching the ripples glittering like molten diamonds. Only the quiet patter of raindrops disturbed the silence. But tonight the silence was not welcome.

Lezlie was restless. She wandered around the house, flipping on the television and then just as quickly turning it off. She straightened the living room even though she really didn't need to. She made tea and didn't really want any. She wished Drew would call, but he didn't. Finally, she decided to go to bed. But her restlessness persisted. She lay awake, staring at the ceiling for a long time, thinking. Her mother hadn't said one word about Drew after they had left the hospital, but Lezlie could feel her mother's silent approval, and appreciated not being questioned. What was she going to do about Drew? How important had he become if she was wishing he would call? Was she putting too much importance on their relationship? She didn't know quite what to think. One moment Drew was like a friend, offering support or help, the other he was a virile, physically exciting man who incited her senses. And that was what frightened her, Lezlie admitted. She could deal with Drew on one level, but not when he appealed to her sensual needs. Why, she asked the darkness, but the only answer that came back was fear—the fear of becoming involved in a relationship where she would have no control of her own life anymore, one in which she'd have to take another person's feelings into account.

Wondering where they were going tomorrow had driven her crazy all week, and to divert her troubled thoughts she wondered what he had planned that required a bathing suit and a hat. She hoped it was nothing too rigorous. Unexpectedly, she found herself thinking about Michael. It was funny how different she and Michael had been, yet they had shared so much.

Lezlie smiled into the darkness. Michael had liked to do things that were good for the body; Lezlie had liked what was good for the soul. She loved to drive along narrow country roads, read a good book or putter in the garden, while Michael adored tennis, racketball and jogging.

The memories soothed Lezlie's fretfulness, and soon she drifted to sleep, but her dreams were not about Michael. He was her past; her dreams led to the future. Sometime during the wee hours of morning, Lezlie woke and heard the rain still coming down. *So much for Drew's prediction,* she thought with a sleepy smile, and she snuggled back under the covers to her pleasant dreams of the golden-haired man with sky-blue eyes.

CHAPTER TEN

THE SHRILL AND PERSISTENT RINGING of a bell disrupted Lezlie's lovely dream. Groaning, she reached from beneath the covers to slap the alarm, only to realize the telephone was making all the noise. She cushioned the receiver against the pillow, answering sleepily.

"Rise and shine," was Drew's chipper greeting. "I made a bet with myself that you would oversleep. I'm right, I see."

"It's raining," Lezlie said.

"Oh no it isn't. I'll be over in thirty minutes, ready or not."

Lezlie still had her eyes closed when Drew hung up. "Thirty minutes?" she cried, throwing back the covers to see the time. "Oh, for crying out loud," she fumed. She had overslept. She looked toward the window and saw the sun shining brightly. She hopped out of bed and raced for the bathroom to shower and wash her hair, fussing all the while about having to rush. But it was her own fault for taking it for granted that anything as unimportant as the weather would deter Drew Bradinton.

Lezlie had given up trying to figure out where they might be going. But she had come to the conclusion that there was one sport that would require a hat, as well as a suit for dunking to ease the heat. "Oh, I hope he's not taking me fishing," she said fervently.

She had just finished French braiding her hair and pulling on jeans, a linen blouse and a khaki jacket when the doorbell rang. Opening it wide, she smiled brightly. "You're late."

"I thought you might need an extra few minutes. I could have been on time and caught you in your skivvies."

"My what?"

"Your skivvies," he repeated. "Unmentionables, I believe they were once called."

"Oh," Lezlie said as a pretty flush crept up her cheeks. Five minutes earlier and he would have caught her in even less. "Well, I'm not wearing any of those," she replied coolly.

"No?" Drew said, his face alight with interest as his gaze dropped.

"Are we ready?"

"Where's your suit?" Drew asked, obviously distracted.

"I'm wearing it." Lezlie grinned, and the look of disappointment on Drew's face was comical. She had a bag by the door that contained a change of clothes and a towel. "Since I don't know where we're going, I wasn't sure what to bring...."

"I have everything you'll need," Drew replied easily. His strong arm circled her waist and he propelled her out the door. "If we don't get out of here, we may not get there," he said gruffly.

It was one of those rare, startlingly clear, bright

days with not a cloud to mar an incredible blue sky. The air was fresh, the grass dewy green and the sun sparkled through the tree branches. The yards of the homes in the neighborhood were filled with azaleas and other beautiful bursts of colors in red, pink, fuchsia and snow-white.

"Where are we going?"

"You'll see," he said mysteriously. "But first we're going to get some breakfast. Hungry?"

Lezlie suddenly realized she was famished. "Starved," she answered as he put the Porsche into gear.

"That's my girl," Drew said with a smile. The comment sounded so pleasant. *His girl,* she thought. She couldn't help wondering what it would be like to be Drew's "girl." But she already knew the answer. It would be all-encompassing, overwhelming and an emotional high that would leave little in its wake when it was over. She hadn't been wrong in her earlier assessment, of that she was certain.

They stopped at a café on Highway 41, a small cinder-block building. The sign in front promised an Old-fashioned Country Breakfast. A variety of pickup trucks and derelict cars filled the parking lot. The red-checkered tablecloths and white-ruffled curtains gave the restaurant a homey atmosphere, and the room was filled with the most appetizing aromas imaginable. Their entrance brought momentary curiosity from the other patrons, who quickly went back to their conversations.

"Have you been here before?" Lezlie asked as they seated themselves at a vacant table.

"I think I'm what Ruby refers to as a 'regular.' Ruby is the waitress. She's one in a million."

Ruby was a small woman of indefinable age, her eyes hidden behind thick glasses, her chestnut hair streaked with gray. She moved quickly but talked very slowly, and the combination was unsettling.

"How're you today?" she asked Drew.

"Fine, and you, Ruby?"

"Same as always." She withdrew her order pad, but her eyes were on Lezlie. "Who's your friend?"

"This is Lezlie. Lezlie, meet Ruby."

"Pretty, ain't she?" Ruby said before Lezlie could acknowledge Drew's casual introduction.

"I think so." Drew smiled.

"Well, what can I get you folks this morning?"

The amount of food Drew ordered amazed Lezlie. "You said you were hungry," he explained when Ruby hurried away, calling out their order in a jargon Lezlie didn't understand. The cook behind the counter turned away with a gruff "gotcha." The workmen seated at the counter where every stool was taken lounged over coffee and talked of the news of the day, the weather or the fishing forecast. She and Drew were the only couple in the place. Lezlie was seeing another side of Drew. His relaxed casualness was a sharp contrast to the successful businessman she knew him to be. He possessed none of the stuffy self-importance that so often accompanied success. Each time she was with him, she discovered some facet of his personality that made him more interesting and more complex.

"Have I suddenly sprouted another head?" Drew

asked, leaning his elbows on the table. His sleeves were rolled up, exposing his muscular forearms as he laced his fingers together.

Startled, Lezlie realized she had been staring. "No, I was just thinking...."

"About what?"

"You...."

"That's encouraging." Drew grinned.

"You didn't let me finish. I was going to say you seem to fit into any situation so easily. I don't know if I've ever seen you uncomfortable or out of place."

"I have been. Uncomfortable, I mean."

"When?" Lezlie challenged, disbelieving.

"Quite a few times where you're concerned," Drew answered with quiet sincerity. Lezlie didn't know if he was referring to the passionate encounters they had shared or something else, but Drew quickly cleared any confusion. "It's more than that," he said defensively. "Meeting your mother was one."

"My mother?"

Drew smiled sheepishly. "Mothers didn't take to me too well when I was younger."

"I wonder why," Lezlie joked.

"It wasn't funny," Drew returned. "I think every mother thought my only aim was to seduce her daughter."

"I can understand the concern."

"Your mother didn't seem to be thinking that."

"My mom is special," Lezlie said.

"So is her daughter," Drew answered. He reached across the table, his finger hooking hers. "You're wrong if you think sex is all I want from you, Lezlie."

The quiet admission was so sincere that Lezlie was forced to look away. She wanted to ask him what he meant, but she was afraid of the answer. Ruby was approaching the table, balancing several plates. With the delicious food on the table, Lezlie placed her napkin in her lap.

"I know you won't say where we're going, since it's such a surprise, but will you at least tell me...it's not fishing, is it?" Lezlie asked cautiously.

"Why, you don't like fishing?"

Lezlie shook her head. "My dad took me a few times when I was little. I found nothing to like about sticking a wiggling worm on a hook and pulling a flopping fish onto the bank. He finally gave up because he always had to throw back the fish he caught."

"Well, to put your mind at ease, we're not going fishing." Drew dug into steaming scrambled eggs sided by grits, sausage and a bowl of white pasty gravy for the biscuits. "You had better eat up or we're going to be late."

Thirty minutes later they were back in the Porsche speeding along Roswell Road, then down Johnson Ferry. Where the road crossed the Chattahoochee River, Drew pulled into the newly graveled parking lot. A wooden booth for raft rental was crowded with people.

"We're going rafting?" Lezlie cried, excited.

Her reaction made Drew turn around. "Don't tell me you've never rafted on the Chattahoochee."

Lezlie shook her head.

"I don't believe it. I used to come all the time, until they started that raft racing thing a few years back. Now that they've done away with it, the river's not quite as crowded."

Excitement and anticipation bubbled within Lezlie. Men, women, girls and boys passed by in cutoff jeans, bikinis or shorts, laughing as they carried a variety of orange-and-black rafts or big black inner tubes twice the size of a car's tire. Sitting in the front seat of the Porsche, she slipped off her jacket and jeans and put on the pair of cotton shorts she had brought. Drew had also peeled off his jeans, and the dark shorts he wore clung to his muscular tanned legs. Lezlie appraised him appreciatively as he unloaded a cooler. He locked the car and they headed toward the riverbank.

"What about a raft?" Lezlie asked.

Drew took her hand, his fingers intertwining with hers. "It's already on the water." He squeezed her fingers.

The gravel crunched beneath their steps, leading to the grassy bank and muddy incline. There was no way to descend the bank without sliding.

"Hey, here they are. We'd about given up on you." A group of people were clustered on the bank. Two of the men came forward and caught the cooler as Drew dropped it down to them.

"Better late than never," Drew replied.

"That's a matter of opinion," the sandy-haired man answered good-naturedly.

Drew grabbed a tree branch and dropped to the bank below. He held his arms out to Lezlie and she followed suit, his hands catching her around the waist to cushion her jump. His arm was still around Lezlie as he introduced her to a group of six people. There was Pete, an accountant, and his wife, Karen; Charlie, a heavyset and well-known developer in Atlanta, and his wife, Maxine; and a third man whom Lezlie had met several times before. The sandy-haired man was Ken Lawson, an attorney, who had known Michael. Of course, he had been married when Lezlie knew him. His date's name was Jamie.

"Hi, Lezlie," Ken said, the only one of the group who reached out to shake hands. "How have you been?"

"Pretty good, and you?"

Ken looked at Jamie and then shrugged. "Can't complain," he said and then he grinned. "How long have you known Drew?"

"Not very long," she answered.

"He's a nice guy," Ken offered. "I've been doing his legal work for a couple of years now."

Drew was a few yards away, anchoring the cooler. Nine big black, doughnut-shaped tubes glistened in the water. They had been roped together in a large circle—a tube for each person and one for the cooler.

Everyone was ready to take a position on the undulating makeshift raft. Drew had stripped off his shirt. The sun played across his broad shoulders, emphasizing his taut muscles and smooth skin. His chest was covered with a heavy matting of hair a darker shade than the sun-streaked gold on his head.

Lezlie quickly discarded her blouse and shorts, ignoring Drew's lengthy stare. But she heard the sharp intake of his breath. Lezlie noted with satisfaction that his eyes had narrowed and darkened into fathomless pools.

"That is some suit," he whispered, his voice slightly hoarse.

"My mother said you would like it," Lezlie said breezily.

"I salute her good taste, but not her good judgment." Drew said, his gaze sweeping the black material that clung so seductively to her fair skin. Lezlie felt the heat rise to her face. "Seems you have your doubts, too." Drew grinned. He held Lezlie's hand as she slipped on the muddy bank. Then he swept her into his arms and deposited her on one of the large tubes. Her arms and knees supported her while her torso slipped through the center of the inner tube. She sucked in her breath as the frigid water splashed her stomach.

"Oh, it's cold," she whispered.

"Not for long," Drew said, hoisting himself into the tube beside her. "Wait until we get out in the middle and the sun gets to you. You should do this the end of April or early May. This is like tepid bathwater compared to that."

The cooler was strategically placed in the center of the circle of tubes, where it could be reached easily. As soon as the others had climbed on, Ken yanked on the rope that anchored the raft to the shore. Slowly the current caught them and they drifted away from the bank. The current was faster and the river muddier because of the previous day's rain, but it hadn't seemed to deter anyone at all. Rafts floated lazily along the river, laughter carrying across the water as a group of boys tried to paddle toward an orange rubber raft filled with girls.

"I think they are pursuing a lost cause," Charlie said. The girls were giggling, but other than that they showed no interest in the amorous young boys.

"It's an upstream battle," Ken added, paraphrasing an old saying.

"Up a creek without a paddle," Charlie continued, laughing at the gangly youths leaning over their raft using their arms and hands in a useless feat. "Hey, what d'you think about the Braves? They had a good exhibition series...."

"That doesn't mean anything," Ken said, disgusted. "They always get off to a good start and then they lose their steam near the end of the season. Every year it's the same thing. Everyone speculates about the pennant about midseason only to watch the team give it away."

"That's not fair," Maxine challenged.

"Fair or not, it's true." Ken reached into the cooler and brought out a beer for each of them. "Leave it to Drew to take care of everything. None of us is going to get hungry. There must be a dozen sandwiches in there."

"I think that's all you think about," Jamie said.

"He's not the only one," Lezlie said for Drew's hearing only.

"You don't do too badly, either," Drew returned quietly.

Ken had leaned back and began telling of a case that was due in court in a few weeks.

Lezlie wasn't really listening to the conversation. Instead, she was absorbing all the wonderful beauty of the river. Ancient gnarled trees leaned out from the bank, their limbs reaching across the water like leafy hands. Just beyond the landing, the group passed some expensive homes built along the river and a long stretch of condominiums where owners sat on the lush grass. The gentle motion of the water rocked the raft and Lezlie sighed contentedly. She leaned her head back against the warm rubber, feeling the sun on her face. The touch of a hand on her cheek roused her. The others, absorbed in their discussion, took no notice of Drew's withdrawal from the conversation.

"You're going to get a heck of a sunburn if you aren't careful," Drew said as he reached into the cooler and brought out a bottle of sunscreen. His touch was gentle as he spread the lotion across her shoulders and then her nose and cheeks.

"Are you always so prepared?" Lezlie said.

"I try to be," he said, his touch lingering on her chin. "I take it you know Ken. You looked a little funny when he started talking shop."

"It didn't bother me," Lezlie said, not adding that at one time she had been very accustomed to hearing about pending cases, to feeling the excitement mounting as a case was developed and evidence compiled. "Ken and Michael used to work for the same firm until Ken branched out on his own."

"That must have been about the time I met him." Drew's warm gaze caressed her. "And he had the advantage of already knowing you. We might have met a lot sooner...."

"I wasn't in the frame of mind to meet anyone then." The thought went through Lezlie's mind before she could divert the kaleidoscope of memories.

Drew took her hand. "That was thoughtless of me," he said gently.

Lezlie studied his hand, the strong tanned fingers tracing the tips of her fingernails. So many times the memories seemed like yesterday; at other times, they seemed from another lifetime. But she had put it in the perspective of "then" a moment ago. The abrupt change startled Lezlie, but the next instant, she was even more surprised. Drew had said she was "in love with a memory of love." But she felt so differently now. She remembered Dr. Harvey reassuring her that in time there might be a love that would dispel the memories. Could Drew be the love he had meant? Could she possibly care more than she was willing to believe? Was that why she felt so much more alive, so confused and distracted? Without knowing why, Lezlie wanted to deny the possibility with vehement certainty, but she couldn't.

"Hey, you two gonna join the group or stay huddled to yourselves?" The question had come from Charlie. "Not that we don't understand, mind you. I can remember when Maxi and I first met. Literally knocked me on my—"

Maxine punched her husband's arm playfully. "Don't you dare!"

"No fair," Ken said emphatically. "You can't lead us on like that and not give."

"It's not that funny," Maxine said.

"Let us judge for ourselves," Ken persisted enthusiastically and Maxine shrugged, leaving it up to Charlie, who was only too happy to recount an episode that turned out to be hilariously funny.

"We met on the side of the road," Charlie started, recounting how he had seen this beautiful young woman having car trouble. Her horn was stuck and blaring. "I pulled over and parked in front of her. I was planning to impress her with my knowledge of cars, but she had some little foreign job. When I reached in to disconnect the horn, I accidentally released the brake. Of course we were on an incline. You can imagine how I felt when her car started to roll... because I was parked in front of her...."

"You should have seen him," Maxine added, and she chuckled despite herself. "Here he was in a three-piece suit, slipping and sliding as he tried to keep my car from rolling. He was cussing and screaming as if the car could hear him and would just stop, right?"

Charlie shook his head. He had stood and watched in utter disbelief as Maxine's dented old little car had plowed into the back of his brand-new Mercedes. Then, to add insult to injury, when he had kicked her tire in frustration, he had slipped and wound up sitting on the ground, in the mud, of course, and his suit had been ruined.

"What about you, Drew? How did you and Lezlie meet?" Ken asked.

"Nothing as exciting as Charlie and Maxine, I will say," Drew started. Lezlie held her breath. "We were introduced by a mutual friend."

Lezlie had had a fleeting fear that Drew might recount their initial meeting and the misunderstanding, but she should have known Drew would not say anything to embarrass either of them.

They drifted past residences. Some sat high on a hill above the river, barely visible behind the heavy foliage, while others were so close to the bank that the residents returned the waves of cheerful rafters. Several people holding fishing lines sat on the limbs of trees that leaned across the water. Wild flowers dotted the bank alongside white daisies and mossy thrift with its cushion of purple blossoms. It was all so beautiful, Lezlie could hardly take it all in. She drifted along happily, exchanging an occasional smile with Drew.

"I don't know about y'all, but I'm going to cool off," Drew announced, slapping at a mosquito that was planning to lunch on his arm.

"Don't you have bug repellent somewhere in the cooler?" Lezlie teased in a whisper. Drew rewarded her with a chagrined grimace.

"Well, I am perfectly comfortable," Ken said, reaching into the cooler for another beer. "Anybody want a sandwich?"

Drew pushed himself up and dropped his legs through the inner tube. He disappeared beneath the water, only to surface just outside the circle of tubes. He shook his head, and the drops of water were a spiral around his shoulders.

While Lezlie didn't feel the heat on the part of her body submerged in the cool water, her face and neck were moist with perspiration. She used her feet to lever herself so that she could slip off the back of the inner tube and slide into the water.

The coolness was delightful, but even more pleasurable was the pressure of Drew's reassuring arm around her. His legs brushed hers beneath the water, an accidental contact that sent shock waves through Lezlie. His eyelashes were in water-darkened clumps, making his eyes even more incredibly blue. He touched her shoulder. Her fair skin was already tinged pink.

"I didn't want to stay on the river all afternoon anyway, but it's a good thing we aren't going to be out too long. A sunburn might mess up the rest of the day."

"What rest?" Lezlie asked.

"You'll see," Drew promised, with his familiar sense of mischief.

"I just thought of something," Lezlie said suddenly. "How are we going to get back to your car? We'll be miles down the river."

"When are you going to learn to trust me?" Drew said easily. "Charlie's van is at Powers Ferry where we'll get off."

"It isn't that I don't trust you," Lezlie started.

"Good, then don't ask any more questions."

Hidden from their companions behind the huge tubes, Drew leaned forward and touched his lips lightly to hers. He stroked the enticing curve of her waist. "Are you enjoying the day so far?"

Lezlie slid her arm along his shoulder. His skin was cool to her touch. "Yes, but you'd be in a lot of trouble if I was the type who despised surprises."

"Nobody really hates surprises, they just don't like to look foolish."

"Am I going to look foolish?"

"Never." Wisps of hair curled around Lezlie's face, having escaped the confines of the braid. "Why don't you wear your hair down more often?"

"It gets in the way," Lezlie answered. "If I wanted to wear it down, I would have to cut it."

Lezlie was holding on to her inner tube when Drew released her, and his intense gaze settled on her eyes. He touched her cheek and ran his hand along her jaw and the nape of her neck. The silent question went unasked and unanswered as he searched the coil for the pins. When Lezlie didn't protest, he began to pull out the pins, dropping them one by one into the murky river. A couple of times he was forced to let go of the inner tube to search out a hidden pin. A groan of success rumbled in his throat when the braid fell heavily against Lezlie's shoulder.

Drew had become fascinated with his task. He removed the rubber band and began to slowly unwind the strands until Lezlie's hair hung free and flowing in the river. The curls danced on top of the water for only a moment before floating out around Lezlie's shoulders, the ends curling around Drew's arm like a live tangle.

"You look like a mermaid," he whispered, his arm again circling her waist as he pulled her against him.

"Mermaids don't live in rivers," Lezlie said, attempting to sound unconcerned by what his nearness was doing to her.

"Mine does," Drew said quietly.

He held the inner tube with one hand, drawing her with him in the current. He paddled lazily and his leg brushed between hers. It was as though no one else existed when he looked at her. They could have been in a secluded glade, concealed from the world as he kissed her, a gentle searching kiss, which became an exploration that left Lezlie breathless. His mouth played on hers, demanding a response Lezlie could not deny. She pressed closer, liking the feel of his strong legs intertwined with hers. Slowly he turned her so that her back was to the current and his body was above hers. The hair on his chest was a soft forest beneath her searching hands. She clung to him for a moment, lost in the wondrous sensations that swept her away as unerringly as the current.

Drew sighed heavily, dropping his head against her damp shoulder.

"I know," Lezlie said quietly, and his head came up sharply. She smiled shyly and he returned it.

Drew kissed her chin, his tongue touching her skin. "I'll say one thing...you're the first mermaid I've encountered whose skin tasted like muddy water."

"Oh, and how many have you encountered?"

"None who look like you," he answered easily.

"That's what I thought."

"But I'll take a river mermaid over a sea mermaid any day."

"Really?"

"Really."

"If I see one, I'll let her know." Lezlie heard Jamie's giggle followed by Charlie's robust laughter. "Now, how do you suggest we get back on the raft?"

"The same way I got in. Dive under and go back up the center. Then lift your legs up."

When they were settled back in their tubes, Lezlie brought her hair across her shoulder to let the warm air dry it. Of course, she would have to wash it again as soon as she got home, but that didn't matter. Nothing did, except that she was truly enjoying herself. Drew had promised her a day of fun and he had certainly brought it about. But the day ended too soon when they neared the landing at Powers Ferry and the three men jumped off the raft to drag it to shore. Other rafters were just getting on the river to travel down to Cumberland Mall.

Charlie, Ken and Drew dragged the raft onto the rocky shore where Charlie began deflating the group of tubes. It would be much easier to take the raft the six hundred yards to the parking lot than to try to maneuver it along the narrow, rocky, tree-lined path with other rafters coming from the opposite direction.

"You have this down to a science," Lezlie told Charlie.

"It almost isn't worth the effort for a two-hour jaunt," he grumbled with a good-natured smile at Drew. "But our friend didn't want to spend a whole day on the river."

"Oh, it would have been fun," Lezlie said, disappointed that the outing had ended so quickly. She hadn't seen Drew approach.

"We'll do it again from Morgan Falls all the way down if you can stand six or eight hours, but today I wanted us to do other things, too."

Lezlie soon found out what one of the "things" was. They had maneuvered along a narrow path and across a bridge to the parking lot. Charlie and Ken dropped their burden to the ground and helped Drew unload two ten-speed bikes from the back of Charlie's van.

"I appreciate your picking these up last night," Drew said.

"I ought to charge you guys rent for all the stuff I haul for you."

There was a stack of towels in the back of the van and Lezlie dried off, retrieving her hat, blouse, shorts and sandals from a plastic bag Drew had put in the cooler. He was still wearing the tennis shoes he had had on at breakfast, but now they squooshed when he walked. Her purse was locked in the back of Drew's car and Lezlie was wondering what to do with her hair. With a gallant smile, Drew handed her the rubber band he had taken from her hair and looped around his wrist.

"I had a feeling you might need this."

"Don't happen to have a comb, by chance?" Lezlie said with a smile.

"Sorry, it's in the car."

Lezlie had slipped back into her clothes. Her blouse stretched tautly across her breasts as she reached back to secure her hair in a ponytail. Drew silenced a groan, but Lezlie saw the look of desire flash in his eyes before he turned away to inspect the bikes. She glanced down to find her wet shirt a perfect outline of her breasts.

"We're ready to go," Charlie said as Jamie and Maxine said goodbye and climbed into the van. "I guess we'll see you later—"

"You bet," Drew interrupted, and Lezlie had the impression he had wanted to cut off what Charlie was going to say. When the van pulled away, Lezlie leaned over Drew's shoulder. He was crouched beside the bikes, checking one of the tires.

"Where are we meeting them later?" she asked.

Drew glanced over his shoulder, but only shook his head.

"Another surprise," Lezlie sighed. "Am I going to go through the whole day not knowing anything until it happens?"

"I hope so," Drew said. "It makes it more fun that way."

"That's your opinion," Lezlie grumbled in frustration.

"Are you ready?" Drew asked merrily.

"I'm almost afraid to answer that. Do you have any idea how long it's been since I was on a bike? And I don't think I've ever ridden a ten speed."

"It's a lot easier than a conventional bike. And it'll come back to you. Just don't expect to be able to stop by backpedaling." Drew showed her how to operate the bike and use the hand brakes.

"I thought we were going to take Charlie's van back to the car," Lezlie said.

"Grumble, grumble." Drew grinned.

"I'm not grumbling," Lezlie defended.

"No?"

"No," Lezlie answered, determined not to say another word that would sound like a complaint. But her patience was tested less than a quarter mile from the Powers Ferry landing when she and Drew rounded a curve onto Powers Ferry Road and started up a steep incline. Cars whizzed past them, veering out, but their speed and nearness made Lezlie nervous.

Drew jumped off his bike and turned back as Lezlie did the same, and they walked the bikes up the hill. "Once we get past Terrill Mill, we won't have to watch for the traffic," he called over his shoulder.

Lezlie nodded, trying to determine how far it was to the car. She had driven this way several times on her way shopping, and she had the sinking feeling that it was better than five miles to their destination. She shook her head, climbing back on the bike at the top of the hill, but a short distance ahead she realized Drew was right. Pedaling the ten speed took a lot less effort than an ordinary bicycle. Riding up the many hills was difficult but they coasted along the stretches of level road. When the traffic became congested, Drew slowed down, glancing over his shoulder. Lezlie was speeding up on him, not paying attention, and he called out.

"Hey, slow down."

As though coming out of a daze, Lezlie immediately squeezed the hand brake, almost upending herself. Her surprised expression brought a hearty laugh from her companion. "You all right?"

Lezlie nodded, trying not to overcontrol the bike as she maintained a slower speed. Lezlie had to be careful not to get too distracted watching Drew's back and his strong legs pumping the bicycle. The breeze ruffled his heavy hair and threatened to take her hat, so Lezlie swept it off and stuffed it in the pocket of her shorts. When Drew rode into a quick-stop market, Lezlie waited outside until he returned with two cans of soda, which he placed in the pack behind his seat.

They had reached Terrill Mill, a congested intersection that gave way to rolling fields on the right and subdivisions on the left. At the Terrill Mill Park, Drew veered right onto a more-narrow but less-traveled road, past a horse farm and stables, and an elementary school named for the narrow creek where a bridge allowed only one car across at a time. Lezlie maintained a safer distance, but it was no easier to keep her mind on where they were going.

Perspiration trickled between Lezlie's breasts and she was breathing hard by the time they reached the other side of the creek to face another incline. At the curve of the hill, Drew walked his bike to a narrow path that widened and led down to Sope Creek.

"How 'bout a breather?" Drew asked, and Lezlie simply nodded, glad for the reprieve as they parked the bikes.

A steep gullied path led down to the rock-strewn creek bed. Drew carried the pack from his bike in one hand, extending the other to Lezlie. The path was little more than a rutted track sided by trees and brambles, and twice Drew's hand tightened on hers when Lezlie's footing slipped. An ancient stone barbecue pit was in crumbling disrepair, but there was evidence of recent use. As they reached a sandy shoal where the water swept around the boulder-size rocks scattered across the creek, Drew sat down, pulling Lezlie down next to him. Other couples dotted the banks or lounged on the rocks in the middle of the stream. A large black dog bounded across the water, scrambling onto the rocks or climbing along the steep bank on the opposite side. A low whistle perked his ears and he headed back, his dark wet coat gleaming.

It was so peacefully quiet that Lezlie closed her eyes, listening to the gentle splash of water. She had lived in Atlanta all of her life yet Drew was showing her things she'd either never known existed, or that she hadn't made the time to notice.

Drew had opened the pack and popped the tops off two soft drinks. Handing one to Lezlie, he smiled as she took a long drink. "How long did you say it's been since you've ridden a bike?

"I didn't say," Lezlie replied, "but it has obviously been too long."

"I don't know," Drew mused. "You look to be in pretty good shape to me."

Lezlie didn't answer, but concealed her discomfort while eating a sandwich he had brought.

Drew had already finished his sandwich and he leaned back on his elbows, crossing his legs at the ankle. He was completely relaxed, but his quizzical stare did not leave Lezlie as she nibbled her sandwich. Every time he offered a compliment, she seemed to withdraw from him. Perhaps she saw compliments as empty flattery, or perhaps she really didn't see herself as others did. And what Drew saw and knew about her kept him totally captivated. She was incredibly beautiful, but hers was not the superficial kind of beauty with no substance. She was sensitive, kind and vulnerable. And he knew, without conceit, that her attitude toward him was changing. He could see it in the way she looked at him, and feel it in her response to his touch.

But Drew's feelings had changed, too, and deepened into an awesome blend of pleasure and torment. He wanted to spend every minute with her, but it wasn't possible; he wanted to shower her with gifts, which he was certain she would refuse; and he wanted to show her the physical side of his feelings, but until lately he had thought she would spurn him completely. One thing he knew without a doubt. She would have to be the one to initiate any intimacy they might share, other than the flirtatious kisses and caresses he had bestowed upon her.

Just watching her, the way the light glinted in her hair and the softness of her smile, was enough to set his pulse hammering in his head. A heavy sigh lifted Drew's chest. He hoped she would give him some indication soon, or he might have to take matters into his own hands and cause her to yield to her own desire.

"How did you find this place?" Lezlie asked, brushing her hands off when she had finished her sandwich.

Drew's distraction evaporated. "I used to come here with some of the guys from Tech." He shifted uncomfortably. "Of course, it was a lot different then."

"Wasn't everything? I can remember when there was nothing this side of Sandy Springs, except a little grocery mart a few miles north. Now there's a fast-food something on every corner and in between, and now all the offices—"

"I hope that isn't a criticism of what I do for a living," Drew offered.

"The builders only build the buildings, it's the county that permits it."

"Very astute, but the county is growing by leaps and bounds. Business is an integral part of it, Lezlie."

"I know, I just hate to see a beautiful area become a mass of traffic and fast-food chains."

"You and everybody else," Drew said. "But we're fast becoming a society of convenience. There's one place I know of where you can forget what is being done a few miles away. That's what I wanted to show you."

"What is it?"

"You'll see," Drew answered with a quick grin. He stood up, his long legs flexing with the motion. "You want to take a dip?" he asked, indicating the swirling creek. Squatting on the warm sand, he splashed water across his shoulders and arms. "It will help the heat."

Lezlie's hair was stuck to the back of her neck and her shirt clung damply to her back. Still, she shook her head, remembering how Drew had looked at her at the river. She had felt a thrill mingled with her embarrassment at the darkening scrutiny before he had looked away, but she didn't want to tempt the fates by tempting Drew too far. She was having a hard-enough time keeping her own thoughts from straying to the sensations he aroused, without blatantly asking for trouble. And his constant affectionate touches kept her at odds, muddling her concentration. On the one hand, she wanted him to kiss her, to hold her and caress her until all rational thought flew from her mind; on the other, she was afraid of the consequences. Because once such a course was set, there would be no turning back, no last-minute reprieve. That particular realization was both enticing and terrifying.

Drew had turned around and noticed Lezlie's preoccupation. She stood and he walked toward her slowly, taking her chin between his thumb and forefinger. "What are you thinking about?" he asked, his voice a low caressing rumble.

Lezlie tried to look away, but he held her chin, forcing her to face him. "I was thinking what a wonderful day it has been."

"You sound as though the day's over."

"Almost, but I have really had fun...." Drew's amused countenance brought her up short. "What?" she demanded with a warning frown. "And if you say 'it's a surprise' one more time, I'll scream."

"You promised me a whole day," Drew said simply. "And, correct me if I am wrong, but a day is twenty-four hours. While I don't intend to hold you to the exact definition, we do have plans for the evening."

"We do?"

"We most certainly do," Drew answered easily.

"And I don't suppose it will do me any good to ask what those plans are."

"No, it's a sur...secret." Drew shrugged sheepishly. "I wouldn't want everyone around to think you're in trouble and come running to your rescue. You don't want to be rescued, do you?"

"Do I need to be?"

"That depends," Drew said, his arm sliding around her waist.

"On what?" Lezlie challenged, answering the teasing glint in his eyes.

"On whether or not you're afraid of me."

"And why should I be afraid of you?" Lezlie asked innocently.

"I would think that is obvious," Drew drawled, his gaze lowering to her curved mouth.

"I don't think you would ravish me right here in front of everyone," Lezlie said smugly.

"Don't push your luck," Drew warned with a playful hug. "You have to be alone with me eventually—" he continued and then, more seriously "—and you'll be the one to start or finish whatever happens between us."

"Somehow, I'm not so certain," Lezlie said warily.

"Well, you can be." Drew kissed her quickly then, a peck on her lips that left Lezlie strangely unsettled.

Without thinking, she reached up. Her fingers slid through Drew's hair. His hair was like silk and she urged him to lean down. Then, with a teasing smile, she returned his brotherly peck. But in the moment when their gazes fused, Drew held his breath. Lezlie's action had taken him off guard, but her next move was even more startling.

The pressure of her fingers beckoned another kiss, but her playfulness had given way to confusion and uncertainty. As her mouth opened, inviting Drew's sensual exploration, Drew's arms closed tightly around her. Her breasts pressed against his rock-hard chest while her thighs were tickled by the hair on his legs. But all sensation blended into one surging ache to be closer, to touch and be touched. Drew's tongue began a sensual dance of delight, darting and exploring until Lezlie moaned, a low cry of pleasure that only added to the fuel of Drew's ardor. Drew held the back of her head, his mouth gently ravaging her senses while his muscular body held no secret of his desire.

"Yahoo! Go for it!"

The yell managed to seep into the consciousnesses of Drew and Lezlie. He raised his head, his eyes hooded by desire. Lezlie dropped her face against his chest, trying to bring her tumultuous feelings under control. Her legs felt as though there was no strength to support her, but she didn't worry. Drew's arms were still holding her. A group of kids lounged on a rock about fifty yards up the creek. The one who had yelled waved, his grin visible.

"How embarrassing," Lezlie mumbled.

"It could have been a lot more so if he hadn't yelled," Drew answered quietly. His stroking hand on her back sent shivers racing along Lezlie's spine.

Drew swept the pack from the ground. He returned the boy's wave before they started back up the path. Her hand was securely locked within his and they walked in silence. Birds and squirrels scampered in the trees around them, and a blue-tailed lizard scurried across their path. As they climbed back on the bikes, Drew's wink released Lezlie's tension.

Proceeding on their excursion, Lezlie shook her head. What in the world had come over her? What had prompted her to act so forward? But she knew the reason. She had wanted Drew to kiss her, to reaffirm what she was too afraid to admit. Could she possibly be falling in love with Drew Bradinton? Somehow, the thought was not as terrifying as she had imagined, though it was unsettling. Loving meant commitment, entanglement and sometimes pain, and that was what she was not ready to experience again...not yet. And maybe she never would be.

Lezlie had fallen back and now she pedaled sharply to catch up to Drew as he rode into an exclusive area of homes. The sloping meticulously kept lawns led the eye to large, custom-built homes of every design. They zigzagged through the winding streets, then over the rolling hills to a steep descent to a road that sided the Chattahoochee River. They had passed the same stretch and seen the homes from the vantage of the river, but Lezlie hadn't been half as impressed as she was now. Each home held an individuality of design and taste, except in the use of elaborate stained-or-beveled-glass treatments on the doors and windows of the entries. Red-brick Williamsburg, white Colonial, French country and designs Lezlie couldn't name blended into an appealing display of taste and affluence.

Drew stopped on a vacant lot where heavy old oaks would fill a backyard with shady tranquillity. As he put down the kickstand, Lezlie glanced around.

"Come on," Drew said, heading onto the property.

"Should we be here? Won't somebody complain?"

"Nobody but the owner would," Drew said, adding, "and since I am the owner, that takes care of that."

Lezlie fell into step beside him, skirting the patches of mud. "Are you going to build on it?"

"I don't know," Drew answered, looking at the sluggish river that backed his property. "Land along the river is really scarce. Originally, it was just an investment, but... I don't know."

Lezlie glanced around, glimpsing joggers and other bike riders on the divided road. The median was dotted with crape myrtles, the slender branches promising to burst into blooms of fuchsia or pink later in the summer. Drew had been right. It was as though the outside busy world didn't exist. There were only a few rafters on the river now that it was late afternoon. Peacefulness settled over Lezlie and she yawned.

"Tired?"

Lezlie looked up at Drew. "It's been a busy day," she said abruptly.

"Complaining?"

"Not me," she said with a grin. "Though I know I'll be sore tomorrow."

"I'll be glad to massage whatever hurts," Drew offered graciously.

"Thanks, but a warm bath will take care of it."

"Not like I can," Drew said with a lecherous smile.

"Bragging again," Lezlie challenged.

"The truth isn't bragging," Drew said airily, and Lezlie made a face of strained tolerance. "Well, I guess I should get you home so you can get ready for the rest of our 'day.' You may even have time for a nap. But I won't be so considerate about arriving late if you oversleep."

"I'll remember that," Lezlie promised.

It had taken them almost an hour to get back to Drew's car, strap the bikes to a rack, then reach Lezlie's house. When he dropped her at her door, he touched her pink nose. "Don't take a hot shower."

"I don't intend to," Lezlie answered, thinking to herself that an icy-cold blast might be just the thing to dispel the warm rush of her blood she experienced when Drew looked at her as he was now.

"I'll see you at eight. Dress casually, jeans will be fine, and don't eat."

Lezlie raised her hand in a mock salute. "Yes sir," she said briskly. "Anything else, sir?"

"I didn't mean it to sound like an order," Drew started, but Lezlie's unsuccessful attempt to conceal a smile made him shake his head in resignation. "All right, you win."

"What do I win?" Lezlie challenged.

"The dry-humor award, but I think you deserve a frustration award, because that's what you're doing to me."

"I don't mean to," Lezlie said more seriously.

"The hell you don't," Drew growled. "After the way you kissed me today?"

Lezlie actually blushed with the reminder, and Drew laughed. He gripped her shoulders, turned her around and swatted her playfully on the bottom before propelling her toward the door.

"And I'm not complaining, either," he commented.

Inside the house, Lezlie closed the door and leaned against it as she watched Drew leave. She turned around, pressing her back into the wood as her stomach did strange flip-flops. But her happiness was interrupted by a sharp cramp. She leaned over, groaning. She kneaded the muscles of her thighs, which were already showing signs of the soreness she had expected.

"I'm going to be in great shape," she grumbled to herself.

Intending to run a warm bath to soak her aching legs and back, she stripped off her shirt and headed into the bathroom. A lighthearted tune was on the radio and she found herself humming along.

CHAPTER ELEVEN

THE LONGHORN SALOON was a recreation of a Wild West town block, though it was only one large building. A rough-plank porch supported a second-story balcony, and bold signs along the saloon's front announced Painless Dentistry, Sutton Gun Shop, Stokes Dry Goods, Hotel, Sheriff McClure and the Prairie Cattle Company. The twang of country music wafted on the warm night air as blue-jeaned patrons entered the nightclub.

Lezlie's mouth had gaped open when Drew pulled into the crowded lot and located a parking space. It all dawned on Lezlie—her reason for her own casual dress and Drew's similar attire of jeans, plaid shirt and smooth leather boots.

"You can shut your mouth now." Drew reached over and gently clipped her chin. "Surprised?"

"It's been one right after another," Lezlie answered. "I've never—"

"You've never been to a country-and-western bar," Drew interrupted.

Lezlie turned toward him, the light shadowing her face and glittering in her eyes. "How did you guess?" she asked wryly.

"Just a lucky stab." Drew grinned. "It seems

there's a lot you haven't been doing. And I want to change that."

Drew had started out of the car and Lezlie opened her own side. "What do you mean, want to? You've done a fair job in one day."

"It's not over yet, sweetheart," Drew answered. His hand rested on her waist as they walked in. Lezlie's hair was brushed back and secured by decorative cloisonné combs. The soft curls reached Drew's hand. "In case I haven't said so, I like your hair down."

"You have said so...several times." But the compliment was pleasant to hear. After her bath, Lezlie had intended to French braid her thick hair when she had succumbed to the sudden impulse to wear it loose. The colorful enameled combs of beige and blue showed well against the auburn waves. She had worn blue jeans and a knobby weave cotton sweater, the boat neckline draping her shoulders and complimenting her small waist and tight jeans.

As she and Drew passed through the glass doors, Lezlie noticed two doormen leaning on stools, their wide hats and beards almost obscuring their faces. Their jeans were faded and their boots scuffed and any minute Lezlie expected one of them to take aim at the brass spittoon that served as a planter. To the right of the entrance was a paneled room with tables, which Lezlie assumed was a restaurant. It was so crowded Lezlie couldn't see the dance floor, but she certainly heard the music. The people shifted and moved, a slow tide of humanity in a smoke-filled room.

"They have some terrific barbecue here," Drew said, steering Lezlie to the right and toward a table where Charlie and Maxine waved. As they approached, Ken and Jamie glanced up.

"Now I understand what Charlie meant when he said he would see us later."

Charlie was decked out in jeans, boots and sported a befeathered hat on his curly hair. "Hi, y'all," he drawled.

Lezlie had just taken the seat Drew had pulled out for her when she spotted Donna and Jim. They glanced around the entrance, then Donna nudged Jim and they headed over. Drew made the introductions and Donna slipped into a chair next to Lezlie.

Lezlie smiled in surprise. "What are you two doing here?"

Donna cast a glance in Drew's direction. He was engrossed in a conversation with Jim, and Donna lowered her voice. "Drew called us yesterday and asked if we would like to meet here. I must have sounded like a real space cadet when he said y'all were spending the day together and then he was bringing you here." Donna's eyebrows rose quizzically. "It seems to me that the last time we talked, you were pretty firm in your decision not to see him." Donna leaned toward Lezlie. "I should have known he would get through to you after the way he was at the hospital the other day. I just wish you had mentioned it so I wouldn't have stammered so."

"It was as much a surprise to me as to you," Lezlie said. "But I've been wanting to ask about Elizabeth."

"She's doing really well, and don't change the subject," Donna admonished warmly. "You know, I get the distinct impression that nothing just happens where your friend is concerned."

"You, too?" Lezlie said, and then glanced at Drew, her expression softening noticeably. "I'm afraid I may be getting in over my head."

Donna laid a reassuring hand on Lezlie's arm. "Don't be worried. I think he just wants you to be comfortable with him. And it isn't your *head* you need to worry about."

Lezlie smiled ruefully, knowing very well what Donna meant. "And I'm the one who advised *you* not to get personally involved."

"It happens on occasion," Donna replied. "And about all you can do is go with the flow. But think about it another time. This place is such fun."

"You've been here?"

"Several times. We just got the hang of the dances a few weeks back."

Lezlie had a suspicion that Drew was attempting to introduce her to his friends and bring her gradually into his life. He knew that she and Donna were good friends, so he had invited them. Beyond his teasing banter and sensual suggestiveness, he appeared to be very attuned to the feelings of others. Lezlie hadn't realized she had turned toward him until he glanced up, his eyes narrowing with his warm smile as he listened to Jim. She felt the pressure of his knee against hers beneath the table. It was a private communication no one else shared. The knowledge that Drew had noticed her and the continuing pressure of his leg bolstered Lezlie's spirits.

Dinner was a pleasant exchange of jokes and conversation over toe-tapping country music. Whatever was going on on the other side of the building brought loud stomps and cheers. Lezlie's curiosity was getting the better of her by the time Drew suggested they join the fun. Beyond the bar, a wooden dance floor was enclosed by a rough plank railing. Barstools lined the rail and there were tables to accommodate larger groups. Lights edged the banistered balcony. A red-white-and-blue flag sporting a huge star hung over the dance floor. Two fans did little to stir the smoke that hung in a cloud above the dancers. Lighted beer signs and confederate flags sided the huge Longhorn Saloon sign at the far end of the bar where a red steer watched over the festivities with a blank expression.

A smooth flow of couples circled the floor, moving in a unison of steps and rhythm. Several couples were more elaborate in their steps and Lezlie was fascinated. Everyone was dressed casually though some of the women wore ruffled blouses and skirts that swirled above intricately stitched boots. Some of the men wore leather vests or felt hats with decorative bands or feathers. The music was loud and infectious.

Charlie had located two tables at the far end, and Lezlie, with Drew at her back, worked her way through the crush of people.

"Somehow, I wouldn't have thought this to be your kind of place," Lezlie threw over her shoulder.

"I have quite varied interests, as you will learn," Drew replied, his breath against her ear. "Except in one important area." His strong hands squeezed her waist.

No sooner had they sat down and ordered a round of beers than Charlie and Maxine disappeared into the sea of people on the dance floor. Lezlie tried to keep them in sight but it was impossible. Drew propped his foot on Lezlie's chair, his arm draped around the back.

"Let me know when you're ready," he said easily.

Lezlie's quizzical stare met his. "Ready for what?"

"To dance," he answered simply.

Lezlie started to shake her head. "Drew, I don't know how...."

"It's a cinch."

"It doesn't look that easy."

"But it is. Come on, I'll show you." He was standing next to her, waiting for her answer.

"Drew, I can't go out there. I'll make a fool out of both of us."

"No, you won't. I'll show you back here." Drew took her hand and pulled her out of the chair. "It's very simple." He looked at the dance floor and pointed out a couple for her to watch. "This is a polka. All it is, is three steps."

Drew held her hands. He stepped back, drawing her with him. He showed her the simple steps and repeated the sequence of one-two-three, one-two-three in a low voice. Lezlie watched his feet, doubtful that she could learn the pattern. But within a few moments she realized it really wasn't difficult at all. At least not at the back of the bar where there weren't other couples to dodge.

"One thing to remember...you really just slide your feet along the floor. There's sawdust in the barrels to make it easier." Drew led her to the opening in the fence around the dance floor. His hand rested easily on her shoulder as he gave her a chance to watch. A polka was playing, a tune Lezlie had heard a few times on the radio.

Drew's voice warmed her cheek as he leaned down to talk to her. "See how the feet seem to slide along the floor? It's like a glide."

That is exactly how the dance looked. The dancers stepped and slid, the top part of their bodies stationary, except for the couples doing the more intricate turns and twirls.

"Ready?"

Lezlie's terrified gaze lifted to Drew's smiling countenance. "Drew, I don't want to make a total ass out of myself...."

"You won't," Drew reassured, his arm sweeping around her waist. "Trust me, Lezlie."

"Do I have a choice?" she groaned.

"No," Drew replied, drawing her onto the dance floor when an opening appeared. His hand slid along her shoulder under her hair and rested on her neck. His other hand held hers tightly. Lezlie's arm was around his broad back.

"This feels really strange," she said, remarking on the unusual stance. Inside, her stomach fluttered nervously.

"Here we go."

After the first few attempts to keep pace with his smooth lead, Lezlie got the hang of the sliding pace. His quiet voice reassured her as she watched his feet, making hers follow, uncertainly at first, but then with more confidence. They circled once and she had not misstepped. She glanced up from the floor, her enthusiastic smile mirrored in her eyes. "Hey, I think I've got it."

"What'd I tell you?" Drew held her securely, no longer counting the cadence of one-two-three. He took her around the floor several times, leading her so she wouldn't be bumped. When she seemed to be gaining confidence, his hand caressed her neck. "We're going to try a turn."

Lezlie's eyes flew to his face. "Oh, Drew, wait a minute...."

"You go into the turn on the step, then one-two-three, and come out of it on a step, then three step." He towered over her, and Lezlie tightened her grip on his hand. "That's right. Just hold on to me."

As the corner of the dance floor drew closer, Lezlie's chest tightened. She didn't want to make a fool of herself, not in front of Drew. She concentrated on following his lead, but she needn't have worried. Drew's gentle, though firm guidance indicated the direction of the turn. She closed her eyes, moving her feet in automatic rhythm, and she felt the gentle turn as it was completed.

Drew smiled down at her. "See? Now we'll do each corner."

Her hair swung behind Lezlie as Drew whirled her,

his hands guiding her body to follow his. After a few turns on the floor, she was beginning to relax, allowing Drew complete control of the dance. The sensation of whirling in the corners made her giddy with delight when they accomplished two continuous turns. When the dance ended she was somewhat disappointed, a reaction that made Drew laugh.

"Don't worry, we have the whole night to dance, if you want."

A cheer rippled through the crowd as a pop tune with a heavy beat replaced the country songs. Dancers clustered onto the floor very quickly, and Drew guided her to their table. Lezlie took a sip from the frosty mug of beer. "What are they doing?"

The dancers had made numerous lines from one end of the floor to the other and all the way across.

"It's exactly what it looks like," Drew answered. "A line dance."

Lezlie had never seen so many people do the same sequence of steps. Each person acted as an individual and danced without a partner.

"It will be a while before couples get the floor back," Drew warned, smiling. "Once the line dances start, the dancers don't want to give up the floor." Drew went on to explain the various dances of twenty-seven steps with dips, shimmies and four-sided turns. After the soulful country tunes, the Michael Jackson song seemed out of place, but it provided the perfect beat for the dance, which was a complex series of steps. When the group gyrations began, Lezlie shook her head in amazement.

"These dances require a lot of practice," Drew added.

"Can you do a line dance?"

"One or two of them, but they lose me with this one. I can't teach you a line dance, but you'll learn at least two dances tonight. We'll try the two-step next."

Lezlie was fascinated by the unity of the line dance. A few mavericks improvised more difficult sequences of steps while keeping perfect time to the music. "When did you learn how?"

"Meredith taught me."

The answer caused Lezlie to look up, but Drew's eyes were fixed on the dance floor.

"Whenever I was in Denver, we would all go out together. There was a club not too far from their house, like the Billy Bob's in Dallas." Drew shrugged, but he seemed more tense than he had been a moment before. "Meredith loved to dance; Greg didn't. So when we went out, I was her partner."

"Greg must have been very understanding," Lezlie said, but the lightness of the comment fell like a lead weight.

"He was in a lot of things, more than anyone can know."

The remark roused Lezlie's curiosity. The very core of her profession was people's emotions and their reactions, and she found her psychological expertise flowed into her personal life more often than she wished. But there was something very odd about the relationship between Meredith, Greg and Drew. Though Lezlie couldn't pinpoint the origin of her opinion, it was a feeling she got whenever Drew talked about his brother. The same questions she had asked silently before went through her mind again. Had Drew been jealous of his brother's family? Was it something to do with his parents? Or, Lezlie thought inexplicably, was Meredith somehow the cause of the estrangement between the brothers?

Lezlie studied Drew, a thousand questions whirling through her mind. He was absorbed in watching the dance. The dim light moved across his features, showing a strong chin, perceptive yet sensitive eyes and a sensual mouth. And as had happened before, there was a silent hint of some hidden pain in his expression. *What?* Lezlie wondered. Chiding herself for her curiosity, she decided she had to stop putting labels on Drew's actions. Whatever the problem had been, it didn't really affect her relationship with Drew, and she had no right to question it, except as a friend. But Drew was no longer only a friend—he was so very much more. The warm pressure of his fingers along her arm was a reminder of his importance to her.

Ken and Jamie were off somewhere, perhaps having their picture made at the improvised studio on the second level. Donna and Jim were dancing side by side and trading comments with happy smiles.

Charlie and Maxine returned to the tables, faces flushed and damp. Charlie swept off his hat. His graying hair was plastered to his damp skin. "We're getting too old for this sort of thing, Maxi," he puffed out, wiping his face and neck with a handkerchief.

"Speak for yourself," Maxi retorted coolly, but she rolled her eyes and expelled a tired breath as she eased into her chair. "But these dances *are* getting more complicated."

"It isn't that the dances are more complicated," Charlie wheezed. "It's that we can't do them as easily as we used to."

"Do you have to rub it in?" Maxi grumbled, tucking her shirt in with sharp jabs.

"If the shoe fits, honey...." Charlie grinned, wrapping his heavy arm around his wife's rigid shoulders. "You aren't getting older, baby, you're getting better."

"Bull." Maxi's caustic comment brought a guffaw of laughter from her husband.

"You've got me," Charlie said tenderly. Maxi's anger, contrived or not, dissolved, and she pressed herself against Charlie's side. "See what you've got to look forward to." He winked at Lezlie and Drew.

The assumption caused Lezlie to look at her hands.

"Hush up, Charlie," Maxi whispered.

"What'd I say?" he demanded.

Drew touched Lezlie's arm. "Let's dance," he said quietly. She put her hand in his. On the dance floor, conversation was related to the one, one-two-three cadence of the two-step. It was more complicated to master and several times Lezlie lost the pace, but easily regained it.

"I hope what Charlie said didn't upset you, Lezlie."

Lezlie lost the step again. "Seems I can't talk and

keep track of my feet on this one," she said with a smile, but it was a distant smile.

"Then just listen. Charlie didn't mean anything by what he said. It's just a standard comment. He wasn't assuming...."

"Oh yes he was. Darn!" Lezlie had lost the pace again. "But you're right, it was a familiar comment."

For the next three dances, Lezlie and Drew remained on the dance floor for another polka, a two-step and a slower polka. Lezlie's hand rested easily on Drew's shoulder until he whirled her into a turn. She was more at ease now. The dancing had reminded her of the soreness in her legs, which seemed to get more noticeable with each dance. When the third song ended, Lezlie groaned, "I can't dance another step," as she leaned against Drew. "My legs are about to fall off."

"It will get easier as you learn to relax more." Drew had a hold of her arm and propelled her through to the opening off the dance floor. The smoke and heat were like a drifting fog over the room. "Why don't we get some fresh air?"

Threading through the talking and laughing groups of customers, Lezlie had become acutely aware of Drew's possessive touch. Considering how some of the men openly ogled her, she was glad for his size and his deterring presence. One man actually reached out and touched Lezlie's hair as she passed, but Drew brushed his hand aside.

The air outside was a welcome reprieve from the stuffiness inside. The coolness as it brushed across

Lezlie's face was as fleeting as the touch of a butterfly's wing. Drew's boots echoed hollowly on the plank porch as he and Lezlie walked its length and then leaned against the railing.

Lezlie breathed deeply, enjoying the comfortable summer night. Drew was propped against the rail, his thumbs hooked in his pockets. He withdrew a cigarette, lit it and inhaled deeply. The tip glowed, brightening his face. As he exhaled, Lezlie gaped at him.

"I didn't know you smoked."

"It's an old habit, one I've found hard to break completely."

"But in all the time we've spent together, I didn't even guess...."

"That's because I don't smoke regularly, only when I feel tense."

Lezlie digested the comment before asking, "You're tense with me?"

A rakish smile drew the corners of Drew's mouth. "Lady, I have been more tense in the past few weeks than in the past few years. And yes, you're a large part of it, to be honest."

But Drew hadn't been completely honest. He had withheld saying that he had been living with a pendulum swinging over his head...the pendulum of the truth Merri might reveal. His large hand cupped Lezlie's cheek and his eyes bored into hers. "You're like a flower uncurling at the first streak of dawn. But the slightest disturbance will send you back into your safe little shell of petals."

It was such a tender parallel, and accurate, Lezlie

admitted. "That may have been true a few weeks ago."

"And now?"

"Now I'm not so certain." Lezlie turned and stared into the starry sky, listening to the music coming from inside the Longhorn. "I don't seem to be certain of very much lately," she commented, her voice so low that Drew had to strain to hear.

"Then we have the same problem." Drew was standing behind her. He put his hands on the railing, trapping Lezlie between his arms. Her hair blew against his face, its warm freshness teasing his nostrils. The thick auburn curls were aflame with highlights under the soft lighting. "Should I tell you how we can solve it?"

Lezlie's glance traveled across his broad chest where hair peeked out of his open shirt beneath the strong length of his neck. The mixture of cologne and smoke drifted across her face. She wanted to close her eyes and bury her face against the wall of his chest. Instead, she noticed the way his shirt was taut across the broad shoulders, outlining the muscles in his arms. "No," she said quietly. "You don't have to tell me. Can we go back in?"

Drew's dejected expression was exaggerated to restore her humor. "You can't elude my clutches forever, ma'am," he drawled in his best Texan imitation.

"Do you have a thing about impersonation?" Lezlie asked brightly.

"I have a 'thing' about a lot of things," he answered easily, adding under his breath, "you included."

When she smiled and shook her head, he slung his arm around her shoulders. "You're impossible."

"Oh, no, I'm not. I'm a real pushover, just try me."

Lezlie chuckled in spite of her futile attempt to redirect the conversation. Returning to the table, they found Ken and Jamie, but it looked as if the couple had probably argued. Donna and Jim sat very close, and for the next half hour they munched popcorn and sipped beer from frosty mugs. It had been the most perfect day, Lezlie was thinking, watching Drew's hand move expressively as his conversation ranged from sports to restaurants to the smooth ability of a particular couple on the dance floor.

When a slow ballad started, Drew turned around, interrupting Charlie's comment to look at Lezlie. The expression on his face made her legs feel weak while her heart raced crazily. Without a word, she took his offered hand and they made their way to the dance floor.

The ballad was a slow tender song that touched a cord of nostalgia as Drew's arm circled her shoulder. But this time he brought her close, so that Lezlie's face rested against his chest and her arm curled around his waist. She fit so well against him, her face turned into the curve of his neck. The spicy scent that clung to him paralyzed Lezlie in a cloud of touch and smell. The muscles in his back rippled as her fingers explored the rigid cords. His shirt was soft against her cheek while there was nothing at all soft about the body that was pressed to hers. She nuzzled into the curve of his shoulder, receiving an answering squeeze from Drew as he leaned over her, his hard chest teasing her breasts and his legs rubbing seductively against her thighs.

Lezlie closed her eyes, lost to the music and the rising desire Drew's closeness elicited. He folded his arm, bringing her hand against his chest while his forearm teased the curve of her breast. It was such an exquisite moment that Lezlie held her breath, afraid that it would all disappear. But Drew's warm breath in her hair, the touch of lips on her forehead and the embrace of his arm verified the experience. As his mouth drifted along her temple, Lezlie's pulse jumped.

The lights had been dimmed, so that the figures on the dance floor were indistinguishable. Lezlie turned her face upward, wanting only to feel the brush of his lips against the heat of her own.

Drew lowered his chin slightly, his own breath trapped within him as he became ensnared by Lezlie's unconscious invitation. His mouth claimed hers tenderly and the room became a blur in the light of the emotions that swirled around them. Lezlie's quiet sigh whispered against his chest as she dropped her face, and he wasn't certain she had spoken until she glanced up at him.

"I want to be alone with you," Lezlie said, shaken to the very core of her being by the intensity of her feelings. There was no uncertainty or hesitation betrayed in her eyes, only a vulnerable request Drew couldn't have refused, even if he had been so inclined. They had stopped dancing with Lezlie's words, but still he couldn't believe what she had said.

Her hand crept up his chest, touching his chin. "Did you hear me, Drew?"

Several flippant answers flitted through Drew's mind to test her certainty, but he couldn't put them into words. He brought her tight against his side as they left the dance floor, and quickly said good-night to their companions, offering no excuse for their early departure.

Hurrying to his car, Lezlie felt light-headed and happy. They piled into Drew's car, and the engine rumbled powerfully as he pulled away from the saloon. His hand held hers tightly as he drove, but a few miles from her house he pulled into an all-night doughnut shop.

Lezlie turned in confusion, but the severity of Drew's expression silenced her question. "I think we have to talk, Lezlie. Why don't we have some coffee."

"I don't want to talk," she returned, "and I don't want any coffee. I meant exactly what I said. I've had a wonderful time today and I like your friends, but I want to be with just you. We could have coffee at my house."

Drew raked a hand through his hair. He didn't know how much longer he could put a damper on his feelings for Lezlie. Being alone with her the way she suggested could tear apart his willpower if she made the slightest indication that she might want to explore the physical side of their attraction. He was no longer simply attracted to her body. He loved her gentleness, her vulnerability and her quick wit. But if he told her, those very words might send her flying from him. Through the darkness, he saw her smile and was lost. He put the car in reverse and backed out of the lot as Lezlie's head came to rest on his shoulder.

The drive passed in a blur of lights as Lezlie closed her eyes, but each time she glanced at Drew she was fascinated by his strong profile. She could feel the tremor in his hand where hers rested, and a smile of compassion lit her eyes. *He is such a wonderful person,* she thought happily. And she was glad to be with him, speeding toward a haven of solitude where she would have him all to herself. They got out of his car and strolled up the walkway in silence, but his hand was a steady reassurance. She opened the door and walked in, turning around as he followed.

"Do you really want coffee?" she asked politely.

Drew was staring at her and he slowly shook his head. He stretched his arms toward Lezlie and she walked into his warm embrace. A quiet sigh escaped Drew as he pulled her against him, his body a shield for her softer emotions, his desire a flame for hers. He hugged her close, his arms wrapping all the way around her slight form as he buried his face in her neck.

Lezlie's hands slid up along his back and clutched his shoulders. A deep peace had settled within her: the peace of acceptance. So when Drew raised his head to voice a silent question, there was no longer any thought of denying what she had wanted so desperately. His head lowered and Lezlie's mouth parted, waiting in suspended agony for the claim of his lips. When the tender assault came, Lezlie's senses flashed to life and a jolt went through her. Her breasts pressed into the muscled wall of his chest, her hips sought the pressure of his, where the evidence of his desire thrilled her. His kiss scorched, branded and set her on fire, her body aching for the intimacy of his touch.

Drew cupped her head, his mouth ravaging hers with an assault as old as time itself. She yielded to him fully, her mouth opening to accept his tongue and its tantalizing exploration. He caressed her back, his hands sliding along the curve of her hips. *She is so incredibly pliant,* Drew thought. Her body reacted to his touch so completely that it fairly took his breath away. He leaned over her, forcing her back, the lower part of their bodies more intimately intertwined as he drew the honey from her mouth, all the while tempering the fierceness of his desire for her.

Lezlie arched her neck, shivers of delight racing along her skin in the wake of Drew's warm lips. She could not suppress a groan as his tongue traced circles on the sensitive skin of her shoulder. Deep within a swirling ache had become a whirlpool, spiraling and twisting through her until she could hardly bear it. But the ache was an exquisite realization of her own needs... needs that would build and bubble until Drew brought forth all she held within, and she would freely succumb.

Drew followed the enticing curve of her back, his hand tracing the gentle curves. His fingers lingered on her neck where he sought evidence of a small gold chain from which a wedding band had been suspended. He hoped he wouldn't find it, but he had to know.

As Drew's fingers caressed and explored, Lezlie sensed his aim. She leaned away from him, just far enough to look into his face. "It's not there," she said breathlessly. "I took it off that day you walked out."

"I thought you might have just taken it off when we reached the river, so you wouldn't lose it."

Lezlie shook her head. Her eyes darkened with her words. "Make love to me, Drew."

"I want to. I've never wanted anything more in my life," Drew moaned, his arms a crushing embrace around her. "But I don't want there to be any regrets, any second thoughts...."

"There won't be," Lezlie murmured, lifting her face to meet his kiss.

Drew's lips claimed hers in a kiss no longer tempered, but filled with all the raw passion that had been held at bay. His fingers speared through her hair, the intensity of his desire drawing a sigh of surrender from Lezlie as she eagerly sought to mold herself to the curve of his body. She clutched him tightly, wanting only to be closer than the barrier of clothes permitted. The next moment, Drew had swept her off her feet and into his powerful arms. Lezlie snuggled against him as he carried her into the darkened bedroom. Drew swept the covers from the bed and gently laid her upon the cool sheets. His gaze pierced hers, but her smile assured him there were no ghosts between them and he lay down beside her.

The moonlight streaked into the room, its silvery rays an iridescent cocoon. Lezlie's eyes glittered as she watched him discard his shirt, then saw the play of emotions upon his face as he slowly stripped her sweater away. Goose bumps rose on her skin as he stared at her, his hands gently following the path his eyes had taken. His touch was a gentle caress tracing the line of her shoulders, exploring the hollow of her throat where her pulse jumped beneath his finger. He didn't want to rush a single part of their intimacy, so he took his time, watching the changing expressions on Lezlie's face.

When Drew replaced his fingers with his mouth, the warmth of his tongue brought a gasp of surprise from Lezlie. Her breasts ached, thrusting upward to meet the touch that flickered closer and then moved away. Lezlie arched her neck as his lips followed the smooth tendons toward her chin. He lay against her side, touching her with his mouth. She wanted to feel the weight of his body as her fingers ran through the curls at the back of his head to bring his mouth back to hers. She turned slightly, her hips arching toward him. His kiss ravaged the sweetness of her mouth and his warm breath heated her already-enflamed skin.

Lezlie's hands shook as he pulled away and sat up, his back bowed as he pulled off one of his boots and dropped it to the floor with a heavy thud before the other followed. He gripped Lezlie's ankles, his gaze raking the length of her slender figure before he began to remove her shoes. He gently kneaded her feet and then her ankles before his hands slid up the legs of her jeans to caress the curves of her calves.

Lezlie's breath caught in her throat as he straddled her hips. Both of them still wore their jeans. The fire in his eyes as he slowly lowered his weight onto her fairly scorched her skin. His hips settled between her legs, and a heavy sigh escaped her with the contact.

Propped on his arms, Drew's opened mouth followed the rise of one breast, lingering for a moment before moving to the other, his tongue tasting and touching but never claiming. His hand was shaking as he unfastened the snap of her silky bra, exposing the fullness of the throbbing peaks. He nuzzled the valley between her breasts and Lezlie writhed, the movement of the lower part of his body taunting her with its promise of ecstasy.

Her voice was a broken whisper as she cried out his name, but the word ended in a sweet sigh when his mouth returned to hers. The heavy mat of hair on his chest tickled the aroused peaks of her breasts. She was aflame with sensation, with desires the depth of which she had never guessed existed. Drew was the total sphere of her pleasure, the focus of her passion and the man of her desire. A shudder raced through her, settling in the hidden part of her that was quickly losing all control beneath his sensual onslaught.

She almost cried out as his lips sought the peak he had deliberately avoided for so long and settled over the tip with moist warmth to trace dizzying circles that sent her insides into spasms of delight. His hips pressed her into the softness of the bed, slowly tantalizing her with a gentle motion, which she answered. She arched toward him, silently cursing the barrier of the jeans, but in the next few moments the barriers were removed, swept away by an unsteady hand that fumbled with the snaps and zippers. Naked beneath his gaze, Lezlie felt no embarrassment as she saw the appreciation in his eyes mingled with a passion that sent her heart racing. This time when his body stretched the length of hers, there were no barriers to hinder their delight.

Lezlie's arms wound around his back. She arched toward him, her hair tumbling across the pillow as she raised up, her face pressing into the furry hair of his chest. She wanted to draw him into her softness to appease the coil of desire twisting within. Heat radiated from him as his body settled onto hers, his mouth claiming hers and his kiss mingling with her moan of surrender. His back rippled beneath her searching fingers, while his mouth elicited a sea of sensations as it traced a fiery path between her breasts and abdomen.

Words welled within Drew, but he was afraid to speak and shatter the rising ecstasy with the words that filled his head. He would show Lezlie how much he cared by sharing himself in a way that would need no definition. He caressed the length of her slender body, a smile touching his mouth at the quiet noises in her throat as she arched to meet the instant when they would, for a moment, become one, joined in an age-old dance of love.

Lezlie's limbs trembled, her desire fanning out to engulf her. Her eyes glittered brightly as Drew rose above her, then lowered to capture the final intimacy, one she happily met. Her breath caught in her throat as she bore his full weight and became part of a union that offered her the heights of desire. A deep inner satisfaction mingled with her passion. She held Drew tightly, her eyes closed as he rained soft kisses the length of her neck, then returned to her mouth for a slow sensual exploration. Nothing about his lovemaking was going to be hurried, Lezlie knew; there was no need. She wanted to savor each touch, each caress in their surrender to each other, and Drew was obviously of the same mind. He stroked her hair, his fingers diving into the heavy mass to raise her face to accept plundering kisses that shattered her thoughts into shards of feeling.

Every inch of her body cried out for his touch, for a release from the tormenting ecstasy mounting within. When Lezlie reached up to touch his face, his hand captured hers and their fingers intertwined while his other hand slipped beneath her, drawing her hips into the perfect mold of his.

Lezlie was soaring, her senses exploding into slivers of ecstasy. Her mind closed to everything except Drew and the incredible fulfillment only a whisper away. Her shallow breathing fanned his face and his name died on her lips beneath a kiss that sent her spiraling toward a dizzying pinnacle of delight. The descent was a blissful return with Drew's arms and kiss prolonging the moment. His warm lips caressed her chin, her cheek, and teased her mouth.

Drew held her close, as the tremors in her body radiated through his. He continued his gentle assault, his body still merged with hers, tantalizing her to soar again. But his tempered fierceness gave way beneath his passion, and Lezlie readily climbed with him, reaching for ecstasy once again. The image of Drew's face exploded into a thousand little prisms as they rose together, each caught in the ecstasy of the other and then slowly reconnected. Still, he did not leave her, but adjusted his weight as his hands cradled her and his breathing became more normal.

Drew cupped Lezlie's chin and planted gentle kisses on her softened lips. "I didn't hurt you, did I?" he murmured.

Lezlie shook her head, still trying to regain her breath. She snuggled into the curve of his neck, kissing the strong cords of his throat.

Drew's husky laugh rumbled in his throat. "Unless you want another round, I suggest you stop." He moved against her, and she sucked in her breath. "Well?"

Wonder filled Lezlie's eyes as she looked straight into his shadowed face. She was suddenly very tired, her limbs caught in a lethargy that made every movement an effort. She wanted to stay like this forever, and fall asleep with Drew still cradling her. As he rolled over to lie beside her, a sudden chill swept over Lezlie. Drew pulled up the covers and tucked them over her. He touched her lips once before his arm circled her waist and he pulled her back up against his chest. His legs fit into the curve of hers, her bottom pressed into his hips.

Lezlie yawned wearily, quickly succumbing to the blissful softness of sleep. She drifted in a dreamlike doze of contentment. A tender whisper tickled her ear. Had she dreamed it was Drew's husky voice and gentle "I love you, Lezlie," that sent a ripple through her consciousness? A vision formed in her mind. In her sleep she smiled at the man with sandy hair and incredibly blue eyes.

CHAPTER TWELVE

LEZLIE AWOKE SLOWLY, the trill of birds and bright sunshine filtering through her sleep and rousing her. A memory of the night before flitted through her mind, bringing a smile in its wake. She rolled over, stretched out her hand and her smile dissolved. The place beside her was empty. Sitting up, she listened for any noise in the house, but there was only silence. If it weren't for the indentation in the other pillow, she might have wondered if she had dreamed it all. A tingle went through her. No, it hadn't been a dream. Still, why had Drew left without waking her? And when had he left?

Before Lezlie could puzzle further, the phone rang and Drew's cheerful voice greeted her.

"And how are you this morning?"

"Quite well, actually," Lezlie answered.

"Any regrets?" Though humor edged his voice, there was a serious undertone to the simple question.

"Only one," she replied. "Why did you sneak off during the night?"

"Sneak off?" Drew answered with chagrin. "Sneak off! What do you mean? I tried to wake you up and I might as well have been trying to move a mountain. You were out like a light."

"I'm a deep sleeper, and that doesn't answer my question."

"Sweetheart, you don't just sleep, you become comatose," Drew teased. "And since I didn't ask you about staying the night before you fell asleep, and I couldn't wake you up, I thought I would leave... and not compromise you."

"Compromise me how?" she retorted playfully.

"Oh, you know, just a worrisome little thought about nosy neighbors who see a man leaving your house early in the morning."

"You didn't want to besmirch my reputation, then. That's very thoughtful, but I had hoped to wake up with you here."

"Next time I'll know," Drew said with a husky promise. "But I could imagine your neighbors' comments...."

"They probably wouldn't have thought a thing about it."

"Don't count on it."

"Is that personal experience talking?"

"Call it what you will, but it's common sense to me. If it doesn't matter to you, then it sure as hell doesn't mean a flip to me."

Lezlie laughed and then became more serious. "Last night meant a lot to me, Drew."

"I know, sweetheart. It meant that much to me, too. Actually, that was the real reason I was trying to wake you up."

"Oh ho, the truth comes out! You had designs on my person, not on my reputation."

"I cannot tell a lie," Drew answered lightly. "I had designs."

"Then why are you there and I'm here?"

"Oh, sweetheart, there is where I want to be." Drew hesitated. "But I promised to take Merri to the Six Flags amusement park today. I was calling to see if you could go with us. She'd get a real kick out of it." His voice lowered to a husky whisper. "I won't say what I hope to get."

"I detect a hint of lechery," Lezlie admonished.

"I never hint. What you hear is an all-out proposition."

"It's a little early in the day for propositions over the telephone." When Drew chuckled, Lezlie could almost envision the small lines creasing at the corners of his eyes.

"I could come over and make it in person...but then we might not make it to Six Flags."

"True," Lezlie mused.

"Will you come with us?"

Lezlie glanced at the clock. "What time will you pick me up?"

They agreed on one hour later, and Lezlie stretched lazily. The retrospection of Drew's lovemaking sapped her will to move. The pillow held his scent as well as the impression of his head. She scrambled out of bed to banish the melting memories.

An hour later, Merri bounded up to the door followed by her uncle. But any display of affection between Drew and Lezlie was transmitted only within the warm glances they exchanged.

The day was humid and hot, but once they arrived at Six Flags Over Georgia the heat was relieved by a good splashing from the churning waters of the Log

Run. Their damp clothes cooled their skin then dried quickly in the warm breezes as they went from ride to ride, sidetracked only momentarily by hot-dog stands and cotton-candy vendors. Merri bubbled like a sparkling stream, her enthusiasm a boundless energy that left Lezlie drained. As she and Drew collapsed onto a bench near the boardwalk and Merri went to explore the game vendors, Lezlie sighed heavily. Absently, she watched a family with a young son pass where they were sitting. The familiar heartbreak she had carried for so long had diminished. In its place was a sad wistfulness perhaps, but there were no unpleasant feelings.

Drew reached over and touched her hand. "Sad thoughts?" he asked compassionately.

Lezlie glanced over at Drew. "Not sad thoughts, just nice memories."

Drew also watched the family for a moment. "Memories are the one thing no one can ever take away," he mused, "and that can never be replaced by anything or anyone." His fingers laced with hers and a smile tilted the corners of his mouth. "That doesn't mean there can't be new memories."

Lezlie contemplated his comments as Drew, groaning wearily, answered an excited summons from Merri to win her a teddy bear at the ring toss. Never had Lezlie seen or heard any impatience on Drew's part at the demands his niece made on him. She had to admire his ability to adjust to circumstances thrust upon him. And she appreciated the difficulty of assuming a parental role. She had been wrong when she thought him insensitive and too tied up in his business to give the child the emotional support she needed. Because that was exactly what he was doing without applying any pressure for Merri to accept him as anything more than an authority figure.

Lezlie was puzzled for a moment until she realized that that same sensitivity had been used with her, only in a different form. And his simple statement had reassured her that he understood her feelings and the fact that her husband and son would always be a part of her. She had certainly underestimated Drew Bradinton, she thought with a rueful shake of her head, but she was glad she had.

By the time they left the park, Merri's energy had waned and she sat quietly in the cramped space behind the car's front seats, holding a fuzzy teddy bear. They returned to Drew's house where Mrs. Cates had left a cold-plate supper of ham, coleslaw and potato salad with a large pitcher of ice tea.

Merri rummaged through the refrigerator, then the freezer. "She made us Popsicles," she said gleefully, keeping up a constant chatter as they set the table.

Halfway through the meal, Merri turned toward her uncle. "Will you ask her, Uncle Drew?"

Lezlie glanced up from her plate. "Ask me what?" she said with a cautious smile.

"Merri was wondering if it would be all right for her to miss Tuesday's appointment. There's a birthday party for one of her friends at the skating rink—"

"And then everybody's going back to Jennifer's house to swim and roast hot dogs," Merri added, unable to contain her excitement.

"Or what about rescheduling for another day?" Drew suggested.

"This week is really booked," Lezlie said. "Besides, Merri and I were going to have a very specific talk." This last remark was directed toward Merri, who dropped her gaze to a spot on the table. "Merri?"

"I don't want to miss Jennifer's party," Merri explained. "We can talk when I get back, can't we?"

The request held a plea for compromise and Lezlie gave it serious consideration. Forcing Merri to keep an appointment that conflicted with what she wanted to do wasn't exactly conducive to a relaxed atmosphere, considering the nature of the discussion they would have. Was there any harm in putting it off, Lezlie wondered. Drew remained silent, not voicing any opinion.

"I have been thinking about it, like you said," Merri pressed. "But do I have to miss the party?"

"Will you promise that we will talk about it as soon as you get back from camp?" Lezlie was uncertain about her suggestion the minute it was out of her mouth. Was Merri using Jennifer's party to put off the inevitable discussion? Or was she merely ruled by her own wishes, as many children tended to be? In any case, Lezlie didn't see any reason to foul up the plans. Merri was adjusting very well and two weeks wouldn't necessarily make that much difference in her progress. Still, a niggling doubt remained in Lezlie's mind.

"I promise," Merri agreed.

After dinner, Merri ran up to her room to call her

friend and accept the invitation. Drew leaned back in his chair, puzzled. "Does canceling the appointment bother you, Lezlie?"

"Not exactly, but we were going to talk about the accident. I can't help wondering if Merri is simply trying to stall. And that worries me."

"Well, I can promise you she will come in to see you as soon as she gets back."

Lezlie smiled. "I don't really think there's anything to worry about." But for some reason she couldn't define, she wasn't 100 percent certain of her young patient's motives. But she couldn't worry about it now. The decision had been made.

"One thing I do know is that if you keep feeding me, I won't keep my girlish figure," she fretted, helping Drew stack the dishes. She was standing at the counter as his arms came around her waist.

Drew kissed the tip of her nose. "And such a girlish figure it is," he murmured, his hand covering the flatness of her stomach.

"I was wondering if you had noticed," Lezlie quipped, placing the plates in the sink.

"Oh, I've noticed, believe me, I've noticed," Drew confirmed, running his lips along the curve of her jaw. "I've wanted to do this all day. Absolute torture having you so close and not being able to touch you."

Lezlie closed her eyes, reveling in the sweet pleasure that coursed through her veins. But Merri could walk in at any moment. "It won't do for Merri to find us cavorting in the kitchen," she admonished, though it took every ounce of her willpower.

"I like the sound of that," Drew whispered, placing a lingering kiss on her parted lips. With a groan, he drew away, snatching up a dish towel. He disappeared into the living room and when he returned, he was grinning like a Cheshire cat.

"You look very pleased with yourself," Lezlie commented suspiciously.

"I just called the girl next door. She's going to come over and stay with Merri while I take you home. I told her it may be a couple of hours... or so."

"The 'or so' sounds interesting." Lezlie grinned. "I wouldn't want you to be pressed for time."

"I'm never that pressed," Drew returned glibly, wrapping his arms around her for a moment.

"I hope you can wait while I take a shower," Lezlie frowned, feeling grimy from their trip to the park.

"Only if you want me to scrub your back."

"You've got a deal," Lezlie replied seductively.

Drew touched her chin, lost in the fathomless depths of her gray eyes. Her hair, left free, flowed around her shoulders, and her cheeks were a rosy pink. She was a completely different woman from the rigid Dr. Garrett he had met a few weeks ago. Her natural sense of humor had surfaced, erasing the seriousness he had seen their first few meetings. Last night appeared to have destroyed the last of her doubts where he was concerned. And he had no intention of disrupting the nurturing trust she had shown him.

IT WAS FOUR HOURS LATER when Drew reluctantly got ready to leave Lezlie's house. Pulling her against him for a final caress, he cupped her chin and stared into her eyes. But Lezlie could not guess his thoughts. They had arrived at her house and had soon become a tumble of limbs as Drew swept her into his arms and swung her around. The moment his lips had touched hers in complete possession, she had surrendered to him and to her own desire.

With actions meant to incite her senses, he had slowly disrobed them both, lingering over his labor until Lezlie could have screamed in frustration. His hands were unsteady as he unhooked the waist of her shorts, which dropped to the floor, soon followed by the rest of their clothing.

The mirror reflected their nakedness, making Lezlie very conscious of his masculine build in contrast to her own slender figure. Her skin was translucently pale beside his tanned torso. Playfully, Lezlie scratched the hair on his chest. She liked the feel of the furry curls and rigid muscles rippling beneath. Her hands were trapped between them as their bodies met in an intimate caress before he pulled her into the shower and under the ice-cold spray.

Lezlie squealed in protest as the frigid water almost took her breath away. Drew laughed huskily until she lurched backward, knocking him against the cold tile. The length of her body slid along his as he crouched down, pulling her down with him to keep her away from the faucet.

Drew's sudden laughter echoed off the walls of the small bathroom. "I thought we were going to take a shower," he stuttered as Lezlie squirmed in his arms.

"It's too cold," Lezlie cried, goose bumps rising on her skin and shivers causing her teeth to chatter.

Drew seemed totally unperturbed by the frigid temperature. "It's supposed to be good for the circulation."

"Not for someone who is naturally cold to start with," Lezlie fussed. "It will take me hours to warm up."

"No, it won't," Drew said with a grin.

The water was still pelting them while she turned on the hot water and warmed the assault.

"Well, you could have warned me," she grumbled, clasping her arms across her chest in an effort to stop shivering.

"Come here," Drew said, pulling her toward him. They were sitting on the bottom of the tub with the shower spraying them. Drew soaped his hands and a fluffy washrag, his eyes sparkling with promise. Between kisses and nibbling on her ear, he slowly and meticulously bathed her. His large hands warmed her skin wherever the smoothing strokes wandered, and soon she wasn't cold any longer. Lezlie's mind was filled with anticipation.

When he was through, he politely handed her a bar of soap. "Are you still cold?" he asked with a grin. Lezlie's luminous eyes met his and she shook her head. "Well then, it's my turn." He smiled, folding his hands behind his head.

Lezlie suddenly felt very shy. The soap was slippery as she lathered his chest, which tapered to a narrow waist and hips. His muscles were taut cords, well-defined in his shoulders as well as in his long legs.

Lezlie was enthralled with her chore. Sometime during her task, he had stopped looking at the wall and his steady gaze had settled on her. Water was beaded on her flushed face and followed an interesting path between her breasts and across her flat stomach.

Her quiet attention to her task was belied by the rapid rise and fall of her breasts as their gazes locked. It gave him profound pleasure to know he affected her in the same way she did him. He stood up beneath the spray and drew her into his arms, the water mingling with a searing kiss.

Thick fluffy towels barely dried their damp skin before they fell onto the bed, Drew's long frame completely covering Lezlie's. He stroked her cheek, mesmerized by the perfection of her face. Her hair clung to her back and soaked the sheets. But neither of them noticed.

Their lovemaking the previous night had been a tentative exploration. Now Drew meticulously sought out each tempting curve. Lezlie's flesh trembled beneath his touch. But she was learning, too, her gentle touch bringing a groan to his throat. Her skin was like velvet beneath his hand and searching mouth. His lips traveled along her shoulder and he turned her over to continue his exploration. He wanted to know every hidden corner, every secret place that brought her pleasure. His hand followed the curve at the small of her back and was replaced by his warm mouth.

"You have the most tempting curve, just... about...here," he murmured, his lips tracing the path of his hand to the dimples at her hips.

Lezlie pressed her face into the pillow. He was doing incredible things to her as his touch lingered on her inner thigh, teasing and stroking. As he stretched beside her, she turned and propped up on her elbows, her face level with his.

Drew lay on his back and pulled her across his heavy chest. Her hair fell around them in a heavy sodden mass as his tongue touched the corner of her mouth and his kiss began an assault that left her breathless. He swept her hair back as she arched to allow him better access to the sensitive skin of her neck. He brought her on top of him so that her hips settled firmly upon his.

Lezlie dropped her face into the hollow of his throat. She could feel the steady beat of his pulse beneath her searching lips. But Drew ended her game as he lifted her easily and brought her breasts toward his mouth. A jolt shot through her and clutched her insides as his moist mouth teased one aroused peak, then moved to the other. Then once again, she lay along the length of him, his furry chest a soft cushion for her head. The hair felt good beneath her face as she burrowed against him, her senses aflame with the tantalizing movement of his hips beneath hers.

He kissed her then, drawing the sweetness from her mouth as his body merged with hers. A gasp died in Lezlie's throat and bubbled into a sigh of delight. He held her hips tightly against him, tantalizing, teasing and demanding a response she could not hide. He stared into her face, watching the play of pleasure across her features before she sought his kiss, totally lost to the desire building within her and seeking relief.

Swept along by their mutual passion, Drew slowly rotated until she was beneath him. She was so beautiful and so responsive, her passion driving Drew beyond the bounds of control. He plunged deeply into her enveloping softness, her quickening breath a ragged whisper in his ear.

Lezlie clutched him to her, her body answering the demand of both their needs. They climbed and soared, racing toward a crescendo of ecstasy that left their skin clinging damply. As Lezlie crossed the threshold, her senses exploding into fragments of lights and feeling, Drew's name was upon her lips and in her heart. He was heavy on top of her, but it was a weight Lezlie gladly bore. His warm lips remained on hers, the gentle probing prolonging the ecstasy and sweetening the descent. They remained locked in the tender embrace for a long time, sharing the joy of mutual fulfillment.

Lezlie closed her eyes, awed by the incredible fervor Drew brought forth. He stroked her flushed skin, his smile sending a bubbling happiness through Lezlie. And she almost sighed with contentment as he began to brush her hair. The slow steady strokes were as sensual as any caress. A quiescent lethargy mingled with the soothing strokes of Drew's hands, and her eyes drooped closed.

Drew impulsively placed a tender kiss on her temple. "You're all I've ever wanted in a lover... and in a woman, Lezlie." His voice was quiet and Lezlie's eyes opened slowly to meet his tender gaze. She reached up, drawing his mouth to hers.

"I'm glad. You please me, too," she whispered, drawing his mouth to hers.

More than anything, Drew wanted to tell her exactly how he felt about her and his speculations about the future. Still, he wondered if it was too soon. Would his declaration of love shatter the tender thread that had brought her surrender?

Instead of revealing the direction of his thoughts, he began to make love to her again, momentarily content with her unbridled response. But he couldn't withhold his hopes for a future, any more than he could stop wanting her. He couldn't get enough of the sweet joy he found in her arms; and she eagerly shared his sentiments. He only prayed she also shared his hopes for the future—a future together as more than lovers.

Later, as Lezlie puttered in the kitchen, she was aware of Drew's scrutiny and wondered what deep thoughts plagued him. She handed him a glass of lemonade and returned his slight smile. "I've been wondering about something you said a while back," she said coyly. "Something about being friends that you would explain. Remember?"

Drew leaned against the counter, a towel draping his hips.

"You said you would tell me someday? How about now?"

Drew caught her as she walked to the sink, and pulled her against him. "There's not that much to tell," he said with a wink. "I was referring to an old saying about friends making the best lovers. In this case, it certainly proved true."

Lezlie stared up at him. "You mean, you knew even then that this would happen?"

"No," Drew drawled, "but I certainly hoped it

would. And I thought given time, you would see things as I did."

Lezlie's glance dropped to the wall of his chest. How could he have known what she hadn't even known herself? He had broken through the protective shell she had built around herself. She had been so secure in her love for Michael that she had feared involvement with Drew might bring with it the guilt of betrayal to her husband's memory. But Drew had dispelled her worry and brought her out of the past. Another thought worried Lezlie. Was theirs an affair that might last a few weeks or months? Then what? The uncertainty flickered through Lezlie's eyes.

Drew touched the small frown that had settled on her forehead. "Let's take it slow for the present," Drew said quietly. "We have all the time we need to discover what we feel about each other, although I already know what you mean to me. I don't ever want to lose you, Lezlie. It's taken me too long to find you."

He swept her into a hug that took her breath away and chased the lingering doubts from her mind. It would have to be enough for now.

THE WEEK swept by in hectic activity. Lezlie and Drew agreed not to see each other the few nights before Merri left for camp. They would have two whole weeks, Drew promised meaningfully. And each night they shared a long telephone conversation that left Lezlie happy but strangely restless.

Lezlie dictated notes of her sessions from the day the previous week when she had hurried to the hospital after Donna had called. The notes included her session with Merri. During the canceled hour of Merri's Tuesday appointment, she reviewed some questionnaires and tests Merri had completed during their first few appointments at Lezlie's office. She reread the brief stories Merri had written to accompany a series of pictures. Some of the writings clearly revealed Merri's loneliness and sense of displacement. But one story brought a smile to Lezlie for it indicated a streak of independence in the girl. She knew Merri's responses would be different now, and that she had at least partially accepted her parents' deaths, but there were still areas she and Lezlie needed to investigate. Lezlie made a note to herself for the direction of their first session after Merri's return from camp.

A quick lunch with Donna one afternoon broke up the week, as did dinner one evening with Lezlie's mother. Donna was happy and relieved. Ann Clarke, Elizabeth's mother, was interviewing housekeepers and actively seeking a job that would take her out of the house. Elizabeth had another chance.

Lezlie's mother was off on another trip the following week. When they met for dinner, Lezlie was strangely silent, listening to her mother's plans for a two-week vacation in the Cayman Islands.

"Your vacation sounds lovely," Lezlie commented.

Her daughter's distraction had not escaped Margaret's perceptive eye. "How did your outing go with Drew?" she asked, unerringly coming to the cause of Lezlie's silence.

Her mother's perception never failed to surprise Lezlie. She could always count on her mother's understanding and support. That never changed. And at the moment, her life was besieged by changes. Her thoughts and feelings were not the same anymore. She laid her fork on the table and folded her hands, her serious gaze meeting her mother's reassuring one. "Mom, how can you know for certain that you're making the right decision...? I mean, that what you feel isn't a substitute for something else?"

"I take it this pertains to Drew."

Lezlie nodded her head. "I thought I had my life all figured out, but he's come along and disrupted everything."

"And that surprises you?" Margaret smiled.

"Not really," Lezlie admitted. "But I thought I would feel some guilt or betrayal about Michael...."

"And you don't?"

"No," Lezlie answered quietly.

Margaret was relieved by the answer. "Lezlie, it has been two years. Perhaps it's time to move on to other things...and other people. Is that the problem?"

Lezlie's tear-bright gray pools lifted to her mother's gaze. "I'm afraid," she said.

Margaret's eyes softened. She knew the kind of fear Lezlie was experiencing. It was the fear of being hurt as deeply as she had been after the accident. Though her daughter hadn't suffered a physical injury, the emotional blow had nearly undone her. And it had left her afraid of commitment.

"Everyone is afraid of change, Lezlie. But you can't let fear rule your life, which you have allowed these past two years. You can't refuse to be a part of life because it has some risks. You had no way of knowing when you fell in love with Michael that your life together would be interrupted by tragedy. Life doesn't come with those kinds of guarantees." Margaret took her daughter's hand. "You're over the hurdle, Lezlie. But don't let an intangible fear ruin it for you. Drew is a very rare type of man. I know some of his qualities from the conversation we had in your office while you talked with Merri. Michael and Mike were a very special part of your life, never to be forgotten, but it's time to let go and move on." Margaret smiled gently. "But you already know that, don't you?"

"I think I had almost come to that conclusion, but it helps to hear it from another perspective."

"So, tell me, how serious is your relationship?" Margaret asked. When Lezlie looked at her mother, an inner radiance touched every feature of her face. Margaret smiled happily. "Never mind, dear. I know. And I am so glad."

"I am, too," Lezlie added, almost in awe of the realization.

Margaret chuckled and soon they were laughing, hugging each other with deep affection. As Lezlie left her mother's house, Margaret watched from her window. Her daughter was a different woman, her jaunty step and swinging hair evidence of her inner contentment. It was so hard to let go...of a loved one, a husband or a child. Lezlie had faced the finality of her loss. Tears tracked down Margaret's cheeks. She understood so well how Lezlie felt. She had listened and comforted her for the lonely months after the death of her son-in-law and grandson and watched in helpless sadness as Lezlie sealed herself off from others. Her tears were brought on by the relief that Lezlie wouldn't spend her life alone, not if Drew had anything to say about it.

The following evening Lezlie left her office quite late. Her phone was ringing as she fumbled with her keys to unlock the door. Merri was calling to say goodbye.

"Are you all set?" Lezlie asked.

"I think so," Merri answered.

"And how was Jennifer's party?"

"Oh, it was great. It went on all day and then Jennifer had a slumber party. It was really a neat birthday. Then I had to come home and help Mrs. Cates pack my stuff."

The lament of the last comment made Lezlie smile. "Well, it will all be worth it when you get to camp and start having fun."

"I guess," Merri said.

"You don't sound very excited."

"Oh, it'll be fun," Merri said, and her voice dropped to a quiet sigh. "But Uncle Drew only agreed so he wouldn't have to take me to Denver."

The admission caught Lezlie off guard. She could sense the little girl's dejection. "Have you asked him?"

"He's too busy right now."

"Well, why don't you ask him when you get back from camp."

"Maybe," Merri said. "I have to go now."

Lezlie hung up, feeling unsettled by the conversation. Drew called as he did each night. They talked for some time about the progress on the Roswell Road complex. Drew sounded tired, and Lezlie debated telling him of her conversation with Merri. But Drew took the decision out of her hands.

"I think now that the time has come, Merri's a little hesitant about this trip."

"I got that impression, too, along with one that she wants to go to Denver."

Drew sighed. "She's mentioned that, too. I told her I would think about it and when she gets home, we'll decide."

"Well, at least you didn't tell her no."

"I might as well have from her reaction. She sulked in her room all evening. But I can't just drop everything right now."

"I know that," Lezlie agreed. "And I told her to ask you again when she gets home. I think she just needs some reassurance."

There was a long pause before Drew said quietly, "I've missed you, Lezlie. Have you been thinking about me?"

"Some," Lezlie replied.

"That's not very reassuring," Drew wheedled. "I could come over...."

"We have Friday night and then the whole weekend." Lezlie gently reminded him of their agreement. Drew had felt he should spend most of his evenings with Merri before she left for camp.

"I'll hold you to it."

You don't have to, Lezlie said silently.

"Do you know what I'm thinking right now?" Drew asked.

"I have an idea...."

"Well, let's just say I have a question for you. Have you ever made love on a water bed?"

A surge of titillation flushed Lezlie's cheeks at the suggestiveness in his voice. "Can I assume you intend to broaden my horizons?"

"Most definitely," he promised.

"How's the dollhouse coming?" Lezlie asked pointedly. The warmth in his voice flowed through her, making it difficult to think.

"You're changing the subject."

"If I don't, I'm liable to find you on my doorstep."

"That idea has terrific potential."

"The dollhouse," Lezlie prodded.

They talked for some time about the finishing touches Drew was putting on Merri's birthday gift, which would be ready by the time she came back from camp. They drifted onto other subjects, including Lezlie's schedule for the weekend.

"Are we on for dinner Friday night?" Drew asked.

"Maybe I should ask what to wear," Lezlie teased, "considering I never know where you're going to take me."

"We're going to one of the hotels downtown."

"I don't believe it!" she cried. "You actually told me. Now it won't be a surprise."

"I didn't say which one. Sweet dreams, Lezlie."

The receiver went dead and Lezlie stared at it in

helpless frustration. She had walked right into his verbal trap. She slipped between the inviting sheets of her bed, hugging her pillow close. Silently, she wished it was Drew she held. She fell asleep, dreaming of Friday.

CHAPTER THIRTEEN

THE CITY SPREAD OUT in a glow of lights beneath the Westin Plaza. In the distance, suburban neighborhoods were illuminated in the darkness; the twin towers of Lenox, the city of Marietta, and a red light blinked monotonously atop Stone Mountain. The rotating restaurant on the seventieth floor of the hotel turned slowly, showing Atlanta's beauty from every direction. The golden dome of the capitol building glittered while its stone structure was illuminated by soft incandescent lights. Atlanta was a blend of old treasured buildings and new skyscrapers, though each old building had to struggle to hold its place or fall prey to the developers as the city expanded. The Fox Theater, a beautiful old landmark, was filled with irreplaceable art in the form of murals, marble, tiles and sculpture. It had nearly been lost in the name of progress. But a small group of people had banded together and saved it from being leveled.

Lezlie and Drew had talked about the past; the places where they grew up, went to school and where their parents had taken them for vacations.

"The house in which I grew up was only a couple of miles from Lenox," Lezlie told Drew. "We lived in Buckhead, which is being called Mid-Town now. Do you know how it got the name Buckhead?"

Lezlie related a tale she had heard when she was a little girl. At a small neighborhood market, the proprietor often entertained the neighborhood children with stories about the area. His name was Mr. Chalders, Lezlie amazed herself by remembering. According to Mr. Chalders, when Georgia was still a frontier, there was a small trading post in the wilderness, which was now the intersection of Peachtree Street and Roswell Road. It was a crude structure of wooden logs and planks and above the door hung the head of a deer, a buck. The trading post was soon called The Buck's Head, and through time was shortened to Buckhead.

"I don't know if it's true," Lezlie explained, "but it certainly enthralled all the children. We could imagine the pioneers, renegade Indians and wild animals stalking just outside where there was a cement parking lot."

"He sounds like an interesting character," Drew said.

They talked about a whole range of things, including each one's very first dates, which for Lezlie had been catastrophe and for Drew had been an evening of sweaty hands and unexpected high-pitched squeaks in his changing voice.

Lezlie couldn't help laughing when he described the party he and his date had gone to, and how, because he had been so uncomfortable, he hadn't asked another girl out for almost a year. "I can't imagine that," Lezlie said, still grinning.

Next, they talked about college, and Drew remarked that only highbrows went to her alma mater, Emory, while the peons were relegated to the other local colleges—at which Lezlie took great offense. They even talked about Michael. Lezlie truly felt that Drew understood and didn't resent the place Michael had had in her life. For the first time she talked very easily about the past, finding him to be a quiet listener.

The conversation they had shared over drinks and through the appetizers made the silence over dinner an easy companionable one, except for one thing.

Lezlie sat across from Drew, her sumptuous dinner barely touched beneath the intense scrutiny he lavished upon her. "If you don't stop looking at me like that—" she whispered, glancing at the tables nearest them "—you're going to short circuit this whole building, as well as make everyone in this place see exactly what's on your mind."

"Am I that obvious?" Drew smiled with a wicked gleam.

"Transparent is more the word. Seriously, Drew."

"All right, sweetheart. I'll at least give you time to finish your dinner before I pounce on you."

"That's exactly what I have felt ever since the appetizers."

"I can't help it if I'm with the most beautiful woman here." Drew wasn't exaggerating. Her flawless fair skin was shown to perfection by the black sheath dress she was wearing with its soft neckline and cap sleeves. A becoming flush accented her cheeks and made her eyes more luminuous. The only adornment that broke the severity of the outfit was a delicate antique brooch with an enameled painting of a Renaissance woman. Lezlie's hair was swept back in an attractive French braid, and a bouquet of tiny flowers adorned the soft coil at the nape of her neck. Small gold earrings dropped from her earlobes.

"Flattery, too?" Lezlie chided, breaking into his thoughts.

"The truth is never flattery," Drew corrected easily, and as his gaze caressed her, Lezlie leaned forward.

"You're doing it again."

"What?"

"Staring."

Drew smiled apologetically. He shifted in his chair and unbuttoned the jacket of his blue three-piece pinstripe suit. Now, it was Lezlie who was staring as he gazed out at the view. He fit into the atmosphere of the Westin as easily as he had Longhorn's. The cream shirt contrasted with his tanned skin, which had darkened with his work at the construction site. He seemed perfectly at ease.

"Like what you see?"

The comment brought Lezlie's gaze to his smiling eyes. Though he hadn't turned his head, she wondered how long he had been watching her out of the corner of his eye.

With an appreciative gleam, she nodded her head. Lingering over coffee, they enjoyed the soft music and the view. When Drew lit a cigarette, Lezlie leaned forward on her arms.

"I thought you only smoked when you're tense," she teased.

"I am," Drew said, taking a deep drag on his cigarette.

"Why?" Lezlie asked gently.

Drew exhaled in a long slow breath. "I had intended to talk to you about something tonight, but I don't think the timing is right."

"Can you tell me what it concerns?"

"I could, but then I'd have to explain the whole thing." Drew reached over and touched her cheek. "And I don't want anything to spoil the time we have together. I can tell you later."

"We can talk now," Lezlie offered, but Drew had crushed out his cigarette and was standing up. He held her chair and when she stood next to him, his pensive mood had evaporated.

"I want to take you dancing until the sun comes up," he whispered. "And then I want to make love to you until the day is gone."

The eloquent sentiment touched a response deep within Lezlie. "I had hoped it would be the other way around."

"Had you?" Drew smiled, looping his arm around her waist. "Didn't anyone ever tell you that anticipation is half the fun?"

"Only to a certain point," Lezlie replied.

"Why don't we test the theory?" Drew suggested and Lezlie readily agreed. Either way, she would be in his arms where she sorely ached to be.

A few blocks from the Westin, a little bistro occupied the basement of an old gray-stone building. Its smoky atmosphere was dim, the music was soft and mellow; perfect for the kind of dancing Drew had in mind. No sooner had Lezlie laid her purse and shawl on the table than Drew took her hand.

Lezlie slipped into his arms, oblivious to the other couples swaying near them. Her arm rested along his broad shoulder while her hand was completely lost in his. The soft music washed over Lezlie and combined with Drew's nearness to warm her senses. As she rested her cheek against his shoulder, his strong thighs brushed against hers while he held her close, so close that her head was swimming with the teasing contact.

Time stood still, and Lezlie was only vaguely aware of the changing tunes. As long as Drew kept his arms around her, she was content. As they moved in slow unison the lights changed color behind Lezlie's closed eyelids while they glided and turned. Drew's warm breath was against her ear and his cheek rested on her forehead. With only a slight tilting of her head, Lezlie raised her lips and felt the tender brush of his. The touch was accompanied by a tightening of his hand on her waist, which brought their lower bodies into closer contact. His strong thigh rubbed against Lezlie's legs, titillating her as her hip received the pressure of a desire he could not conceal. Her breasts were pressed against the firmness of his chest and she inhaled the warmth of his skin beneath the sheath of clothes.

"So much for testing the theory," Drew said, his voice raspy.

Lezlie leaned back to look up into his shadowed face. "Have you had enough anticipation?"

Drew still held her tightly, but they were swaying

together more than dancing. "Do I get an 'I told you so'?"

"No, but you get an 'I was right.'"

"You sound awfully smug," Drew teased. "Let's see how you hold up."

With that, he leaned over and captured her mouth, which was opened to protest. But Lezlie's words died beneath his thorough possession. They were in the far corner of the dance floor, which was a small corner of dark refuge from prying eyes. Drew swayed with the music, his leg firmly between hers as he slowly turned, drawing her with him. He continued to kiss her, his tongue ravaging her mouth and scorching her senses while their intimate contact turned Lezlie's insides to liquid. She leaned into the curve of his body, her mind swirling and tumbling in an abyss of delight. She never wanted the kiss to end, so when he raised his head, a sigh of disappointment escaped her.

"I know I want you," Drew said huskily, "and you know it. But if we don't get out of here, everyone else will know it, too."

With that, he turned, his arm scooping her along before he gathered her things and put them in her shaking hands.

The cool night air blew a refreshing breeze across Lezlie's heated skin. They hurried to Drew's car, holding hands and pausing to kiss under the heavy branches of a magnolia tree. The sweet fragrance surrounded them for a moment, its allure seeping into their senses.

"If I was smart, I'd take you right back to the Westin," Drew breathed.

"But we'd have to check out in the morning," Lezlie answered, "and deal with maids or room service...."

"Well, there's one place where we won't be disturbed. I gave Mrs. Cates the weekend off." Drew hurried her along to her car. "I was just thinking that the hotel was closer."

"Anticipation is half the fun," Lezlie mimicked.

She succumbed to bubbling laughter when he looked at her and ground out, "Very funny."

The drive to Drew's house passed with Lezlie's head resting on his shoulder while his strong fingers caressed her thigh.

"Do you know what you're doing to me?" Drew groaned as she nibbled at his jaw. He was trying to watch the road, but her seductive attention wasn't making it easy.

"It's the same thing you did to me," Lezlie whispered. "Remember?"

"I remember," Drew admitted, and he couldn't contain a smile.

A welcoming light shone from within Drew's house as they hurried up the walk, laughing and holding hands. Beneath the porch light, Drew pulled Lezlie into his arms. He stared down at her for a moment until all the laughter died in them and was replaced by the intensity of what they were feeling. There was no longer any uncertainty in her eyes, but a womanly acceptance of her passion. She gave of herself with a generosity that surpassed what Drew had hoped for. Gently he caressed her cheek, and her eyes darkened in immediate response.

"Once we go in, I can't be responsible for when you will leave," he murmured. "I may never let you leave."

"Who says I would want to?" Lezlie countered, the flicker of a smile twitching her lips. "At least until Monday morning, that is."

"Then I don't want to waste another minute." Drew leaned over, surprising Lezlie as he swept her into his arms and carried her into his house. She was cradled against him, her arms wound around his neck as he headed straight into the bedroom.

When he set her on her feet and brought her into his embrace, Lezlie's heart was hammering. He kissed her slowly, his lips exploring her cheeks, the curve of her eyebrows and the softness of her bottom lip. Her eyes fluttered closed as she raised her face to his. Drew pulled the earrings from her lobes and dropped them into his pocket. As he shrugged out of his jacket, Lezlie had begun to loosen his tie and unbutton his shirt. His strong hands encircled her waist then caressed her sides, his palms brushing the swell of her breasts. He pulled her hips against his, slowly sliding down the zipper of her dress. Lezlie held his shoulders as he bent over and unhooked her strappy sandals, his touch warming her skin.

Drew's shirt slipped off beneath Lezlie's trembling fingers, followed by her dress. A lacy teddy ended at the top of her long legs. The texture of the material Drew pushed from her shoulder was like a silky scarf. The mat of hair on his chest was crisp to Lezlie's touch and tapered to a thin line across his flat stomach.

A moment later, naked, they faced each other and Drew took her into his arms, a sigh of happiness whispering against her cheek. Her hair tumbled down her back as Drew removed the pins, unconcerned where they fell. Lezlie's skin tingled wherever his touch wandered. His lips settled over hers with a possession she welcomed eagerly.

Drew sat down on the edge of the bed, drawing her between his legs. The flesh of her stomach quivered beneath his lips. As he lay back, he pulled her along with him, then rolled over to trap her body beneath his. The bed bore their weight with a rippling wave that startled Lezlie, but her concern evaporated as Drew assaulted her senses, his body wooing her with a promise of ecstasy.

Lezlie arched against him, her mouth opening beneath his. But as his kiss wandered to the smoothness of her shoulder, a strange sensation bubbled in her stomach. The bed was undulating, pitching and rolling with each movement as Drew's body pressed hers onto the bed. She closed her eyes, trying to ignore the queasiness. Her fingers snaked into his hair and she lifted his head.

Her voice was a raspy whisper. "Drew, the bed—"

"Wonderful invention," he said, but his suggestive words were cut short by the frown settled between her eyebrows. "What is it, sweetheart?"

"It's the motion," Lezlie murmured.

"You're kidding," Drew said in disbelief, but she shook her head. "No, you're not kidding."

Drew's exit from the bed caused it to rock crazily. He leaned down and gathered her in his arms. Once on her feet, she breathed a sigh of relief. "I never realized a water bed was so disorienting."

Drew had opened a trunk at the foot of the bed. "Have you ever been on a water bed?"

"No, but...."

"It takes some getting used to," he said easily, and a moment later a downy comforter covered the floor. Lezlie came down beside him and he brushed tiny curls from her damp forehead. "Better?"

"Much," she whispered.

"Are you sure?"

"I'll prove it," she said huskily. Her hands slipped into his hair and she pulled him to her. Her senses were once again incited to fever pitch as he took her in his arms. Their bodies intertwined intimately as she arched against him. She reveled in the feel of his strong body covering hers. Everything had been forgotten except the breathtaking delight Drew stirred within her as his body merged with hers, sweeping her into the vortex of sensations that left them clinging to each other in their climb. Lezlie turned her face into the hollow of his shoulder, her lips tasting the salt of his skin as his fingers intertwined with hers and they soared, the ceaseless rhythm building into waves that washed over them, cresting in the heights of ecstasy and dashing them to earth in blissful harmony.

Drew's mouth clung to the sweetness of Lezlie's as she trembled, her breathing ragged and short. Her damp skin glowed in the soft light from a bedside lamp. Her dark lashes caressed a flushed cheek and her teeth had caught his bottom lip. His teasing movements elicited quiet sighs of pleasure.

Drew covered them with one side of the comforter. Propped on his elbow, he stared down at her while he twisted a curl around his finger. The depth of her response never failed to make his own passion much more satisfying. She radiated in the pure pleasure of their desire. "You are incredible," he whispered, appreciating all that she gave of herself.

Lezlie smiled, almost feeling shy. She snuggled into the warm curve of his body, perfectly content on the soft comforter on the floor. Her body still tingled and she sighed contentedly. "I think Meredith had the right idea but the wrong word when she said a water bed was depraved," Lezlie mused.

Drew was suddenly very still. His hand had stopped in midair. "What are you talking about?" he said.

"Oh, it was something Merri said," Lezlie said, and she chuckled at the memory. "Except that she got the pronunciation fouled up...."

"Will you tell me what you're talking about?" Drew said more sharply than he had intended.

Lezlie turned to meet his questioning eyes. There was a tautness in his expression she hadn't seen before.

"It isn't really important, Drew."

"It is to me," Drew corrected.

Hesitantly Lezlie explained what Merri had told her, reiterating that it wasn't that important. "Has she told you anything else about Meredith?"

"Very little, actually." Lezlie could have sworn Drew's sigh was one of relief. "Drew, I'm sorry. I shouldn't have said anything. Of course, it would strike you differently than it did me. Although I do recall thinking that it was an odd thing to say about a brother-in-law...." A teasing glint appeared in Lezlie's eyes. She wanted to remove the seriousness from Drew's expression. "Unless Meredith knew something about you that I don't."

"Please stop," Drew said, sitting up and raking his hand through his hair.

His reaction immediately set Lezlie on her guard. She sat up and tentatively touched his shoulder. But it was as though a wall had risen between them. Drew, who was usually so disarming and at ease, had retreated and withdrawn from her. And that frightened Lezlie. "Drew?"

"Meredith did know me—" Drew said quietly, his gaze fixed straight ahead "—probably better than anyone. It may have been a subjective opinion, but considering the circumstances, it was probably valid."

Drew shook his head, reminding Lezlie of the defeat she had seen when she had first agreed to treat Merri.

"And above anyone, Meredith had a right to resent what she called my misplaced ideals. I've wondered for years if she was right when she once said I was too filled with ego and selfishness to care about anyone or anything but myself. There are a lot of things a person can take for granted until they come face-to-face with themselves. War is a good mirror. I really had a good hard look at myself in Vietnam. Because of it, I've changed a lot over the years." Drew was lost in his own thoughts. "But it didn't make any difference. The damage had been done, and I couldn't undo it. At least Meredith was willing to give me a another chance. That was more than Greg could do."

"A chance for what?" Lezlie asked quietly.

"To prove I wasn't the same as I was in college... that I had changed." Drew looked directly at Lezlie, his voice giving no indication of his feelings as he said, "Meredith and I were lovers once."

Lezlie stared at him, unsure that she had heard what he'd said. But slowly, the words seeped into her mind. He and Meredith, his brother's wife, had been lovers.

"It was while we were in college." Then Drew added quickly, "But before she married Greg."

"Did Greg know?" Lezlie asked, still too stunned to comprehend all the implications, but his next comment made a lot of things very clear.

"He knew."

Drew's relationship with Meredith had been the wedge between the two brothers. No matter how Greg had fought it, the knowledge that his brother had known his wife intimately must have been hard to deal with. And it had eventually destroyed the closeness the brothers had shared as children.

"Did you ever talk about it?" Lezlie asked.

Drew was so close to telling her all of it, the whole mess and all the repercussions, but he had seen the shock in her eyes. He couldn't bear the thought that she might judge him as harshly as Greg had done all these years. He brought her into his arms, hushing her questions and his own doubts. He kissed her fiercely, pressing her back onto the comforter. He needed Lezlie, needed her nearness and acquiescence more than he had ever needed anything or anyone.

As his lips clung to hers, seeking a response, Lezlie realized his need for her closeness. She wrapped her arms around him, silently offering the solace he sought. This was no tender exploration, but a feverish race toward a precipice that offered an oblivion. Their bodies strained together and their breath mingled in raspy gasps. The intensity of their lovemaking purged all doubts for Lezlie. She met Drew's demand with an ardor of her own, assuaging the need he had shown.

As they lay spent and exhausted in each other's arms, Lezlie fully realized just how much she loved Drew. She loved his strength as well as the vulnerability he had briefly shown her. She loved him completely. And somehow, the emotion didn't terrify her at all. He had shared a part of himself, more than in the physical sense. But something had stopped him from telling her what was troubling him so deeply. He hadn't mentioned his brother's attitude, or what must have been a painful rejection.

Drew held her tightly and Lezlie stroked his hair. The tension drained out of him. The details of what had happened didn't matter. He would tell her in time, and she would show him the same understanding he had shown her. Cuddled against him, she fell asleep.

LEZLIE LAY VERY STILL for a long time. She had been awake nearly an hour. Drew slept on, his face relaxed in deep slumber. She studied his peaceful features, love swelling within her. But she couldn't stop her mind from racing. Questions that hadn't occurred to her the previous night now jumped into her thoughts, threatening her confidence, and not without cause. Because she loved Drew, she now felt even more vulnerable in light of what he had told her. He had accused her of keeping the past in the present, but had Drew done the same thing? Was Meredith the reason Drew had never married? Had losing Meredith been even more difficult because she had married his brother? And what had Greg felt all those years, knowing the relationship that had once existed? Was that why Drew had limited his visits to his brother?

None of the questions had an answer. Lezlie slipped out from under the comforter to stop the nagging queries. She would wait, she told herself firmly. She would wait until Drew was ready to tell her.

Putting on Drew's shirt, Lezlie grinned ruefully. The sleeves draped inches beyond her hands. Rolling them up, she headed into the kitchen to make coffee. She checked in with her answering service, happy that no one had called but Donna, and she hadn't asked to be called back. "She said she just wanted to chat when you have some time," the receptionist said.

Lezlie was smiling as she located the coffee. *That may not be until Monday,* she thought. She jumped as Drew's arms circled her waist, pulling her against the solid wall of his chest.

"I wondered where you went," he murmured, kissing her temple. "How long have you been up?"

"A while," Lezlie answered, her hands clasped around his forearms.

"Lezlie, about last night...."

"Last night was wonderful," she interrupted, turning her face to kiss him. "All of it."

Drew squeezed her tightly, immensely relieved that he hadn't been too overzealous in his lovemaking. Or at least if he had, she hadn't minded. And she didn't seem inclined to continue their conversation.

"So, tell me, what's on the agenda for today?" she asked. He was still holding her as she measured the coffee and put the basket into the percolator.

Drew was staring down at her, totally fascinated by his view. His arms pressed her breasts upward and the shirtfront gaped open. "I think the plans may change drastically," he said thickly.

Lezlie glanced over her shoulder, then followed the direction of his gaze. She blushed furiously.

"You look better in that shirt than I ever did," Drew whispered. The shirttail dipped over her derriere and curved enticingly along the top of her thigh.

"Are you hungry?" Lezlie asked, trying in vain to ignore the way his lips trailed along her shoulder.

"Not for food," Drew mumbled against her skin. But there was some unfinished business he didn't want standing between them. He had been awake long before Lezlie thought he had and he had noticed her contemplative frown. He would give her a chance to ask whatever she wanted to. "We didn't finish our discussion last night," he said quietly. "I didn't give you much of a chance to ask me...."

Lezlie turned and reached up, placing her hand on his mouth. "I don't have any questions, Drew. Whatever happened is in the past. I'm sure you'll tell me when it's easier." She smiled reassuringly. "But I know that it's not the right time."

"I don't know if there will ever be a right time," Drew commented. But the trust and understanding Lezlie offered, both now and last night, lessened his worry about the truth coming between them. He kissed her then, a slow sensual mingling of tenderness and affection.

"If you want breakfast, I...suggest...you...stop...." Lezlie spoke between nibbling kisses and then giggled, a girlish sound to Drew's ear.

"You win," Drew said, then smiled. "For now."

They shared the duties of making a breakfast of scrambled eggs, toast and sliced tomatoes. Several times Lezlie smothered a chuckle as the towel draped around his hips worked loose and threatened to fall. Drew retucked the edge, winking in response to her thwarted expectations. But while he was buttering the toast, the towel did slip, dropping to the floor before Drew could move. He stood there in all his naked glory as Lezlie's laughter bubbled forth. His chagrined expression intensified her mirth and she doubled over, holding her side as he tried to pick up the towel, but it slipped between his fingers. She squealed in surprise as he grabbed her, but her laughter did not subside.

"Laughing at me, huh?" he said playfully as he swung her up. His arm scooped under her legs so that his hand could explore her inner thigh and bottom. He held her across the back, relentlessly raising her toward his face. Lezlie was helpless as she continued to giggle, but her amusement dissolved when his mouth nuzzled her throat. His finger was circling her bottom, her whisper-thin panties no barrier as he squeezed the firmness of her buttock. He held her tightly, his chin pushing the material of the shirt out of his determined path toward the rosy peak hiding from him. A grunt of victory rumbled in his throat as his lips settled on the target and the soft flesh tautened beneath his sucking motion.

Lezlie held her breath as a shock raced along her nerve endings and settled in the pit of her stomach. His mouth and tongue provoked an exquisite torture while his hand worked ever closer to another target. She squirmed in his arms, but he did not release his hard-won treasure. Lezlie threw back her head, clinging to his shoulders. Her hair swung out behind her, but Drew's second target was beyond his reach. He gave his avid attention to the soft mound beneath his mouth, hearing the quiet sighs bubbling in her throat.

When he raised his head, Drew was met by Lezlie's flushed face and half-closed eyes. "You stopped laughing," he said, pleased with his success.

As he let her slide the length of him until her feet touched the floor, a wide smile curved Lezlie's lips. "So have you."

When he started to kiss her again, he was interrupted by the sizzling of the eggs.

"The breakfast!" Lezlie cried, spinning around to see if their meal was ruined. "I hope you like your eggs well-done."

"I like everything well-done," Drew drawled.

Lezlie slanted a chastising glance over her shoulder, but it dissolved as he stood proudly in front of her, the towel still on the floor. They lingered over breakfast, then straightened the kitchen before showering and dressing.

It was late afternoon by the time they had left Drew's house, driven to Lezlie's so she could change, and started through the countryside north of Roswell with no particular destination. The narrow road, sided by farms and fields where cows grazed lazily in the shimmering afternoon heat, stretched out in gentle curves and hills.

Several times along the way, they stopped to poke around small country stores or antique shops. Lezlie had worn shorts and a thin cotton blouse because Drew had said he preferred to ride without the car's air conditioning. At each store, they thirstily guzzled a soft drink. At one store, which was little more than a shack set back from the road by a gravel drive, Lezlie tentatively accepted a cup of chilled apple cider. Its refreshing tanginess tickled her throat and quenched her thirst.

As Drew talked to the man behind the counter, she wandered through the narrow aisles of groceries and small farm tools. Toward the back of the store, the shelves were dusty and covered by an assortment of items that defied definition: things that appeared to be pieces of lamps or lanterns, rusted metal disks, and so on.

But when she found an unusual pink bottle to add to her collection, Drew gladly paid the proprietor's ridiculous price of fifty cents.

"These sell for a great deal more," Lezlie advised the man behind the counter.

"Don't know why," the grizzled owner answered, disinterested. "I got no use for it. You like it, it's worth fifty cents."

It was the most pleasant day Lezlie could ever remember. She laid her head back on the seat, the warm breeze blowing across her face as they headed home. She glanced over at Drew, his strong profile bringing a rush of emotion. She returned her gaze to the fields, which rippled and bowed to the wind, feeling very much in tune with the inability of the meadow grass to stand against the power of the wind.

Dinner was a pleasant unhurried cookout of steaks, salad and French bread, which they ate on the deck, with the starry sky and descent of night as entertainment. As Drew stretched on a lounge, he patted the place beside him. But when Lezlie started to lie down, he brought the full weight of her body atop his, sighing contentedly as she snuggled closer. He stroked the bare skin of her arm.

Lezlie was completely content. She closed her eyes, the thud of Drew's heart just beneath her ear, and the warmth of his arms around her. She awoke to the loud chirping of June bugs and the gentle caress of Drew's lips. Lifting her face, she surrendered to the warm comfort of his arms and his desire, their mouths tasting and savoring with unhurried appreciation. *It will always be the same,* Lezlie thought dreamily, her senses responding without reserve.

The night enveloped them, offering its gentle melody and soft glow as a haven for a passion that knew no bounds, but that deepened the love so generously given and received, though no words were spoken.

CHAPTER FOURTEEN

CHARLES SANDERS EMERGED from a private room on the second floor of Riverview Hospital. Preoccupied by his note making, he caught only a glimpse of the woman who passed him with a breezy hello. He swung around as recognition dawned on him. He hurried down the hall to catch up to her.

"Hey, Lezlie, wait up!"

Lezlie turned, halting her steps until Charles was only a few feet away. "I didn't want to disturb you." She smiled.

Charles could hardly believe his eyes. He couldn't define it, but there was a drastic difference about Lezlie. He scrutinized her closely, trying to discern the change. It was not a physical difference. She wore the familiar white coat, her hair was in place, the usual wisps defying containment. Finally, it dawned on him. The difference was not on the outside, but radiated from within. She actually glowed with happiness. Her eyes sparkled and her smile was easy and unstrained.

"I tried to call you several times over the weekend," he started, still amazed by the change. "Myra and I wanted to have you over for dinner Saturday, and when I couldn't reach you, I tried again Sunday."

"I was away for the weekend," Lezlie said with a vague smile. It had been a terrific two days. On Sunday, she and Drew had slept late, waking with slight backaches from sleeping on the comforter on the floor.

"I can see I'm going to have to find another bed...and soon," he had grumbled, rubbing the small of his back.

"That or someone who can tolerate a water bed," Lezlie replied.

"The bed will have to go," Drew told her firmly.

They had made love in the morning and then sprawled on the floor to read the *Sunday Journal Constitution*. While Drew glanced over the Sports section and grumbled about the baseball team's persistent losing streak, Lezlie had laughed at the antics of Garfield. Later, they had gone over to the construction site. Lezlie had wandered through the eerily empty buildings while Drew checked over some papers in his trailer. When Drew had come to find her, they had kissed on the fifth floor of the building's shell, the wind whipping through the open walls and blowing her hair around their faces. Just thinking about it brought a familiar tingle to Lezlie's lips.

"Wherever you went certainly agrees with you," Charles commented, and he thought Lezlie's smile was a trifle secretive. "But what are you doing here?"

"I'm working," Lezlie answered. "According to the head nurse of Pediatrics, there is only one tonsillectomy scheduled for Wednesday morning. It's going to be a slow week, unless something comes up."

"I reiterate, what are you doing here?" Lezlie's

blank stare caused him to shake his head. "Have you been to your office?"

"I got in a little early but was just on my way back...."

"Good. I'll let Jean tell you that you are scheduled for vacation this week."

Lezlie's mouth opened, then clamped shut.

"You may as well go on home, unless you want to tell Dr. Anderson he doesn't need to cover for you." Charles chuckled and started off, glancing over his shoulder. "Boy, it must have been some weekend if you completely forgot the fact that you're supposed to be on vacation."

His laugh drifted back along the corridor. Lezlie shook her head. She checked the date on her watch, suddenly remembering the vacation she had scheduled almost three months earlier. Why hadn't Jean reminded her, she thought, then immediately diverted the blame to herself. She started in one direction down the hall, then changed her mind and headed to her office. But her smile was bright as she stripped off the white smock.

She couldn't believe that since giving her schedule to the hospital administrator's assistant, she had not made any plans. She had gone over some brochures around Christmastime, but had quickly put the worrisome details out of her mind. Besides, vacations the past two years had only meant too much time to herself, and she was always anxious to return to work. Now, however, a full week of freedom stretched before her, and she could think of a hundred things she would like to do. And most of them involved Drew.

Jean normally used the time Lezlie was away to update the filing system, bring the accounts up-to-date and do a biannual accounting. By the time Lezlie returned, everything that had been put aside or put off had been brought to a current status before Jean left for her own time off.

When Lezlie walked into her office, Jean glanced up from the stacks of paper on her desk, her wide stare evidence of her surprise.

Lezlie held up a hand as she walked through to her office. "I know, I know," she said quickly. "Charles just reminded me I was on vacation."

Lezlie hung her smock on the back of her door as Jean began to laugh. "I left a note on your desk Friday," she called.

"I didn't see it," Lezlie answered, glancing around her office. Her appointment book was a glaring affront to her foul-up, the pages clearly marked No Appointments.

"I take it you haven't made any plans," Jean said, leaning against the door.

"That can be remedied," Lezlie answered. Picking up her purse, she headed out of the office. "But you can bet this is the shortest day I've ever worked."

"I would be envious, since I'll be up to my ears in paperwork for the next three days. But my turn is coming. Have fun."

"I'll do my best," Lezlie replied, waving as she pulled the outer door shut.

The day loomed emptily ahead as she reached her car. Drew would be tied up at the construction site, and she didn't feel comfortable with the thought of just stopping in. Impulsively she turned in the opposite direction of her house. She drove along Highway 41 until she reached a narrow side street that led to a one-level house that had been converted into a school for autistic and mentally retarded children.

Since the students who attended Donna's school did not understand or had little comprehension of the dangers beyond its walls, a high fence surrounded the large, beautifully planted yard. The flower beds had been planted and were tended by the students themselves. Huge hydrangea bushes sat proudly alongside the porch, the heavy mauve clusters of flowers adding their sweetness to the breeze.

The door had a buzzer that required one of the faculty to use a key for admittance of any visitors. Lezlie waited patiently for her summons to be answered. It was Donna herself who peered through the curtain and smiled.

"Well, hi stranger," she said cheerily. "I thought you would be well on your way...somewhere."

Lezlie stepped across the threshold. She waited until Donna had relocked the door and they were heading into the office, which occupied the front corner of the school. An array of plants clung precariously to the narrow windowsill. The furniture, though not a decorator's choice for a modern office, was comfortable and nonthreatening in its blandness.

"It seems that everyone was aware of my vacation but me," Lezlie said ruefully, repeating the episode with Charles. Donna laughed uproariously. "And I thought you would take pity on me and we could go to lunch."

"It's only ten o'clock," Donna cried. "You are at loose ends."

"Not really, but we've both been tied up the past few weeks."

"I've missed you, too," Donna said quietly. "If you can hang on for a little while, I should be able to get clear, at least for an hour or so."

"I'm in no hurry," Lezlie said with a smile.

Unlike conventional schools, Donna's classes ran the year through, except for the month of August. Even though the instructional training was curtailed, the children who needed to be cared for during the workday could still be brought to the school. Several of the staff and Donna's assistant played games and made up picnics, which the children adored.

Lezlie wandered around Donna's office, noting the additions to "Donna's wall"—pictures taken each July of the children who had attended that year. Some of the students had been with Donna for several years, and the change that shone in their faces was evidence Donna was providing much more than custodial care.

When Donna returned, she gave a thumbs-up sign. "I'm all yours for a couple of hours. Maybe we could do some shopping at Cumberland Mall before we have lunch. I haven't done that in ages, and Jim's birthday is coming up soon."

Lezlie was reminded of another birthday that was also near, and she decided to try to find a special gift for Merri, perhaps something for the dollhouse, which was finished and would be ready for Merri as soon as she got home from camp.

Lezlie struggled with her packages and her keys before she finally managed to open the door to her house. She had found Merri a special gift indeed. She had known how much the girl would value her purchase the moment she had seen the miniature furniture, especially the imitation French provincial four-poster with minute canopy, chest, chair and little pictures in metal frames for the wall. She laid her packages down, having bought some material to make a small bedspread and canopy scarf. At least Merri would have one room to set up before she and her uncle began the process of furnishing the rest.

With a burst of restless energy, Lezlie hurriedly changed her clothes. She considered calling Drew, but decided not to chance interrupting him. So, donning her heavy gardening gloves, which hadn't been used since one day last spring, and a visored hat, she headed into the backyard to put some order to the overgrown and weed-ridden garden. She had been in the yard but a few minutes when Beelzebub strolled through a gap in the fence, jumped onto a huge rock in the center of a flower bed and stared at her with wide unblinking yellow eyes. As she dug and tugged at the tenacious roots, she talked to him, receiving a disinterested meow every so often. When she went into the house to get a cold drink, Beelzebub followed. Then he returned to the yard with her, taking up his proprietorial position on the rock.

"If you were smart, cat, you'd find a cooler spot," Lezlie puffed, wiping the beads of perspiration from her forehead and feeling some trickle between her breasts.

When she had done as much as she could to rid the flower bed of its invading growth, she sat back on her haunches. A pungent warmth emanated from the overturned sod, while the sublayer of brick-red clay was crusted on her knees and gloves. She felt the sting of the sun when she flexed her shoulders. Beelzebub alertly watched the fluttery flight of a white butterfly, his sharp eyes never losing sight of the insect until he became bored with the effort.

Lezlie returned the tools to the small shed at the back of the house, then she swept the patio. When she pulled off her gloves and looked at the spot where Beelzebub had been, he had wandered off. She went inside, leaving the sliding doors open as she showered. Dressed in a light flowing lounging shift, she stretched on the sofa to read, but soon dozed off.

A quiet twilight had darkened the room when she awoke. Her hair, though spread out across a towel, was still damp. Yawning, she went into the kitchen to see what her refrigerator could offer up for dinner. Deciding on a salad, she was just sitting down where she could look out the window when the phone rang. A smile immediately touched her mouth when Drew's gruff voice answered.

"You sound tired," Lezlie said.

"That's an understatement," Drew grumbled.

"I've had a fairly interesting day myself," Lezlie started, intending to tell him about the stupid mistake she had made. But the frustration she discerned from Drew's next comment wiped what she was about to say from her mind.

"I wish mine had been interesting rather than just

infuriating. Would you believe the company supplying the tile sent the wrong order for two of the buildings? Even if it wasn't a cheaper grade, the company that has contracted for the buildings had very definite specifications for the interior. And to top it off, the company in Macon can't accept a return without approval from the sales manager, and he's on vacation until Thursday."

"What can you do?"

"If the problem isn't straightened out by tomorrow morning, I'm going to drive to Macon and *get it* straightened out. My men are ready to lay that tile now. The last thing I need is to get behind schedule." He sighed heavily. "I had hoped to spend a lot of time with you this week, Lezlie, but I'm getting bogged down."

"I understand," Lezlie said sincerely.

"What were you going to tell me?" Drew asked.

"Nothing that can't wait. Have you heard from Merri?" Lezlie had decided it wouldn't serve any purpose to tell him she had the week free. It would only add to Drew's frustration that he couldn't break clear.

"I talked to her last night. Overall, she said camp is 'okay,' the food is 'awful,' but it's 'fun.'"

"Well, that's encouraging." Lezlie chuckled.

"She sounded funny. She's a little lonely, I think. She mentioned Jill has made friends with some of the other girls in their cabin."

"Merri may be feeling a little threatened, Drew. But she became friends with Jill. She'll make other friends as time goes on."

"I know, but it's hard watching her struggle through this all on her own."

"She's not alone, Drew. And you have to consider that she may be finding it hard to share Jill. But this is the way it is with every childhood friendship. You remember...."

"Yes, but I still feel for her."

"All parents do," Lezlie said gently. "You have entered a twilight zone of helpless sympathy. You can advise, comfort and console, but there's so little you can do to shield children from the hurts of growing up."

"Merri has had enough hurt to last a lifetime," Drew said.

"She's a strong girl, Drew."

"You have enough confidence in her for both of us," Drew said amiably. "I miss you."

"We were just together yesterday," Lezlie laughed.

"That was yesterday. I'm talking about today, now, this minute, and every other minute all day. Getting bogged down in details on the job puts a real crimp in what I had planned for the evenings this week."

"I've been thinking about you, too," Lezlie admitted.

"Ah, finally," Drew sighed in exaggeration. "I was beginning to wonder."

"Well, you needn't."

Drew's voice sounded resonant and cheerful. "I'll call you tomorrow night. It may be late if I have to drive down to Macon."

When Drew had hung up, Lezlie leaned back in her

chair. It was going to be a different vacation entirely from what she had planned earlier in the day. But it didn't really matter. She had plenty to keep her busy through the week, and she would talk to Drew in the evenings. There was always the weekend, she consoled herself.

THE WEEK PASSED QUICKLY, even though it wasn't particular exhilarating for Lezlie. Drew had made the trip to Macon, calling her at almost midnight, but she hadn't minded. He called her each evening, but she felt her hopes dashed for the weekend when Drew said the crew would have to work Saturday to make up for lost time during the week. He hadn't heard from Merri again, and Lezlie assured him no news was a good sign that she was having fun.

Lezlie had spent the days giving her house the spring cleaning she had neglected. She washed windows, took down curtains and drapes and had them cleaned. She scrubbed and vacuumed until she thought her arms would fall off. She straightened and rearranged cupboards, cabinets and closets until the order made it almost impossible to find a particular thing. But the sense of accomplishment she derived from her work was reward for her efforts as she looked around. She had even picked fresh flowers from the rosebushes near her fence. Their sweet scent filled her kitchen and bedroom.

Each afternoon she took a couple of hours to lie in the sun and be completely lazy. She drove her mother to the airport to catch a flight to the Cayman Islands. It had been tempting to take up her mother's offer to accompany her, but Lezlie had declined. There was too much happening in her life at the moment. And without even realizing it until her mother's request, she was using the time alone to make some adjustments.

Each night when she talked to Drew, they had long lazy conversations, which eased the harried tone in his voice and softened the strain both of them felt at not seeing each other. But on Thursday afternoon, it all fell apart.

Lezlie was cleaning out the last of the closets the first time she heard the phone ring. But by the time she reached it, whoever it had been had hung up. Later, in the shower, she thought she had heard the phone ring again, but when she turned off the water, only silence greeted her quiet attention. She doubted it was the hospital, and if it was Donna or her mother, her service would have taken a message. Lezlie planned to return the call in the early evening, before Drew's usual call. She went to the grocery store, then picked up the drapes at the cleaners. And just as she was coming in the door, the phone stopped ringing. As soon as she put the groceries away, she would check with her service, she decided, inexplicably uneasy.

Drew slammed down the receiver of the telephone. Frantically, he wondered what in the hell to do, but as he rushed out of the house, he already knew. He was furious. Why hadn't she told him she wouldn't be in her office for the week? Now when he needed her the most, he couldn't find her.

Lezlie heard the rumble of the car engine just as

she hung up from talking to her answering service. A sense of dread filled her. The receptionist hadn't been able to tell her anything more than that a man had called, several times, demanding to know where he could reach Dr. Garrett.

Lezlie was just about to dial her office when she heard pounding on the front door. She ran through the house, knowing the car engine she had heard was Drew's. Something was wrong...something was very wrong. Lezlie's foreboding mounted and threatened to suffocate her as she opened the door.

Drew stormed into the house, a complete stranger from the man she had come to know these past weeks. "Where in the hell have you been?" he demanded. "I've been trying to reach you for hours!"

"I've been here," Lezlie answered, too stunned by the almost ragged desperation in Drew's face. "Most of the time," she clarified.

"I just talked to some bat brain at your office who tells me you're on vacation for the week. She doesn't know where to reach you and keeps trying to put me off to some joker named Anderson. And your answering service was damn little help."

Drew was pacing, glowering at her with a frustration she couldn't comprehend.

"I can't believe you didn't even tell me," he raged, noticing the suitcases standing in the hall. "Are you on your way out of town? Is that why you couldn't be bothered?"

"I'm not going anywhere," Lezlie retaliated. "I'm giving some things to Goodwill, the suitcases included. And bothered about what?" Lezlie ended shortly.

The intensity of Drew's resentful temper kindled a defense mechanism, and she faced him squarely.

Drew rubbed the back of his neck. "It's Merri," he said, slamming his fist onto his open palm. "I thought everything was great, or at least heading that way, and now this."

"What?" Lezlie demanded.

Drew looked at her and all the anger seemed to drain away, leaving his face haggard and strained. "She's run away. I got a call from the camp just before lunch."

Lezlie shook her head, momentarily numb. "But why? I mean, did they tell you anything?"

"Only that they've searched the grounds thoroughly. But nobody can remember seeing her since yesterday afternoon. And it wasn't until this morning that they realized she was missing when the counselor found a note on her bed. They've called in the police...."

"A note? What did it say?" Lezlie clutched his arm, as the desperation he had felt transmitted itself to her.

Drew waved his hand. "I don't know. It was some cryptic message about saying goodbye and going home, but I've called Mrs. Cates and she hasn't seen her. The police are putting out a description, but she could be anywhere...."

Something in the words of the note struck a familiar chord within Lezlie. She searched her memory and remembered the last session with Merri. Her eyes opened wide. "I know where she is," she said decidedly. "That last session we had, the one where Donna called from the hospital, remember?"

Drew was staring at her and when he nodded, Lezlie hurried on. "Merri and I were talking when Jean put the call through. We had been talking about her parents, and she had asked me a question about how I had forgotten about my family. I told her I hadn't forgotten them, but that my family life was in the past. The phone call interrupted us, so I didn't think anything about it when she pressed me to know how I stopped thinking about it."

"What does this have to do with now?" Drew interrupted.

Lezlie sighed heavily. "I told her that I had gone back to the place of the accident to say goodbye, because in the confusion after the accident, I hadn't had the chance." Lezlie ran a shaky hand across her brow. "That's what Merri meant in her note. She's gone to say goodbye, don't you see? To say goodbye to her parents, the way I did to Michael."

"That doesn't make sense," Drew argued. "She's never shown any inclination that she would strike out on a whim—"

"It isn't a whim, Drew. Didn't she recently ask you about going to Denver? When you said you couldn't take her, what if she took it to mean you wouldn't?" Lezlie challenged. "And Merri is more independent than you might think, Drew. I have indications of it in some of the tests I did."

"Then why didn't you warn me this might happen?" Drew questioned accusingly.

"If she had given me the slightest idea that she was going to take what I said literally, I would have told you," Lezlie said defensively.

"What in the world is she thinking, to go off halfway across the country on her own?"

The question hung between them, and Lezlie tried to suppress the wave of guilt that washed over her. By confiding her manner of handling her own grief to an impressionable young girl, she might have provided the catalyst for Merri's impulsive action. Perhaps it wasn't an impulse, she thought, but a well-made plan. If only she had been more observant, she might have seen some indication of Merri's intention.

"I think what we have to do is find out if we are right and how she could manage it," Lezlie suggested.

"You're serious? You think she's on her way to Denver?"

"Can you think of anywhere else that would apply to what she said in her note?"

Drew raked a hand through his hair. He had begun to pace again, his forehead furrowed with thought. "So we need to figure out how she's getting there," he mused, no longer doubting Lezlie's theory, "and when she left the camp. If she took the money she keeps at home, she would have had enough to get there... not by plane, but by bus, maybe, if she could've made it to the station."

"Did they do a bed check or something last night? Was Merri there?"

Drew shook his head. "When the counselor went in, Jill covered for her and said she had gone to the bathroom. I talked to Jill this morning. She doesn't know exactly when Merri left because she was horseback riding most of the afternoon. All that Merri told Jill was that she was going home. Jill assumed she meant she was coming to our house."

"Then we know she left the camp sometime after lunch. Could she have hitchhiked with anyone?"

"I talked to a man named Richard Allen at the camp. He felt fairly sure she would have been spotted on the road. But then he remembered that one of the counselors was coming into Marietta to pick up some equipment they had ordered. He said it was possible that she might have slipped into the truck without the driver knowing. He was going to check it out."

"All right," Lezlie mused, "suppose Merri did hitch a ride with the counselor. You say she couldn't afford a plane ticket...."

"And the counselor was only going as far as Marietta, so that lets out the bus station, unless she hitchhiked into Atlanta." The mere thought of Merri on the road with a complete stranger and what could happen to her made Drew sick inside. "I can't believe this," he whispered.

Lezlie jerked around. "But she wouldn't have had to go into Atlanta for a bus. There's a Greyhound and a Trailways station in Marietta on Highway 41. She could have bought a ticket. She could be on her way now to Denver."

"Well, there is one sure way to find out," Drew said decisively. "We'll check the bus stations. You had better get a few things together in case we have to go after her."

Lezlie quickly changed out of her lightweight apparel and threw some clothes into a suitcase. When she returned to the living room a few minutes later, Drew was hanging up the phone.

"I called the bus terminal in Marietta. The man who was handling the tickets yesterday said there was a girl there late in the afternoon. If it was Merri, she got on the six forty-five bus. He said he would recognize her from a picture." Drew took Lezlie's arm and propelled her out the door. "I also called Mrs. Cates. She's going to stay by the phone in case the police call."

"What time would she reach Denver?"

"There are several stops, including a bus change in Saint Louis. The scheduled arrival would be six tomorrow morning."

As they raced along Lower Roswell Road toward Highway 41, Lezlie silently prayed that it was Merri on that bus. At least then they would know where she was. And she would be in a lot less danger on a bus than on the street or on a highway. Like Drew, that thought made her stomach queasy.

Drew stared straight ahead, but near Clay Street he scanned the intersection, swung right, then left to the street that led into the bus terminal.

The clerk was a heavyset man with tired eyes. He glanced up as they walked in, noticing immediately that they were different from the people who came into the station to purchase tickets and wait for the bus. There was a desperation in the man's eyes that made the clerk sympathetic when Drew pulled out a picture and laid it on the counter.

"I called you a while ago about a little girl...."

The clerk was already nodding. He picked up the

picture and stared at it for only a moment. "That's her," he said easily. "She came in about five o'clock asking for a ticket to Denver. I can usually spot a runaway, but when I asked her if she was sure, she said her mother had sent her in to buy the ticket and she was waiting in the car."

"And you believed her?" Drew demanded.

"No," the clerk admitted slowly, "but if I hadn't sold her a ticket, she would've gone out of here and found another way. Besides, there was an elderly lady waiting for the same bus. She started talking to your girl here, and they were sitting together when the bus pulled out." He looked at Drew and then at Lezlie. "What'd she run away from?" he asked nosily.

"Camp," Drew answered succinctly. "Would you show me the route and stops the bus makes?"

"Sure," the clerk answered. A map hung on the wall behind his counter. There were stops in Chattanooga, Nashville, and a couple of small towns before the bus reached Saint Louis. There Merri would have to change to another bus for Denver, or wait during a layover until the final leg of the trip.

"Where is the bus now?" Drew asked, his gaze glued to the map as if the red lines were a thread to Merri.

"Let's see," the clerk mused, calculating in his head. "She would be a little ways out of Saint Louis by now on the way to Denver. There are quite a few stops along the route, and the bus should pull into the Denver station about six in the morning."

"Come on," Drew told Lezlie. "We have to get a road map."

"If you're planning to catch up to the bus, you would do better to fly and meet it at the station," the clerk suggested, but Drew didn't respond.

When they reached the parking lot, Drew was riddled with indecision. He wanted to get in the car and drive to try to intercept the bus.

"Maybe he's right," Lezlie said gently. "It would take too long to drive to Denver, Drew. Our one chance of catching up to Merri is at the station. If you catch a plane this afternoon, you can be at the station in the morning when the bus pulls in."

Drew looked at Lezlie then, a shattering look of desolation that penetrated to the core of Lezlie's being. "I can't go this alone, Lezlie. I don't even know what to say to Merri, but I think I had better figure out how I can approach her. And I need you to help me."

"It isn't as serious as you first thought, Drew. Merri isn't running away from you. She's ready to bury the past, and while I wish she had said something, this was the way she thought of taking care of it."

"But there's more to it than that," Drew said. He opened the car door for Lezlie. "I'll tell you on the way to the airport."

As Drew maneuvered through the midafternoon traffic and caught the Interstate 285 Perimeter, which circled Atlanta, Lezlie remained quiet, waiting for him to say more.

"Boy, I have really made a mess of everything," Drew said.

"You're being too hard on yourself. Becoming a

parent isn't a cut-and-dried situation. Everyone makes mistakes, and I don't think anyone could fault you for doing the best you could."

"Oh, Greg would fault me all right," Drew remarked.

Lezlie had given some thought to how Greg might have carried some bitterness because his brother had known his wife intimately. It was bound to have been in his mind at certain times, especially when Drew was visiting. "Drew, what happened between you and Meredith happened before she married Greg? It may have caused some insecurity on Greg's part—"

"Insecurity had nothing to do with it," Drew said shortly. "The fact was Greg hated me for what I did to Meredith."

"But he married her," Lezlie said.

"I don't think Greg saw it as a choice." Drew was staring straight ahead, his hands gripping the steering wheel so tightly that his knuckles were strained white. "And every time he looked at Merri, he was reminded of it."

"Of what?" Lezlie asked, confused.

"Of the fact that he wasn't Merri's father." Drew glanced at Lezlie, answering the question before she asked it. "I am."

Lezlie stared at him, incredulous. She struggled for words to voice her stunned confusion. "Merri is your daughter?" she stammered. "But I don't understand...."

"It's very simple actually," Drew said with self-scorn. "Meredith and I were...involved when I received my draft notice. We had talked about getting married, but that notice changed everything. My reasons for not getting married seemed very noble and valid at the time. What I didn't know was that Meredith was pregnant when I left for Vietnam. If she had told me, I would have married her. Instead, it was Greg who took care of her and Merri."

Lezlie was trying to absorb the enormity of what Drew was telling her.

"Meredith and Merri became Greg's whole life in the three years I was gone," Drew continued. "When I came back, it was surprise enough to learn that they were married. They had received word that I was missing, and that was the last they heard. I had been captured and was rotting in a stinking prisoners' camp just outside of Hanoi. Sometimes I think that it was only holding on to the future that kept me alive, a future with Greg and Meredith. I was in that camp a little over a year before several of us managed to escape and get back to South Vietnam. We were shipped straight home."

Drew sighed, a deep shuddering explusion of breath. It was as though the mere memory of his capture brought a tremendous weight to his shoulders. His voice was quiet and reflective. "I was never so glad to see anyone in my life as when I went to Denver to visit Greg and Meredith. Somehow, seeing them again was more important than the fact that they were married. But I could feel the tension. They seemed to be waiting for something, expecting some confrontation. I could tell that they loved each other, so somehow it didn't matter. The three years I was gone had been hard for them, too, but what I didn't realize until later was that my coming back was worse.

"Then I saw Merri. I simply assumed she was Greg's child, until I asked how old she was. It was a natural question, but their reactions revealed a great deal. It didn't take much after that to figure out why they were so ill at ease. When I confronted Meredith, she admitted that Merri was my child." Drew shook his head. "I can't describe how I felt, but I was both elated at being a father and appalled that I hadn't borne any of the responsibility. I would have done anything to make it up to them. But Greg didn't want me in Merri's life. And he was adamant that she not be told I was her father."

They had reached the Camp Creek Parkway, an access to the airport. A thousand questions went through Lezlie's mind, but one held precedence. "Is that what you were afraid Merri overheard in the car that night?"

Drew nodded. "She was so withdrawn after the accident. I couldn't be sure if it was grief or that she knew the truth."

It hadn't been Meredith who stood between the brothers, Lezlie realized, but a set of circumstances that had caused anger, resentment and bitterness. Greg had married Meredith, then fallen in love with her and accepted Merri as his own child. But Drew had returned from Vietnam and intruded upon the tranquil existence Greg had established.

"When Meredith first told me about Merri, I agreed that she was too young to understand. She didn't even know me. So I didn't press the issue. But as she got older, I wanted to have a place in her life. Meredith was willing to let Merri spend some time with me, to give her a chance to know me before we made any decision about telling her the truth. Greg objected furiously. He felt that my intentions were more selfish; that once I had Merri with me, I would fight to keep her, or tell her the whole story. Maybe he wouldn't have felt so strongly if they had had children of their own. But during Merri's delivery, something went wrong. Meredith couldn't have another child. Greg never said it, but I'm sure he blamed me for that, too."

"You should have told me all of this at the outset," Lezlie said quietly.

"You said you didn't want to know," Drew reminded her. "And, to be perfectly honest, I didn't want to tell you." His laugh was bitter and hollow. "It doesn't make me out to be much of a person. I deserted a girl I had gotten pregnant...."

"You didn't know," Lezlie said kindly. "And I'm not certain Merri knows, either, Drew. I think her attitude is based on Greg's bitterness and his objection to her being with you. Merri said as much in one of our sessions. But if I had known all of this, I might have responded differently, or at least prepared her in some way."

"What did Merri say?" Drew asked pointedly.

"Drew...."

"What did she say?"

There was no way to soften the comments about Greg's assumption that his brother knew nothing about children, and the effects Drew's presence had on them, or Greg's anger and Meredith's sick headaches. Lezlie repeated Merri's words, watching an almost melancholy sadness envelop Drew. "Drew, I'm sure Greg was doing what he thought was right for Merri, and you have to admit, he would have felt threatened that you might become more important to Merri."

"That's something we'll never know now," Drew said. "All I want to do now is find Merri."

"We'll find her," Lezlie said. She reached across and touched his arm, wanting to reassure him, but not knowing what to say.

Lezlie could only imagine how Drew had felt when he returned home and learned that not only was the woman he loved denied to him, but he had also been denied all rights to his child. Yet, Greg, his own brother, had condemned him and misunderstood his motives for wanting his daughter to know the truth. It had not been a selfish act when Drew put his own wishes aside for Merri's well-being. He had remained in the background, accepting the role of uncle because it was for the best. And intentionally or not, Greg had made the situation even more awkward. His words, spoken in frustration and anger, had made Merri wary of her uncle. But then, Greg hadn't anticipated that Merri would become Drew's ward should anything happen to him and Meredith.

Suddenly, Lezlie saw so many other ways she might have helped Merri if she had insisted that Drew tell her Merri's complete background. But she had had no idea of the serious repercussions of the past. One fact was glaringly clear. The truth had been suppressed too long. And she knew exactly what had to be done.

CHAPTER FIFTEEN

THE RUSH of passengers arriving and departing at the airport chafed Drew's sense of helpless inactivity as they waited at the gate. Luckily, the nonstop flight to Denver at 4:12 had seats available. Drew had charged their tickets, mumbling under his breath about the much-maligned benefits of plastic money. After they had taken the train to Concourse A, Drew stopped at one of the numerous coffee shops.

"Do you want anything to eat? It may be a while...."

Lezlie shook her head. "Maybe just some coffee."

Drew ordered the coffee and then pumped the change into a vending machine of cigarettes. He lit them with alarming frequency.

Lezlie sat in the waiting area at the gate. She didn't notice any of the people who shared their wait for the same flight. She sipped the strong coffee with a thoughtful expression. Drew's attention was focused on some point beyond the expanse of runway and airplanes being serviced. He was absolutely motionless, his nerves strung taut. Time passed slowly, testing his forcibly restrained restless energy. Lezlie's heart ached for the anguish he was suffering and had suffered in the past.

Walking beside him, she shared the view of an endless stretch of concrete and planes. But looking up at Drew's haggard face, her own sense of failure assailed her.

For the past hour, she had scrutinized her sessions with Merri, trying to discern what she might have done differently had she not been so certain of her course of therapy. One fact remained: she had become personally involved and had lost her objectivity.

"You've been awfully quiet," Drew commented.

Lezlie's smile was wan. "Maybe if I had been more observant, all of this could have been avoided. I broke my own rule and got involved...."

Drew was squinting against the glare from the large-paned windows. "Do you mean with me, or Merri?"

Lezlie could feel the intensity of his scrutiny. "With both of you," she admitted. "Not very professional, I will admit."

Drew touched her cheek. "Is it all that important, Lezlie?"

"It should have been. When I chose to disregard what was becoming a personal involvement, I failed both of you."

"I disagree." The comment offered quiet reassurance. "Listen, Lezlie, Merri has been happier these past few months than she's been in a year. She has made a lot of progress, not because she was handled with an emphasis on professionalism but because of your patience and compassion. You couldn't have done more."

"I wish I could believe that," Lezlie said. "If only I hadn't—"

When Lezlie stopped abruptly, Drew surmised the train of her thoughts. "Do you think if we hadn't become involved, you would have been more aware of what Merri was intending to do?"

"It has entered my mind," Lezlie replied. "And this was exactly what I was afraid of...that my perspective would be diminished by my own personal feelings for you."

"We talked about it...."

"Well, it didn't do much good, did it?" Lezlie said derisively.

"You're really taking the burden of responsibility on yourself," Drew said.

Before Lezlie could comment, the call for boarding was announced over the loudspeaker. There was a lot she hadn't said. If anything happened to Merri on this impromptu excursion across the country, Lezlie would never forgive herself. Her involvement with Drew might not have harmed the situation, but it hadn't done anything to help. If she had insisted that Merri keep that last appointment, she might have learned, or at least gotten some inclination of what Merri was planning. Then she might have been able to intervene and bring about Merri's wishes in a safer way.

"If, if, if," she mumbled to herself as she picked up her small bag, which Drew immediately took from her.

As they went aboard and located their seats, Drew kept silent. But when Lezlie was strapped into her seat beside him, he took her hand. He struggled to say what was on his mind.

"Has anything changed, Lezlie?"

Lezlie stared at their hands. His were tanned and strong as they enclosed her slender fingers. She realized what it had taken for Drew to put his doubts into words. "Telling me about Merri doesn't make any difference except in the way I would have treated her. Surely you don't perceive me as being so shallow that I would judge you for something you couldn't have changed?"

"Not shallow, Lezlie," he answered quietly, his gaze filled with sincerity and kindness. "But you were so apprehensive about involvement that we may have been finished before we ever began. Maybe that's why I didn't push telling you," Drew admitted. "I wasn't sure how you would react. And today, when I couldn't find you, I had the horrible feeling that somehow I was losing both of you."

"I don't think my secretary would appreciate being called a bat brain."

Drew smiled, and the tension in his face eased. "No, I guess not. But I was a little confused. Why didn't you mention you were on vacation?"

"If you will remember what was happening with you the first part of the week, it should be self-explanatory. I knew there was no way you could get away...."

"So you spared me the aggravation of knowing you were free all week?"

"In a manner of speaking."

"Well, that's one reason that didn't even occur to me." The teasing faded as Drew stared into her face, his own features exposing his uncertainty. "I'm glad you're with me, Lezlie," Drew said, squeezing her hand.

"It'll all be straightened out," she said with a confidence that wavered. Some of the outcome would depend upon Merri and her reaction to the truth. What would happen once she was told, Lezlie had no way of even guessing.

"Denver is an awfully big city. I just hope we catch her at the bus station," Drew said.

Lezlie hoped the same thing with all her heart. As the plane climbed, Lezlie stared out the window. The ground dropped away until the roads were thin ribbons and the countryside was a neat patchwork of farms and fields appliquéd with trees. But there was one thought nagging her.

When Drew had mentioned his coming home to Meredith and Greg, there had been a certain change in his expression, a look of wistfulness. He may have accepted Greg's marriage to Meredith because it was done, but what of his feelings for Meredith? His love for her wouldn't necessarily die simply because she had married someone else—even his brother. Meredith was the girl he had loved and she had borne his child. Was he tied to her more strongly than he had admitted through the years? Was that the reason Drew had never married? As much as Lezlie wanted to deny all her questions, in good conscience, she knew she could not.

When the stewardess came by to smilingly ask if they would care for a drink, Lezlie declined, and Drew ordered a Scotch. Lezlie closed her eyes, trying to shut out the persistent questions about Meredith.

She had seen her pictures many times: a petite blonde with soft features, so different from Lezlie's own tall figure and more sharply defined bone structure. She couldn't divert a mental picture that formed of Drew and Meredith together. It was an agonizing image. If only Drew had told her he loved her, perhaps she wouldn't feel so threatened. She had only dreamed the words the first time they had made love, or he would have repeated them, wouldn't he? He had told her she was special, that he cared about her, but never once had he mentioned love, except to say he wasn't sure he knew what love was. But what about Meredith?

All the doubts brought by the vulnerability of being in love with Drew confronted Lezlie, and she felt the sting of tears. She squeezed her eyes tightly shut, and kept her head turned toward the window, all the while aware of the pressure of Drew's fingers interlaced with hers.

DREW GENTLY SHOOK LEZLIE. She had fallen asleep soon after they had left Atlanta. Her mumbling when he had brought her head to rest on his shoulder had caused him to smile. And her slow steady breathing had slowly calmed Drew's ragged nerves. He had finished his Scotch and, after watching the changing terrain below them, he had also managed to catnap. As Lezlie stretched against him, he watched her silently.

It took a second for Lezlie's thoughts to clear. When she opened her eyes and met Drew's smiling blue gaze, she remembered they were on their way to Denver.

"Hi, sleepyhead," he whispered, dipping his head to touch her lips with a brief kiss. "We'll be touching down in a few minutes."

Lezlie sat up and ran a smoothing hand over her hair. "I feel like a rumpled rag doll."

"You look fine to me," Drew commented. "But then you could be wearing a potato sack and you'd still look good."

Lezlie's glance met his incredibly blue stare. They shared a mutual reassurance that all would turn out right.

If it had been pleasure or even business that had prompted the trip to Denver, Lezlie might have been impressed by the sweeping expanse of the flat dry plain giving way to the burst of green and tall buildings. The city seemed to sit like an oasis in a totally isolated plain, with the backdrop of the craggy black Rocky Mountains rising proudly against the blue sky. In the far distance to the south, partially obscured by a halo of clouds, was the famous Pikes Peak. The city with its high-rise buildings showed a modern progress. The only evidence of the bygone gold-rush days was the shimmer of Colorado gold on the capitol's dome.

Drew retrieved Lezlie's bag and his own, which he had thrown into his car before racing to Lezlie's house. They hurried through the airport terminal, ignoring the excited embraces and conversation surrounding them. Drew avoided the baggage bays and headed straight to the car-rental counters.

As they waited in line for a car-rental agent, Drew paced and fidgeted, drawing impatient glances from the other customers. Lezlie had some insight about what their time together would be like until the bus arrived in the early morning. Somehow, she had to keep Drew's mind off his worries or he would be exhausted by morning.

After the paperwork was done, they caught a shuttle bus to the car-rental lot and climbed into the compact sedan parked in the rental zone. Drew seemed ready to explode. He slid the seat back and quickly became familiar with the dash.

It was comfortably warm and the sun was still shining brightly as Drew stopped at the red light on Quebec Street.

"Where are we going?" Lezlie asked.

Drew glanced to the left, then the right, trying to get his bearings. "To the bus station," he answered shortly, and then glanced at her curiously.

"It's a long time until tomorrow morning, Drew. We can't just sit around waiting for the bus to come. It's like a watched pot...it'll drive you crazy just sitting there with nothing to do all night but wait. Besides, the station may close sometime during the night."

Drew considered what she had said and then nodded. "What do you suggest?"

"I think we should get a room somewhere, have dinner, and if rest is impossible, find something that will make the time pass easier."

Drew turned left, and then onto East Colfax Avenue. They were going against the evening traffic. Lezlie stared out of the window, the older street and sections giving way to the more-modern buildings closer to town. The gray capitol building reminded her a great deal of Atlanta's own capitol. Curtis Street cut along the western edge of the city, and at the intersection of Curtis and 19th, Drew pulled over.

A beautiful new high-rise hotel occupied the corner. Its gray stone and black windows were very modern, and an air of luxury was evident as liveried bellhops hurried to assist arriving patrons.

"We'll stay here," Drew announced. Before Lezlie could question the obvious expense of such a place, Drew pointed to a single-story building across the street—the Denver Bus Center.

The Park Suite Hotel was one of the most elegant hotels Lezlie had ever seen. Drew had told the valet-parking attendant that they would be leaving again in a few minutes. He took Lezlie's arm and escorted her into the hotel's lobby.

Lezlie felt as though she was walking into an apricot-colored satin powder puff. The immediate impression the hotel gave was one of soft comfort. Mirrored walls, satiny apricot-colored wallpaper and a rose floral carpet were a feast for the eyes. But more important was the graciousness of the staff. They sensed the fatigue of some of their arriving guests and offered their assistance for any need.

"All they have here is suites, Lezlie," Drew whispered as they approached the desk. "Would you prefer one with two bedrooms?"

"Still trying to save my reputation?" Lezlie quipped. Drew shrugged, but amusement sparkled in his eyes. "No, I don't want separate rooms, so you needn't worry about my reputation."

"I won't," Drew answered with a promise glittering in his blue eyes. "I plan to make it all legal just as soon as you'll agree."

"Really?" Lezlie commented succinctly. "It might be nice to be asked...."

"I'm just giving you fair warning that you will be asked, and asked and asked." Drew smiled, his face taking on an air of pained tolerance. "I only hope you won't make it as tough as you have so far."

"Are you tactfully trying to say you think I'm stubborn?"

"If the shoe fits..." Drew drawled, and Lezlie punched him playfully with her elbow.

But the truth was she was anxious to be alone with Drew, to ease the lines of worry that had settled over his eyes. Lezlie wasn't fooled by the joking tone Drew employed. He was deeply worried and was attempting to cover the depth of his anxiety about what lay ahead—the inevitable confrontation with Merri.

Drew was too keyed up to go to their room. As soon as their accommodations had been guaranteed and the bellhop had taken up their bags, he headed back out to the car with Lezlie in tow. She didn't ask where they were going as they circled the one-way city blocks to reach Colfax Street, and went the way they had come, passing streets with lyrical names such as Dahlia, Eudora, Jasmine and Kameria, before Drew turned left onto a parklike street.

The older neighborhood had a quiet dignity. Many of the houses had been refurbished or converted to more modern homes, with the emphasis on retaining the original beauty of the area. A wide grassy median of trees divided the street and gave it a spaciousness Lezlie hadn't seen in other areas where the yards were small and somewhat barren. Though traffic was fairly heavy less than a block away, it did not encroach upon the quietness of the street.

Drew stopped before a lovely brick home with black shutters. Heavy evergreen trees sided the house, giving it an air of seclusion. The back of the house was hidden behind a high fence. But Lezlie recognized the design immediately. It was almost exactly like the dollhouse Drew had built.

As Drew went up the walk and searched a large urn by the door, Lezlie glanced around, knowing this was Greg and Meredith's home. It was a logical choice for an architect, an older home he could renovate to his own taste and specifications.

Lezlie walked into the house behind Drew, feeling somewhat like a trespasser. She looked around the beautifully decorated home. Hardwood floors and oriental carpets contrasted with soft shades of cream, beige and ivory. Silk flower arrangements were bright bursts of color in the living room, dining room and entry. Chinese vases, brass bookends and figurines occupied a bookcase unit and brought out the colors in the pale floral silk drapes. But everything was covered with a thin layer of dust, and the air was hot and close.

Drew was walking several steps behind her. "I guess I should have hired someone to come in every so often. One of the neighborhood kids comes by and mows the yard during the summer."

Except for the dust, the house was neat, but there

were reminders of an interrupted life. Dishes were still propped in the drain in one of the sinks, while in the master bedroom an opened magazine on the bedside table was an eerie reminder that the house had once been a home. Merri's bedroom was the only one that had been disturbed. It was empty except for a few boxes and some paper wadded in one corner.

Drew glanced around the still silent house, his expression blank. Lezlie could imagine the anguish he felt seeing all the reminders. He stood at the patio doors leading to a sculptured garden and the pool. Lezlie wondered if he was thinking about Meredith and her life here with his brother.

Lezlie brushed her hands on her slacks, trying not to cough from the disturbed dust that filled the stuffy air. "Why didn't you sell the house, Drew?"

"I haven't really had a chance," he said absently. "I was thinking about leasing it out, but I didn't know what to do with all the furniture. All I could think about at the time was Merri."

"You could have it packed up and stored. Then when Merri's older, she could decide if there are any pieces she would like to keep."

"I suppose," Drew answered.

Lezlie wandered around the living room. "This house reflects Meredith's personality," she commented. "I suppose you have a lot of memories...."

"This house shows only the softer side of Meredith, not the bitter side," Drew returned. "Usually, she was pretty even tempered, but whenever I was around, she let me know just what I'd done to her. She only put it into words a few times, but I could always feel her anger, at least the first few years. I couldn't seem to make her understand that if only she had trusted me enough to tell me of her pregnancy before I'd left for overseas, I would have made it right. But eventually, she did try to put it all behind her."

Compassion for what Drew had gone through overwhelmed Lezlie. She was only a few feet from him, but she felt as though miles separated them. She walked into the arms that received her easily and buried her face in his shoulder. He had been treated so unfairly.

"It must have been so hard dealing with it all, especially coming from someone you once loved," she said, her voice muffled and strained.

"I cared for Meredith, Lezlie, because of what we had together and what came out of it. But what I didn't really realize until much later was that maybe we were too young for the commitment we made in some ways.

"I have only truly loved one woman other than my mother—" Drew continued, his voice a low rumble to Lezlie's ears "—and I'm holding her in my arms right now and wondering if she can love me as deeply as I love her, or if she is still too afraid of a commitment."

Lezlie felt as if the last bit of air had been sucked out of the room. The words washed over her, seeping into her own tormented thoughts. She leaned back to see his face. The look there held all the love she had been so afraid of.

"Me?" she whispered.

"Do you see anyone else standing next to you?" Drew questioned, a grin twitching his mouth.

"I thought maybe there was," Lezlie replied honestly. "I thought you loved Meredith even though you said you didn't. And you never said you loved me...."

Drew's expression softened and caressed her face. "I let it slip once, but you don't seem to remember."

"The first time we made love," Lezlie breathed.

Drew nodded. "Since then, I've told you in a thousand ways. I've showed you in every way I know how while inside I wanted to shout it until you heard me," he breathed. "But I thought the words might force a commitment you weren't ready to make, so I've waited." Drew draped his arms over her shoulders. "If you think about it, you may begin to understand that I've fought it almost as hard as you have. The first time I kissed you, I knew...oh, not that it was love, but that what I felt was much more than attraction. And I really tried to convince myself that was all it was.

"You're everything I've ever wanted in a woman, Lezlie. You're sensitive and kind, more than anyone I know. I've watched you with Merri and seen her respond to you so easily. And I even envied your husband for stirring such a loyal love that even after he died you went on wearing his ring and loving him."

Drew smoothed a curl at her temple. "When I saw that picture of your son, I knew what you had gone through. You lost your family while I could never have mine. But we have another chance, Lezlie, together. And you don't need to be worried or anxious...."

"You make me sound so timid," Lezlie said.

"I don't mean to," Drew said. "But once I knew about Michael and Mike, I understood what you were feeling. I knew why you had shut yourself off. Before that, it drove me crazy because there just wasn't any logical explanation."

"I'm glad you didn't give up, Drew, because I love you, too," she said softly, her eyes luminuous and steady. "There aren't any ghosts between us. And I'm not afraid." Drew pulled her head to his chest, his hands stroking her hair as his heart hammered with happiness.

"But you were right, Drew. I had put myself in an emotional vacuum. Sometimes you don't realize just how important someone is to you until they're gone. And then it's too late to say all the things you've left unsaid. There were so many things I might have told them if I had known.... When they died, I felt guilty that I was still alive and even resentful that I was alone. I decided I wouldn't be hurt that way again."

"I know, sweetheart, I know." Drew folded her into his arms. "I think I was what you needed, and I know for a fact, you are what I've wanted for a very long time. And I'll tell you every day...."

When Drew's lips touched hers it was the sweetest kiss Lezlie had ever known...filled with love, trust and understanding. If Drew had told her he loved her before, it would have been a happy revelation, but the fact that he had told her in the house Greg and Meredith shared made her secure that his past was behind him, just as hers was.

"What do you say we get out of here?" Drew suggested.

Lezlie nodded, her arm still around his waist as they left the house. At the door, Drew glanced back, then closed the door firmly. They returned to the car, their hearts less burdened, their minds less cluttered. Whatever came, they would handle it together, each giving and seeking strength from the other. But there was one important task yet to do.

DREW DROVE AIMLESSLY, giving Lezlie a running travelogue of Denver. They rode through a small suburb of Glendale to the farthest tip of an area called Aurora. Construction was going on everywhere and he pointed out several office parks, buildings and a hotel Greg had designed, as well as two of the new schools. On a vacant side street, Drew pulled to the dead end where a flat plain stretched for miles. The solitude of the view seeped into Drew's very being, and even Lezlie felt the relaxing calm as the evening breeze became cooler. They sat for a long time as the sun dropped in the west, giving the still terrain a fleeting golden sheen.

It was nearly dark when Drew started the car and silently headed back to the hotel. The long wait was only partly over. Their suite was as elegant and welcoming as the rest of the hotel. The warm roses and blues and muted patterns of drapes, bedspreads and carpet were restful to the eye and pleasing to the senses. Their clothes had been unpacked and neatly put away. Their showers were separate, and so different from the fun-filled shower they had shared at

Lezlie's house. Lezlie dressed while Drew showered, feeling refreshed after the long hours on the plane and in the car.

The second-floor lobby of the Park Suite Hotel was even more elegant than the registration area on a lower level. A mirrored fountain babbled quietly beneath a pear-shaped crystal chandelier. Windows with Roman shades covered the side of the building that looked out on 19th Street and the bus station. Cozy sitting areas, a piano, a lobby bar and tables with green-velvet chairs offered guests a place to gather other than the cocktail lounge or restaurants.

Drew chose the more casual atmosphere of the small intimate restaurant called Burgundy's over the more elaborate Plaza View Restaurant. Velvety booths wrapped them in a half circle of privacy. Though Drew ordered a complete meal, he ate very little. Lezlie tried to fill the silence with idle chatter or questions about Denver, which Drew answered quietly. But his continued distraction was obvious. By the time dinner was over, Lezlie was at her wits' end about how to keep Drew from sinking deeper into the despair that was gaining on him.

Back in their room, Lezlie changed into her nightgown in the bathroom. She returned to the bedroom and found Drew seated at the window. The complete dejection surrounding his motionless silhouette clutched her heart. She moved to stand behind him, dropping her hands lightly on his shoulders. He reached up and touched her fingers.

"Drew, it won't do any good to sit and brood," she said quietly.

"I just can't stop thinking about Merri sitting on a bus and going to face something like this all alone. I wonder what she's feeling...."

"She won't be alone when we find her in the morning," Lezlie reminded him.

"I just wish I knew how she's going to feel when she sees me."

"Very relieved, probably. Often when children strike out on some decision, their pride won't let them give up. But inside, they wish there was someone to chase the fears away. Merri has that someone; she just doesn't know it yet."

Drew glanced over his shoulder. "I can't believe I ever questioned your insight about children," he said quietly. "Until she came to you, we were going along day-to-day without any real relationship. I've been thinking about this all evening, Lezlie. I want her to know who I am, but for the life of me I don't think I can tell her."

Drew shrugged and shook his head. "After all that's happened, I honestly don't think she will be able to accept the truth from me. It could make her even more angry and withdrawn than she has been in the past because she may feel I am trying to displace Greg. That's the last thing I want to do. He was her father in every way that I wasn't."

"But Merri has something very few can have, Drew. She's lost one father, but has another who loves her. She will understand. There may be a lot of questions later, but by then you'll both be able to deal with the answers."

"Will you tell her?" Drew sat absolutely still,

waiting anxiously for Lezlie's reply. When it came, he breathed a sigh of relief.

"Yes, I will tell her, Drew. And I'll do my best to make her understand."

A slight smile tilted Drew's mouth. "If anyone can, you can."

Lezlie smoothed the worried frown on his forehead. "I love you, Drew, and I've come to care a lot about Merri...more than I thought I could two months ago."

Drew pulled Lezlie into his lap and burrowed his face into the curve of her shoulder. "We are so lucky that Charles called you that day," he murmured, his lips seeking the pulse suddenly springing to life in Lezlie's throat.

With unhurried tenderness, he stroked her hip and thigh as his lips explored her fragrant skin. As his mouth settled over her parted lips, Lezlie's gentle sigh fanned his cheek. Her arms circled his neck and she welcomed the slow exploration of his hand along the length of her body.

Drew stood up, lifting Lezlie in his arms to carry her to the bed. Between caresses and long melting kisses, their clothes were removed with a leisureliness that made Lezlie shiver. The strength of his muscular frame trapped her in a web of sensation that transcended worldly worries by the promise of fulfillment. Their lovemaking was so much more than physical need; it was an instinctive joining of two hearts, two bodies and two souls needing solace. Both lovers found reassurance in their simple sharing.

Lezlie clung to Drew, offering him the oblivion of ecstasy and finding her own in return. His tender words of love were answered, and his name burst from her lips in a gasp of pleasure.

Drew brought her gently back to reality with velvety kisses. Her luminous eyes betrayed the love and trust he had hungered for so long. He cradled her against him, aware of all she offered him, and he was, for the moment, at peace.

Lezlie stroked Drew's hair as he fell asleep, his arms firmly wrapped around her and his head resting on her chest. When he stirred, she whispered reassurance until his heavy breathing told her he was again asleep. But she could not sleep. She studied the pattern in the salmon-colored wallpaper, her mind filled with awe by the depth of her love for Drew. He was a complex man, capable of great strength, equal tenderness and a tempered fierceness. She smiled into the dim room. She closed her eyes, completely happy. Tomorrow would come soon enough.

CHAPTER SIXTEEN

A WAKE-UP CALL came at exactly five o'clock. Drew jerked awake, the lethargy of sleep leaving his face the moment he hung up the telephone. Without talking, both he and Lezlie hurriedly slipped into their clothes. Room service delivered the coffee Drew had ordered as they waited for the last few minutes to pass before walking across the street. Lezlie had been right. The bus terminal closed for several hours during the early morning, not reopening until 5:40.

The sky was just lightening when she and Drew emerged from the hotel. Lezlie shivered in the unfamiliar chill of Denver's weather. The bus terminal was a new, one-level building, housing both of the major bus lines and several smaller tour lines. Already there were people purchasing tickets for the early buses. The coffee shop and the Rocky Mountain Café wouldn't open until ten.

Drew went straight to the ticket counter. The agent answered his questions and pointed toward a series of doors on the right side of the terminal. Lezlie was glad the waiting was almost over as Drew prowled around the seats, stopping before the glass walls where the buses parked in diagonal spaces. The rumble of the bus's engine signaled its arrival. As the door whooshed open, Drew stood just outside the double doors and Lezlie followed.

The passengers disembarked and Drew looked beyond each one for a glimpse of Merri. But his hope suddenly faded when the bus driver stepped off with a small satchel.

Drew grabbed the driver's arm. "Where's the little girl that got on in Marietta?" he demanded.

The bus driver was momentarily confused, and he glanced at Lezlie. "She's blond, twelve years old," Lezlie explained. "We spoke to the agent in Marietta, Georgia. He sold her a ticket and she was supposed to be on this bus."

"Oh, yeah," the driver said, eyeing Drew warily. "I let her off a few miles back."

"You what?" Drew almost shouted.

"Drew, that won't help," Lezlie said quickly.

Drew took a ragged breath. "Where did you let her off?" he asked, more in control.

"At the intersection of East Colfax and Boston streets in Aurora."

"Why didn't you make her stay on the bus?" Drew snapped, frustrated. "And why would you let her out before the station?"

"Listen, mister," the driver said defensively, "I'm sorry if you were waiting here. I asked her if anyone was meeting her and she said no. And she said she had somewhere to go in Aurora and it was closer than coming all the way into town. I figured she knew what she was doing. And I didn't just let her off. There's a station in Aurora, at Boston and East Colfax."

Drew turned away, his thoughts scattered. "Where could she go?" he asked quietly. He had been so certain she would be on the bus, and the fact that she was not exacerbated all his fears. Merri was alone in a large city, vulnerable to the many dangers that could beset a small girl. He took Lezlie's hand and hurried through the terminal. "If she got off in Aurora, there's only one place she would go."

"Where?" Lezlie asked, almost running to keep up with his long strides.

"The house."

"But how could she have made it there?"

"By taxi, by the city bus...I don't know," Drew said with anxiety and then hope. "She has to be there."

Drew maneuvered through the city streets with alarming speed. The first stages of morning traffic were building, and he switched lanes recklessly.

"Drew, we'll find her, wherever she is," Lezlie said anxiously, grasping his arm. He looked at her, a tormented expression in his eyes. "But not if we're killed in the process."

Drew immediately slowed down, but there was an intensity in his face that alarmed Lezlie. What if Merri wasn't at the house? And another thought occurred to Lezlie. "Drew, where did the accident happen?" she asked suddenly.

"Out on the highway," he answered, glancing to the left as he made a right-hand turn.

"Would she go there?"

Drew shook his head. "I doubt she even knows where it happened. No, she has to be at the house."

But as Drew pulled up in front of the house on Monaco Street, Lezlie was already sure they wouldn't find Merri there. They hurried up the walk, and Drew checked in the urn for the key he had used yesterday. His face dissolved into a frown of worry when he extracted the key. He went inside and checked the house anyway, returning a few minutes later and shaking his head.

"I guess all we can do now is wait," he said quietly. "I should call the police...."

"There's one other place to check," Lezlie said gently. "Where are Greg and Meredith buried?"

"The cemetery?" Drew asked doubtfully.

"It's the only logical place, actually, Drew. She has come to say goodbye."

The Fairmount Cemetery was only a few miles away, and they reached it within minutes. An old stone building sat near the street by an iron-gated entrance. A narrow pebbled road led inside, branching off in several directions.

Lezlie had never seen such a beautiful cemetery. While all around it the area was flat with few trees, heavy bluish evergreens of indefinable age lined the fence and dotted the drive, their heavy limbs almost reaching the ground. It was as though the whole property was from another place and another era. The graves were marked by stones that could only be called works of art, statues and gracefully carved marble of many colors. The narrow drive wound around elaborate crypts—some gabled, some turreted with fretwork or wooden-and-glass doors—all of them had an air of quiet serenity.

"How lovely," she breathed, her eyes sweeping across the headstones. Birds chirped softly from the trees and a quiet breeze rustled the branches.

The Ivy Chapel, a lovely ivy-draped stone building with a delicate spire, was to their right. Drew scanned the expanse of countless headstones, but a large ornate crypt blocked his view of Meredith's and Greg's graves. He pulled to the side of the road and stopped.

"What if she isn't here?" he said in hushed tones.

"It's the only place she can be, Drew." Lezlie craned her neck to see beyond some of the larger headstones. The sun was bright and she squinted just as a movement caught her eye. Then she saw the glow of sun on a blond head.

"There she is," she cried in a whisper. Their relief mingled with delight and Drew kissed her soundly before they tumbled out of the car and hurried across the grass, careful to avoid the graves.

Merri's head was bowed and her mouth was moving as she talked to the silent graves. A lump rose in Lezlie's throat. She put a restraining hand on Drew's arm. They stopped and waited, and Drew's hand gripped Lezlie's.

The two graves had gracefully carved headstones. A delicate ribbon connected them, a symbol of how Greg and Meredith had been connected in life. Lezlie did not know how long they stood there, surrounded by tranquillity. Drew's eyes never left Merri.

Merri stood up and her thin shoulders lifted in a quiet sigh. As she turned around and spotted Drew and Lezlie, her surprise melted into relief, and then tears.

"Uncle Drew," she cried, breaking into a full run. He opened his arms to her and she flew into them, her slender arms wrapping around his waist.

Drew hugged her fiercely. He wanted to tell Lezlie this was the first time Merri had put her arms around him for comfort; the first time she had turned to him to share her tears, but his throat was closed.

"What are you doing here?" Merri asked.

"I might ask the same thing of you, young lady," Drew answered, his stern reprimand not quite coming across.

Merri glanced from one of them to the other. "I'm sorry," she said quietly. "But it was something I had to do."

"If you had told me this was the reason you wanted to come to Denver, I would have brought you, Merri," Drew said.

"But you're so busy...."

"I'm never too busy if you need me," Drew interrupted. "All you have to do is ask and maybe give me a reason. I would have understood, pumpkin."

Merri nodded quickly, her face brighter, her eyes happier as she wiped away her tears with the back of her hand. "Boy, am I glad to see y'all," she said breathlessly.

"No more than we are to have found you. You really had us worried, but there was no harm done. But next time—"

"I promise, Uncle Drew. I'll ask first."

Lezlie shared a glance with Drew and then reached out to take Merri's hand. "Let's take a walk, Merri."

Merri sighed wistfully. "I guess you're going to fuss at me, too."

"No, I want to tell you something that may be hard for you to understand, but that you should know. You're a young lady now, and old enough to hear the truth."

Merri glanced over her shoulder as she walked away with Lezlie. They disappeared from view and Drew wandered to sit on a marble bench near the car. It was the longest, most difficult wait of his life. He watched the two people he loved most walk away, and there was a chance that only one of them when they returned would ever accept him for what he was. It was a risk, but the truth had to win out... it just had to.

Merri walked beside Lezlie expecting a scolding. It never came. The wind whispered across the soft grass, and the sun turned Lezlie's hair the color of molten copper. "Boy, you sure look different with your hair like that," Merri commented.

"That's what Drew says." Lezlie smiled.

"You like my uncle, don't you?"

"Yes, Merri, he's a fine man in many ways, but like everyone else he has made mistakes and has done things he regrets, but can't change."

"Like me," Merri said with honest insight. "I've been a real brat, haven't I?"

"In some ways, but you had to come to grips with a very hard fact of life."

"Is Uncle Drew really mad at me?" she asked timidly.

"No, he was just very worried," Lezlie said, adding, "as any parent would be."

"I never thought of Uncle Drew as a parent," Merri mused.

"Well, I think it's time you did, Merri." Lezlie turned Merri to face her. "I don't know if you can understand what I'm going to tell you, Merri, but I want you to try."

Lezlie began the delicate process of telling Merri about her mother and the man she had always known as her uncle. The emotions showing on Merri's features were curiosity, caution and disbelief. But as Lezlie continued to talk, to explain and to soothe her doubts, Merri listened quietly, and after a few questions and tears, acceptance of the truth was in her clear blue eyes.

"He's my dad?" she asked quietly.

Lezlie nodded. "What happens from here, Merri, is up to you. Your un...Drew stayed out of your life because he was convinced the truth would only have confused you. The arguments your parents had when Drew came to Denver all centered around telling you the truth, but they hadn't come to a final decision before the accident. You didn't hear any of that argument?"

"Some, but it didn't really make any sense. I just thought they were mad at Uncle Drew again." Merri chewed her bottom lip for a moment. When she turned and walked quickly in the direction they had come, Lezlie hung back, giving the child a chance to talk with Drew alone.

The sun beat down upon Drew's back as he sat hunched over, his elbows leaning on his knees. His gaze was fixed on the ground, while his thoughts scattered in all directions. But as a pair of sandal-clad feet came into his vision, he glanced up.

Merri stood a few feet away, tears swimming in her eyes. "Is it true, what Lezlie told me?" she asked hesitantly.

Drew nodded, surprised when she walked slowly toward him. Her arms wound around his neck and her tears fell on his shirt. He held her tightly, comforting Merri as Lezlie approached, her hands clasped behind her back. Her smile was reassurance that though it might be a long road, the first mile, often the hardest, was now behind them.

When Merri's tears had subsided into little hiccups, Drew stood up, drawing her against his side. Lezlie slipped within the protection of his other arm. Merri glanced back for only a moment, before she turned her attention to Drew and Lezlie.

They had reached the car before Merri looked up at Lezlie. "I think he likes you, too," she said mischievously.

"You might say that," Drew said with a grin. "In fact, sweetheart, you could even say I love Lezlie. And if it hadn't been for you, we would never have met."

"Really?" Merri breathed.

"Really," Drew said, leaning over to first kiss his daughter's flushed forehead, then Lezlie's. Gratitude was mirrored in his eyes. Someday he would tell Lezlie just how much what she'd done had meant to him.

"Oh, neat," Merri chirped. "Maybe Lezlie could be my substitute mom."

"I wouldn't doubt it for a minute," Drew drawled. "What do you say, Doc?"

"Well, it looks like it's two to one. I don't stand a chance, so let's just say it's unanimous," Lezlie teased. "And if we're going to have a democracy, I vote we stay in Denver for the weekend instead of heading back home today."

"Oh, yes," Merri agreed. "Could we, please?"

"Two to one." Lezlie grinned. "You lose."

"Oh, no I don't," Drew whispered. "I can't lose now." As they walked to the car, he held each of them close. "But I think we're going to have to get this democracy thing worked out, my girls."

His eyes sparkled with promise as Merri climbed into the car, and he turned to Lezlie to seal their agreement with a kiss that left Merri gaping at them from the window.

Lezlie's protest died in her throat. Drew's mouth was only a breath away from hers. "You had better get used to it, just as Merri will," Drew murmured. "I am a very affectionate person, and I don't intend to suppress it."

"So, who's asking you to?" Lezlie challenged, bringing his face to hers.

The future loomed brightly ahead, and she would go toward it happily with two very special people. Like Merri, she had another love, and another chance at happiness.

Drew drove out of the cemetery holding Lezlie's hand as Merri chattered excitedly about all the places they should see during their vacation. They would never have time for it all, Lezlie thought smiling, seeing the day differently than she had only yesterday.

She would have a lifetime of memories with Drew

and Merri, and perhaps other children who would have crystal-blue eyes and blond hair, or gray eyes and mops of auburn curls. And every day would add to her store of memories, mingling with those of another love—though gone, not forgotten. Her life would be complete.

**August's other absorbing
HARLEQUIN *SuperRomance* novel**

THE GENUINE ARTICLE by Pamela M. Kleeb

Tessa always felt like Alice tumbling down the rabbit hole whenever she encountered Jean-Paul Heidemann, the austere new president of a Swiss bank.

Despite Jean-Paul's insistent advances, she was determined to conduct herself professionally in the restoration of the bank's art treasures. She was hardly prepared for discoveries so shocking she hesitated to bring them to light.

As pawns in an ugly scheme of art fraud, both lovers had truths to reveal. But rather than face painful consequences, each gambled that silence would ensure the joy they found in each other's arms.

A contemporary love story for the woman of today

These two absorbing titles
will be published in September
by

HARLEQUIN
SuperRomance

SONG OF THE SEABIRD by Christina Crockett

Suffering from a failed marriage and broken dreams, Claire Parnell returned home to Palm Shores, Florida.

She had begun to think she would never sing again, until she met Dylan Jamison. This gentle and caring man recognized the song in Claire's soul. All he asked her to do was trust him – for Claire, that was the hardest thing of all.

Like the injured seabirds Dylan mended and returned to the wild, she could eventually fly away. But if she stayed, he would prove that love could truly set her free. . . .

THE RISING ROAD by Meg Hudson

When Timothy Flanagan came to her rescue in a pub in south Boston, Anne Clarendon couldn't believe her luck. She was even more surprised when she discovered this man with the twinkling green eyes and coppery hair was the lawyer handling her father's estate.

By the time she sorted out her impressions she had fallen in love with the charming Irishman. But Timothy felt he couldn't return that love—not until he found out about his family, and his past. . . .

These books are
already available
from
HARLEQUIN
SuperRomance

RETURN OF THE DRIFTER Melodie Adams
LITTLE BY LITTLE Georgia Bockoven
A MOMENT OF MAGIC Christina Crockett
DELTA NIGHTS Jean DeCoto
TASTE OF A DREAM Casey Douglas
WHEN MORNING COMES Judith Duncan
MOUNTAIN SKIES Sally Garrett
CHAMPAGNE PROMISES Meg Hudson
CRITIC'S CHOICE Catherine Kay
THE AWAKENING TOUCH Jessica Logan
A LASTING GIFT Lynn Turner
THE HELLION LaVyrle Spencer

If you experience difficulty in obtaining any of these titles, write to:

Harlequin SuperRomance, P.O. Box 236, Croydon, Surrey CR9 3RU

HARLEQUIN *Love Affair*

Look out this month for

DAYDREAMS *Rebecca Flanders*

Reality was always disappointing and Stacey had no desire to spoil the image of the Jon Callan of her daydreams. Stacey protested vigorously as she was ushered backstage to Callan's dressing room. When she stood before Callan himself, Stacey felt embarrassed and nervously wished she had never attended his Boston performance.

Jon had never really known a fan before; his schedule didn't permit it. The quiet woman in the simple linen suit was alien to the glittering, hectic world he lived in. She wasn't what he expected... but he sensed she was what he needed.

MEASURE OF LOVE *Zelma Orr*

Nothing in her experience had prepared nurse Samantha Bridges for the situation at Bumping River. The cramped cabin possessed Stone Age facilities, and Sam's two charges were beyond belief: the ugliest dog she had ever laid eyes on and an unconscious logger of giant size. Surveying the scene, Sam knew her life had hit an all-time low, for if the dog didn't attack her, the unsanitary conditions would kill them all....

But the situation would soon go from bad to worse: Nicholas Jordan was about to regain consciousness.

PROMISE ME TODAY *Cathy Gillen Thacker*

Detective Tom Hennessey cared. He cared enough to confront teacher Merritt Reed about his nephew's grades. He cared enough to notice the little things about Merritt that signalled half-buried sorrow. Tom cared enough to try and heal Merritt's wounds—even if the process was painful for them both.

Tom Hennessey cared enough to risk his life daily for the citizens of Cincinnati. And that was just the problem, for Merritt had learned that you could trust a cop with your life—but not with your heart!